MURDER
MOST GRAVE

Books by G.A. McKevett

Savannah Reid Mysteries

JUST DESSERTS
BITTER SWEETS
KILLER CALORIES
COOKED GOOSE
SUGAR AND SPITE
SOUR GRAPES
PEACHES AND SCREAMS
DEATH BY CHOCOLATE
CEREAL KILLER
MURDER A` LA MODE
CORPSE SUZETTE
FAT FREE AND FATAL
POISONED TARTS
A BODY TO DIE FOR
WICKED CRAVING
A DECADENT WAY TO DIE
BURIED IN BUTTERCREAM
KILLER HONEYMOON
KILLER PHYSIQUE
KILLER GOURMET
KILLER REUNION
EVERY BODY ON DECK
HIDE AND SNEAK
BITTER BREW
AND THE KILLER IS . . .
A FEW DROPS OF BITTERS

Granny Reid Mysteries

MURDER IN HER STOCKING
MURDER IN THE CORN MAZE
MURDER AT MABEL'S MOTEL
MURDER MOST GRAVE

Published by Kensington Publishing Corp.

G. A. McKevett

MURDER MOST GRAVE

Kensington Publishing Corp.

www.kensingtonbooks.com

KENSINGTON BOOKS are published by

Kensington Publishing Corp.
119 West 40th Street
New York, NY 10018

All Kensington titles, imprints and distributed lines are available at special quantity discounts for bulk purchases for sales promotion, premiums, fundraising, educational or institutional use. Special book excerpts or customized printings can also be created to fit specific needs. For details, write or phone the office of the Kensington Special Sales Manager: Kensington Publishing Corp., 119 West 40th Street, New York, NY, 10018. Attn. Special Sales Department. Phone: 1-800-221-2647.

Library of Congress Card Catalogue Number: 2021953425

The K and Teapot logo is a trademark of Kensington Publishing Corp.

ISBN: 978-1-4967-2909-5

First Kensington Hardcover Edition: June 2022

ISBN: 978-1-4967-2911-8 (e-book)

10 9 8 7 6 5 4 3 2 1

Printed in the United States of America

Lovingly dedicated to Bruce,
who doubles my joys and halves my sorrows.

Acknowledgments

I wish to thank Leslie Connell, forever a beloved member of the Moonlight Magnolia Detective Agency and a dear friend.

I also wish to thank all the fans who write to me, sharing their thoughts and offering endless encouragement. Your stories touch my heart, and I enjoy your letters more than you know. I can be reached at sonja@sonjamassie.com and facebook.com/gwendolyn narden.mckevett.

Chapter 1

"That's it, you little turkey butt. Snooze away. Regain your strength so's you can torment me at dawn-thirty, when the rest o' the world's sound asleep and sawin' logs. Ever'body but you and me, that is," Stella Reid said as she gently and oh so slowly laid her sleeping six-month-old grandson in the bassinet next to her comfy chair in the living room.

Once she had the infant settled and covered with his blue flannel blanket, she couldn't resist one light stroke of her fingertip on his silky cheek.

Baby skin. Softest thing on earth, she thought, feeling a flood of affection flow through her, warming her heart and reviving her exhausted body and mind.

She smiled, whispering, "Even at four in the mornin', I wouldn't take a billion dollars for ya."

Glancing at the tarnished sunburst clock on the wall over the couch, she realized that this peaceful interlude wasn't going to last long. Any moment now, the rest of her grandangels would return from school and tear through the front door like a pack of prairie coyotes with a brush fire at their heels.

Make the most of it while you can, Stella May, she told herself as she settled down for a brief rest in her old, avocado leatherette recliner. *Sit a spell and stick yer feet up. Lord knows, breaks from all this grannying business are few and far between these days.*

Like an instant fulfillment of her prophecy, she glanced out the window and saw a big yellow school bus slow down, pull over to the edge of the highway, chug to a stop, and swing its door open.

A million children poured forth and began to race up the long, dirt road toward the tiny shotgun shack that had been Stella's home for decades. Now, thanks to a compassionate sheriff, who had interceded on their behalf with the local judge, the humble house was their home, as well.

It seemed like a million kids, though it was actually only a gaggle of grandyoung'uns.

The Good Lord had blessed her with eight in total.

Well, the Lord above and my horny son and his ding-a-ling wife, who still ain't figured out that it ain't the stork who brings babies into this world, she thought, shaking her head. *Babies that need tendin' and a heap of lovin' and guidance for the next twenty years or so.*

But she couldn't help laughing as she watched them kick up clouds of dust and listened to them whoop and holler as they rushed toward the house, eager for a welcome hug and some sort of after-school treat.

A few months ago, their snack would have been fresh-from-the-oven chocolate chip cookies. But since Macon Jr., the baby, had joined his brother and sisters in her custody, most of the cookie baking was being done by a fellow named Famous Amos, assisted by the Keebler Elves, depending on which brand was on sale that week. These days, Stella barely found time to grab the store-bought goodies off the grocery shelf, let alone whip up a batch herself.

Fortunately, the children didn't seem to care who made their refreshments, as long as they were readily available, especially after school, when they truly believed they were likely to expire from hunger at any moment.

With a keen grandmother's eye Stella observed her brood tripping over their own feet, not to mention each other, in their mad dash to the house. Suddenly, she had an inkling.

Something was wrong.

They were always eager to get inside, but they were usually laughing, at least grinning, as they fought to be the first to breach the door. But not with this degree of urgency.

Also, a quick head count told Stella that somebody was missing. Besides the one sleeping next to her chair, there were only six.

"I wanna tell her first!" she heard the second oldest, Marietta, yell as they bounded onto the porch.

Seven-year-old Jesup was shoved aside as Marietta scrambled to enter the house first. But, as usual, the eldest grandchild took charge of the situation.

Thirteen-year-old Savannah wrapped a protective arm around Jesup and told Marietta, "Don't go yanking on your sister like that, Miss Mari. She's little, and you might hurt her, manhandling her that way. Besides, you've got no more right to be the one to tell Granny than she has. Just leave her be."

Sliding deftly between Marietta and the front door, Savannah cleared the way for Jesup, who scurried past her disgruntled sister and into the house.

Stella stood and steeled herself for what she was about to hear. She had already figured out that the missing person in the mess of grandkids was her other grandson, Waycross.

He was conspicuous in his absence because everyone rushing through the door was female and had dark hair like her own, a testimony to Stella's mother, a full-blooded Cherokee.

Waycross was exceptional in the family for two reasons. First, until baby Macon Jr. had arrived, he had been the solitary male child. Second, he was distinctive as the only carrottop. And no simple, subtle auburn shades for Waycross Reid. He had a flaming copper, wild and wooly head of hair that one could spot a mile away in a crowd.

But today, not one ginger kid came through Stella's door, and that was alarming, as the one child most likely to get into deep trouble was poor Waycross.

He wasn't a bad kid. Just fond of mischief and resourceful at creating it.

"Okay, where in tarnation is that brother of yours?" Stella asked the eager-faced Jesup, who ran up to her grandmother, wrapped her arms tightly around her waist, and stared up at her, big blue eyes wide and concerned.

"He done run off, Granny," Jesup proclaimed.

"Yeah!" shouted another voice in the crowd, followed by more excited pronouncements.

"We tried, but we couldn't catch 'im!"

"I had him by the shirt for a minute, but he wriggled out of my—"

"Even the principal tried to lay hands on 'im!"

"Some of the teachers, too!"

"But he got clean away! Made hisself a proper es-cape, he did."

"You know how fast he can run when he's a mind to!"

Stella held up both hands and donned her best, "Don't-worry, pressure-on-that-cut-will-stop-the-bleeding" look.

She used it frequently, whether she felt optimistic about such remedies or not. With eight grandchildren under her roof, optimism had to prevail at all times.

"This ain't the first time Waycross has run away," she told his excited, worried sisters. "Cain't really blame the boy if he decides he's had his canful of all of us females at least once a month."

"Yes, he does run away on a regular basis," Savannah said softly, a calm contrast to the rest of the gang. "But he always takes time to pack a pillowcase with some of his Transformers, his G.I. Joe, *and* a pair of clean underwear for each day he intends to be away."

"Yes." Stella nodded. "Waycross is big on personal hygiene. It's true. An admirable quality, 'specially in a boy child."

She reached for the baby, who was wide awake now and beginning to fuss. As she clasped the child to her chest and patted his behind, she turned back to Savannah and said, "Where was he last seen and what happened right before he made his git-away?"

"It was at school!" Marietta interjected. "Made a dang fool of hisself right there in front of ever'body. Embarrassed the family somethin' fierce. Like he always does."

"I figured it was at school, Marietta, since the principal and teachers chased 'im," Stella told her with a tone far more patient than she felt.

Marietta made a practice of standing on her grandmother's last strained nerve and dancing an Irish jig on it. "I'll thank you not to refer to anybody in this family as a fool. We're all doin' the best we can, day to day, includin' Waycross. Sometimes we do well and sometimes we fall flat on our faces, but there ain't no fools under this roof."

Marietta stuck out her lower lip. "'Cept Waycross."

"Go to your room, Miss Marietta Reid. Right this minute, and don't come out till I tell ya to."

As Marietta flounced off toward the bedroom she shared with the rest of her sisters, stomping and huffing, Stella added, "You'd better stick that bottom lip of yours back in place, too, before you trip over it."

Stella heard a disgruntled mumbling. Something about old ladies tripping if somebody pushed them hard enough. But she decided to let it go. She had to pick her battles with Marietta Reid. Otherwise, her home would be a constant war zone.

She turned back to the group of girls and said, "Everybody go into the kitchen, raid the cookie jar, and get yourself a cup of milk. Vidalia, you pour for the little'uns. Savannah, darlin', you stick around. Alma, please bring your big sister some refreshments."

The room cleared out in an instant, leaving only Stella, Savannah, the baby, and a rare moment of peace and quiet.

"Tell me ever'thing, sweetheart, and don't leave out nothin'," she told her firstborn grandchild, the girl who was having to become a woman far too quickly.

Savannah sighed, walked over to Stella, and took the baby from her.

As soon as the exchange was made, Stella realized how good it felt to have her arms empty for a moment. Little Macon Jr. only weighed seventeen pounds, but after a few hours, it took a toll on his grandmother's arms.

She had once told her best friend, Elsie, "There's a reason the good Lord don't give women our age little children to care for. We just ain't up to chasin' after 'em, like when we was younger."

Of course, that had been before Stella's son had decided he didn't need to bother raising the children he'd brought into the world and her daughter-in-law had gone to prison for neglecting and endangering them.

Savannah kissed her little brother's forehead and held him close to her chest. He reached up and laid his chubby baby hand on her cheek.

"The problem with Waycross," the girl began, "got started by that nasty ol' Jeanette Parker."

Stella sighed. "Now why doesn't that surprise me? I wish that girl would find herself somebody else to torment for a while and give our poor Waycross a break. He could sure use one."

A look crossed Savannah's face ever so briefly. Uneasiness along with something perhaps akin to guilt.

Stella's sharp eyes caught it, and her grandmotherly suspicion was aroused.

"Is there somethin' else you wanna tell me, sweetheart?" she asked the girl. "Somethin' you got to say about Miss Jeanette maybe?"

Savannah shrugged and the sheepish look deepened. "Um, well, Gran, I . . ."

"Yes. Spit it out, child. You got nothin' to fear in my house by speakin' the truth."

"Okay." Savannah drew a deep breath and said, "I think Jeanette's really mad at *me*, but she's been taking it out on Waycross, because he's little and he won't fight back like I do."

"Hmm. Okay. We'll discuss the ins and outs of that later," Stella said, pushing her own suspicions and misgivings aside for the time being. "What did she say or do to Waycross that upset him so?"

"I'm not sure. I didn't hear it all. But I think it was something about his hair being red."

Stella shook her head. "That child does shoulder more than his share of grief because of that colorful hair of his. Why, I'll never know. He's beautiful and easy to spot in a crowd. There's somethin' to be said for that in a passel o' kids this big."

Savannah just smiled and nodded. She still had that air of sadness about her, and something told Stella there was more to it than just concern about her brother. Later, Stella would have to shake her tree a bit and see what fruit fell to the ground, if any. Now that Savannah was a teenager, she held on to her secrets a tad more tightly than before adolescence had changed her, both body and mind.

"I'll watch the kids while you go look for him," Savannah offered. "I'm sure he's eager for you to find him. He always is."

Stella hesitated. While she knew that Savannah was far more mature and capable of caring for her siblings than most of the adults in their tiny town of McGill, Georgia, she hated to saddle a child with such a chore.

Stella had left the gang in Savannah's custody when emergencies had occurred. But that was before baby Macon Jr. arrived. Stella was reluctant to burden the child with an infant as well as her sometimes unruly siblings.

Stella glanced at the sunburst clock again. "Okay. Elsie should be finished workin' there at Judge Patterson's place. I'll call her and ask if she can come over. Then I'll go scour the countryside for your wayward brother."

"You can go on ahead. Let me call Elsie. I'll tell her about Waycross and that you had to go. You know her. She'll be here in three minutes flat. I doubt anything bad will happen that quick, what with Marietta on time-out in the bedroom."

Stella chuckled. "That's true. But call Elsie right now. I wanna know she's on her way before I leave."

Savannah laid the once-again asleep baby down in his bassinet, then rushed to the phone and dialed. As Stella collected her purse and car keys from the piecrust table next to the door, she heard her granddaughter say, "Thank you, Miss Elsie. Granny appreciates it. We all do. See you in a minute."

Savannah hung up the phone and turned to her grandmother, who was waiting by the open door. "Okay, Gran, she's on her way. I'd check the graveyard if I were you. He was headed that direction."

"Thank you, darlin'."

"Tell him Elsie's bringing one of her coconut cakes. He'll be making tracks toward home in a jiffy."

"Will do, sugar. Thank you." Stella blew her granddaughter a kiss, then scurried out the front door and down the rickety porch steps.

The graveyard. The girl's right. That's the first place I'll look, Stella thought as she rushed across the yard to her old panel truck and climbed inside.

Stella knew her grandangels well and understood they were creatures of habit. When Savannah was upset, she would head for the library to lose herself in a good mystery book. Marietta would run to the drugstore to buy a candy bar, if she had enough money, and to pilfer one if she didn't. Jesup would huddle deep in the corner of her lower bunk bed with a doll clutched to her chest. Cordele would find someone to boss around or complain to. Vidalia would soothe herself by writing a record of her woes in her diary. Alma would go looking for an unfortunate animal somewhere that, at least in her opinion, was "in desperate need of some lovin' and doctorin'."

But Waycross, Stella's sweet grandboy, with the sun's fire in his hair and the gloom of a dark, rainy night in his soul, would head for the old cemetery and the unique comfort he had found there so often among the ancient gravestones.

Stella was pretty sure that was where she would find him.

"Bless his heart," she whispered as she drove. "And bless ever' red hair on that precious head o' his."

Chapter 2

As Stella drove through the downtown area of McGill, pausing at the town's only traffic signal, a four-way blinking light, she glanced around at the unsightly litter of red, white, and blue campaign posters and decided she would be glad when this election hooey was finally over and done with.

Once Stella had cared deeply about who occupied the White House, but with her current distractions of raising grandkids, she had little interest in whether Mr. Bush or Mr. Dukakis won.

She was more focused on which of the town's two gas stations was the cheapest. With any luck, she might not have to pay over a dollar for a simple gallon of gas. That might make the five dollars in her purse stretch far enough for her to buy milk, bread, and, if Wakefield's grocery store had a sale on, maybe even some eggs.

She just wanted the clutter of banners and signs gone from the lawns, business windows, and billboards. Even more, she wanted McGillians to find something else to complain and fight about among themselves. All this uproar and the hard feelings politics aroused played havoc with folks' digestive systems. It wasn't good for their nerves, either, already frazzled after the unusually hot summer that had burned the crops and left them scorched and crisp in their brown fields.

Of course, not everyone was a farmer. The folks who lived in town had even more important concerns to argue about. At least, in their own opinions. Like what color to repaint the gazebo and whether or not the town should subsidize Mayor Larry Kramer's extraordinarily high gasoline bill. After all, he preferred to just walk from one place to another. In a downtown area that was only three blocks long, cranking up the car and driving from city hall three doors down to the Burger Igloo for a double chili cheese-burger lunch was hardly practical.

It was Mayor Larry's wife, Penelope, who racked up the miles, driving in and out of Atlanta to go clothes shopping.

Then there was the matter of whether Sheriff Manny Gilford would win his umpteenth reelection or if he would lose his long-held position to his deputy, Augustus Faber.

That particular race interested Stella far more than all the others put together. She was a big fan of Sheriff Gilford's. Had been most of her life.

As Stella passed the sheriff's station house, she couldn't resist glancing down the narrow space between it and the next building to see if Manny's cruiser was parked there.

It was, and she couldn't help feeling a tingle of excitement that seemed to accompany any sort of "Manny sighting."

While she didn't exactly welcome her reaction to all things Manny, Stella also knew it was inevitable. The sheriff was a handsome man, extremely kind, at least to law-abiding towns-folk, and they were close friends. Had been for years.

Some in McGill speculated that they were more. But although they were a widow and a widower and therefore technically "ro-mance eligible," they were also a grandmother and the sheriff. Stella and Manny had enough on their plates at the moment. Neither of them needed the complications of an amorous liaison.

Or so they told themselves.

With that in mind, Stella resisted the urge to stop at the station, run inside, and ask Manny to help her find the missing Waycross.

The sheriff was busy with real cases to solve, and criminals to locate. Surely she could find one tiny boy on her own without calling in the law. Especially since the missing kiddo was the only true redhead in town.

As she drove by the park, Stella glanced at the swing set and monkey bars. Waycross wasn't among the numerous children playing there, but she hadn't really expected him to be.

She knew her little grandson better than that. Like Savannah had suggested, Stella figured he was probably at the cemetery, and she knew why. The boy would be talking to his grandpa.

Arthur Reid was a good listener. He always had been but was even more so now, as he had taken up residence among the town's dearly departed.

Stella didn't visit his resting place all that often on her own. She had never felt the need.

Anytime she closed her eyes and took a breath from the day's hustle and bustle, she could feel her Art right beside her. Especially at night, when the house was finally quiet, and she was snuggled in her feather bed, covered by the Cherokee wedding quilt her mother had made for her. The one she and Art had slept beneath every night from their honeymoon until his untimely tractor accident that had taken him from her.

As she pulled off the highway and onto the one-lane, asphalt drive that led into the cemetery, she wondered, not for the first time, about her grandson's connection to his grandfather. She doubted that Waycross actually remembered him, as the child had been so young when Arthur had passed. But in a house filled with women and his absentee trucker father on the road nearly all the time, the boy was in sore need of a male figure in his life.

Stella's heart ached to think that the child attempted to fill that need in an ancient cemetery with only a patch of grass and a gravestone to confide his troubles to.

She pulled her old panel truck up to the gate and parked next to an equally decrepit blue pickup with STANLEY HORTON III, LANDSCAPING SERVICES printed on its door.

In Stan's case, "Landscaping Services" was code for "grave-digging."

Stanley Horton had been burying the residents of McGill for as long as she could remember, and that was a pretty long time. His daddy, also named Stanley, had held the job before him, and his grandpa, the original Stanley, before that.

Stella doubted the tradition would be handed down to the next generation. Stan Horton IV was known more for his skill at sinking balls at the town pool hall and shoving quarters into the Pac-Man machine at the pizza joint than for any sort of sweat-producing, let alone backbreaking, labor. Since he was now pushing fifty and hadn't developed any visible sign of a work ethic, Stella doubted Stan Version Four was likely to get fired up and work-brickle all of a sudden.

Neither she nor the town was sure what McGill would do once the currently employed Stan retired his shovel. Apparently, they'd just have to figure out a way to stay alive and above ground, since there'd be no one to bury them.

Stella didn't see the hardworking, elderly Stan as she walked through the wrought-iron gates and approached the statue of Michael the Archangel, who guarded the entrance.

He had been protecting the cemetery, while subduing the mighty, writhing serpent beneath his feet, since before the Civil War.

With a grimace on his face and a spear in his hand that was longer than he was tall, the archangel appeared fiercely deter-mined to continue his ages-old fight with Satan, even if it took all eternity.

As Stella walked by him, she kissed her forefinger and lightly brushed it across his big toe, showing her appreciation for his diligence. It was a common custom among McGillians and, as a result, Michael's great left toe was considerably shinier than the rest of his digits, having been worn smooth over the years.

She passed through the older part of the cemetery, with its fine marble statues of life-sized angels, saints, and cherubs holding their silent vigils over the area's founding families.

The Spanish moss dripping from the trees, like the tattered, lacy petticoats of ladies long gone, lent the sacred, silent place a soft and gauzy, otherworldly ambiance.

Stella wasted no time as she moved among the ornate monuments, past the ancient antebellum gravestones whose names and dates had worn away until one could hardly read them.

She was headed to the rear, where the newest inhabitants were interred.

Walking by the graves of her parents Stella felt the familiar, painful emotions the setting never failed to evoke. Grief, for the mother taken far too young under tragic circumstances, leaving her only child without protection in a harsh world. Despair, for the father whose passing marked the death of any hope that they would ever find a way to establish a strong and loving father/daughter relationship.

"Losses come in lotsa forms," Stella whispered as she reached down and patted the top of her mother's headstone. "If we aim to be happy, we've gotta keep looking at what we've got, not what we lost."

Stella had only to think of the eight blessings beneath her roof. Even when they had their problems, as they did on a daily basis, she could barely contain all the joy they gave her.

No, she had nothing to complain about. Missing freckle-faced boy or not.

As she neared the shaded area where Arthur lay, she heard Waycross even before she saw him.

To her great relief, he wasn't crying, as he often was when she retrieved him from this unusual sanctuary of his.

He was just talking. Calmly. Quietly. Matter-of-factly.

She couldn't distinguish his words, but she would describe his tone as "man-to-man," and she felt better instantly.

She rounded a particularly large Celtic cross monument and saw him, sitting on a grave, leaning back against its stone, looking down and chattering away.

"You never told me *that* before," he was saying to the ground beneath him. "I had no idea that was the case." The boy drew a deep breath. "I feel heaps better now."

He seemed to be listening for a moment, his head cocked to the side like a robin trying to catch the sound of an earthworm crawling beneath the soil.

"Oh, I'm gonna tell her the first time I see her! She's got a lotta nerve that ol' Jeanette, sayin' stuff like that!" He listened again, then giggled. "That's true! That girl *don't* know her backside from a hole in an outhouse seat."

No sooner had he uttered that last phrase than he saw his grandmother looking at him with as disapproving an expression as she could muster while trying to suppress a snicker.

He tucked his chin, looked up at her with all-too-innocent wide eyes. "*Grandpa* said it first. Not me."

Unable to decide how to respond to that, Stella simply said, "O-kay." She walked over to the boy and sat beside him on the grave.

"I'm not in trouble for sayin' it if Grandpa said it first, right?" he asked, smiling the delightful, gap-toothed grin of a mischievous ten-year-old boy.

Stella reached over, wrapped her arm around his thin shoulders, and drew him close to her side. "Grandpa Art was talking about Jeanette Parker's backside? Is that what you expect me to believe, grandson of mine?"

He nodded vigorously, his wind-tousled curls bobbing.

"Well." She cleared her throat. "I was married to Mr. Arthur Reid for many a year, and truth be told, not once did I ever hear him compare somebody's rear end to an outhouse seat."

"That's 'cause you're a lady," Waycross shot back. "He talked one way to you, and he talks another way to me, 'cause we're both guys."

"Hmm. Manly-man talk, huh?"

"Yep."

Stella stared at him, and as always in these circumstances, she wondered if Waycross might actually have some sort of connection with his grandfather that neither she nor anyone else enjoyed. Most of what the child said, she chalked up to his overactive imagination and a deep need for this attachment. But sometimes he came up with something that seemed beyond even his flights of fancy.

"I won't ask what you and your grandpa were jabberin' about," she told him. "But your sisters said you were feelin' pretty poorly and now you seem mighty chipper. I guess the little chat you had helped a bit, huh?"

"They always do," he replied, most solemnly. "He's a fart smeller; I mean a smart feller, Grandpa."

She laughed. "He is that, for sure."

"He tells me stuff that nobody else ever thought to tell me. Stuff I need to know."

"Like what, if you don't mind me askin'?"

"Like that he was a redhead, too. That stuff's important. You or somebody shoulda mentioned it, one time or another."

His words took Stella aback, and she searched her memory for a time when she might have told the boy that Art had copper hair. But she couldn't recall having done so. Maybe he was right.

With all the hustle and bustle of their daily lives, meals to cook and laundry to wash, not to mention doling out discipline and bandaging scraped knees, that tidbit of family trivia must have fallen by the wayside.

"I beg your forgiveness, darlin'," she said. "I sure should've told you. Your grandpa did indeed have a fine head of hair and ever' one of them hairs was as red as yours. Maybe even redder, truth be told."

"I don't remember that at all," the boy said. "I only saw him that one time, and his hair was all white then."

"You remember seeing him? What time was that, honey?"

"When he was in his coffin there in the living room."

Stella's heart caught in her throat, and she fought back the tears that were blurring her sight as she stared down at the boy. It was the first time she had heard this, and it saddened her greatly.

"I didn't know you saw him in his casket," she said, when she finally found her voice. "I thought your mom was keepin' you littlest kids out in the backyard, all of y'all except for Savannah and Marietta."

"She was, and we were. But she wandered off to get a drink, and I snuck in and took a peek."

"I'm sorry, honey. I wish you hadn't seen him. Leastways, not like that. He was always such a handsome man, all lively, healthy, and strong."

"That's all right. I thought he looked nice, all dressed up and layin' in that pretty box with soft, shiny cloth stuff inside. He didn't look dead. Just asleep. All peaceful like. It was the first thing I remember in my whole life. I'm glad it was somethin' nice."

Stella thought of the simple coffin, the only one she had been able to afford at the time, and saw it through a child's eyes.

The satin lining and pillow. Arthur dressed in his Sunday suit. His only suit. The suit he had worn on their wedding day.

"I'm glad you remember him that way," she told him, smoothing the child's curls. "He was a mighty handsome man. Stole my heart away when we were just young'uns."

"In spite of his hair?"

"*Because* of his hair, and a lot of other fine qualities, as well."

"Like what?"

"Your grandpa was a kind man. He was funny, smart, generous, and hardworkin', and honest as the day's long."

Waycross nodded approvingly. "Those're important things to be."

"They sure are. 'Specially for a husband."

Waycross sighed and a sad expression crossed his little-boy face. "My dad's funny. He told me a joke one time. I reckon he's pretty smart, too. You have to be if you're gonna drive a big truck all over the country. Otherwise, you'd get yourself lost and wind up in some other state."

Stella felt yet another wave of grief sweep through her. She fought to keep her voice even, her tone neutral as she replied softly, "Yes, darlin'. Your daddy's smart and funny and hardworkin'. Like his daddy, he's handsome as the day's long."

She didn't include "generous" or "honest." There was no point in lying to the child.

Unfortunately, he knew better.

"He is handsome. Strong too," the boy added, looking into the distance, as though searching for the semitruck that might be coming down the highway. "But Grandpa's always here when I need him."

"That's right, and he had red hair, just like you!" she said, too enthusiastically, eager to change the topic back to Arthur.

The boy's grin reappeared, and he said with a proud lift of his chin, "That's right! Grandpa Art was a ginger! So dumb ol' Jeanette Outhouse-Bottom Parker was just *wrong, wrong, wrong*! I ain't no bastard after all!"

Chapter 3

Stella gasped. "A bas—? What did you say, child?" She reached down and placed her finger on her grandson's lips. "Never you mind. I heard what you said. You don't need to repeat it." She sighed and leaned back against her husband's gravestone for support. "Good heavens above, what is this world comin' to?"

"That dumb ol' Jeanette, she said it right there on the playground, too, in front of everybody," Waycross complained, on a roll. "She said anybody could just look at our family and tell I wasn't part of it. She said my momma must've done somethin' bad with somebody besides my daddy when she got me. Some guy with red hair, not black like Dad's and yours. And I couldn't argue with 'er, 'cause Momma did do a lot of bad stuff with a lot of guys, right there in our house, and now she's coolin' her heels in jail. The proof's in the puddin'."

"You listen to *me*, Mr. Waycross Reid, not that silly girl who's always got her gums flappin' about some nonsense or the other. You *are* your daddy's boy. Nobody else's. You're Arthur Reid's grandson, and my grandson. Ever' precious bit of you."

He looked up at her doubtfully. "Precious? Even my freckles?"

"Especially your freckles. I love ever' single one of 'em. How many times have I told you, them freckles are angel kisses? They show where a low-flyin' angel leaned down and planted a smackeroo on your nose."

He sighed. "And on my cheeks and on my forehead and on my arms and . . ."

"They're plenty fond of you, them angels. They're partial to redheads, I've heard."

"Hmm."

Stella stroked his cheek, which was nearly as soft as his baby brother's. "You are a Reid, darlin' boy, through and through, and Miss Jeanette don't know nothin' 'bout nothin'. She's a silly goofball of a girl who couldn't find that outhouse hiney of hers if you tied her hands behind her back."

They both giggled, but only Waycross was amused.

Stella was inwardly fuming and trying not to let her anger show.

For a moment, she pictured Jeanette's adolescent face, with its perpetual pout and mocking smirks. The term *box her jaws for her* crossed Stella's mind, but she quickly discarded the notion.

It wasn't the girl's fault.

Her parents were some of the most affluent in the tiny town, and Jeanette seemed to believe that gave her some sort of "princess" status.

The child had always possessed an unkind streak and appeared to enjoy bullying smaller, less advantaged kids.

Stella couldn't help disliking the child . . . and feeling bad about it. One had only to look at the haughty mother to see that it hadn't been a windy day when that particular Jeanette apple had fallen from her family tree.

Besides, as the not-so-proud grandmother of her own Marietta, Stella couldn't exactly judge.

But still . . .

"I'm gonna have a serious talk with Miss Jeanette's momma about this," she told Waycross.

"It won't work. That booger-rat Jeanette, she'll just aggravate me more if you do."

"Booger-rat?" Stella gave him her most disapproving, Granny-ain't-happy scowl. "Really, Waycross?"

He snickered and blushed. "It ain't that much worse than 'turkey butt' and you say that all the time."

Stella opened her mouth to argue with him but quickly closed it. The kid had a point.

"Okay," she said. "We both could stand to watch our language a bit more. Let's just say, if givin' that prissy gal's momma a talkin'-to don't work, then I'll address Miss Jeanette herself directly."

"Address her?" He thought it over a moment, then grinned broadly. "Is that anything like takin' her behind the chicken coop and introducing her to Miss Switch?"

Stella sighed. "Don't I wish, darlin'. Don't I wish. It'd do her and me both a heap o' good."

"Me too! I'd pay a nickel to see that!"

They laughed together and hugged each other.

Stella pushed the mop of red curls out of his eyes and planted a smack on his forehead, among all the angel kiss marks. "You know," she said, "we asked Elsie to come to our house to watch your brother and sisters, whilst I came out here to fetch you. Happens, she brought us a special treat. It's waitin' for us on the kitchen table."

His eyes widened and so did his tooth-deprived grin. "Oh, wow! Is it cake?"

Stella nodded.

"Is it *coconut* cake?"

Stella opened her mouth to answer, but before she could reply, a horrible sound echoed across the otherwise quiet cemetery.

21

An alarming sound.

A man's voice. Crying out.

The yell was followed by a string of colorful curses.

"What . . . who was that?" Waycross asked.

"Sounded like Mr. Horton to me," she told him.

"If it's him, he sounds *all* in a dither!"

The swearing continued, and Stella's concern mounted as she realized his tone was far more frightened than angry.

"Which way is it comin' from?" she asked herself.

Waycross answered for her. "Over thataway." He nodded in the direction of the cemetery's largest family mausoleum. "By that big ol' tomb house thing!"

"I think you're right. The Patterson crypt!"

She stood, pulled Waycross to his feet, and headed in that direction. Then she stopped, realizing she was possibly heading toward danger with a child in tow. A young child, at that. She froze, unable to decide what to do next.

"We gotta go help him!" Waycross told her, literally jumping up and down with excitement and pulling at her hand. "Now, Granny! Some skeleton might be stranglin' the life right outta him or eatin' his brain or worse!"

She wanted to ask him what could possibly be worse than having one's brain eaten by a skeleton in an ancient cemetery, but she decided not to. He was a wildly imaginative child whose fantasy life did not need encouragement.

The yells had subsided, but Stella heard the pounding of running feet coming in their direction.

She grabbed Waycross and shoved him behind her.

He didn't go willingly.

When she finally managed to get in front of the boy, so he was shielded by her full skirt, she turned once again toward the old crypt and saw Stanley Horton, gravedigger extraordinaire, racing in their direction. He passed them with only one quick glance their way.

His face was white and sweaty, and at first glance, she feared he might be suffering a heart attack. But he was running a bit too fast for an old guy who was about to expire from a coronary.

She was in the process of discarding that theory and coming up with an alternative when she heard him shout, "Get outta here, Miz Reid! Fast as you can! Git a move on!"

She reached behind her, grabbed her grandson's hand again, and hurried after Stan. She felt foolish to be running with no idea why. But the terror in his voice lent an undeniable credibility to his warning.

With a job such as Stanley Horton's, a family business at that, he wasn't a man easily spooked. She decided not to stick around and investigate.

Not at the moment, anyway, with a grandkid in hand.

"What is it, Mr. Horton?!" she shouted as they scurried after him, darting between the gravestones, racing toward the gate.

"Yeah! What's up?" Waycross called, as he stumbled over a tuft of grass, then scrambled back to his feet with his grandmother's assistance.

"Awful!" Stan shouted over his shoulder as he passed Michael the Archangel and the writhing satanic serpent. "Just plumb awful!"

They caught up to him as he was going through the gate.

For a moment, it seemed the three of them would clog the entrance, trying to exit all at once.

After a bit of jockeying for position, they burst through and raced to the two trucks, parked side by side.

"What was it, Stan?" Stella asked him as he collapsed, huffing and puffing, across his pickup's hood. "What in tarnation happened to scare you so?"

She saw raw horror in his eyes when he managed to gasp out, "Dead . . . man. Crypt."

Confused, she was contemplating her next question when she heard her grandson say, "But it's a cemetery, sir. There's dead men aplenty hereabouts. Ladies too. Even a few kids."

"Yeah," Stan replied, finally regaining a bit of his composure and his breath. "But most of 'em departed this world on account of accidents, or illness, or old age. But the one stretched out on the steps of the crypt, let's just say it's mighty obvious . . ."

"What is, Stan?" she asked, dying by degrees from curiosity. "What's obvious?"

"That he sure as shootin' didn't die of no *natural* causes!"

"What are you sayin', Mr. Horton?" Stella asked. But she knew the answer, even before he uttered the word. Only one thing could have upset the well-seasoned, hard-as-coffin-nails gravedigger to this extent.

"Murder!" he said, rubbing his forehead as though trying to erase something that had been seared into his mind's eye forever. "He ain't just dead. That fella's been plumb massacreed!"

Chapter 4

"Murder? Really?"

"That's what he said. Sure as I live and breathe."

"Wow!"

"Yeah! I know!"

Stella sat in her kitchen, fork in her hand, half a mouthful of Elsie's coconut cake making it difficult for her to tell her story to the rapt audience who had joined her around the old red Formica and chrome-trimmed table.

"I was there, too, don't forget," Waycross said, shoveling in more of the delicious dessert than he could chew.

Overloading one's plate, fork, and mouth was a family tradition. One Stella had attempted many times to squelch. Without success.

"I heard and saw ever'thing that Granny saw," Waycross added. "It was downright awful!"

"Ain't like *you* actually *saw* a dead body or nothin' totally grody like that," Marietta said, her arms crossed over her chest, her lower lip pushed out to a new, record-breaking extreme.

When the world experienced an extraordinary event and didn't furnish her with a front-row seat, Marietta Reid took it personally.

"Actually, finding dead bodies isn't all it's cracked up to be," Savannah added, her voice soft, her pretty face solemn, as she stared down at the empty dessert plate in front of her.

Stella reached over, covered her granddaughter's hand with her own, and gave it a squeeze. "You know a bit too much about that subject, don't ya, sweetcheeks?"

Savannah looked up at her grandmother and nodded.

For a moment, they held each other's gaze and remembered the Halloween night that began with fun and ended with a soul-scarring discovery that none of them would ever be able to forget.

Certainly not Elsie.

They looked over at their most treasured family friend, sitting at the other end of the table, her own plate empty, as well. They gave her a sympathetic smile. Her sweet, coffee-colored face softened as she returned their smile, though her dark eyes still reflected the pain of those events.

That experience had been a hard one for everyone, and not enough time had passed to even dull the pain, let alone heal the wounds.

But the moment of heavy, awkward silence ended quickly with Marietta firing yet another volley in her brother's direction. "So, big whoop-de-do," she snapped. "You're just makin' a big ol' honkin' deal outta nothin', like you always do, Waycross Reid. Some guy hollered, and y'all hightailed it outta the graveyard. Big duh. Who cares?"

"Marietta, if and until you can think of somethin' kind to say, I want you to say nothin'," Stella told her. "And while you're busy not talkin', I'd like you to clear the table, carry the dishes to the sink, and wash 'em."

"But it ain't my day! It's Vidalia's!" Marietta shot back with a defiant toss of her head.

"If you sass me once more or try to pick another fight with your brother," Stella said softly, "it's gonna be your *week*."

"Yay!" Vidalia interjected, clapping her hands at the very idea. "Go on, Mari. Sass her again! Quick, before she changes her mind!"

As always, Elsie stepped in to restore the peace. As she rose from her chair, she turned to Marietta and said with her sweet, soothing voice, heavy with Southern charm, "I'll do the dryin' for ya, sugar. We'll have them dishes washed and put away lickety-split."

Savannah stood, walked around the table to Elsie, and placed a gentle hand on her shoulder, nudging her back onto her chair. "You baked the cake, Miss Elsie. Besides, you're our guest, and company's not allowed to do chores in this household. I'll dry the dishes for Mari, while you have another cup of coffee."

Stella refreshed Elsie's mug, the one with Mickey Mouse on it, Stella's personal all-time favorite. A Christmas gift from Savannah. Elsie was one of the very few human beings who were allowed to drink from it. Elsie and Manny, of course.

Marietta and Savannah gathered the dishes and emptied the table, Marietta expressing her displeasure with every movement, nearly breaking the glasses and managing to ding Waycross on the ear with his plate as she whipped it away from him.

On the other hand, Savannah accomplished three times as much with grace and skill, maintaining a smile the whole time.

As she had many times before, Stella wondered at the difference in the two girls. From the moment they had come into the world, Stella had tried to teach the same life lessons to both, showing each one as much unconditional love as she could while administering occasional gentle discipline when needed.

She was sure that, to the degree any human could, she had treated them the same.

To the best of Stella's knowledge, their mother, Shirley, had done likewise. While good ol' Shirl might not have handed out a lot of love or carefully measured, thoughtful discipline, at least she appeared to have neglected them equally.

Try as she might, Stella could think of nothing to account for the differences in the two girls.

She glanced over at Elsie, who was also watching the girls as they began their dishwashing process, and Stella wondered if her friend was thinking the same thing.

Little escaped Elsie's watchful eyes. Although she had raised no children of her own, she had a gift for dealing with the younger set. Her ability to calm the wildest child was a divine talent that rivaled her ability to bake a perfect cake and to hug anyone fortunate enough to be in her presence. Her famous Elsie Dingle embrace had a magical quality about it. One all-enveloping cuddle from her had the power to squeeze away the huggee's troubles along with the frown from their face.

Daily, Stella enjoyed and appreciated the gift of her friendship.

Once the girls settled into a relatively peaceful washing/drying routine, Elsie turned back to Stella, her eyes aglow with what could only be described as morbid curiosity.

Elsie's a proper saint, Stella thought, snickering to herself, *but she's only human*.

"Then what else did Mr. Horton say?" Elsie wanted to know. She glanced around the table at the youngest faces. "That you can discuss here at the table anyway, that is."

"He was all upset, I can tell you. As he scrambled to get into that pickup of his, he said he was headed for the sheriff's station to fetch Manny."

Elsie gave her a knowing look, as she always did when Stella mentioned Manny. Even though Elsie had never been married or, to Stella's knowledge, even experienced a romance of any kind, she seemed particularly astute when it came to discerning the particulars of other people's relationships.

Often to Stella's consternation.

"Reckon you wanted to follow him to the station," Elsie said with a twinkle in her eyes and a smirk on her round face.

"I had other things to do," Stella said, giving a slight nod in Waycross's direction.

"Yeah," the boy said, eyeing the remaining slices of cake on Elsie's cut-crystal plate. "She would've been there quick as a duck on a June bug if she hadn't been saddled with the likes of me."

Stella grinned, reached over, and ruffled his hair. "I was not 'saddled' with nothin' and nobody. Least of all, *you*. I just had responsibilities of my own to attend to. Higher priorities and all that."

Waycross grinned at Elsie and nodded. "Yep. Like I said, stuck with a young'un. With this many of us, she's always got at least one of us, stuck like a sticker-burr on the backside of her breeches."

"That ain't so, boy. You and the rest of you kids are more like flowers on my bonnet than stickers on my rear end. I wouldn't have it any other way." Stella stood, walked to the stove, and turned on the heat under the old percolator coffeepot to rewarm it.

This was going to feel like one very long night. Unless, of course, Manny gave her a call or, better yet, dropped by to fill her in on all the gory but oh-so-interesting details.

As she passed Savannah, Stella heard her whisper, "You'd give your eye teeth to be at that cemetery right now."

"Would not."

"Would too." Savannah flipped the dish towel at her as she passed. "Don't lie now, Gran. You're always tellin' us how you can't abide lyin'."

"Hush up and git them dishes dried, girl. Time's a-wastin'," Stella said with all the pseudo indignation she could muster as she refilled the creamer.

Savannah giggled. "Oh, don't worry. I can tease you, dry dishes, and chew gum at the same time."

Of course, Elsie had heard the exchange. So, when Stella bent over to pour a generous amount of cream into the Mickey mug, Elsie nudged her with her elbow and said, "Do us all a favor and skedaddle back to that graveyard."

"I can't, Elsie. You know that."

"I don't know no such thing. Yes you can. Manny'll be out there by now, so it'll be safe, no matter what happened. You can snoop around and then hightail it back here and give us all a report."

As Stella took her seat at the table again, she glanced up at the cat clock on the wall. Savannah had bought the clock for her when she was much younger with her hard-earned and diligently saved pennies. The black cat's green "diamond" eyes moved from side to side, and its tail twitched back and forth as it kept the Reid household informed of time's relentless passing.

"It'll be dark in a few hours," she said.

"All the more reason to be makin' some tracks in that direction," Elsie said with a grin. "You don't wanna be out there in that graveyard when the haints git to stirrin'."

"Yeah!" little Alma piped up. "I know what haints is. They's ghosts and you don't want no part o' them!"

"'Specially after dark," Vidalia added with a knowing nod.

"There's no such thing as ghosts," Marietta interjected, pushing a dripping plate at Savannah. "Nobody but a stupid dummy would believe in stuff like that."

Stella gasped and shot a quick look at Elsie, who was a firm and outspoken believer in all things spectral.

She searched her mind for an appropriate response to the girl's outburst. But before she could think of one, she noticed that, as usual, the gentle Elsie hadn't taken offense.

Elsie just gave Marietta a long, searching look and said, "A dummy might believe in ghosts. So might a person who lives in an old plantation mansion filled right up to the brim with haints. A person who's met a few of 'em face-to-face. Even had conversations with 'em from time to time. Mighty interestin' talks they were, too, I must say. Especially since some of 'em have been dead since before the Civil War."

Every child at the table, Savannah, and even Marietta gaped at Elsie, open mouthed and wide eyed at this pronouncement.

"Wow!" Alma whispered. "I'd've liked to've heard them talks you had with 'em. Must've been mighty interestin'."

"Me too," breathed Jesup.

"Not me," Cordele added.

"Me neither." Vidalia shuddered. "I got enough problems messin' with live folks, never mind the dead ones."

Stella noticed that, unlike his sisters, Waycross was silent, gazing at Elsie with what looked like a new, even higher level of respect. Stella wanted to question him a bit, see what might be on his mind, as well, but the cat clock on the wall was ticking away. If she was going to go to that cemetery, and she knew she was, she had better get a move on.

At that moment, she heard an all-too-familiar sound. A baby crying. Macon Jr. was awake and fussing in his bassinet in her bedroom, next to the kitchen.

"So much for adventures," she whispered as she rose from her chair to head in that direction.

"Oh no you don't!" Elsie was out of her own seat and across the room before Stella could take two steps. "I'll take care of the baby and see to it that the rest finish their homework and git their baths. You skedaddle out that door this minute, Sister Stella, and find out what's goin' on over in that graveyard."

Stella grabbed her friend and drew her close for a tight embrace, then a peck on the check. "I owe ya, darlin'. Big-time."

"You sure do, and don't you forget it. Babysittin' seven kids and a baby is worth a whole heap o' gossip. You better come back here with a truckload. You hear me good now! Lots of it!"

As Stella grabbed her purse and headed for the door, she heard her friend call after her, "The juicier the better!"

Chapter 5

One of the best things about living in the mini-town of McGill was that it never took longer than six minutes to get from one end of the village to the other. Unless it was Easter morning, and there was a traffic jam in front of the old Baptist church at the corner of Main Street and Douglas.

Stella made it from her house back to the cemetery in record time. The body truck was old, but, like her, it could move along at quite a clip when somebody stepped hard enough on its accelerator.

The thought of murder was certainly a pedal-to-the-metal of her imagination. She had a passion for solving crimes, catching bad guys, and occasionally gals, and getting some degree of justice for those who had been robbed of piddling things like a dollar bill or everything. Some even their very lives.

For such a small town, McGill had seen more than its share, statistically speaking, of mayhem and murder. Most of the town's small population attended the community's two churches as often as three times a week, where they listened to lessons about how to love their neighbor as themselves. Considering that,

Stella thought they should be better able to resist the temptation to slaughter one another on a regular basis.

Even Sheriff Manny Gilford, excellent law enforcer that he was, had been unable to keep the homicide rate down to the national average in little McGill. Much to his consternation.

It didn't help that his deputy, Augustus Faber, managed to mention that fact every time he made one of his political speeches about all the law and order he intended to bring to the town once he himself was sheriff.

In the course of those dissertations, Augustus didn't mention the obvious: As one of McGill's two deputies, he had already been given the opportunity to perform the miracle he was promising he would manifest as sheriff.

But he had not.

However, two nights ago, when Manny had dropped by Stella's house for a friendly chat and a cup of her famous coffee, they had discussed how quiet things had been lately in the community.

No one had been murdered, no thievery, not even a bottle of nail polish shoplifted from the dollar store, and nary a bloody nose in sight.

The town had been remarkably law abiding for quite some time. So, they should have been on the alert that some skullduggery might be lurking just around the corner.

"We done spoke too quick," Stella muttered to herself as she pulled off the highway and headed down the one-lane road into the cemetery. "The devil heard us braggin' and, bingo, there's a fresh, new murder."

She couldn't help wondering who the victim was when she pulled up to the sheriff's black and white cruiser, parked at the cemetery's entrance, next to Stan the gravedigger's battered truck.

Though she knew it wasn't a particularly generous thought,

she couldn't help hoping the freshest corpse in the graveyard wasn't someone she loved. Or even liked, for that matter. Hopefully, the Lord had chosen to take someone less kind, innocent, and law abiding than the average McGillian.

"Heaven knows, we got enough rapscallions amongst us who You could pick and replant in your garden up there," she whispered, sending the suggestion skyward. She recalled some particularly ugly acts committed by some of McGill's "worst of the worst" over the years, and she quickly added, "Or wherever, in your great wisdom, You decide where they deserve to spend all eternity."

Although she couldn't resist the temptation to ask for divine intervention in the matter, Stella doubted her prayer would have much influence with the Almighty. Among the folks who had left the earth at another's hand, she had numbered more innocent souls than guilty ones among them.

Sadly, homicide spared no particular group of persons.

She got out of her truck and headed through the gate. This time, she didn't pause to tweak Michael the Archangel's toe. Though she did glance down at the serpent and briefly wonder if he had escaped the angel's custody sometime during the past day or so to wreak unholy havoc inside the normally peaceful graveyard.

As she neared the elite area of the venerable cemetery, with its elegant statuary and imposing, marble mausoleums, she could hear Stan blabbering away in the distance, his tone excited and shrill as he reported his story.

"I was just walkin' through, Sheriff, mindin' my own beeswax, when I saw that there mess on the steps," he was saying. "At first I thought somebody had vandalized the Patterson crypt. Lord knows it wouldn't've been the first time, what with Judge Patterson bein' the tough ol' gizzard that he is. But then I got a better look and knew it wasn't a simple case o' garbage and red paint."

She also heard Manny reply in a far calmer and more even tone, "How close did you get to the body, Stan?"

"Close, sir. I mean, I had to see if he was still alive and in need of assistance, didn't I?"

"Of course you did, Stan. Thank you. But, after getting close, you realized there was nothing you could do."

The sound of Manny's deep voice went through Stella like a warm cup of cocoa with a generous dollop of whipped cream on a winter's day, soothing, rich, and satisfying.

As she rounded a hedge of carefully trimmed boxwoods, she saw as well as heard him, and the sight of him had the same effect on her as his voice.

Stella was pretty sure she would have felt the same way about Sheriff Manny Gilford if he hadn't been tall, broad shouldered, with a bass voice, thick silver hair, and a quiet, confident way about him that made her and the citizens of McGill, Georgia, feel they were safer for having him nearby.

She would have harbored feelings of deep affection, immense gratitude, and abiding respect even if he hadn't been one of the handsomest and most admired men in town.

But she had to be honest; it certainly didn't hurt that he was.

Her husband, Arthur, had been an attractive man. A loving husband. A devoted father. A truly good human being.

But Manny Gilford had a charm all his own that caused her pulse to quicken and her knees to weaken any time she was near him.

Something told her he felt the same. In spite of her best efforts, suspecting that her feelings were reciprocated caused her to feel positively giddy inside any time she was in his presence.

Now, even with the expectation of seeing a murdered body within moments, she felt the familiar, almost overwhelming sense of pleasure when he turned and smiled at her.

He had one of those disarming smiles that was more than a

simple curving of the mouth. It lit his eyes, as well, and they twinkled at the sight of her.

"Why, Miss Stella May Reid, as I live and breathe," he said. "Fancy meeting *you* here." While he was obviously pleased, she could tell he wasn't the least bit surprised to see her.

"I was by here earlier, fetchin' Waycross," she told him. "He'd come to say how-do to his grandpa." She nodded toward the still badly disheveled, pale, and sweaty Stan. "We heard Mr. Horton here holler and saw him makin' some fast tracks to the gate. He said somethin' about a murder."

"Yes, Mr. Horton has already informed me of your shared adventure," Manny replied. "I'm glad everybody's safe and sound."

"I got her and the boy outta here quick-like," Stan told Manny with a lift to his stubbly chin. "Didn't know what we had here exactly, but I figured it wasn't a fit place for a woman and child to be."

Manny nodded solemnly. "Thank you, Mr. Horton. I appreciate you taking care of them like that."

Turning back to Stella, Manny wore a smirk that told her he was aware she had not needed rescuing.

Manny and Stella had shared plenty of adventures themselves over the years for him to know she was made of tough stuff. If anyone had needed assistance, it would have been Stanley Horton in dire straits and her attending to him.

With a tone that was suspiciously grave Manny added, "Sounds like you all had a close call. I'm just happy you managed to get out alive by the skin of your teeth."

She glanced over at Stan and could tell from his blank look that he had no idea the sheriff was pulling his leg.

Just as well, she thought. *This is probably the biggest adventure of Stanley's life. Why throw mud on a guy's hot fudge sundae?*

She looked around, curious but afraid of what she might see.

The first thing she noticed was the police crime scene tape that Manny had strung in a square shape, by winding it around four trees. That bright yellow tape always sent a chill through her when she saw it marking the boundaries of a particular location where something distressing and probably criminal had occurred.

In the center of the now-secured area stood the largest and most imposing marble mausoleum in the century-plus cemetery. It was a work of art, created by the most skilled marble masons of their time. The structure stood apart from the rest because of its highly detailed workmanship. Its unique embellishments included jewel-toned stained-glass windows, an arched bronze door engraved with intricate filigree, and four graceful Corinthian pillars, not unlike those that lined the front of the antebellum mansion the Patterson family had owned for many generations.

As always, when Stella saw the highly decorated tomb, she couldn't help recalling how hard it had been to raise the money for Art's tombstone. His resting place might still be identified by the small, generic metal marker provided by the funeral home had it not been for the special offering taken by her church congregation and Manny's own quiet contribution. He had discreetly left a generous amount of cash inside the Bible she had carried to the funeral with a note that read, "Arthur Reid was a fine man. He deserves a nice stone."

Manny hadn't signed it. But Stella had recognized his handwriting. He'd sat next to her in third grade and then again in fifth. She had seen enough examples of his barely legible scrawl to know it anywhere.

Now, standing near the Pattersons' palatial mausoleum, she felt a prickling of envy, that folks who had done more harm than good to their community over the years had such an elegant resting place, compared to a man like hers, who had left his small corner of the world far better than he had found it, but was remembered with less.

As always, Stella quickly chastised herself and pushed the thought from her mind. Coveting was a sin. One that led to a lot of pain for the one who harbored it. No one could be happy without gratitude and peace, and the act of coveting destroyed every vestige of both in the human heart.

Besides, what greater testimony to a man's well-lived years could there be than having a small boy run to his grave, hug his stone, tell him all his troubles, and even share a few man-to-man laughs with him?

She hadn't seen any troubled Patterson descendants sitting beside that fine marble tomb, seeking comfort and advice from their ancestors interred within.

Turning to Manny, she donned her most professional let's-get-down-to-business scowl, put her hands on her hips, and said, "So, where's this here dead body I've heard tell of?"

Chapter 6

Manny gave a quick glance toward the mausoleum, cleared his throat, and told Stella, "The body's on the other side of the Patterson crypt there. Stretched out on the steps. I'm not sure you want to see this one, darlin'. It's a bad one. He was . . . Well, let's just say, he didn't leave this world naturally or gently. Not by a long shot."

"That's for sure," Stan piped up. "I've seen a lotta dead bodies in my day. Way more'n most. But I gotta say, he takes the cake." He puffed out his chest, shoved his hands into his pockets, and pronounced, "Ya live by the sword, yer sure as shootin' gonna die by the sword. That there's straight from the Good Book itself, ya know."

Stella smiled, deciding not to correct Stan's rough paraphrase of St. Matthew's gospel. Stanley Horton III, a normally humble and rarely celebrated man, was having a big day, basking in his newfound limelight. Stella figured there was no point in dimming the beam on him.

Again, she turned back to Manny. "I reckon I can handle it, Sheriff," she told him in the most patient voice she could muster.

"I've seen more'n my share of mayhem in this world. A bit more won't wreck me."

She could tell Manny was mulling it over and was still reluctant. So, she added, "After that 'live by the sword' comment, I figure it ain't no sweet soul that I'm overly fond of. Not that I'd wanna see *anybody* smashed to smithereens, but . . ."

"It's one of our least popular citizens," Manny said, as he took her by the arm and led her closer to the mausoleum. "Let's just say he won't be missed at Wednesday night prayer meeting or Sunday school."

Stan snorted and followed after them. "Heck, that one won't even be missed at the Bulldog Tavern or the pool hall, and that's where he spent the better part of his days and nights. That fella worked hard at playin' the criminal. He thought he was Mr. Al Capone hisself. Leastwise, the closest we got here in little ol' McGill."

From Stan's description, Stella realized instantly who was lying just around the corner of the mausoleum.

It was Dexter Corbin.

Just had to be.

Corbin was the self-appointed town ruffian, the community's top gangster. At least in his own less-than-humble opinion.

She had to agree with Stan and Manny. If the murder victim was Dexter Corbin, his absence would be more of a blessing than a cause for grief. There probably wouldn't be much of a crowd at his funeral. Among the citizens of McGill, he was one of the least likely to be mourned.

"I'd feel sorry for ol' Dexter," she told her companions, "if he hadn't worked so hard over the years to be so unpopular."

Manny nodded thoughtfully. "He was particularly zealous about maintaining that nefarious reputation of his."

Stan added, "I reckon nobody in town'll be observin' that old rule about not speakin' ill of the dead."

"That's so true," Stella said. "If his ears were still workin', they'd be ringin' overtime, for sure, with all the bad gossip that's gonna be swapped concernin' him in the very near future."

"Did you ever get one of his famous phone calls?" Manny asked Stan.

"Of course I did. From what I hear, ever'body in town did at one time or another."

Stella hadn't been "gifted" with the dubious honor of hearing from Dexter Corbin personally, but she knew about his nasty habit. One of his favorite pastimes was to get rip-roaring drunk and start making threatening phone calls to folks he'd once disagreed with about something of little or no importance to anyone but Dexter.

Most of the townsfolk had crossed swords with him a time or two in the past and knew they could receive such a call at any hour of the day or night. Dexter's favorite time for such recreations was 3:00 a.m.

Most McGillians found their powers of discernment to be low or nonexistent at that hour, and they had a hard time deciding if Dexter Corbin was genuinely a deadly threat to humanity or a nitwit bully with nothing better to do between the closing of the local bars and the rising of the sun than terrorize his fellow man.

To their knowledge, he had never actually carried out his threats of murder and mayhem. There was never any proof that he had killed anyone, but they didn't exactly rest easy, never knowing when he might escalate from verbal abuse to the real thing and follow through with his dark promises.

"I don't reckon there'll be nary a soul at his burial," Stan said.

"Maybe a few," Stella said. "A handful or so who just wanna make sure he's under the grass and gone for good."

Stan chuckled. "We could put, 'Glad yer finally dead, you nasty, rotten son of a sidewinder' on his grave marker."

"Naw." Stella shook her head. "The headstone carver wouldn't have the space or the patience to hammer out all that."

"Sad commentary on a life," Manny added solemnly. "That guy spent more time behind the bars of my jail than anybody else in McGill history. Unfortunately, I couldn't prosecute him for just threatening to do something criminal. I wish they'd change the laws in that regard. But I did pick him up, throw him in there, and leave him to reconsider the folly of his ways any chance I got." He sighed. "For all the good it ever did."

As they rounded the corner of the mausoleum, Stella got her first look at the body sprawled facedown on the front steps, between the Corinthian pillars, beneath the engraved and gilded name above the door that read simply, PATTERSON.

Manny was right about the sight being more gruesome than the average death from illness, accident, or even murder.

Someone had wanted Corbin dead. That much was obvious. So was the fact that they had directed their considerable rage at his head.

Had Stella not heard Stan's description and recognized his pinstriped suit and high-heeled crocodile shoes, she would never have known the dead man was Corbin.

"Mercy," she whispered. "Looks like he might've threatened the wrong person!"

"Yeah," Manny replied.

She heard a gagging sound and turned to look behind her at Stan. He had turned an ugly shade of green that she had seldom seen on anyone who hadn't eaten a bad hot dog at the Burger Igloo.

"I can't," Stan said, shaking his head and turning away from the sight on the stairs. "I'm sorry, Sheriff, but I just—"

He left them, ran over to a nearby grove of trees and surrendered whatever remained in his belly.

Manny watched him for a moment, then looked away and shook his head. "I hate it when a civilian comes upon this sort of thing before we do. It's hard enough for us."

"Y'all see it way more than us average folks do," Stella replied. "Though it can't be easy for law enforcement folks, neither."

"It isn't," he assured her. "We have nightmares for years about what we've witnessed. But that's the job. Poor Stan there, he didn't sign on to find a murder scene where he earns his living. He's never going to be the same, and I hate that."

He patted her hand and said, "Stay where you are, darlin'. I'll be right back."

She nodded, and he left her to walk over to Stan.

Stella watched as Manny wrapped his arm around the older man's shoulders, gave him a gentle shake, and asked, "You gonna be all right there, good buddy? I'm a bit worried about you, what with that high blood pressure of yours."

Stan nodded feebly and wiped a shaking hand across his face. "I'm all right, Sheriff. Don't you worry about me. Just get on with . . . whatever you're fixin' to do for him over there."

"You go on home," Stella heard Manny tell him as he offered him a piece of mint chewing gum from his shirt pocket. "If I need anything else from you, it's not like I don't know where you live."

Stan brightened a bit, took the gum, and offered his hand to Manny. "I thank you, Sheriff Gilford," he said. "I truly do. I want you to know you've got my vote in this here upcomin' election. Always did have it and always will. I swear on my momma's best pecan pie."

Manny shook hands with him and gave him an affectionate whack on the back. "I appreciate that, Mr. Horton. You run along home, settle down in your easy chair, throw back a beer, and watch the ball game. That's what I'd be doing right now if I could."

Stan gave him a hint of a smile and nodded vigorously. "I'll drink two then, Sheriff. One for each of us."

"You do that. I'll give you a ring if I need anything else from you."

Stan wasted no time scurrying toward the exit as Manny rejoined Stella.

This time, with no one around, he took her hand and led her to the yellow tape.

Glancing back toward the road, he said, "I'll take you inside for a minute or two, if you want to go."

"You know I do, Manny," she replied. "I ain't the kind to sit a dance out, crammed up against a wall, feelin' sorry for myself, when I can be on the floor in the middle of the mess."

"I'm all too aware of that." He chuckled, then cast another wary look toward the road. "But if we get any more visitors, you're out of there pronto. Got it?"

"I do," she said. "I 'got it' more than you think I do."

He gave her a quizzical look, then chuckled. "Of course you do. Not much gets past you, girl."

Stella took a pointed look down the road herself and said, "Especially if we see a car comin' down the road, and it's a cruiser with Deputy Augustus Faber inside it. Right?"

Manny nodded. "Exactly. I overheard him on Sunday telling somebody how I 'play loose with crime scenes, letting civilians tromp all over them.' He even mentioned you by name as the primary offender."

"Offender? Well! *I'm* offended! I don't tromp nowhere, let alone around a body who's been murdered. I've been known to tippy-toe from time to time, but I'm as careful as any of you law enforcement types. I don't go handlin' bloody rocks or lead pipes that might be layin' about or steppin' on shell casings. I sure as shootin' do not lay a finger on the dearly departed. I might have a couple of threadbare holes in the bottom of my marble bag, but I ain't lost 'em all just yet."

"I know that, and you know that, and I told him so in no uncertain terms." He grinned down at her, then reached over and gently brushed one of her wayward curls out of her eyes with his fingertips. "Don't worry, darlin'. Nobody bad-mouths you in my presence and gets away with it. I'll defend your sterling reputation to my death, I swear."

She snickered. "I don't know how sterling my reputation might be, and you don't have to challenge Augustus to a duel or nothing deadly on account of me. Just a sock in the eye would do."

"I'll keep that in mind. A pleasant prospect." He nodded thoughtfully. "Yes. Something to look forward to."

He glanced down at his watch. "I'm surprised he didn't beat me to the scene. He's usually so gung ho about every call."

Stella laughed. "That knucklehead, he'd put on his siren and lights to answer a jaywalk complaint if he thought he'd get any attention."

"Don't I know it."

"He's a lot worse now even than before the campaign," she added. "He's plumb chompin' at the bit to show you up any way he thinks he can and ever' chance he gets." She gave a snort and a toss of her head. "Like he could hold a candle to you."

Manny grinned, then leaned down and planted a quick kiss on her forehead. "I think you might be a bit prejudiced when it comes to my abilities and charms, Stella dear." He paused, took a moment to search her eyes, and added, "At least, I hope you are."

"Maybe just a wee bit biased." She batted her eyes and gave him her best Southern coquette impression. "You know darned well, Manny Gilford, that I'm your number one fan. I always will be."

They stood in companionable silence for a moment.

Then they both cast quick, guilty glances toward the still-empty road.

"Let's go," he said, reaching for the tape and pulling it up for her to pass beneath it. "We've got a murder scene to process before Officer Gung Ho Gus shows up."

She passed beneath the tape, then held it up for him. "He's quite skilled at makin' a nuisance of himself, that deputy of yours. If you had a penny for every time that boy got on your bad side . . ."

"I'd put those pennies, every dadgum one of them, inside my biggest hunting sock, and I'd beat him to a frazzle with it."

They laughed. But only for a moment.

Then they walked to the front of the mausoleum and turned their attention to the mortal remains of Mr. Dexter Corbin.

Such as they were.

Chapter 7

"It was either somebody who managed to sneak up on him or someone he felt comfortable around," Manny said as he and Stella bent over the body and peered down at the wounds that had been inflicted on Dexter Corbin. "Somebody he felt safe with."

"How do you figure that?" Stella asked.

"For them to hit him on the back of the head, he must've been turned away from them when they attacked."

Stella nodded thoughtfully. "True. Dexter here wasn't the sorta fella to turn away from an enemy."

"He certainly had enough of them."

"I don't recall him having a friend in the world except maybe that Grymes boy. Tyrell's his first name, I believe. I did see them two hanging out together a few times, but they didn't seem to like each other."

"I'm quite sure they didn't. They busted each other's heads a few times, though neither one of them would ever press charges against the other."

"Then why did they keep company?"

"Illegal activities, I'd say, rather than genuine affection. Tyrell and Dexter were more like partners in crime than buddies. I busted them several times for drugs and such. Always got the idea that Dexter was the brains and Tyrell the fall guy. Tyrell didn't strike me as mean. More like just stupid. Gullible, too, at least as far as his choice of companions went. Where Corbin, on the other hand . . ."

"Was meaner than the disappointed bobcat when the fox snatched his rabbit."

"Precisely." Manny looked around and waved a hand to indicate the surrounding area. "Yes, I think it was someone he knew and trusted. It's pretty open right here. Nothing to duck behind. I guess it's possible but unlikely that someone was able to sneak up on him."

Stella studied the one particularly wide and deep laceration on the head, across the base of the skull. "That must've smarted somethin' fierce," she said. "Makes ya feel sorry for the guy, even if he wasn't worth a plug nickel as human bein's go."

"Yes. It's likely the fatal blow. The other one appears to be fairly superficial. But we'll be able to tell better when we get him on Herb's table with all that blood cleaned off."

Stella held an affectionate thought for her friend and fellow church member Herbert Jameson. Herb's wife had died young and unexpectedly, leaving him to raise their daughters on his own, as well as perform the duties of the town's only mortician and coroner. He enjoyed few spare moments but mostly spent those on his girls and his community.

She didn't envy him having to deal with this situation. This body.

"I reckon you already called Herb about this mess," she said.

"He'll be here before long. I rang him as soon as I got the call from Stan, but he was in the middle of working on Jake Robins. Said he'd get here quick as he could."

Manny pulled a small camera from his jacket pocket and leaned over the body to take close-ups of the carnage.

"Sweet little Jake," Stella said. "That fella was cursed with such lousy vision, bless his heart. A blindfolded lawn mole had keener eyesight than that poor guy."

"I know. But you'd think, in broad daylight, he would've been able to see something as big as a barn and not plow into the side of it."

Manny snapped another picture, then moved to the other side of the body and knelt on one knee to take more. "That guy got bullied a lot over the years. Those Coke bottle glasses with the thick black frames didn't help him a bit. The bow tie and plaid pants, either."

"Or bein' short as a flea, but not able to jump near as high."

"Working for the sewer department didn't help."

"His occupation did lend itself to a lot of ugly insults. Even folks with stunted imaginations can come up with some doozies when they've got that much to work with."

"Fertile ground, indeed. And now, Jake's stretched out—well, as far as he can stretch—on Herb's table, getting prepared for his funeral. Life sure isn't fair to some folks. Especially good, gentle fellows like him."

Stella stepped away so her feet wouldn't show in Manny's picture. "Reckon Jake'll be wearin' them glasses? In his coffin, I mean."

"No. Herb says Jake asked him years ago not to bury him in those rotten glasses. Though he didn't say 'rotten.' You being a lady and all, I won't repeat what he actually said."

"I can imagine, and I don't blame him. I hope he's got twenty/twenty vision in heaven right now."

Manny chuckled and smiled up at her. "You're a good woman, Stella May. I'm proud to know you and prouder still to keep company with you."

She glanced around the graveyard, then down at the body. "You call this 'keepin' company'? I thought you were only supposed to use that term when those whose company was being kept were enjoyin' themselves and each other."

He stood, brushed the dirt off his pants leg, and gave her a look that went right through her, warming every cell as it passed. "I'm enjoying your company, darlin'," he said, his voice soft and low. "As rotten as this sort of thing is to have to deal with, I'd rather be doing this with you than anything else with any other lady."

She blushed. She could feel the heat of it in her cheeks and knew he was noticing.

Nothing got past Sheriff Manny Gilford.

"Same here," she whispered.

Of course, he caught that, too, and he laughed heartily. "Ah, Stella. What am I gonna do with you, gal?"

Several tantalizing possibilities materialized instantly in her mind. But as quickly as they appeared, she shoved them aside.

She was the grandmother of eight grandchildren, all of whom were living under her roof, eating at her table, and right this moment, they were being tended by someone other than herself, just so she could be with this man who set her heart aflutter with a simple smile.

You should be plumb ashamed of yourself, Stella Reid, she thought, as she looked up into those intense gray eyes that were studying her closely. No doubt, knowing everything she was thinking.

"The kids are fine, sugar," he said. "Next to you, Elsie's the best person on the planet, and she loves them dearly, like they were her own. They're perfectly safe and happy with her watching over them."

"I know, but—"

"But nothing. Everybody needs a break once in a while. Even grandmothers. Especially ones like you, who pour so much of themselves into the little ones in their care. Once in a while, you need something else to think about besides those children. It's good for you, and what's good for you is good for them, too, in the long run."

He draped one arm over her shoulders and gave her an affectionate squeeze.

Waving his hand toward the body, he said, "Tell me what you think about this."

She glanced around at the cemetery. "I don't recollect Dexter havin' any kinfolk buried here that he'd be visiting. Plus, we already discussed that he had no friends to speak of. I can't think of any normal reason he'd pay a visit to this place. So, I figure he came here to meet somebody."

"Okay. I agree. He and someone else arranged to meet here for some reason."

"Probably no good reason."

"Because?"

"If it'd been on the up-and-up, they could've met in town at the Burger Igloo, or on a street corner, or in the gazebo in the middle of town. It would've been more convenient than drivin' out here."

"True. What else?"

She knew that he already had answers to the questions he was asking her. Manny Gilford didn't need Stella Reid to solve his case for him.

It was more like being quizzed by a teacher. But that was fine with her.

Fun, in fact. At least, as fun as it could be, considering there was a murdered man lying, mangled and bloody, at her feet.

Stella looked around at the grass, which was kept pristine in this area of the graveyard. There was nothing out of the ordinary to mar its perfection. Not even a wayward dandelion.

"There's nothin' layin' around close that's big enough to kill somebody with," she said. "If the murder weapon was left here at the scene, it sure ain't nearby."

"We're starting to lose the light. I'll search the area as soon as the sun rises tomorrow," Manny told her. "I'll get Augustus out here with me. Mervin too. But I have a feeling we aren't going to find anything. I suspect the killer took it with him."

"I reckon he brought it with him, too," she said.

"Why do you figure that?"

She shrugged. "Look around you. There's not a lotta stuff in a cemetery that'd do the job. The gravestones are too heavy. The caretaker picks up any branches that break off in a storm, and we ain't had no high winds in a month or more. He got rid of any rocks long ago, so's he wouldn't mow over 'em. Other than the monuments and the grass, there ain't a lot here. 'Cept the wilted bouquets, and you'd have to be mighty mad to beat somebody to death with one of those!"

"Good work, Detective Reid," he said with a wink. "What does that tell us about our killer?"

"That he probably brought the weapon with him, which means he knew what he was gonna do before he got here."

Stella felt a cold shiver go through her. "It means, this weren't no accidental killin'. Or even a momentary act of passion that turned into a fistfight with a bad end. It wasn't even plain ol' murder. No, this here was most likely what you call 'premeditated murder.'"

Manny's face grew grim as he looked down at the victim on the stairs with his ruined head and his flashy, expensive clothes that were now stained with a gruesome quantity of blood.

"Yes," Manny replied, "and premeditated is the worst kind. In the heat of a moment, in a fit of rage, most people can lose their minds for a few seconds and do something they'll regret for the rest of their lives."

Stella shivered, moved closer to Manny, and leaned against him. "For somebody to think about it ahead of time," she said, "to plan it, and then to carry out those plans . . . now that's a whole other level of evil."

Chapter 8

Normally, by ten o'clock at night, Stella was exhausted and on her way to bed. But relaxing in her living room with Manny, Elsie, and Savannah for company, not to mention baby Macon Jr., who was snoozing in her lap, she was still going strong, as bright of eye and bushy of tail as any squirrel gathering autumn nuts for his winter stash.

But Stella was gathering memories. Ones she would cherish, pull from her mental treasure troves, and savor over and over again for years to come.

There was nothing quite like knowing that someone else had died young and unexpectedly to affirm the fragility of life. It made a person fully appreciate the fact that they were still above ground and breathing fresh air.

"I know you're not supposed to say bad things about people who've died," Savannah said as she handed Manny and Elsie fresh glasses of lemonade from the kitchen, "but if I was honest, I'd have to admit that I never really liked Mr. Corbin all that much. Not a bit, in fact."

"Why is that, sugar?" Stella asked her, as she shifted the sleeping baby in her lap, trying to restore the circulation in her left arm, where his head was resting.

Savannah considered her reply thoughtfully before answering, "I'm not exactly sure. I suppose it's because he had a weird, dark way about him. He kinda radiated bad vibes. He gave me the creeps."

Instantly, she had Manny's attention. As he took the glass from her, he thanked her and said, "Why do you say that, Savannah? What do you mean by 'the creeps'?"

Having distributed the drinks, Savannah walked over to Stella's chair, and as was her custom, she sat on the floor at Stella's feet and leaned her head on her grandmother's knee. Savannah had done that since she was a tiny girl, and Stella had always found it endearing.

With her baby-free hand, Stella reached down to run her fingers through the girl's glistening black curls. "We know what 'the creeps' means, but what does it mean to *you*, sweetie? Did Mr. Corbin ever say or do anything inappropriate in your presence?"

Savannah shrugged. "Not exactly. Nothing you could really hang your hat on. But a few times, when I passed him on the sidewalk or in the grocery store, he'd look me up and down in a way that made me uncomfortable."

Stella glanced over at Manny and saw his face grow dark and his jaw tighten.

Manny was protective of Stella and her entire brood, but especially Savannah, who was, undeniably, his favorite among the grandchildren.

Stella wasn't sure why the sheriff was keeping such a close eye on Savannah. Perhaps because the girl had shared with him, more than once, her fervent dream of someday becoming a law enforcement officer, like him. Savannah took a great interest in

Manny's work and frequently stopped by the station house to chat with him and ask questions. Questions he seemed happy to answer.

Or maybe he was watching out for her because, at the tender age of thirteen, Savannah was entering adolescence with an exceptionally beautiful face and the body, not of a girl, but of a decidedly curvaceous woman.

Facts that were not lost on the male citizens of McGill, both young and not so young.

"O-kay," Manny said slowly. "But did he ever actually say or do anything he shouldn't?"

Savannah shook her head. "No. It was more like I could see it in his eyes, like he was thinking stuff about me that he shouldn't have."

Elsie chuckled and took a sip of her lemonade. "You're a mighty pretty little gal, Miss Savannah," she said. "You're gonna have to get used to menfolk gawking at you and thinking things they shouldn't. Best you just ignore 'em and look the other way. That sends 'em the message you ain't thinkin' the same thoughts. That's enough to put most of 'em in their place. The decent ones, anyways."

Savannah blushed and cleared her throat. "I know about that stuff, Miss Elsie. I've been getting those sorta looks for some time now. Usually, I just give them a little frown, like they should be ashamed of themselves, and they cut it out. They even seem a mite embarrassed that I caught them."

"But not Corbin?" Manny said, still radiating an intense disapproval.

"No. Not Mr. Corbin," Savannah replied. "He didn't seem the least bit embarrassed or uncomfortable when I gave him my 'Take a hike, buddy' look. With him, it wasn't just a man looking you over, thinking you're pretty, and maybe having a dirty thought about you. It was that, but more. He wanted me to notice him looking. He liked it that I knew he was thinking bad stuff. But what he really liked was that it embarrassed and scared me. That was the creepy part. Only a bad guy enjoys scaring a girl that way."

Manny shifted in his chair and leaned forward, closer to Savannah. He reached out and placed his big hand on her shoulder. "Savannah, honey, I want you to promise me something, okay?"

She nodded. "Sure. What?"

"If any man, or even boy, in this town makes you feel creepy again like that—at all, even a little bit—I want you to come straight to me and tell me about it."

Savannah smiled up at him from her seat on the floor and blushed a pretty shade of rose. "Why, Sheriff? Are you gonna go beat them up for looking at me cross-eyed?"

"I most certainly will," he replied instantly with a mock-stern tone. "I'll lock them in my cell, feed them moldy bread and water, and make them write, 'I'm sorry, Savannah,' a thousand times a day for the rest of their lives."

She laughed. "Thank you. I appreciate your enthusiasm and your kind offer. But I'm pretty sure you can't arrest somebody for looking at a girl the wrong way. Otherwise, your jail would be packed, a dozen to a cell. You'd have to use a shoehorn to get them all in, and the streets of McGill would have only women on them . . . no males at all."

"Okay, I might not be able to arrest them, but there's a big difference in a decent guy noticing a pretty girl and one who's deliberately making a female feel like she has something to fear from him. If anybody gives you cause to feel uneasy, unsafe, you let me know. If you have an intuitive notion that there's something not quite right about any guy in this county, you trust that feeling. Take it seriously and tell me about it. I'll take some sort of action on your behalf. I promise."

Stella patted the top of her granddaughter's head. "You listen up, Savannah girl. Sheriff Gilford's right. The good Lord gave you that intuition for a reason. Make sure it's your best friend. The one you always listen to. It's meant to help young women . . . young men, too, for that matter . . . get through this life with as little trouble as possible."

"I did, Gran. I stayed away from Mr. Corbin," Savannah insisted. "I had a feeling he wasn't going to live to a ripe old age and then die in his sleep, peaceful like."

"I think we all had that feeling about him," Manny replied. "I don't need Herb's report tomorrow to tell me he didn't pass away quietly while taking a nap on those mausoleum steps."

Stella wished that she could have stayed with Manny longer in the cemetery. At least until Herb Jameson arrived to collect the body. But she'd worried that she was taking advantage of Elsie's generosity and had returned home before the mortician arrived.

As it happened, she could have stayed longer. Elsie was in no hurry to rush home, as evidenced by the fact that she was still sitting on Stella's couch, sipping lemonade, and trying to coax even more information out of both Stella and Manny.

"Do you think he fought back, that weasel Dexter?" Elsie asked Manny. "Can you tell that sort of thing just by lookin' at a dead body?"

"It was pretty dark out there, Miss Elsie, when we moved him," Manny told her. "The few lights Herb brought with him weren't that powerful, so there was a limit to what we could see. Plus, we didn't want to undress him until we had him in the mortuary, in case something important might fall off him and onto the ground."

Elsie looked disappointed and sighed as she ran her finger around the top of her frosty glass. "Guess we'll have to wait 'til Brother Herb's done with his exam then. I don't know if I can stand the suspense. It just might be more'n I can bear."

Everyone chuckled except Elsie. She glanced from one to the other, as though wondering what the joke was.

Savannah spoke up. "But once Mr. Jameson starts looking him over there in the funeral parlor's preparation room, he should be able to tell if Mr. Corbin fought his attacker. The victim might have bruises on his forearms, where he tried to hold his arms up to protect his head and face. Or he might have skin or hair under his fingernails if he scratched someone. Or . . ."

Stella caught the little grin that Manny gave Savannah. Obviously, she had been learning under his tutelage and retaining what he'd told her.

At this rate, Stella thought, *that child's gonna be a full-blown detective with a gold badge and ever'thing by the time she turns fourteen.*

Savannah turned to Manny. "Mr. Jameson will make sure to check for hair between Mr. Corbin's fingers, won't he? That could help. Especially if it's a color other than brown. Like blond or red."

"If it's red, it ain't mine," came a young male voice from the other room. "I ain't your man, Sheriff, red hair or no."

Stella laughed. "You're supposed to be sleepin' in there, Master Waycross Reid. You've got school tomorrow."

"Just wanted you to know, I'm innocent as I can be," was the childish reply. "I was just there chewin' the fat with my grandpa, and he didn't say a word about no dead guy layin' nearby." There was a brief pause, then, "Now that I think about it, I'm surprised Grandpa didn't mention it."

"Okay, okay," Stella said, trying not to laugh. "Enough outta you, young man. Close your eyes and your ears and get to sleep, before I hafta come in there and jerk a knot in your tail."

"Oh, yeah. That'd put me in a nice, peaceful, sleepy mood. Good thinkin', Granny."

"Waycross!"

"I'm sleepin'! Startin' to snore right now."

A round of giggles could be heard from the bedroom, followed by a series of loud, deep, gasping "snores."

"Good grief, Waycross," Stella called out. "Knock that off. You sound like a Louisiana swamp bullfrog with a sinus infection."

The snoring ended abruptly, followed by more titters, then silence.

Manny glanced toward the bedroom, lowered his voice, and said, "I don't want to haul him out of bed at this hour. But tomorrow morning, if you think he could miss a couple hours of school, I'd appreciate it if you'd bring him to the station for a while. I'd like to question him about what he might've seen while he was there today."

"Anything I can do to help, Sheriff," Stella said in her most businesslike voice, trying not to sound too thrilled at the prospect of spending time with him again so soon. "I'd be happy to."

"Good. I can use all the help I can get," he replied, looking and sounding tired. "Once Merv and I get back from the cemetery in the morning, I'll give you a call, and you can go pick him up from school then. I don't want him to miss a whole day on account of me."

"I wouldn't mind takin' off the whole day," came a small voice from the other room. "I really wouldn't, as long as it's for a good cause."

"Good night, Waycross," they called out in unison, only to be answered with a fit of giggles and more fake snores.

"I'll send him off as usual," Stella told Manny. "By the way, did you ever get hold of Augustus?" she asked.

"I didn't, and I'm not happy about that, either. I radioed Merv, and he said Augustus hasn't checked in with the station house for hours. I sent him to do a wellness check on Widow Hayward hours ago, and I haven't heard from him since. How long does it take to find out if an elderly lady is still on her feet or not?"

Elsie piped up, "Oh, I hope she's all right. She was lookin' and feelin' poorly at church on Sunday. Now I feel bad I didn't go out there to check on her myself."

"I hope there's not a problem at her farm," Manny said, looking even more concerned than before. "Her daughter, the one who lives in Atlanta, rang the station and asked us to look in on her. She calls her mom every afternoon, and today the widow didn't pick up. So, I sent Augustus out there to make sure there wasn't anything seriously wrong. I can't imagine what he'd be doing that would take so long."

Stella felt Savannah stir at her feet. Then the girl turned and looked up at Stella with a strange look in her eyes that Stella couldn't quite interpret.

She appeared to have something she wanted to say but, for some reason, was holding back.

"Um, I, uh . . ." Savannah murmured.

"Yes, child? What is it?" Stella prompted her.

The baby woke and started to fuss. Stella lifted him, draped him over her shoulder, and began to pat his back.

"I'll get his bottle!" Savannah said, far too enthusiastically, as she jumped to her feet and rushed off to the kitchen.

Stella watched her disappear, then noticed that Manny was taking it all in, as well. His expression was curious, as though he, too, sensed something was up but going unsaid.

"Boy howdy," Elsie said. "You couldn't ask for a better helper than that Savannah. What a dedicated big sister she is! Did you see her fly outta here like her tail feathers were aflame?"

"Yes, I did," Stella replied with a far less enthusiastic tone. "I gotta wonder if—"

"What in tarnation?" Manny jumped to his feet and hurried to the front living room window.

Stella leaned forward to look at what he was seeing.

A vehicle was turning off the highway, then coming down her dirt road toward the house.

It wasn't hard to tell whose car it was, as the top of it had red and blue lights that were flashing, signifying some sort of emergency or serious situation, and it wasn't large enough to be an ambulance, let alone a fire truck.

"Deputy Augustus Faber," she heard Manny mutter under his breath. "Boy, you'd better have a good excuse for going AWOL or your ass is gonna be shoved through a wringer."

He turned back to the women in the room, seemed to realize he wasn't alone, and said, "Beggin' your pardon, ladies."

"Under the circumstances, all's forgiven, Sheriff," Elsie assured him, her dark eyes sparkling with excitement. "Go whup his lazy bee-hind and don't hold back on our account!"

"Yes siree bob," Stella added. "All's well here. You get on out there and rain some hellfire and damnation down on that there conceited, cabbage head deputy of yours! Spare the rod, you'll spoil that boy!"

Manny looked at Stella then Elsie in turn, out the window at his deputy, who had parked in front of the house, lights still flashing, then back at the two women.

"Wow," he muttered under his breath. "Remind me never to get on the bad side of you two demure Southern belles!"

That said, he hurried out the door to confront his deputy.

In his wake, Elsie and Stella, who was still holding the baby, jumped up from their chairs and rushed to the door. Once there, they jostled for positions, each trying to get the best look at what was about to happen outside through the lace-curtained window in the door's upper half.

"Can we open it a crack, so's we can hear what they're sayin'?" Elsie asked Stella.

She thought it over for a moment. "Naw. That wouldn't be polite, eavesdroppin' like that."

With some difficulty, considering the child in her arms, Stella pressed her ear to the door.

But whatever Manny said in his gruff greeting to his deputy, she couldn't discern, because his words were too muffled for her to understand.

"Okay," she told Elsie. "A crack. We'll open it an itty-bitty crack."

"What are you two doing?"

They turned and saw Savannah standing behind them, holding the baby's bottle, wearing an amused smirk on her face.

"Nothin'!" Stella said. "Gimme that and pipe down!"

Savannah surrendered the bottle, then tried to see through the door's window. "Is that Deputy Faber out there?"

"Yes," Stella whispered, "and Manny's gonna read him the riot act for disappearin' all afternoon and bein' outta reach when he needed him."

"Oh, um . . . yeah, that . . ." Savannah replied, again with a funny look on her face.

"Shh, both of you," Elsie said. "I cain't hear a word they're sayin' out there for you two's jabberin'. Sister Stella, hush up. Savannah, you wedge in here between us and keep quiet! I do swear, both of y'all have got a lot to learn about eavesdroppin', and I aim to teach it to ya!"

Chapter 9

"Don't stand there with a straight face, Augustus Faber, and tell me it took you four hours to perform a simple wellness check on one old widow woman," Sheriff Manny Gilford told his deputy, who was leaning back against his patrol car, as though trying to distance himself from his irate boss.

"It did!" Augustus protested. "That's how long it took. I swear!"

"Then you'd better tell me that she had a heart attack right in front of you, and you had to perform emergency bypass surgery there on her kitchen table. Because anything else, including driving her all the way to the hospital in Franklin, wouldn't have taken half that long."

Stella, Savannah, and Elsie listened to the heated conversation, taking place in Stella's front yard, from their carefully chosen positions just inside the front door of Stella's house. The door that had been oh-so-carefully opened just a crack to ensure they didn't miss a word.

"It's not like she lives inside the city limits," Deputy Faber whined. "It's a ways out to her farm."

"Yes. It takes ten minutes to get there, instead of two, like it does to answer a call that's in town," Manny shot back as he leaned closer to Faber, invading his personal space.

From her vantage spot, peeking through the lace curtain, Stella couldn't help noticing how much taller Manny was than Augustus Faber. Or almost any other man in town.

Long ago, Stella had decided that, as males went, Manny Gilford was a fine specimen. She also liked his confidence and how easily he slipped into the role of alpha when the situation warranted.

She couldn't help being proud of him, as he refused to accept the obviously lame excuses his deputy was offering.

"That's it, Manny," she whispered. "Don't let that polecat wriggle outta this. Tell 'im what's for."

"Shh, Gran." Savannah nudged her in the ribs with her elbow. "If they hear you, we won't be able to listen to the rest."

"Ten minutes there, ten minutes back," Manny was saying, "and, say, five to get out here. That leaves you another three hours and thirty-five minutes to account for your whereabouts."

Faber took off his hat, ran his fingers through his thick blond hair, and replaced it carefully, obviously buying time as he did his own quick mental calculations.

"I stopped by my house on the way back," he finally offered. "I hadn't eaten any dinner and was about to starve. My old lady, she's a real slow cook."

"What the hell did she make you? Beef Wellington?"

Augustus squirmed and stared down at his shoes. "Um, a bologna sandwich."

"You're telling me it took her over three hours to put together a bologna sandwich?"

"With cheese."

Manny glared at him, and Stella winced. She could tell by the tight set of his jaw that Manny was about to lose his patience, and

Deputy Faber was skating on spring-thawed ice. Ice with sharks circling beneath.

"What time?" Manny asked.

"What time did I eat the sandwich?"

"What time were you at home? From when to when?"

Again, Faber fidgeted with his hat, then his tie. Finally, he said, "From, say, five-thirty until, oh, about six o'clock."

"I called your house at ten to six and your wife said you weren't there. She also said she hadn't heard from you all day."

"I guess she forgot."

"It's hard to imagine that your wife, bright as she is, would forget something as monumental as making you a bologna sandwich. *With cheese*, no less. Also, I'm pretty sure she's observant enough to know whether there's a husband in her house or not."

Faber gave a little smirk, looked down at the toes of his boots, and said, "Well, sir, being newlyweds and all, we might've enjoyed . . . had a bit of . . . dessert, if you know what I mean."

Faber laughed uproariously at his own joke, but Manny's expression remained grim as before.

"Okay," Manny replied, "you had a roll in the hay with your new wife. So, that was another three minutes of paid duty the county's never gonna get back."

With a deep sigh, Faber sagged against the cruiser, and in a tone of voice used by felons confessing murder, he said, "Okay, boss. You got me. Let's just say I went a bit out of my way to help the widow today, and since I know how you are about us squandering the taxpayers' dollars, I didn't want to admit it."

Still, Manny appeared unmoved. "How?"

"I fixed her toilet. It was overflowing like crazy, and she was knee deep in the backwash. A serious toxic dump. That's why she didn't answer the phone when her daughter called."

Stella stifled a snicker, but Elsie couldn't. She snorted, then laughed, loud and hard.

Both men turned to look toward the house. The three females ducked their heads, and Stella reached out and clapped her hand over Elsie's mouth.

"Quit that gigglin'," Stella whispered. "So much for you being the snoopin' expert around here."

She waited for Elsie to stop shaking with laughter and said, "You got control of yourself now, girl?"

Elsie nodded, and Stella pulled her hand away from her friend's face.

"Okay, okay," Elsie said, out of breath. "I'm all right now. Sorry."

Stella glanced at Savannah, and, to her surprise, the girl wasn't laughing or even smiling along with them. She looked quite somber, troubled even.

But Stella didn't have time to wonder why for long, because the conversation outside was getting louder by the moment.

"You fixed the woman's toilet?" Manny was asking. "You expect me to believe that?"

"And helped her clean up the mess."

Manny looked him up and down. "Then why do you look and smell fresh as a bar of lavender soap?"

"I changed clothes and showered while my wife made the bologna and cheese sandwich."

"But you couldn't just tell me this in the beginning? You couldn't have radioed the station and informed Merv where you were and what you were doing?"

"No. I couldn't. I was up to my eyeballs in—"

"Yeah, yeah. Okay. Whatever."

"You do believe me, don't you, sir?"

Manny shook his head slowly. "No, Deputy Faber, I do not believe you. And I'll tell you right now that when I find out what you were really up to, you and I are going to have another conversation that won't be nearly as cordial as this one."

Manny gave him a smile that was anything but friendly. It reminded Stella of a junkyard dog baring its teeth.

"So," Manny continued, "think about that. It'll give you a little something to look forward to."

Stella didn't like the look that Augustus gave Manny in return. It seemed threatening to her. She knew Manny was attempting to put his deputy in his place, to affirm who was the boss and who wasn't. Even if Augustus was running for the position in the local election, he wasn't sheriff yet.

But she could see that the deputy was far from apologetic or submissive. The look he gave Manny frightened her, even if it didn't Manny.

In that moment, it occurred to Stella that Deputy Augustus Faber could make an unpleasant enemy.

Not that ol' Gus makes that good of a friend, she added to herself.

In that moment, she wished with all her heart it was someone else who was running against Manny in the election. After all, many an election had been won through less than honest means, and something told her Augustus wasn't above resorting to unethical tactics to get what he wanted. Like a sheriff's badge on his chest.

But for the moment, Manny appeared to still be firmly in charge as he told his deputy, "Since you were AWOL all afternoon, supposedly performing latrine duty, eating fancy bologna sandwiches, and romancing your wife, you get to spend the night in the cemetery, making sure no one crosses into that crime scene."

"But, sir!"

"It's going to be a chilly night, so I recommend you take a warm jacket, two large thermoses of coffee, and a big, empty jar. There's no sort of restroom in that area, and I don't want to hear that you 'watered' anybody's grave while on duty out there. Merv and I will relieve you at sunrise, when we come to search the out-lying areas of the scene."

"I'm not going to get to search the scene with you?"

"You had the chance to do that this afternoon and evening, but you were doing whatever you were doing that you don't want to admit. So no. Merv and I will handle it without you."

"Merv's an idiot."

"His biscuits are a bit doughy in the middle. Everybody knows that. But most of the time he's where I tell him to be, doing his duty. To my knowledge, he's never lied to me about anything but the quarters he takes out of petty cash to play Pac-Man at the pizza joint."

Stella watched tensely as the two men stared at each other.

She heard Elsie whisper, "I think they're gonna fight."

"What will we do if they start pounding on each other?" Savannah asked, sounding genuinely afraid.

"I don't know," Stella replied. "It's not like we can call the police to come break it up. They *are* the police. Of course, there's Merv."

Stella tried to imagine Mervin, the sheriff department's official goofus, trying to pull a man as large as Manny and one as ill-tempered as Augustus Faber apart.

She nudged Savannah. "Darlin', go sit on that telephone. You know how we do it."

Savannah nodded solemnly and headed for the end table next to Stella's easy chair, where the telephone rested.

As Savannah placed the phone on the seat of the chair, Stella squeezed past Elsie and threw the front door open wide.

Hurrying out onto the porch, she said breathlessly, "Evenin', Deputy Faber. Nice to see you this fine night. I'm sorry to interrupt the two of you, but somebody's on the phone, Sheriff, and I believe it might be important. Could you come inside quick?"

A gleam lit Manny's eyes, and Stella could have sworn she saw the ghost of a smirk crook one corner of his mouth. But he turned to Augustus and said, "I'll see you at dawn, Deputy. Have a pleasant night."

Without another word, the disgruntled, outranked lawman climbed into his cruiser, slammed the door, and started his engine.

Stella laced her arm though Manny's and nudged him toward the house.

As they climbed the porch steps, he chuckled and said, "Nobody called this house looking for me, did they, Stella May?"

"Nope."

"Don't tell me a good, church-goin' woman like yourself just told a bald-faced lie to get me inside before I decided to clean my deputy's clock."

"I didn't lie. I didn't speak one solitary untrue word. Someone's on the phone, and they do want to talk to you."

Manny mulled that one over as they walked to the door.

He paused before going in. "Then tell me, who is it that's actually 'on' that phone? Elsie or Savannah?"

She grinned, held the door open, and waved him inside.

"Step right in and see for yerself," she told him.

He did as she told him and stopped short when he saw Savannah parked in Stella's recliner. She had a big grin on her face and was holding the phone cord in her right hand, swinging it in circles like a jump rope.

The cord led beneath her bottom.

"Okay," he said with a sigh. "I suppose we've established that she is, indeed, technically 'on the phone.' But I'm not sure that would hold up in a court of law as 'the truth, the whole truth, and nothing but the truth.'"

"It'd be pretty flimsy, evidence-wise," Savannah told him with a sly wink of her eye, "but we won't tell anybody if you don't."

He shook his head and laughed. "You Reid gals are full of sass and vinegar, you know? I'm just mighty glad you're on my side."

"They are," Elsie assured him, "and so am I. We were watching and listening at the door."

He sniffed. "Figured you were."

Stella said, "We was afraid you and Gus there were gonna get in a tussle, right there in my front yard."

"You didn't have to go to such extraordinary measures," Manny assured her. "I could take Augustus every day and twice on Sunday."

"But you might skin your knuckles in the process and mess up that perfect hair of yours," Stella said with her best Dixie coquette toss of her head and dimpled smile. "We cain't be havin' *that*, now. You gotta stay lookin' your Sunday best ever'day this close to the election."

He thought it over, nodded, and said, "Good point. Thank you for looking out for me."

As Savannah stood and lifted the phone from the chair, her smile faded. When she turned to face Manny, her expression was quite sober.

"I was on the phone, and I did want to talk to you, Sheriff," she said softly. "I have to ask you something."

"What's that, darlin'?"

"I think I know your answer already."

"Ask it anyway."

"Okay." She drew a deep breath. "Would you like to know where your deputy really was this afternoon and early this evening? Because, as it turns out, I know."

Manny stared at the girl, as though taken aback. "I certainly would. I'd be most grateful, in fact."

Savannah swallowed, lifted her chin a notch, put on what Stella called her "determined" look, and said, "Okay. Then I'll tell you."

71

Chapter 10

"A rally?" Manny asked Savannah, who had delivered her news as somberly as if she had been reporting a heinous felony. "What kind of rally? A pep rally? A monster truck rally?"

Stella's head spun as she stared at her granddaughter and wondered what they were about to hear next. That child was simply full of surprises. Fortunately, most of them were pleasant. But Stella wasn't sure if this new revelation was going to be easy on the ears or not. Savannah was, after all, a teenager now.

Apparently, that changed things.

When Savannah didn't reply right away, Manny turned to Stella with an inquisitive expression.

She shrugged her shoulders and said, "Don't look at me. I got no idea at all what she's goin' on about, how she came to find out about it, or why she didn't tell any of us earlier."

He looked at Elsie, who shook her head, spread her hands wide, as though to show she was empty-handed, and said, "I got no notion, Sheriff. None at all. But I'm as curious as you are to hear about it."

Manny turned back to Savannah, then placed his hands on her shoulders and pulled her a bit closer to him. Looking down into her eyes, which were suspiciously wide with pretend innocence, he said, "Just say it, honey. You have nothing to fear from me. Ever. You know that."

Savannah cut a quick look in Stella's direction, then down at the floor. "It's not *you* I'm concerned about," she mumbled.

Stella weighed her options carefully before deciding which was most important—getting information to assist Manny versus disciplining Savannah for something she obviously wasn't proud of having done.

Finally, Stella made up her mind and said, "Savannah, if you help the sheriff here with his problem, I'll forgive you for any nonsense you might've done in advance."

"Really?" Savannah looked suspicious but hopeful.

"It's a done deal. Spit it out. Time's a-wastin' and our nerves are gettin' plumb frazzled waitin'."

Apparently satisfied with the generous offer of proactive clemency, Savannah lifted her chin, fixed Manny with her laser blue eyes, and told him, "Your deputy Faber was attending a campaign rally out of town. *His* campaign. Seems he's bound and determined to take your place as sheriff."

Manny thought it over for a few moments, then said, "Okay. It's no secret that he wants my badge. A drive down any street in town would tell you that, considering all the signs he's put up everywhere. You can't take a step without tripping over one and banging your head on another."

"That's for sure," Elsie piped up. "For a feller who throws a dyin' duck fit over somebody tossin' an empty gum wrapper on the sidewalk, he's made a mess of this town with all his political litter."

"And them posters have all got his ugly mug on 'em, too," Stella added. She clucked her tongue and shook her head. "That boy may be smart, but he sure is homely. Bless his heart."

Manny chuckled. "Why, Stella May, I believe that's the most critical thing I've ever heard you say about anybody."

"Oh, I've heard her say way worse," Elsie interjected with a giggle. "You should hear her after choir practice, going on about the soprano section."

Stella laughed. "That's true, Sister Elsie. Those gals do get on my nerves." Turning back to Manny, she said, "I know. 'Twasn't my most Christian moment there, speakin' of your deputy. But that's what he gets for thinkin' he can oust the best sheriff this county ever had, who also happens to be a good friend of mine, who's near and dear to my heart."

Manny looked pleased but also uncomfortable. Stella thought she saw him blush a bit under his tan.

She hadn't intended to embarrass him, but she had to admit it was a bit endearing to think this big, confident man could turn shy in a heartbeat over some words she'd said in a moment of candor.

But she decided to give him a break and bring the conversation back to Augustus. "I just hope that puddin' head's got someone to help him tear all them ugly signs down once this hoopla's over with."

"I'll see to it that every single poster's gone before sundown the day after the election," Manny told her. Turning his attention back to Savannah, he said, "But a campaign rally? This is the first I've heard about that. Tell me everything you know about it, sugar."

She sighed, then said, "I heard that Deputy Faber and some other guys who don't like you, probably because you arrested them at one time or another, wanted to get together without you knowing about it and plot to see how they can get Deputy Faber in office and you out."

"Okay. They're welcome to try. They're even entitled to have a rally if they want to raise funds or whatever, but I don't understand why they didn't just have their meeting here in town."

"Like I said, they didn't want you to know about it," Savannah told him. "They were afraid you might attend and hear all the bad things that're being said about you behind your back."

"True things or lies and rumors?"

"A mix of all three, I'd say."

"I don't care about the lies and rumors. But what's the true stuff?"

"That there's been three murders here in this little town in the past year and a half. They say, considering how few people live here, per capita, that's way higher than the national average."

Manny considered that dismal fact for what seemed like a long time, then nodded solemnly. "They've got me there. It's true. We've had a run of bad luck in the homicide department here in little McGill. You'd have to be living under Hooter Russell's barn to've missed that statistic."

"That's exactly what it is, too, Manny. Nothin' but a run of bad luck," Stella told him. "You didn't cause them murders, but you did solve them, and that's what matters."

"With your help and the rest of your family," he reminded her.

"It don't matter how you pulled it off. You did it. That's what a sheriff's job is. You can't force folks to do the right thing. Even the good Lord above lets us mess up our lives, if we're determined and dumb enough."

"Thank you, Stella. I appreciate that. It means a lot, coming from you." He gave her a smile that warmed her heart far more than she figured was advisable under the circumstances, with her raising a passel of Reids and him trying to keep a town full of cantankerous people from killing each other.

Considering their schedules and responsibilities, Stella figured that any sort of romance between them had to take a backseat. Or, better yet, just step right off the bus.

He patted the top of Savannah's shoulder and said, "Thank you very much, young lady, for reporting that pertinent bit of information to me. I could tell he was lying, but I didn't know why. I'm looking forward to confronting him about it, now that I know."

She grinned. "Glad to be of assistance, Sheriff. We think very highly of you in this household. So, of course we want to help you any way we can."

"Good. Because I have a couple more questions for you, concerning this business."

Savannah gave Stella a quick, wary glance and said, "I was afraid you might. Go ahead. I'm listening."

"Who told you about this rally?"

Again, another guilty look in her grandmother's direction. Then she cleared her throat and said, "Uh, Tom . . . Tommy."

Now why ain't I surprised? Stella asked herself. *Like I didn't know it had somethin' to do with that nincompoop. If that boy wasn't a head taller than me, I'd take a switch to him.*

Of course, Stella made a thousand threats about switching for every time she actually did so. In fact, she couldn't exactly recall the last time she'd cut a switch from the hazel tree and gotten someone's attention with it. But that didn't keep her from enjoying a momentary fantasy of having Mr. Thomas "Peckerwood" Stafford do a little disco dance there behind her henhouse as she taught him the value of keeping his cotton-pickin' hands off her sweet, innocent—or so she hoped—granddaughter.

Savannah had always been such an honest child, but the moment she had reached puberty and that rapscallion of a boy had made goo-goo eyes at her, a wrinkle had appeared on Savannah's otherwise pristine record for truth telling.

Only last week, Savannah had told Stella that she was going

to the library, which wasn't entirely a lie. Stella later heard from the librarian that Savannah had raced inside the establishment, tossed some books into the "Return" bin, then fled back through the door without as much as a "How's the world treatin' ya, Miss Rose?"

This was highly irregular for Savannah, who not only spent every spare moment she could in the library, but also regularly volunteered to reshelve the books for her beloved Miss Rose.

With typical small-town curiosity, the librarian had hurried to the window to see what Savannah might be up to, only to witness her climbing onto the back of Tommy Stafford's scooter and taking off down the street, heading for the highway.

Ordinarily, Stella would have given the child only a minimal grounding for telling the half-truth, but she couldn't bear the thought of Savannah on the back of that scooter, roaring down the highway, clinging to the backside of a miscreant boy who didn't even have a license to operate a roadworthy vehicle.

Stella had forbidden her to even speak to Tommy Stafford until further notice.

Apparently, Savannah had held out for four days.

At most.

"Tommy?" Manny was asking the red-faced girl. "Do you mean that Stafford boy?"

She nodded.

Manny looked over at Stella and the disapproval in his eyes just confirmed what Stella suspected. That lad was trouble.

It made Stella feel sick at heart and afraid to think of her sweet girl involved with a boy whom even Manny Gilford disapproved of. That just couldn't be a good sign, no matter how the cake was cut.

"Are you keeping company with him now, Savannah?" Manny asked.

She nodded, then ducked her head and added, "Well, I was. But then Granny brought a halt to it."

"Or so I thought," Stella muttered under her breath.

"I'm sorry, Gran. I avoided him as much as I could at school, but then he came up to me when I was getting my books out of my locker and invited me to go with him and his dad and his brother to that rally. I told him I couldn't." To Manny, she added, "Not that I would have wanted to go even if I could have. If I was able to vote, Sheriff, you know I'd vote for you. All day long!"

"I know you would, sweetie." He gave her a kind smile, then continued his fact-finding. "Do you happen to know where this rally took place and when exactly?"

"He said it was at the feed store in Pineville, there on Main Street, next to that fried chicken and waffle place." She glanced over at Stella. "I remember because he said we could sneak out of the meeting and go get something to eat, if I was hungry."

"Somethin' to eat, my butt," Stella grumbled. Silently, to herself, she added, *A good-lookin' boy like that 'un, with no more sense than God gave the average goose, he'd go straight for the dessert tray ever' time and get second helpings from most gals.*

Stella was glad she had forbidden Savannah to go out with him. At least, the girl had abided by that, even if she couldn't resist chatting with him beside her locker.

"I know the place," Manny was telling Savannah. "You could get a pretty big crowd in there."

"I don't know about that," Savannah said. "I haven't spoken to Tommy since our little talk there at my locker. But he was pushing pretty hard to get me to come. Said his dad told him to tell everybody, that they wanted as big a crowd as they could get."

"Do you know what time this rally started and ended?"

"Tommy said it started at six this evening. He didn't mention how late it would last. I don't suppose he knew."

"Is there anything else, Savannah? Anything at all that you think I might need to know?"

Savannah thought long and hard, then shook her head. "That's all, Sheriff. But if I think of anything else, I'll give you a call."

"You do that, honey. You know you can call the station house any time, day or night, my home, too." He pulled one of his cards from his pocket and placed it in her hand. "My house number's on there, too. If I'm out in the field, you ask whoever's at the station desk to patch you through on our radio system, okay?"

Savannah smiled up at him with a sassy little smirk and said, "You've told our whole family that a bunch of times, Sheriff. We know you're there for us. It makes us feel better, too. Not just everybody has a real, live sheriff they can call if they need a quart of milk at two in the morning."

She giggled. He tweaked her nose, then headed for the doorway.

"I've got to let you people go to bed," he said. "I've kept you up past your bedtimes already."

"We wouldn't have been sleepin' anyway," Elsie told him. "Not with all this excitement goin' on."

"Hopefully, tomorrow will be even more exciting than today," he said, sounding more tired than optimistic. "When you fine ladies say your prayers tonight, be sure to mention how nice it would be if either Merv or I find a murder weapon tomorrow morning."

"Will do," Elsie said.

"Sure will," added Savannah, "and when I pray, I'll even ask that it has fingerprints on it."

"That's my girl. Good night, Stella, Elsie, Savannah. Sweet dreams. Or at least, sweeter than I'll probably have."

He started to open the front door, but Stella beat him to it.

"I'll walk you out," she said.

"You don't have to, but I'd be mighty happy if you did," he replied, his voice so dark and smooth that it somehow reminded Stella of midnight blue satin.

As they walked through the door, and Stella turned to close it behind them, she heard Savannah whisper to Elsie, "I'm glad she's walking him to his car. Heaven knows, he'd never find that big ol' cruiser sitting right there in front of the house without her assistance."

She heard Elsie giggle. Then both her granddaughter and dear friend began to laugh hysterically, as though they had just heard the funniest joke of their lives.

Stella shook her head and closed the door with a bit more vigor than usual.

When she looked up at Manny, she saw that he, too, was grinning.

He slipped his arm around her waist, she put hers around his, and together they strolled across the porch and down the steps.

"You know," he said, giving her a little sideways squeeze, "I don't think we're fooling anybody."

Except maybe ourselves, she thought, as she returned the embrace, breathed in the sweet, pine-scented Georgia night air, and enjoyed the sensation of him, so close, so warm.

When they got to his cruiser, he turned her around to face him.

With one hand, he pulled her closer. With his other, he pushed some wayward curls back from her face.

Looking deeply into her eyes, he whispered, "I would die for you, Stella May Reid. You *do* know that, don't you?"

For some reason, she could hardly breathe. Something in his eyes was so intense that she couldn't bear to return his gaze, but at the same time, she couldn't stand to look away.

Finally, she found her voice and said, "I know you would, Manny. I know. But I don't want you to. Please promise me you won't ever die. Not for me or anybody else."

He chuckled. "Well, I wasn't figuring on doing it right away."

"I don't want you to die for me. I want you to live for me."

She heard him catch his breath. Again, those gray eyes searched hers. She was sure they saw too much.

With a little laugh of her own, she said, "You have to stay alive and well, Sheriff Gilford. Heaven knows, we might have an emergency in the middle of the night and be in desperate need of a quart of milk."

He glanced back at the house. The living room curtain suddenly slid closed.

"A quart?" he said. "With eight growing kids? I'll bring three gallons."

Chapter 11

Shortly after eleven o'clock the next morning, Stella was hanging sheets and pillowcases on the clothesline in her backyard when she heard the phone ring inside the house.

Scooping Macon Jr. up from a second clothes basket with a pillow and several of his favorite toys inside, she perched him on her hip, one arm around him, and hugged him close to her side. With a kiss to his forehead, she said, "I'll betcha I know who that is, kiddo. Are you ready to go to the sheriff station with me and your big brother?"

When, as expected, Macon's response was little more than a goo and a grunt, she said, "Don't worry. I won't leave you there. We'll be in and out quicker than green grass through a goose. No jailbirds allowed in this here family. You be a good boy when you grow up, you hear? Stay outta trouble, and you'll have nothin' to fear from the powers that be."

She hurried up the rickety steps and through the back door, letting the screen slam behind her.

"You be quiet now," she told the baby as she darted around

the table and struck her hip on a chair in the process. "Granny needs to hear what this gentleman's got to say. Might be important. So, no squawking outta you, young man, or you and me . . . we're gonna tangle."

The child laughed at her and slapped her cheek with his chubby baby hand.

She could tell he was terrified at her threat.

She grabbed the phone off the wall and plopped down on the chair that had, no doubt, just left a big bruise on her hip.

"Hello," she answered, breathless from the run, the stair climb, the painful encounter, and the delightful burden that was now in her lap, cooing up at her.

"It's me," she heard Manny say.

"Hi, me," she replied playfully. "I had a feelin' it was you."

"Sorry. You're huffing and puffing. Sounds like I caught you at a busy time."

"We both know there ain't no other kinda time around here. At least I'm sittin' down now for the first time all day. Reckon I got you to thank for that."

"I try my best," he said. "Getting you to sit down and take a break is the hardest thing I have to do on any given day."

"Ah, it ain't that bad. I do all right."

"All right? You're fantastic! But you never have to hurry for me, Stella. I'd be happy to wait for you any time, night or day. You certainly don't have to run to the phone. Not ever."

"But then, I didn't know for sure it was you, did I?" she said, teasingly.

"Good point. Maybe someday we'll have fancy phones that tell us who it is before we rush to answer it. Then maybe we won't even pick it up at all. Wouldn't that be nice?"

"I can't even imagine such a thing," she said. "How on earth would the telephone company know who was callin' us, let alone tell us ahead of time? It just ain't even possible. Next thing you'll tell me is that we'll have phones we can take out in the yard with us."

"I think they have them now, but they cost about as much as a new car."

"Maybe I'll only buy two of them then."

"I'll buy you three, so you'll have two spares."

"You spoil me, Sheriff Gilford."

There was a long silence on the other end, and for a moment, Stella thought they had lost the connection.

Then he said, "I'd love to spoil you, Stella. I've never known a person who's less spoiled than you and deserves it more. I'd spoil you rotten if you'd let me."

For a moment, she could hardly breathe, let alone speak. She wasn't sure exactly what he meant by that. Or how he expected her to respond.

Finally, she collected herself enough to reply softly, "Lord knows, you do enough for me and mine, Manny. I couldn't expect more. I've never had such a kind, generous friend in my life."

Again, there was a weighty silence. She wasn't sure, but she had the feeling she had said the wrong thing. Not what he was wanting or expecting to hear.

But then she heard him chuckle and say, "Except Elsie. Nobody ever had a better friend on earth than Elsie Dingle."

She thought it over for a moment, laughed, and said, "You're right. She bakes amazing coconut cakes, so she's number one. But you come in a very close second."

"Glad to hear it. I don't mind playing second fiddle to Miss Elsie."

Stella sighed and felt her body sag with relief. Somehow, she felt she had just navigated a particularly difficult river rapid on a flimsy innertube floater.

"Are you ready for me to go fetch that boy and bring him to you?" she asked.

"Yes. Merv and I just returned from the cemetery. I sent him home for a nap, and I'm stuck here until Augustus relieves me."

"Didja find anything?"

"Nothing you and I didn't see yesterday."

"No murder weapon?"

"Nope, not a dadgum thing."

"Sorry."

"Eh, it's all right. You win some, you lose some. Can't always expect the perpetrator to be polite enough to drop their wallet on the ground while fleeing the scene."

She laughed, remembering that Ernie Harkins had done that exact thing when he had broken into his boss's house and stole his precious 1897 Winchester shotgun.

Ernie had dropped his wallet on the pizza restaurant owner's living room floor in the process. As a result he had lost his job flinging dough and chopping pepperoni and onions, had gone to jail for six months, and was now considered the least competent burglar in the county.

"Crime just don't pay," she said. "Ask Ernie Harkins."

"Not if you're as bad at it as he is," Manny replied. "Thankfully, most criminals aren't nearly as smart as they think they are."

"Hopefully, this one won't be, either," she said. "I'd hate to think anybody'd get away with somethin' that violent and still be walkin' among us."

"That's for sure."

"I'll go fetch Waycross and run him right over."

"Thank you, Stella. I'd interview him there at your house, but I have to write this report, and I need to be here if any important calls come through. At least until Augustus decides to show up and relieve me. He's due back at noon."

"I don't mind a bit. Feels good to get out and about."

She looked down at the baby in her lap, who was peacefully playing with the buttons on the front of her dress. "My boys and me'll be over lickety-split."

"Don't rush. Take your time."

Stella looked down at her kitchen floor, sprinkled with wayward cornflakes, a bit of toast crust, and a spot that looked suspiciously like a blob of lime gelatin that had melted into a half-dried puddle.

Time, she thought. *Of all the things I ain't got, that's probably what I got the least of, except maybe energy.*

"I will, Manny."

"That's my girl."

His simple words made her feel warm all over. But they also made her think she needed to go fetch her grandkids from school, put them in her old panel truck, and head out of town.

Way out of town. To another county that didn't have a sweet, good-looking hunk of a sheriff who filled out his uniform in such a nice, masculine way, who had a head of thick silver hair and piercing gray eyes, and who told her in a deep, husky voice to take it easy and not hurry. Or said even worse things like, "That's my girl."

A guy like that could interfere with a gal's concentration.

"I *have* to take my time gettin' over there," she finally told him, when she got her breath back. "If I show up too soon, you'll know I was speedin'."

When Stella arrived at the school, Waycross was waiting eagerly for her next to the flag post, right in front of the building.

The instant he saw her panel truck pull over to the curb, his ruddy little face widened into a huge smile, and he raced across the playground to meet her.

He jerked the front door open, scrambled inside, and after a quick glance around to make sure none of his fellow students were watching, he gave her his usual, affectionate peck on the cheek.

Stella understood his need for discretion. It was bad enough being the only boy in town with flaming red hair. The last thing he needed was to add "kisses his grandma right in front of God and ever'body" to his job description.

"Boy, I thought I was in trouble when the principal called me to his office," he began, after reaching around and patting the head of his little brother, who was strapped into his baby seat. "Then I remembered you told me about goin' to talk to Sheriff Gilford today, and I wasn't worried no more, 'cause I figured that's what it was about."

"I'm sure it'll be fine, grandson," she told him as she watched him put on his seat belt. "The sheriff's just gonna ask you a few questions about anything you might've seen yesterday there in the graveyard."

"Seen? I didn't see nobody, 'cept you and Stan the grave-digger man."

Stella gave him a little cluck of disapproval and a slight shake of her head. "That's Mr. Horton to you, grandson. I know a lot of folks in town call him 'the gravedigger man.' But that gentle-man's got a rough job, and he's always done it to the best of his ability. Which is more'n we can say of a lot of folks these days. We owe him some respect for his service and dedication to the community."

"I'm sorry."

"That's okay. You didn't know no better. Now you do."

She could tell by the frown that wrinkled his forehead he was still considering the topic.

"Anything else you wanna say on the subject, kiddo?"

"I was just thinkin' there's worse jobs than standin' in a peace-ful place and diggin' a hole."

She grinned. "Like what?"

"Like Mr. Herbert Jameson's job, 'cause he's the guy who's gotta get 'em gussied up so Mr. Horton can put 'em in the ground."

"You wouldn't want to be a mortician, Waycross?" she asked, nudging him in the ribs with her elbow.

"No way! Not for all the money in the world. Considerin' all the ways people expire, some of 'em are bound to look pretty rough when he gets 'em. I wouldn't do that for love nor money."

"What *would* you like to do . . . for love or money . . . when you grow up?"

"I wanna be a guy who fixes old stuff up and makes it look all new and shiny again. Maybe cars, or, if I've got enough money, houses that are fallin' apart. But not dead people. I mean, I feel sorry for 'em and all, and they need somebody to help 'em out, but it's gonna have to be somebody other than me."

He looked up at her with soulful eyes filled with remorse and said, "Does that make me a bad person, Granny? That I don't want to mess with dead folks?"

She reached over and stroked his hair, then his cheek. "No, darlin'. You don't have a bad bone in your body. You grow up and fix them cars or them houses if that's what's in your heart to do."

"Really? That's okay?"

"It's more than okay. It's important. Ever'body's got a reason for bein' in the world. A job to do during the time they're alive."

"How do you know what your job is?"

"It's the one that sets your heart afire when you think about it."

His eyes twinkled, and he shifted anxiously in his seat. "I get all aflame inside when I think about takin' a wrecked-up car and makin' it all perfect and pretty again."

"Well, there ya go. That's one of your passions."

"One of? Can you have more than one?"

"Sure you can. You might not make a living following some of them, but you can do them, just for the joy of it, on the side, if you've a mind to."

"So, you're sayin' I could fix houses for a livin' and cars on the weekends just for fun?"

"You certainly could. Waycross Reid, you can do anything you can dream of as long as you're willing to work at it and not give up till you get the job done."

He was giving her a strange, quizzical look, so she said, "Anythin' else, puddin'?"

"I was wonderin' if you've got a passion, Granny. Some job you gotta do that burns up your heart."

She laughed. "I most certainly do."

"I think I know it."

"I'll just bet you do."

He gave her a tender, loving smile. "It's takin' care of us kids, ain't it?"

"It most certainly is. I'm the luckiest woman in the world, gettin' to follow my heart's desire ever' day of my life."

He sighed, as though from relief, and said, "Boy, I'm sure glad your heart likes to fry chicken and do laundry and don't wanna be a ballerina or marry Magnum, P.I. and move to Hawaii."

Giggling, she replied, "I think it's a safe bet I ain't gonna leave you kids and go be a ballerina. The days when I would've worn a tutu and toe shoes, they've come and gone. But I'm warnin' ya, if Mr. Magnum proposes to me, we're packin' up the truck and movin' to Hawaii!"

As he shared her laughter and reached over to pat her forearm, Stella sent a quick, silent prayer that in the years ahead Waycross would remain the sweet child he was now. It was a big favor to ask, she knew. It seemed to her that few children retained their innocence and innately kind natures into their adulthoods.

Life and its cruel trials had a way of souring a person's nature, causing one to forget that the world has many good things to offer including love, honor, loyalty, and respect. But Stella held out hope for this one beside her, and all the rest of her brood, for that matter.

Hope was another one of those precious things she refused to allow the years to take from her. Like love and faith, hope was a powerful substance. One drop could move mountains.

Occasionally, things got rough, difficult, nearly impossible to handle. But even during a really tough time, Stella figured she could muster at least one teeny drop of each one of those priceless commodities, and that got her through the day.

The drive was a short one. In less than two minutes they were pulling in front of the old two-story building that had served as the sheriff's station house and the jail for the citizens of McGill for as long as even the oldest person among them could remember.

It wasn't the largest building in town. The kindergarten to twelfth grade school claimed that distinction. But by far, it appeared to be the sturdiest.

Built of red bricks and square with no ornamentation whatsoever, the station would never be featured on the cover of "*Sheriff Headquarters Beautiful.*" But it did the job.

Stella couldn't recall a single breakout. Not even a riot, if you didn't count the ruckus that had landed half of McGill's population in jail, following the wake of the town bad girl.

Several wives had discovered items from their own jewelry cases on the formerly loose lady's person as she lay in her casket, and that had created quite a scandal that was still frequently spoken of. Especially between those particular wives and their wayward husbands. The ones who had remained married.

But overall, the sheriff's station was known as a peaceful, well-run place. Its major function was to provide overnight room and board for those who had consumed far too much alcohol at one of the two taverns and, as a result, were too angry or joyful to suit their neighbors.

Stella parked and got her two favorite boys out of the truck. Waycross needed no coaxing. He was excited and happy.

Macon Jr.'s personality was less effervescent, as he had decided it was nap time and told her so by baby-grumbling and rubbing his eyes with his tiny fists.

"I know. I know. Life's rough, ain't it, darlin'?" she said, handing the diaper bag to Waycross so she could pull the baby against her chest, where he could rest his head on her shoulder. "Don't worry, honeybunch. Once we're inside, you can snooze away to your little heart's content."

"He won't wanna," Waycross said. "I know a lot about babies, and they don't sleep, eat, or poop when you want 'em to. In fact, I think they work at doin' all that stuff at the worst times possible."

Stella laughed and winked at him. "You *do* know a lot about babies, kiddo. You've had a lot of practice. You'll be an expert by the time you're a grown man and a daddy yourself."

Instead of the complaint she was expecting, he gave her a bright smile and said, "I can't wait. I wanna be a dad. *So* much! I think it'll be a lotta fun."

But as they walked down the sidewalk toward the station house, his face grew more somber. "I won't be no truck driver or pilot or South Pole explorer, neither," he stated quite adamantly. "I ain't gonna have no job where I have to be away from my kids."

They had arrived at the station's door, but Stella hesitated before opening it. She reached down and put her hand under the boy's chin, coaxing him to look up at her. "Waycross, there are lotsa men who drive trucks and fly airplanes for a living, and probably even a few South Pole explorers, for that matter. I'm sure many of them fellas are fine fathers in spite of their occupations. But I appreciate what you're sayin', darlin', and I know without a doubt that you're gonna be the best daddy ever."

His smile returned. "Maybe I'll have a kid who's got red hair like mine! Maybe even freckles!"

"If you leave 'em outside in the sunshine where the angels get sight of 'em, it's bound to happen. Those angels love little redheads, and ever' time they catch a glimpse of one, they swoop down and kiss 'em on the nose."

"I will! That's what I'll do!"

"I believe you will, darlin'. I can see it in my mind's eye right now. It's gonna happen."

Chapter 12

Stella opened the rusty screen door of the sheriff's station house with its perennial crisscrosses of cellophane tape, applied to keep out ravenous Georgia mosquitoes.

With a wave of her hand, she ushered Waycross inside, then resettled baby Macon Jr. in her arms. He had already fallen asleep.

No sooner had they approached the reception area than she saw Manny jump up from the large desk and hurry toward them. From behind the desk came the largest dog who, to anyone's knowledge, had ever set paws on McGill soil.

He was as tall as a Great Dane, but had a thick, muscular body and the face of a German shepherd. Manny had rescued him several months ago, and Stella could tell by the sheen of his glossy coat and the sparkle in his intelligent eyes that the dog was faring quite well in the sheriff's care.

"Hey! Look who's here!" Waycross shouted in delight when he saw his furry friend.

The dog seemed just as happy to see the boy. Long, feathered tail wagging furiously, he bounded across the room and gave

Waycross a lick that wet the entire right side of his face with a co-
pious amount of saliva.

"Eww! Dang it, dog! Don't do that!" the child protested, gri-
macing as he wiped his cheek and chin with the tail of his favorite Teenage Mutant Ninja Turtles T-shirt. "You do that ever'
time I see you. One of these days you're gonna drown somebody,
you flea-bitten mutt!"

"Valentine, sit!" Manny roared, his voice filling the room.

In an instant, the scolded dog did as he was bid, his rear dropping to the floor, his tongue lolling, a slightly apologetic look on
his face.

"Wow! That's impressive," Stella said. "You're turning him
into one of them official, trained K-9 critters."

"I'm doing my best," Manny said, reaching down to stroke the
dog's silky head. "He sits and stays on command now. We're
working on him sniffing out drugs, but I'm afraid it's going to be
a while before he's got the hang of it. He's easily distracted by
squirrels."

Reaching into his pants pocket, Manny pulled out a couple of
clean tissues and handed them to Waycross. "You okay there,
son?" he asked him.

Waycross took the tissues and said, "Aw, that's all right. He
didn't mean no harm. He doesn't lick any more than any other
dog, but with a tongue that big, he tends to overdo it."

"That's true," Manny said. "He overdoes everything. You
should see the size of the feed bags I buy for him every week."

Waycross finished wiping his face and handed the tissues back
to Manny. "You don't gotta worry about me, Sheriff. I'm tough.
It'd take more than a bath in dog slobber to end me."

"I'm glad to hear it." Manny tossed the tissues into a nearby
wastebasket, then stretched out his hand to Waycross.

The boy looked confused for a second, then grabbed it and
the two shared a hearty shake.

The sight touched Stella's heart in a way that she found both endearing and unsettling.

"Sorry I called your dog a flea-bitten mutt, Sheriff."

"No problem. He *is* a mutt. That's part of his charm. And I suppose most dogs you run into have a flea or two on board."

The two smiled at each other. Then Manny told him, "I appreciate this a lot, Mr. Reid, you coming in today to be questioned, fulfilling your civic duty to aid us in our investigation."

"Naw, I didn't do all that. 'Tweren't no big sacrifice, me cuttin' school. They's havin' a history test, and I'm glad I'm gonna miss it. Them dates, they all sound like each other: 1987, 1897, 1789. How's a body supposed to keep 'em straight?"

"I know exactly what you mean," Manny said. "Did Columbus sail the ocean blue in 1492 or 1942?"

"It was 1492," Waycross told him quite proudly. "Even I know that one!"

"I'm sure you do. So, don't worry about it too much, son. I'm certain you can still amount to something in life. I had trouble with dates, too, when I was your age." Giving Stella a wink, he added, "Just ask your granny if that's not so. Her desk was next to mine during fifth grade history class, so she knows all too well it wasn't my best subject."

"You did fine in all your schoolwork, as I recall," Stella replied, remembering those long-ago days as though they had been last week.

The softness in his eyes told her that he was remembering, too.

Manny nodded toward the baby in her arms. "Would you like me to hold the little guy for you? I'd be glad to give your arms a rest."

"Ordinarily, I'd take you up on it, but you're gonna be questioning this hostile witness here." She nodded toward Waycross. "It'd be hard to look tough and intimidating while you're holding a baby. Plus, the little stinker's asleep, and it'd probably be a good idea to just leave 'im where he is for the time bein'."

"Okay. I understand. But if he wakes up, I'll take him. I can pull off the tough-guy thing as long as the kid's awake."

Waycross snickered. "Lookin' after a baby's a lot harder than robbin' a bank or knockin' over a liquor store."

Manny's eyes widened. "Oh really? Is that a fact? You've done a lot of that robbing and knocking over miscellaneous establishments, have you, young man?"

"No, but I've changed a mountain of dirty diapers in my day," the child replied with a lift of his chin and a sparkle in his eyes. "I'll tell ya now . . . it ain't for sissies."

"I believe you, son," Manny replied with a solemn nod. "You have my utmost respect."

Once again, Waycross looked confused. Stella assumed he was having a problem with the word *utmost*, but he quickly recovered and thanked Manny for the compliment.

"And you have mine, Sheriff," he replied with dignity and grace beyond his years.

Stella felt her heart swell with pride as she watched the sheriff lead her grandson over to the desk, with Valentine plodding along obediently at his master's heels.

"Please have a seat," Manny told Waycross, motioning for him to sit on one of the old, metal folding chairs beside it.

Waycross settled himself on the chair, then motioned for Valentine to join him. The dog happily hurried to him, sat at his feet, and laid his big head on the boy's lap.

As Stella watched how gently and affectionately he petted his big friend, she felt a sense of quiet satisfaction.

Daily, she poured her time, her love, her very heart into her grandchildren. All of those carefully planted seeds appeared to be taking root.

For a second, Marietta crossed her mind, and Stella had to remind herself that there was only so much a parent or a guardian could do.

"May I get you a cup of coffee, Stella?" Manny asked, as he ushered her toward the chair on the opposite side of the desk, then seated her with all of the aplomb of a butler attending a royal guest.

"I'd love a cup," she told him. "But I don't dare with this wriggly youngun in my lap. He wakes up quick sometimes and kicks somethin' fierce."

"I understand. How about a soda? If that spilled, the worst you'd get would be wet, cold, and sticky."

"Sure. That'd be dandy."

Manny took her order of a Dr. Pepper, and Waycross's of a root beer, and a couple of minutes later, they were getting refreshed while Manny finished the mug of coffee that had been sitting on his desk.

Stella sat as still as she could on the cold, metal chair, wishing that city hall would allot a few more dollars to the Sheriff's Department.

Even if they won't spring for comfortable chairs with warmers in the seat that vibrate and give back massages, you'd think they could provide chairs that don't leave you with rust on your backside, she thought.

But she didn't share her ruminations with Manny. Being male, he probably hadn't noticed the state of his guest chairs, or the fact that the green gooseneck lamp that illuminated his paperwork was leaning and about to topple over at any minute, or that his desk had seen better days . . . back when Noah had used it during the flood.

Basic sanitation appeared to be the only standard upheld at the station house.

But she did notice that his desk was quite orderly, with very few papers and only two folders on it.

One of those papers appeared to be the report he had mentioned earlier. She didn't want to appear nosy, but she kept sneaking peeks at it.

Stella didn't mind being nosy. Couldn't help it in fact. Being overly curious and snooping to scratch the itch it caused was second nature to her.

But actually *appearing* to be nosy . . . no, that wasn't acceptable. Not at all. So, she tried to be as discreet as possible and still manage to discern a few sentences of what he had written:

Extreme trauma to victim's head; Profuse bleeding evident around and under body; Considerable blood spatter indicates attack occurred at the scene.

Manny saw her sideways glances and grinned.

Whoops, she thought. *He caught me. Nailed for the snoop that I am.*

But instead of scolding her, as he had Valentine, Manny slid the paper across the desk to her and said, "While I'm busy questioning Mr. Reid here, would you do me the honor of reading this, Mrs. Reid, and see if you believe it's an accurate description of what we witnessed out there in the cemetery yesterday?"

"I . . . well, sure, Manny. I mean, if you want, I could do that. As a favor to you."

"I'd be most grateful."

When he turned his attention to Waycross, the boy said, "Why do you keep calling me Mr. Reid? And why did you shake my hand when I came in? It's not like we don't see each other almost ever' day. You're treatin' me like I'm a stranger or somethin'."

Manny cleared his throat and replied with a perfectly straight voice, "You most certainly are a friend of mine, Waycross. As such, on most days, you and I address each other informally as buddies would. But today, you're a citizen of this town, who's set his normal, daily duties aside for a time so he can come here to this station house and perform a vital task. I'm only showing you the respect that you deserve."

"I don't know the word *vital*. Does that mean 'hard'?" the child asked.

"No," Manny replied. "*Vital* means 'important.' Like, so important we can't do without it."

"Wow. That's just totally cool."

"It is. But it's not hard to tell the truth. It's a lot harder to lie, because then you have to work to keep all the details of your false story straight. I'm sure your granny told you that already."

"Oh, sure. She mentions it all the time. I won't lie to you, Sheriff. I wouldn't dream of it!" Waycross shot a look at Stella and gave a quick nod of his head in her direction. "Sure as shootin' I wouldn't even tell a little-bitty fib with my granny sitting right there. Gran's death on lyin'."

"Good for her," Manny said. "That means you're being raised right."

He gave Stella a smile, but she was absorbed in her reading. So far, she was impressed with the details he had written and how graphically and accurately they described the horrors they had seen the day before.

It brought it all back to her.

For a moment, tears stung her eyes, and she felt the need to pull the baby in her arms a bit closer to her chest.

Life was cruel. But there were the little ones to give you hope.

She half listened as Manny questioned Waycross and jotted his answers down in a small notebook with a black leather cover.

"When did you go to the cemetery yesterday, son?" Manny asked.

"After school. Right after."

"Why did you go there?"

"To get away from dumb ol' Jeanette Outhouse-Seat-Bottom Parker."

Manny looked up from his writing for a moment, shot a quick

look at Stella, then said evenly, "Oh. I didn't realize that was Miss Jeanette Parker's middle name."

Waycross snickered. "Well, it oughtta be."

"Okay. If you say so. I'll take your word for it since you know the young lady better than I do. But why did you choose the cemetery for your escape? You could have avoided her by just going on home like you usually do after school."

Stella steeled herself, knowing what was next and wondering how it would go over with Manny.

"I went to the graveyard to talk to my grandpa. His name is Arthur Reid. He was a carrottop, just like me, and he's buried there."

Stella saw a look of deep sadness come over Manny's face, and he took a while before he replied, "I know, Waycross. I visit his grave from time to time myself."

"You do?"

"Yes. I miss him, too. Your grandpa Art and I were best friends from the time we were your age until the day he passed away."

Waycross looked stunned. "You were? I didn't know that!" He whirled around to Stella. "Wow, Granny! Grandpa had red hair like me, *and* he was best friends with a real live sheriff! Lately, I've been findin' out all kinds of stuff about him that I didn't know before."

"I'll tell you something else," Manny said. "You have a lot more in common with your grandfather than just your red hair."

"What's that?"

"You're a good man. Art was a good man. You and he were both blessed with a great sense of humor and a lot of compassion toward your fellow man."

"Compassion means feeling sorry for people when something bad's happened to 'em, right?"

"Yes. That and a lot more."

Manny paused, and Stella had a sense that something significant was coming, although she wasn't sure what.

"You two have something else in common," Manny continued. "Or I should say, 'some*one*.' That's your granny here. She loved your grandpa more than life itself, and she loves you just as much. She took good care of him, and now she takes care of you and all your sisters and that little baby in her arms."

Waycross nodded, glancing at his sleeping brother. "That kid's a handful."

"I'm sure he is. But my point is, she and your grandfather looked out for each other. Now he's gone. So now she's taking care of you, and you need to do what you can to take care of her."

His words brought tears to Stella's eyes and seemed to astonish Waycross. The boy looked at Stella and said, "But my granny don't need much takin' care of. She's got a big ol' skillet and, boy, does she know what to do with it! In this town, people are scared of *her*, not the other way 'round!"

Stella laughed. She couldn't help it, in spite of her tears.

So did Manny as he said, "Yes, Mrs. Stella May Reid has a bit of a reputation around McGill. The whole county, for that matter. She's fought a few battles, usually defending innocent folks against people who were hurting them. It's true she's used some unusual weapons."

"Like her biggest pan!" Waycross added proudly.

"Yes, she's used whatever weapons she had within reach at the moment. She's resourceful that way. But she still needs all the help she can get."

Stella decided to add her bit to the conversation. "I'll have you know that between you two gentlemen, Sister Elsie, and once in a while even Florence, I do all right. I get all the help I need, and it's always graciously given."

"'Cept from Miss Florence," Waycross grumbled. "She'll help ya but, boy, ain't five minutes till ever'body in town knows she did."

Stella and Manny laughed. Both knew Waycross's words were

an incredibly accurate and insightful evaluation of her next-door neighbor.

When Art had died unexpectedly, Florence had been kind enough to drive to Atlanta and buy Stella a nice black dress. To this day, it remained Stella's only nice dress, black or otherwise. But everyone who attended Arthur Reid's funeral left knowing exactly at which prestigious store Florence had purchased his wife's dress, how much she had paid for it, with tax, and that, by doing so, Flo had destroyed her own personal clothing budget for a month.

"I think the boy knows your neighbor all too well," Manny told her. "But I'm glad to hear you're getting the help you deserve from those who love you."

The words *love you* seemed to hang in the air after he uttered them. At least, she seemed to keep hearing them.

She wondered if he did, too.

Oh, cut it out, girl! she silently scolded herself. *You're as bad as Savannah is with that nitwit Tommy fella. Manny could be reading a phone book, and you'd get your knickers all in a twitter about it.*

She was grateful to hear the front door open and close. Someone had entered the station, and no matter who it was, in her opinion, they were welcome.

Anything or anyone who took her mind off Manny and her twittering knickers was a good thing in her present state of mind.

But when she saw a dark look pass over Manny's face, she turned to see who had entered, whose arrival had prompted such an expression.

It was Deputy Augustus Faber strolling in, with a confident stride that suggested he owned the place.

She had never thought all that highly of Augustus Faber. Mostly, because he seemed to think so much of himself, and she felt he had too much unconditional love and unwarranted approval already.

A swelled head don't look good on nobody. Not even a guy as good-looking as Augustus there, she thought, not for the first time, as he gave a curt nod in their direction and headed for the soda machine.

Manny looked up at the clock, mounted on the wall over the file cabinets. It was a quarter past twelve.

"Good *afternoon*, Deputy Faber," Manny said. "I certainly hope you didn't rush in on my account," he added evenly, with only the slightest hint of sarcasm in his voice.

"I had to stop and get gas," Augustus replied, not looking in Manny's direction, as he made a big show of removing the cap from his soda bottle. "I figured you'll have me out in the field all day, and I wouldn't have time to then."

"Yes," Manny replied, his voice low, suggesting he had something of consequence on his mind. "Those trips to Franklin can eat up a whole tankful of gas before you know it."

Augustus whirled around and stared at him, obviously shocked to the core that the sheriff was aware of his recent trip.

"Maybe next time you want to hold a fund-raiser, you can just do it here at home," Manny said. "I'm sure the grange would be happy to rent you their hall. Especially for a midweek event like yours."

Augustus took a long, deep drink from his bottle, nearly emptying it before coming up for air.

Stella thought it rather obvious that he was using the moment to collect himself.

He did. Rather quickly.

That was the thing about Augustus Faber: He never took long to recover his sense of himself, inflated though it might be.

When he finally finished drinking, he lifted his nose a couple of inches and ran his fingers through his long, blond mullet, which reached beyond his collar in the back and was cut extremely short on the sides.

Stella struggled not to snicker. No doubt, Marietta would have been impressed with his style, which could only be described as "bold."

The week before, Marietta had announced that her next hairstyle was going to be a mullet like Joan Jett's. At the dinner table, the girl had proclaimed the cut to be, "Badass, just like *me*," and had been sent away from the table without dessert.

The punishment wasn't for her taste in haircuts, but for the word that Stella had hoped the brood wouldn't have learned for a few more years.

Moderately amused, Stella watched as Manny observed his deputy swagger over to the bulletin board and stand, perusing the wanted posters, public notices, and cards and letters of gratitude from various town folk, students, and civic groups.

Manny gathered up his paperwork, including the report he had been writing, and shoved them into a drawer to his right. He took his keys from his pocket, chose the smallest one, and locked the drawer.

Then he stood and took his jacket from the back of his chair. Turning to Stella, he said, "Now that Deputy Faber has graced us with his presence, I can leave. I'd like to grab some lunch at the Burger Igloo. Would you three do me the honor of being my guests?"

Before Stella could answer, Augustus whirled around and, leaving the bulletin board and its fascinations behind, strode over to stand near the desk, an angry scowl on his handsome face.

"Why can't Merv watch the desk?" he complained. "I'm no house mouse, you know. I work in the field."

"Merv is home, sleeping."

"I was the one up all night. If anybody gets to be home in bed, it should be me."

Manny was silent for a moment, but Stella could tell by his breathing and the scowl on his forehead, he was growing more and more angry. She noticed, not for the first time, how much taller the sheriff was than his deputy, and she wondered if Augustus was aware of that at times like this, too.

She had a feeling the deputy was well aware of the fact and resented it . . . along with all of the other inequities between the two men.

She also suspected that was part of the energy behind his campaign to take Manny's badge.

In her opinion, that was another strike against Deputy Augustus Faber. She considered one-upmanship a lousy reason to do anything.

Manny's steel gray eyes locked with his deputy's. He gave a slight nod in Stella's direction, then at Waycross. "Do you really want to have this conversation now, Deputy Faber, or can it wait?" he asked.

As Stella anticipated, Augustus chose the path to conflict rather than peace.

"Right now's just fine," he shot back instantly. "I don't care if they hear or not. Maybe they need to know how unfair their present sheriff is. Especially Mrs. Reid there, since she'll be voting."

"I've already decided who I'm votin' for, Deputy," she said. "Made up my mind ages ago." Turning to Manny, she said, "Don't hold back on account of me, Sheriff. Say what you gotta say so's we can go grab that burger. I'm fixin' to starve to death."

"Me too, Sheriff," Waycross offered far too eagerly. "Read 'im the riot act, and let's go eat."

Even Valentine added his bit by standing, giving Augustus a low growl and then a deep, loud bark that reverberated across the room.

Having received such benedictions all the way around, Manny turned to Augustus and said, "Your all-night shift was disciplinary, and I'm sure you know that. You'll be expected to carry on today as though you had performed your duties conscientiously yesterday."

"Merv's an idiot and you treat him better than me," Augustus began.

Manny cut him off. "Merv, challenged as he may be in many ways, doesn't *lie* to me. His worst offense has been sneaking quarters from petty cash to play video games, and when it got to be too much, I docked his paycheck. So he and I are even. But you . . . you disappeared off the face of the earth while on duty, Faber. You were incommunicado for hours when we had to investigate a *damned murder*!"

Manny glanced at Stella and said, "Begging your pardon for the language, Mrs. Reid."

"You're forgiven, Sheriff, under the circumstances."

But Augustus wasn't to be denied his indignation. With hands on his hips and a distinct lift to his deeply cleft chin, he replied, "You're just mad because you found out I had a fund-raiser. A super successful one, too. A lot of people from this town turned out to donate and show their support, because they're sick and tired of people getting murdered around here."

"I don't give a hoot if you had a million-dollar fund-raiser and everybody and their cousin's uncle's dog went to it, Deputy. I truly don't. Most days, I'd be happy to pawn this badge off on anybody dumb enough to take it. In case you haven't noticed, there aren't a lot of rewards in doing this job, other than the occasional opportunity to help somebody who deserves a hand."

Manny reached into a drawer, pulled out his revolver, and slipped it into his holster. Then he put on his jacket.

Pointing to the vacant desk chair, he told Augustus, "You either sit yourself down right now and perform your duties for the rest of your tour, Deputy Faber, or lay your badge and gun on the desk there and walk out that door. I'd be pleased to announce to the citizens of McGill that their fine candidate for sheriff just got fired for incompetence, being AWOL during an emergency, lack of integrity, and insubordination. Let's roll the dice and see if this little hissy fit you're throwing will cost you any votes next week."

For what felt like a terribly long time, the two men stood staring at each other.

Manny's eyes had turned positively glacial, as he glared at his deputy, who eventually caved. With an indignant grunt, Augustus deposited himself on the chair. He sighed deeply, his body sagging like a deflating Macy's Thanksgiving Day balloon at the end of a parade. Then he yanked the center drawer open, pulled out a calendar, and pretended to study it with great concentration.

"Good," Manny said. "If you hear anything about anything, I want to know immediately. Page me."

Turning to Stella, Manny reached down and scooped the baby from her arms. "Let's get to the Burger Igloo," he said, "before this young man of yours starves to death."

As they headed for the door, Valentine tagged along.

"Can he come, too?" Waycross asked, delighted.

"Valentine loves going to the Igloo for lunch. He'd never forgive me if I left him behind," Manny told him as they headed outside into the hot midday sun. "He's particularly fond of their chili dogs."

"That's gnarly." Waycross reached over and petted the animal's back, which was shining blue-black in the sunlight. "But if I was you," the boy added, whispering, "I wouldn't call them 'dogs' when you give 'em to him. He might get offended."

Manny laughed and slapped Waycross affectionately on the back with his baby-free hand. "I never thought of that. From now on, it's 'chili frankfurters.'"

Stella smiled as they strolled down the sidewalk, this strange but wonderful entourage. Herself, Manny, two of her grand-angels, and even a canine escort.

It felt right.

It felt like . . . *family.*

Chapter 13

Stella took the baby from Manny's arms, and she waited with Waycross as Manny tied Valentine's long leash to a fence post that was away from the sidewalk, but close to the Burger Igloo's large front window. A nearby maple shaded the spot and a patch of thick grass provided a soft place for him to sit or lie.

"There you go, young man," he told the dog as he patted his head and scratched behind his ears. "We'll be right inside, keeping an eye on you. So don't bite anybody. Unless you've seen their picture in the office on a wanted poster."

"Better warn him about that lickin' mess, too," Waycross said with a snicker.

"Oh, yeah. No licking, either." He gave the dog one final pet and said, "Just keep your jaws closed, and you'll stay on my good side."

Together, they left him and walked into McGill's premiere dining establishment.

Besides its famous double chili cheeseburgers and hot dogs, the Burger Igloo boasted three things: the coldest air-conditioning in town, the loudest jukebox, and vintage decor that hadn't changed since the place had opened back in 1957.

Every time Stella stepped inside the little café, she instantly felt thirty years younger.

The red mother-of-pearl tabletops matched the one she had at home, only the Igloo's were in far better shape. The leatherette booths of the same vibrant shade of crimson, and the black and white floor tiles with their checkerboard layout provided a sense of nostalgia that reminded Stella of Art and the happy times they had spent here, back in the day.

But then, it had been Elvis on the jukebox or the Everly Brothers. Now it was Whitney Houston's voice, filling the room with her new hit, "I Wanna Dance with Somebody."

New times, she told herself. *Same life, but a new, very different chapter.*

Jean Marie, the waitress with the highest peroxide-blond hair and the shortest pleated skirt in the place, hurried over to them, her eyes brightening at the sight of Manny.

"Well, good afternoon, Sheriff," she said, her voice half an octave higher than usual.

She gave Stella, Waycross, and the baby a curt, dismissive nod, then laid her hand on Manny's forearm and said, "I saw you tying up that sweet doggy of yours outside, Sheriff, and I figured you'd want your favorite seat up by the window so's you can keep an eye on him. I got it all ready for you."

"That's mighty kind of you, Jean Marie," he said with a distinct lack of enthusiasm that belied his words. "But that's a table for two and, as you can see, there are three of us here. Four if you count the little one. May we have the larger table next to it?"

Again, she gave Stella and Waycross quick glances and looked more than a little annoyed. "Yeah, yeah. I guess you can see the dog from there, too. Lemme clean it off."

Stella watched as Jean Marie moped over to the other table, trudging along as though each step were a chore. Gone were the bounce and the overt sashay. Suddenly, Miss Jean Marie was a completely different woman from the feisty femme fatale she had been only moments before.

Stella stepped close to Manny and whispered in his ear, "You sure took the starch outta her shorts there, Sheriff Gilford. I reckon she was hoping you were dining alone today so's she could chat you up."

He draped his arm over her shoulders and gave her a hearty, sideways hug. "I stopped worrying about what Jean Marie was hoping for years ago. If she hasn't gotten the message by now, she never will, and that's her problem. For me, I'm delighted that you and your boys are joining me for lunch."

Stella couldn't help noticing that the moment Manny put his arm around her, every single diner sitting at the tables and in the booths stopped in midchew to observe and, no doubt, form an opinion on his action.

Sheriff Manny Gilford was the closest thing that McGill had to a celebrity, and everyone kept tabs on him at all times. Even the other waitresses working the room were watching, as well as the short-order cook in the kitchen, who was peering through the service window.

Stella looked up at Manny and searched his face to see if he was aware of the attention.

She knew he was. Sheriff Gilford was aware of absolutely everything and everyone around him at all times. It was a job requirement.

So, she decided he just didn't care what folks thought or said about him. Apparently, not even days before an election.

She thought how nice that would be, not to care about the opinions of others. How liberating.

"I think I'm going to be like you when I grow up someday," she told him.

He looked confused. Then he grinned, glanced up and down her figure, and whispered, "I'd much prefer it if you'd just stay *you* from now on. That way, our lunches will remain far more interesting."

"Hey!" said Waycross, who had been watching the progress of Jean Marie's table clearing with a keen eye. "She's done! She's wavin' us over."

"Are you hungry, boy?" Manny asked him.

"Enough to chew the south end off a north-going skunk."

"Waycross!" Stella said. "Do you realize what you're sayin' there, grandson?"

"Sure I do."

She sighed. "That's what I was afraid of."

"But I *am* hungry!"

"Then get your tail end over there on that chair before I jerk a knot in it!"

Waycross looked up at her with a smirk, made all the more delightful for its plentiful "angel kiss" freckles. "Do you realize what you're sayin' there, grandmother?"

"Waycross."

"Okay."

It took him less than four seconds to get to the table, sit down, and start making faces at Valentine through the glass. The dog jumped to his feet, rushed to the window, and began to lick it furiously.

As Manny took the baby from Stella and pulled out her chair for her, she said, "You're gonna have to muzzle that mutt when you take him out in public, Manny. If he licks somebody to death, you'll have a lawsuit on your hands."

"Or start carrying a spray bottle of disinfectant in my holster," he said with a sigh as he settled into his own seat and tucked the still sleeping Macon Jr. into the crook of his left elbow.

"You should let me take him," she said. "I know how to eat and hold him at the same time."

"Don't fret, Granny Stella. He's just fine where he is." Manny laid his forefinger against the baby's open palm and smiled when the child's tiny fingers curled around it. "I'll let you know if he becomes more than I can handle."

After a few minutes, Jean Marie sauntered back to the table. As she handed them menus, she looked down at the baby and said, "Who's that you got there, Sheriff, a new deputy?"

"Yes. Swore him in just this morning," was Manny's reply.

She leaned down and said quietly, "You might need him if Augustus loses the election. I heard tell he'll quit if he does."

"One day at a time, Jean Marie. What will be, will be." Manny nodded toward Waycross, who had finished communing with Valentine and was wriggling in his chair, anxious to get on with business. "My young friend there wants a double chili cheeseburger with extra fries and a chocolate malted as soon as possible, to keep all north-bound skunks in the area safe. And my lady friend is having . . . ?"

Stella filled in the blank. "A bowl of your chili with cheese on top and some corn chips, please."

"You'll be having your usual, Sheriff?" the waitress asked, still sounding a bit miffed.

"I will, and a soft swirl vanilla ice cream cone and a bowl of water for my friend out there when we leave. I'd like the water now, if you please."

Jean Marie wrote up the order, walked to the service window, and clipped it on the ticket wheel.

A moment later, she returned with their beverages and placed them on the table along with a large Styrofoam bowl filled with water.

Manny picked it up and handed it to Waycross. "Would you mind much, son, taking that out and putting it down for Val?" he said. "I'd be much obliged."

"Sure!" Waycross sprang to his feet, took the bowl, and disappeared with it.

Meanwhile, Jean Marie stood by, looking as though she had something on her mind. Finally, she said, "There's a good reason I was extra happy to see you today, Sheriff."

Manny looked a bit wary, but he had to take the bait. "Oh? Why is that?"

She seemed quite satisfied with herself when she said, "Because I have some information for you about that new case of yours."

"You've heard about that already?" he asked.

"Of course. You know I hear everything in this place. Folks gossip a lot when they're eating, and they don't pay any mind to us who work here. They think we're just furniture who ain't picking up on what they're saying."

"What did you hear?"

"Dexter Corbin's wife came in this mornin' for a waffle, and she was throwin' a conniption."

Manny nearly spit out his iced tea and Stella gasped.

"Dexter Corbin was married?" they both asked in unison.

Jean Marie couldn't have been more pleased with the effect her words had on her audience. "Sure was."

"To whom?" he asked.

Stella scanned her brain for the name or face of any woman in McGill who might have taken a liking to a rattlesnake in crocodile shoes without the whole town knowing about it.

"A gal who's not from around here," Jean Marie was saying. "Her name's Cindy."

"What else do you know about her?" Manny asked as, through the window, he and Stella watched Waycross set the bowl of water on the ground beside Valentine and receive another enormous slobber kiss for his efforts.

"She was a showgirl in Vegas," Jean Marie was saying. "They met and got married there in one of them drive-up chapels. 'Bout two weeks ago, I think it was."

Jean Marie leaned closer, glanced around, and lowered her voice, saying, "She ain't all that pretty, though, not her face or her body, bless her heart. Reckon it wasn't a very good show she was in, there in Vegas. Probably one of them joints that's not much more than a glorified strip cl—"

"Gotcha," Manny said, cutting her off as Waycross returned to the table, slid back into his seat, and began to slurp his chocolate malt.

"Are you sure they were married?" Manny asked.

"They better've been. She's wearing a wedding ring on her finger that's got a diamond the size of a doorknob."

"Where's she living?"

"There in his house down by the river, I guess. Upstream from your place, Sheriff."

"Is there anything else you know about her?" he asked.

Jean Marie shrugged. "Just that she likes waffles for breakfast with a side of lean ham and two cups of strong, black coffee. Oh, and she's mad at you. Hoppin' mad. Doesn't like you one bit!"

"She's mad at me?" Manny looked confused. "How can she be mad at me when we've never even met? It usually takes a few minutes for people to dislike me."

"She thought it was rude of you not to notify her all official-like that her husband had been murdered."

Stella couldn't keep quiet any longer. "How the heck was the sheriff supposed to notify someone he didn't even know existed?"

"Don't ask me. I just listen and learn." Jean Marie smiled

down at Manny. "Then I pass it along to people I figure need to know it. People I like."

There it is again, that stupid, flirty grin, Stella thought, feeling the inexplicable, almost irresistible urge to pull out every one of Jean Marie's highly processed hairs, split ends and all.

But she also noticed that Manny appeared not to have even registered the comment. He was looking down at the baby, who was beginning to stir in his arms. He picked the little one up and placed his tiny head on his shoulder as he patted his back.

Finally, once the child had settled again, Manny looked up at the waitress and said, "Thank you, Jean Marie. I appreciate you telling me that."

"Are you gonna go notify her, official-like?"

"I am, if I can find her. I'll tell her and interview her while I'm at it. Thank you."

Jean Marie grinned and struck what she, no doubt, thought was a provocative pose with one hand on her extended hip and the other hand behind the enormous poof of her hair. "No problem, Sheriff. I'd be happy to help you any time. You can pay me back whenever you like. Just crook your little finger, and I'll be there so fast it'll make your head spin."

Stella grimaced. Even Waycross rolled his eyes. Manny sighed and reached for his iced tea.

After a long drink, he wiped his lips with his napkin, looked up at Jean Marie, and said, "I'll compensate you right away. I'll leave you an extra good tip today. Then we'll be even."

The crestfallen look on her face was testimony to her disappointment, but a table in her section had just been occupied by six people, so she didn't have a lot of time to pout.

As she strolled away, someone put some coins in the jukebox and Cyndi Lauper began to croon one of her biggest hits.

The cheerful tune filled the dining room, lifting the diners' spirits.

Waycross reached over, nudged Manny's arm, and said, "That Jean Marie, she's just a girl who wants to have fun, Sheriff, and apparently, she wants to have it . . . with *you*!"

Stella laughed. Loudly enough to make the entire restaurant turn in their direction and gawk.

Manny just shook his head and groaned. Then he gave Waycross a long, searching look, the kind Stella had seen him give to many folks in town, but never a member of her family.

She knew he was switching into "sheriff mode."

"Okay, Mr. Reid," he said. "Miss Jean Marie aside, our food's going to be here pretty soon, and then you'll be shoveling it into your mouth as quick as you can, so we'd better talk now."

"That's for sure," the boy replied. "If I talk with food in my mouth, Granny hollers at me."

"I don't exactly holler," Stella objected. "Just a gentle reminder."

Waycross giggled, then delivered his best granny impression. " 'Stop that jabberin' with your mouth full, Waycross Reid! I don't wanna be lookin' at no done-been-chewed food at my breakfast table.' Yeah, gentle like that."

"That's good advice, son," Manny told him. "Take it to heart. Someday a nice woman you like will be impressed that you chew with your mouth closed. Mark my words."

Pulling his small notebook and a pen from his jacket pocket, Manny said, "Okay. We haven't gotten very far with our interview, what with Deputy Faber and our fun-loving waitress interrupting us, but let's get down to business. Okay?"

Waycross nodded enthusiastically. "Yes, sir. Let's do."

"Your school bell rings at two o'clock, and you say you took off right away?"

"Yes. I took off fast, too. Right after that mean ol' Jeanette Parker called me a bast—" He gave his grandmother a sideways glance. "Well, Granny don't like me speakin' bad words, so we'll just say she called me a mean name."

"Any particular reason for her doing that?" Manny asked.

"'Cause she's a mean kid."

"Okay. Gotcha. Did you run away as soon as she called you that?"

The boy snuck another quick look at his grandmother, then said, "I might've said somethin' about her teeth."

"Her teeth?"

"Yeah, I might've mentioned a little somethin' like . . . she could eat corn on the cob through a picket fence."

"To get her back for the bad word she called you?"

"Yeah."

"Was it worth it?"

Waycross's face split with a grin. "Oh yeah! It made her mad as a cat tryin' to cover up his poop on a cement floor."

"Waycross!" Stella reached over and poked his shoulder with her finger.

"Well, it did, and the sheriff says I gotta tell the whole truth and nothin' but the truth."

She sighed. "Okay, continue, Sheriff."

Manny nodded. She could tell he was trying not to smile. "Thank you, Stella." To Waycross he said, "Did you walk to the cemetery, or did you run?"

"Oh, I ran. I was mad, too."

"I won't ask how mad."

Waycross snickered and nodded toward Stella. "Probably just as well."

"Okay. The bell rang, you started to leave, but you bumped into Miss Jeanette Outhouse-Seat-Bottom Parker, she called you a name, you commented on her ability to eat corn on the cob in an unusual way, and then you ran straight to the graveyard."

"That's right."

"So, let's try to figure out what time you got there."

"I'm a fast runner."

"Hmm. Taking that into consideration and the fact that your argument with Miss Parker was fairly straightforward, I'd say you probably arrived at the cemetery around two-fifteen. Does that sound about right?"

"Yes, sir. It does."

"When you first got there, did you enter by the front gate or the one on the side by the peach orchard?"

"I went in the front way, and I pinched that Michael angel guy's big toe for good luck."

"Of course you did. We all do." Manny scribbled something on his pad. "What did you do after you tweaked the angel's toe?"

"I headed back there to that big ol' tree where Grandpa Art's at."

"Did you see anybody at all when you walked through?"

"Nope. Not a soul. The only people I saw there that day was Granny and Mr. Horton, who was *all* in a dither!"

"He sure was," Stella added, "but the poor man had a good reason to be discombobulated. It's not every day that you come upon a dead body where there ain't supposed to be one. Especially one that got murdered."

"That's for sure, thankfully." Manny took a sip of his iced tea and said, "Okay, Waycross, you didn't see or hear anybody there at the graveyard that day except your grandmother and Mr. Horton."

"Nope. That's not true."

Manny looked confused. "Why?"

"They's the only people I saw. But not the only ones I heard."

Stella cringed a bit, dreading what the boy would say next and worried about how Manny would take it. She wasn't even sure how she felt about Waycross supposedly communicating with his grandpa.

Manny was sensible and down to earth about most things. She couldn't imagine him buying into the boy's fantasy.

She hoped he would be kind and not mention any misgivings he might have to the child.

"Who did you hear out there in the graveyard?" Manny asked, suddenly far more alert.

"My Grandpa Art," was the simple, straightforward reply.

Manny studied the little face with its open, innocent expression a few seconds before he asked, "You heard him?"

"I do. He talks to me all the time when I visit him there."

"Oh. I see."

It was Waycross's turn to be confused. "Doesn't he talk to you when you go see him?"

"Not that I've noticed."

"Oh, you'd notice if he did. He ain't shy about it."

"I see."

Again, Manny paused, and it occurred to Stella that, in all his years of conducting interviews and interrogations, this was probably the first time he had encountered something like this. He looked taken aback.

She decided to intervene. "Sheriff, Waycross and his grandfather share a special bond. They spend quite a bit of time together there in the cemetery, discussing what's on their minds, man to man. If you know what I mean."

Manny nodded. "Yes. Of course. I'm glad you have that connection to him, Waycross. I'm sure you . . . you both . . . enjoy it."

Glancing down again at his notebook, he said, "Stella, when would you say you arrived at the cemetery?"

"Well, let's see. . . . When he didn't get off the bus with the rest, and I heard why, I told Savannah to call Elsie and ask her to come over. Once I knew Elsie was on her way, I drove straight to the cemetery. I'd say I got there around two-thirty."

"Okay, then, Waycross," he said, "from the time you got there, around two-fifteen until your grandmother arrived at two-thirty, you didn't see or hear anyone other than your grandpa?"

"No. That's not the truth."

His little brow wrinkled into a frown. "I didn't see anybody, but I heard five people in all."

Manny glanced up quickly from his writing. "Five?"

"Yes."

"I thought you said you didn't see anyone there."

"I didn't see nobody but Granny and Mr. Horton. But I heard Grandpa Art and Granny and Mr. Horton hollerin', and two other people."

Instantly, Stella sat up in her chair, excited. She could tell that Manny was, too. He laid down his pen and leaned closer to Waycross. "Then someone else was there in the graveyard, but you didn't see them, only heard their voices?"

"Yes. They were talkin' to each other, and they weren't very happy. Sounded mad."

"Do you know who it was? Did you recognize their voices?"

"Nope. I don't think it was anybody I talk to, like every day."

"Okay. What were they saying?"

"They were talkin' about some guy they were mad at. They were sayin' that the next time they saw him, they were gonna stomp a mud hole in 'im for standin' them up."

"Did they use those exact words?"

"The man did."

Manny thought that over for a moment, then said, "One was a woman?"

"Yeah."

"Are you sure?"

Waycross nodded vigorously. "No guy has a voice that high and squeaky. She sounded like a cartoon mouse with its tail caught in a mousetrap."

"That's pretty high. How about the man?"

"He sounded grumpy. I got the idea they'd been waitin' a long time for somebody, and he hadn't showed, and they had better things to do than hang out in a graveyard. He said that, in fact, right before he said the business about the mud hole."

"Could you tell which part of the graveyard they were in?" Stella asked.

"Over closer to the gate that's by the peach trees. I remember 'cause I'd been thinkin' that after me and Grandpa was done talkin' I might sneak over there and nab me a peach before I went home. But I didn't wanna take the chance of gettin' caught by people who were mad already and might take it out on a kid who was borrowin' a peach that didn't belong to him."

Stella shook her head. "How many times have I told you, Grandson, that it ain't borrowin' if you can't give it back."

"Well, yeah, and there was that, too."

Apparently, Manny had no time for talk of borrowed fruit or stolen, because he cleared his throat loudly and gave Stella an "If you don't mind" look.

"Sorry, Manny. Go on." She glanced up at the service window and saw the cook shoving their orders out to a waiting Jean Marie. "You best hurry, though, grub's a-comin', and then you won't get a word outta him."

Quickly Manny turned back to Waycross and said, "If you were to hear this woman's voice again, do you think you would recognize it?"

"I'd know it was her faster than the one-legged man who won the butt-kickin' contest."

"Waycross!"

Chapter 14

"Wow! Wouldja look at that guy chow down on that there ice cream cone!" Waycross exclaimed as the confection slid down Valentine's throat in one massive gulp. "I never saw one disappear that quick in my whole life! Wonder if he's gonna get brain freeze?"

Stella stood between Waycross and Manny and marveled at the efficiency she had just witnessed. Turning to Manny she said, "Does he always eat that quick?"

"Always. I swear he doesn't even take the time to chew anything once. Apparently, those big, sharp-looking teeth of his are just for show."

Manny bent over, picked up the now-empty bowl, then tossed it into a nearby trash can.

Having finished his ice cream treat, Valentine began to wag his long, graceful tail furiously.

"He's a super good eater," Waycross said. "If you could ever train him to catch bad guys that good, the world'd be a safer place!"

"I'm working on it," Manny said as he untied the animal from the fence post. "Any day now, I'll release him, and criminals every-where will quake in their boots."

At that moment, a couple of people walked by them on the sidewalk.

Stella turned to see who it was, ready to greet them warmly, as was the McGillian custom. Even if you loathed the person and had vowed to clean their pipes for them the next time you saw them.

Good Southern manners required it.

But she was pleased to see it was two ladies, and she very much liked them both. Though, under the present circumstances, it felt a bit awkward to encounter them.

"Good afternoon, Mrs. Faber," she heard Manny saying as he tipped his hat to the first woman. She was lovely, feminine, with soft chestnut curls and wore a floral print sundress that showed off her slender but curvy figure.

That ignoramus Augustus don't deserve a sweet gal like her, was Stella's first thought any time she encountered Gloria Faber on the street or in a store.

Stella couldn't help wondering if Gloria had married Augustus just because he was handsome. Not as handsome as Manny, of course, but attractive nevertheless.

Stella thought of Savannah and how taken she was with that Stafford boy, and she wondered why young women were such easy prey for a good-looking, sweet-talking guy.

But all she had to do was look back on her own teen years and re-call that in most young females' lives, discernment tended to arrive later than the onset of puberty. Young men's, too, for that matter.

Nature's timing seemed a bit off in that way.

When Stella had heard that Gloria was marrying Augustus, she had wondered if the marriage would last.

It had so far.

She wasn't surprised that Augustus had hung on to a peach of a girl like Gloria. But she wondered how any woman, even one as patient and long-suffering as Gloria, could live with an ego as large as his and not feel the need to kick his backside from time to time.

Possibly right out the front door.

But then, Stella reminded herself that no one could truly know what went on behind the closed doors of any given household. Both good and bad. None but the individuals themselves could understand what bonds held marriages together.

Stella suspected, in most relationships, it was a bit of a mystery even to those involved.

"Hello, Sister Gloria," Stella said, holding out her hand. Gloria attended church with her, and it was yet another Southern custom to address fellow worshipers as Sister or Brother when greeting them. Even if they only attended once a year on Easter morning.

"Good afternoon, Sheriff, Stella," Gloria responded, omitting the "Sister" part.

Ordinarily, Stella would have considered it a slip of the tongue, but considering the upcoming election and the rigamarole last evening and again today between Manny and her husband, Stella thought the slight might have been intentional.

The sad look in Gloria's pretty green eyes told her all was not well.

Stella turned to the woman standing behind Gloria and said, "Hello to you, too, Norma. Good to see you out with your sister this fine afternoon."

Norma smiled, her expression more open and inviting than her younger sibling's, but she seemed a bit guarded as well, which was unusual for the outgoing, bubbly Norma.

She, too, was pretty, but not in a soft, delicate way like her baby sister. She wore a bright red business suit and oversized earrings that reached from her earlobes to her enormous shoulder pads.

Although her sister's makeup was understated and natural, Norma's cat-eye liner, bold red lipstick, and heavily penciled, highly arched black eyebrows were a sharp contrast.

Gloria's grooming whispered, "Demure." Norma's shouted, "Look out!"

"Are you ladies having a late lunch together?" Manny was asking them. But even though his tone was casual, Stella saw him studying Gloria's face closely.

Even the simplest question, when asked by Sheriff Manny Gilford, was little less than an interrogation.

"Yes," Gloria said, her eyes not meeting his. "It was her birthday yesterday, so . . ."

"Happy birthday, Norma," Stella said. "I hope it was a good one and somebody made sure you had a tasty cake."

"My sister did," Norma replied, her voice deep and husky for a woman. Stella had always suspected it might be the result of a lot of cigarette smoke and even more hard liquor.

Norma gave the impression of being a tough gal, but her eyes were soft as she looked at her sister. "I can't cook," she said, "so I buy Gloria bakery cakes. But she makes me a carrot cake every year for mine."

"Wish I'd had a piece of that. Happy belated birthday, Norma," Manny said.

Turning back to Gloria, he held out his hand to her. "I do hope there's no hard feelings about what happened yesterday, Mrs. Faber. I want you to know that Augustus and I came to a . . . meeting of the minds, so to speak. I hope you and I are okay."

"We're fine, Sheriff," she said, looking down at the small purse she was clutching tightly with both hands. "I'm sorry I li— that I wasn't forthcoming with you when you called."

"Think nothing of it, ma'am," he said. "I know I don't."

Gloria looked like she was about to burst into tears when she said, "I'm just so ashamed."

He withdrew his outstretched hand but took one step closer to her. In a soft, quiet voice he said, "Really. You don't need to be ashamed about anything. You aren't the first wife who's covered for her husband, I can assure you. Let's just forget all about it and move on, okay?"

She looked up at him, her green eyes filled with tears, and nodded vigorously. Reaching out, she grabbed his hand and said, "Thank you, Sheriff. You're a true gentleman."

"Well, I don't know about that," he said, giving her hand a quick, gentle shake, then releasing it. "But I'm delighted that a lady such as yourself thinks so."

He reached down and pulled Valentine aside so they could pass on their way to the café's door. "You ladies enjoy your lunch, and again, happy birthday, Miss Norma."

They thanked him, nodded to Stella and Waycross, and continued on their way.

Stella studied Manny as he watched them go inside. *Never off duty*, she thought. *Always aware of everyone around him and what they're doing at all times.*

"She's a sweet gal, that Gloria," she told him. "You handled that well."

He nodded thoughtfully but said nothing.

Stella looked down at Waycross. "I know you're just dyin' to get back to school," she said.

"No I ain't," was the rapid reply. "I was hopin' you'd forget and let me stay out all day."

"I'm not that forgetful just yet, young man."

Manny looked at his watch. "Herb called me earlier. Said he was about done with the autopsy and asked me to drop by the funeral home in a little less than an hour."

He reached out and laid his hand on Waycross's shoulder. "What do you say, Miss Stella, if the four of us pile into my cruiser.

I'll drive this young fellow back at record speed, so he won't miss that important history test that he's so looking forward to."

"Gee, thanks." Waycross sounded anything but grateful.

Manny continued, "Then you and little Mr. Macon there can go with me out to apologize to the newlywed, recently widowed Mrs. Corbin for not informing her in a timely manner."

When Stella hesitated, he quickly added, "*I'll* be the one apologizing, of course. Not *you*. It shouldn't take long, so you can wait in the car with the baby."

"Well, I . . ."

"Then you can go with me to see Herb."

"Really?" Stella asked, trying not to sound too anxious or pleased.

"Why not? I'm sure you'd like to hear what he found as much as I would."

"True, but . . ." She looked down at the baby in her arms, who appeared to be stirring a bit more than usual. "He's going to want to be fed soon."

"Then you can feed him. I'm sure you have bottles with you, and no doubt Herb's got a comfortable chair there that he'll let you use."

"But a baby . . . in a funeral parlor?"

"Why not?" Waycross added. "He don't give a hoot if he's there or at Disneyland as long as he's got his bottle and a dry diaper."

Stella felt as though the sun had risen over the horizon and shone its warm, invigorating rays on her face.

Maybe, just maybe, having a new baby in the family didn't change absolutely everything in her life.

Perhaps she could help Manny with his investigation and still be a grandmother, too.

A good, responsible grandmother. Or close enough anyway.

She grinned up at Manny. "You talked me into it," she said.

He smiled back. "I had a feeling it wouldn't be all that hard. Let's go."

Chapter 15

A quick head count told Manny he had one too many passengers, so he decided to leave Valentine at the station house with Augustus.

The task took only a few moments, but when he exited the building and hurried over to his cruiser, he saw that Stella was in the front seat, and Waycross was in the back with Macon Jr. strapped securely into his baby seat.

"Wow, you guys work fast," he said as he climbed behind the wheel, closed the door, and started the engine.

"Was Valentine disappointed?" Waycross asked. "I'd hate it if he was sad, gettin' left behind."

"It was necessary," Manny said as he pulled away from the curb and onto Main Street.

"Don't you trust Valentine with a baby?" Waycross wanted to know. "I don't think he'd hurt him for nothin'. He probably thinks Macon's a puppy."

"I wasn't afraid of him biting him," Manny told him, watching the boy in his rearview mirror. "But he might lick him to death."

"That's true! I never even thoughta that!"

"He also likes to jump from side to side, to see everything he can," Manny said. "If he caught sight of a rabbit or a squirrel, he might trample a little guy like that, not even noticing he was there."

"Okay. I understand. I just hope he does."

Manny smiled at him in the mirror. "He'll be fine. But thank you for your concern."

"I'll make sure I've got a piece of Granny's Sunday breakfast bacon in my pocket for him the next time I see him."

"He'll love that for sure."

By the time they reached the end of their short conversation, they had arrived at his school.

"Can you drop me off over there by the playground?" Waycross asked. "It's recess, and my friends are out. I want them to git a load of me crawlin' outta a police car."

"Sure." Manny flipped the lights on and took his time pulling slowly to the curb. "But promise me that you'll remember what I said before."

"The stuff about keeping ever'thing we talked about under my hat, 'cause it's top-secret sheriff stuff?"

"That's right. It's extremely important, Waycross. We don't want it spread all over town that you and your granny were in the graveyard yesterday. We're just going to keep that to ourselves for now."

"I remember. I swear I won't say a word about it. Not even if somebody threatens to make me eat a live spider or kiss a snake, I still ain't gonna blab. I double-dog promise!"

"Good boy. Run along now and stay out of trouble. I've got enough to do without having to arrest you."

Waycross laughed and reached over to rub his brother's little head before he got out. "This is the Reid boy you have to look out for. No tellin' what he'll get up to one of these days."

Waycross waited until quite a few of his classmates had run

across the schoolyard to the cruiser, their eyes wide. They were even more surprised and impressed when they saw Waycross climb out.

Manny got out, too, gave Waycross a hearty handshake, and said, "Thank you, Mr. Reid." Then he nodded to their audience, got back into the vehicle, and pulled away.

Stella reached over and placed her hand on his forearm. She could feel the warmth of him through the fabric of his shirt and jacket. "You know you just made that boy's day, don't cha?" she said. "His year, in fact. He'll be flyin' high on this until, well, till he's our age."

"Oh, Lord. Not that long, surely."

She poked him in the ribs and laughed. "Speak for yourself, old boy. Me, I'm still a spring chicken."

She sank back into the big, comfy seat of the powerful car, enjoying the luxury of being driven by someone else.

Her baby-carrying muscles were tired. Her laundry-hanging legs were complaining.

"Okay," she said. "I might not be a spring chicken. Maybe a late summer one. A fall one? No way am I a winter one. Not yet."

"Not even close, darlin'." he told her. "But when you are, you're going to be as gorgeous and just as much of a pistol as you are now."

"Why, thank you," she replied, far more pleased than she wanted to be. "You ain't so bad yerself, for one of them August or September kinda guys."

"Wow! You'll turn my head with compliments like that."

When he got to the highway and turned north, she asked, "That Dexter fella, he was livin' out in the old Becker place, right?"

"So says our overly friendly waitress. The place is a bit of a dump. You'd think a guy who could afford crocodile shoes and designer suits would have a roof over his head that didn't leak."

"I hear old Humphrey Becker wasn't much on house repair, and he's been dead twenty years, so . . ."

"Exactly. Wonder what Dexter's new, Las Vegas showgirl wife thought when he carried her over the threshold."

"If it was a rainy day, she was probably wishin' she had an umbrella . . . or married somebody else."

"I just hope she's there. I'd rather not spend my day tracking her down."

"It ain't gonna be much of a notification if she already knows."

"It's a formality."

"One you hate, I bet."

"Yes, I do, usually. But if she was up to going into town and getting a waffle breakfast from Jean Marie this morning, I don't suppose she's too badly cut up about it."

"Either that or that gal's mighty fond of waffles."

"Boy, howdy! This house has gone from bad to way, way worse!" Stella exclaimed when she and Manny reached the end of the dirt road that led to the riverfront and the "old Becker place," as residents of McGill not-so-affectionately called the former residence of Humphrey Becker, moonshine distiller extraordinaire.

"I've seen worse," Manny replied, looking for a spot to park the cruiser among the derelict vehicles that littered the property. "But it's been a long time, and that place wasn't inhabited."

"Here I thought my porch was rickety and my roof's saggin'. After seein' this, I'm gonna be more grateful for what I've got."

Driving around the right side of the house, Manny passed a decrepit Massey Ferguson tractor with a missing rear wheel. A sawhorse had been shoved beneath the axle for support.

A bit farther, they saw a 1959 Cadillac that, with its enormous fins, looked like a rusty, broken old bird with no hopes of ever flying again. Its engine hung on chains from the limb of a sturdy oak above it.

"I don't see any signs of life," Manny said. "For all I know, Dexter hasn't lived here for ages. The only time I arrested him here at home was several years back. After that, I've picked him up in town or on the road."

"What with him gettin' arrested twice a week, don't you have his address on file somewhere?"

"I checked before we left. This is his last address of record."

Stella knew by the dejected look on his face and his tone of voice that he wasn't happy about this latest development. "I'm sorry, Manny. We'll figure it out. Somebody in town's gotta know where he's been holed up."

"Yeah, a vain guy like that living in a dump like this? No. It doesn't make sense, and I can't imagine him bringing a new wife to this place."

"Or her stayin' if he did," Stella added.

They rounded the back corner of the house and received a surprise. Another vehicle, but one that couldn't be more different from the ones they had seen.

A bright red late model Corvette was being washed by a curvaceous blonde wearing a barely there hot pink bikini. Her golden hair was thick and disheveled, spilling about her shoulders and down the front of her. But it wasn't quite long enough to serve as a Lady Godiva costume or provide any degree of modesty.

"Holy cow!" Stella exclaimed as the woman bent over to toss her sponge into a plastic bucket and pick up the hose at her feet. "If that's her," Stella said, "I can certainly see what ol' Dexter saw in her!"

Carefully, thoroughly, lovingly, she began to pass the stream of water over every inch of the car's hood, rinsing the soap suds off its glossy, red finish.

Manny watched for a few seconds, transfixed, then averted his eyes and added, "Considering what she's wearing, or isn't wearing, I reckon the *whole world* can see what he saw in her."

"Is that her car or Dexter's?"

"I heard he was shopping for a Corvette not long ago. I didn't know he'd bought one, or that it was a brand new one."

As they drove a bit closer, the blonde must have heard the cruiser, because she turned off her hose and spun around to face them, a hostile look on her otherwise pretty face.

Stella was shocked to see how young she was. Early twenties at the most.

"Now that *there*," Stella said, "is a spring chicken if ever I saw one."

"She sure is, and our dear buddy Corbin was a late summer sorta rooster, at best."

"Even if he was to put on that git-up she's wearin' and bent all the way over, I don't think we'd see what she saw in him."

"No. I suspect his appeal had more to do with what was in his wallet."

"Or what she *thought* was in it when she married him back in Las Vegas."

"Before she saw his house."

"Exactly."

The young woman tossed the hose to the ground and started walking toward them.

"This might get unpleasant, darlin'," Manny told Stella. "You stay in the car with the baby. I'll leave the keys so you can roll down the windows or turn on the air-conditioning."

Stella opened her mouth to protest that she wanted to be in on the action, too. Then she snapped it closed, realizing that she had other responsibilities now that trumped her amateur sleuthing.

She could hear Macon Jr. stirring in the back, waking from his nap.

Yes, it was time for a diaper change and a bottle.

"I'll be in the back with the doodle-bug," she told Manny as he opened his door to get out.

"Shouldn't take long," he said. "It's not like I'll have to search her for weapons or whatever."

Before Stella got out herself, she reached over to the driver's armrest and used the buttons to roll down all four windows.

She knew she wouldn't be turning on the air-conditioning. No siree bob.

One more look at the blonde told her there was going to be an affray of some sort, and she didn't want to miss a solitary word of it.

Chapter 16

Even though Stella was sitting in the rear seat of the squad car, changing a wet diaper at the time and cooing sweet nothings to her little grandson, Stella had no problem at all hearing every word the new Mrs. Dexter Corbin shouted at Manny from where they stood in front of the cruiser.

Her opening remarks were less like words and more like high-pitched shrieks of rage, a verbal assault that Stella could swear was violent enough to make her ears bleed.

"So now you come around here!" she screamed as she charged up to him, her fists clenched, her pretty face contorted with fury. "Now, nearly twenty-four hours later, you come by to tell me my husband's been murdered! Well, I already heard, thank you very much. I had to hear it from that stupid knucklehead of a deputy of yours, who gave me the news like he was reading the damned weather report."

"Deputy Faber informed you?" Manny asked, sounding confused.

"Who? What?"

To Stella, she looked equally nonplussed. Then she said, "No. The fat, stupid one."

Merv. Had to be.

Stella shook her head, wondering at such a change of circumstances that the big, bumbling Mervin could have become the better choice between Manny's two deputies.

Mervin might not be the most graceful bearer of bad tidings, but at least he still showed his sheriff a great deal of respect, which was more than she could say for Augustus.

"I'm sorry, Mrs. Corbin," Manny was saying. "You *are* Mrs. Cindy Corbin, right? Married to Dexter Corbin?"

"Yeah. I guess."

When he looked at her strangely, she added, "It's not like I even had time to get used to the name or being a wife, before . . . this."

"I apologize to you that my deputy didn't appear compassionate when he notified you, Mrs. Corbin," Manny was saying, his voice as soft and gentle as hers was loud and abrasive. "But I've known Mervin Jarvis for years, ma'am, and I assure you that he has a lot of compassion for people. I know he felt bad for your loss. As I do."

"The hell you do. Dexter told me all about you, Sheriff Gilford. Instead of flying here from Vegas, we drove all the way, and we did a lot of talking on the trip. I know you and this town had it out for him most of his life, never gave him a chance. In fact, we were going to pack up his stuff here and move back to my apartment in Vegas next week. But now . . . ."

To Stella's surprise, the woman began to cry hysterically.

Of course, she was a widow who had just lost her husband to murder, so she was certainly entitled to her expressions of grief.

But then, just after Stella tucked the wet diaper into a plastic bag and shoved it to the bottom of the diaper bag, she noticed something strange about the grieving widow.

There wasn't a single tear glistening on her cheeks. Not even the slightest moistening of the eyes.

For a woman who was in a fit of hysteria, sobbing her face off, she appeared to be utterly tear-free.

Dry as a potato chip on a picnic table at high noon in the desert, Stella thought.

"When was the last time you saw your husband, Mrs. Corbin?" Manny asked.

"The night before last."

"About what time?"

"Late."

"How late?"

She hesitated, then said, "Maybe four."

"Four in the morning *is* late. What was he doing?"

"Leaving the house."

As Stella lifted Macon Jr. from his car seat and cuddled him close to give him his bottle, she felt a pang of guilt.

Normally, she would be chattering to him, even singing him a song. But she didn't want to miss a word of what was being said outside the car.

"Lord, forgive me. I'm a bad grandma," she whispered as she put the bottle nipple into the hungry little mouth and hoped he would slurp a bit less loudly than he usually did. "Oh, Lordy be, I ain't just *bad*, I'm an *awful* grandma," she added with a sigh.

But Manny was continuing to fire off questions, and Stella could feel her own ears practically standing out on stems to eavesdrop.

"Mr. Corbin left the house around four in the morning to conduct business?"

"Yes."

"Did you ask him what he was doing that was business related at that hour?"

"Of course I did. He was my husband!"

"What did he say?"

"He said he had to meet somebody. When I asked him who he was meeting, he told me to shut my mouth, it was none of my business."

"Those are some pretty harsh words there, Cindy," Manny said.

She nodded slightly, and Stella thought she saw a moment of genuine pain cross the young woman's face. "Dex had quite a mouth on him. He could do 'harsh' when he wanted to."

"Then you saw that side of him, did you?" Manny asked, his tone gentle, as though inviting her to trust and confide in him. "The side that we saw around here. Frequently."

"Yeah," she admitted, looking down at the ground. "I saw it. *After* the wedding, of course."

"Of course."

"Guys like him, they don't show their true faces until the ink's dry on the paper, I guess."

"I'm afraid so."

Seeing the look of true sadness on the young woman's face, Stella felt a sharp pang of pity for her.

So many gals don't get what they bargained for, she thought as she saw Manny reach into his pocket and pull out a tissue. *But then, neither do a lotta guys.*

"Cindy, I know this is a terrible time for you," Manny said as he handed her the tissue. "I hate to ask you such a thing, but do you have any idea who might have wanted to harm your husband?"

She stared up at him and clasped the tissue tightly in her fist. "Then it's true? He was *murdered*?"

"We don't know for sure yet. The coroner is examining him right now. But you should prepare yourself, if you can at all. It may have been a homicide."

"Oh, it probably was," she said, in between making quite an act of wiping away her invisible tears and blowing her nose. "I wouldn't be surprised at all."

"Why would you say that, ma'am?" he asked.

"Because, mad as I am that somebody killed him and nobody bothered to tell me till the next day, I knew Dex wasn't a good man. I don't know who it was that murdered him. But I figure they probably had a good reason."

"Good reasons to take another person's life are few and far between, ma'am," Manny said. He reached into his pocket and pulled out his card. Handing it to her, he said, "I'm sorry to have met you under these circumstances. If I'd known Dexter was married, when he was discovered yesterday, I assure you I would have come out here and informed you myself."

"Thank you, Sheriff," she said with a sniff.

"Once again, I apologize for my deputy. He's truly not a bad guy. He's just a bit clumsy about some things. Giving news like that, it's hard for all of us, as you can imagine. Nobody wants to have to tell someone something that's bound to break their heart."

"No, I guess not." She tucked the used tissue into the left cup of her bikini top along with his card.

"If you need anything at all, or if you think of something that might help me catch the person who did this, you call me. Day or night. Okay?"

"Okay."

"Is there anyone you'd like me to call for you, somebody who can be with you? This has to be a hard time to go through alone."

"No. I don't have anybody. But I'll be okay." She was quiet for a moment, then added, "I was all right after I had my waffles this morning. Bad news always makes me hungry."

Chapter 17

No sooner had Manny climbed back into the cruiser than he looked around for Stella and was surprised to see her still in the backseat, feeding the baby.

"How's it going back there?" he asked.

"Fine. We just finished," she said. Kissing one of Macon's cheeks, then the other, she told the baby, "Your hiney is nice and dry, and if you drink any more from that bottle, you're gonna pop."

She tickled his belly for a moment and was rewarded with a bright baby smile that lit her heart with love.

"Now, it's back into your baby seat for you. The sheriff has places to go and people to see, and we get to go with him! Beats stayin' home and hangin' laundry any ol' day."

As she gently placed the child back into his baby seat and buckled him in securely, she told Manny, "You can go ahead and git goin' if you need to. Don't wait for us. I'll be okay back here."

"I'm not in that big of a hurry. I'd rather wait a couple of minutes and have you sitting next to me."

He grabbed his radio microphone from its holder on the dash. "I will take care of one bit of business, though, while you finish up."

As she gave her smallest grandangel a kiss on his nose, she heard Manny say, "Yeah, Augustus, I need you to run a check on Corbin's wife."

"Wife?" was the reply. "He had a wife?"

"Seems so. For the past few weeks anyway. Met her in Las Vegas, married her there, and brought her home with him. Her married name is Cindy Corbin. Blond, blue eyes, about five feet eight. She was a showgirl of some sort, I understand."

"Ten-four, sir," was the curt reply.

Manny replaced the microphone with a bit more vigor than usual as Stella slid into the passenger's seat next to him.

"Still got his bloomers in a bunch?" she asked with a little grin that was intended to cheer him up a bit.

It worked.

He returned the smile and said, "The last thing I want to think about right now is the state of Deputy Augustus Faber's lingerie, be it bunched, wadded, crumpled, or freshly ironed."

"With extra starch."

"Now you're talking."

As Manny turned the cruiser around to leave the property by the path they had come, they saw Cindy Corbin reach for a towel inside the Corvette's trunk and start to lovingly dry off the car.

"Reckon she gets that car, him bein' deceased and her bein' his wife now?"

"I suppose so. Lucky gal."

She was a bit surprised. "You'd want a car like that? A bright red 'Vette."

He laughed. "Us guys have a thing for Corvettes, Stella."

"Lord, if I ever got down inside one of those low-slung things, I'd need a tow truck with a boom and a winch to get me back out."

"Tell you what," he said, laying his hand over hers. "If I should happen to lose this election to that nitwit Augustus, I'll get myself a shiny red Corvette, or maybe blue, for a consolation prize.

Then we can practice you getting in and me helping you get out. Like Prince Charming helping Cinderella in and out of the pumpkin carriage."

"Well, when you put it like that . . ."

Once they were back on the highway and headed for Herbert Jameson's funeral parlor, Manny said, "By the way. I noticed something back there at the widow Corbin's place. I was wondering if you did, too."

"You mean, that when she's calm and being nice, she sounds plumb normal, but the minute she starts pitchin' a fit, her voice is so high and shrill-like that it shoots into a body's ears and goes right to their brain and freezes it?"

"Exactly. Or that it could even be described as 'like a cartoon mouse.'"

"Yep, I thought of that right away."

"Me too."

They grinned at each other. His hand squeezed hers, and she squeezed back.

As Manny guided the cruiser around the circular driveway in front of the lovely brick building with its graceful white columns, black shutters, and window boxes overflowing with pink geraniums, white alyssum, and deep blue lobelia, Stella said, "Other than the old Patterson mansion, this here's the prettiest building in town. Too bad it's a danged mortuary."

He parked the vehicle in front of the hand-carved wooden sign that read simply, JAMESON'S FUNERAL HOME.

He turned off the engine and studied her face carefully. "Why would you say that, darlin'?" he asked.

She shrugged. "It'd make somebody, like Herb and his girls, a fine house to live in. A mansion, in fact. This way, it's just sorta wasted on the dead."

"O-kay. Never thought of it that way."

"Do you agree?"

"Not really. I figure the people of McGill benefit by having a pretty place to come to when they have to say good-bye to a loved one or comfort someone else who's lost somebody. It's a lot nicer than, say, a big barn, or a parking lot, or . . ."

Stella sat in silence so long that Manny finally asked, "Are you okay, darlin'? I know this isn't your favorite place in the world, because of Art and all, but the last few times we came here to talk to Herb about someone's passing, I thought it got a bit easier for you."

"It did. A bit."

"You don't have to come inside. Really. You can wait out here in the car if you want."

"No way! I don't want you to hear somethin' that I didn't get to hear. You might forget to tell me. Men aren't as good at keepin' account of juicy details as womenfolk are."

Manny laughed heartily and said, "You've got me there. I'm sure you're absolutely right about that."

Suddenly, there was a shriek from the backseat that sounded like a six-month-old growing impatient with his present circumstances.

"If you're going in with me," Manny said, taking the car keys from the ignition and slipping them into his pocket, "I think we'd better get going. Sounds like my detainee back there in the cage is about to protest. Maybe even demand a lawyer."

"Don't worry. I got somethin' that's bound to keep him happy."

Stella reached into the diaper bag at her feet and took out a small jelly jar and a tiny baby spoon.

Manny looked at the pale, mushy stuff inside and grimaced. "What the heck is that? Gruel?"

"Mashed bananas. He's just started eating people food, and he loves 'em. He especially likes to rub 'em on his face and in his hair if I look away for even a second."

Manny turned toward the bored, hungry little squawker in his backseat. "I guess the threat 'Eat it or wear it' won't work on you, young man."

The baby's face lit up with a wide grin, as though he had understood Manny's words. Then the child laughed so loudly that the cruiser's interior was filled with the happy sound.

"It's been a long time since anybody laughed that hard in my ride," Manny remarked. "It's usually pretty sober business back there. I should bring my little buddy along more often."

"Just drop by and pick 'im up anytime you've a mind to," Stella said with a grin and a nod toward the bag at her feet. "I'll be sure and pack a ton of diapers for you. He goes through a lot of 'em."

Manny got out of the car before Stella could and opened the back door. As she grabbed the diaper bag and followed his lead, he took the child from his seat and said, "You think that's gonna scare me, woman? The prospect of a wet diaper? Did I ever tell you about the time I faced down a rabid bobcat?"

She was headed around the car to take her grandson from him, but she stopped, stared at him, and said, "No! You never said a word about no bobcat, rabid or otherwise."

He hugged the child close to his chest and kissed the top of his head. "I haven't told you, because it hasn't happened yet," he said with a wink. "But when it does, you'll be the first to know."

Fifteen minutes later, Stella and Manny were seated in Herb Jameson's elegant office on softly cushioned wingback chairs upholstered with deep blue mohair velvet.

Hers was the same chair she had sat in years before when she had been choosing a coffin for her husband, who had left the world far too soon.

But she found it didn't hurt so much today, because she was holding a precious bit of Arthur Reid in her arms.

Sometimes, you gotta put the past behind you, where it belongs, Stella girl, she told herself. *You keep lookin' back, you miss today's many blessings that are spread out there on the table right in front of you.*

"He's one fine-looking boy there, Sister Stella," Herb said. "I would've known he was one of your grandbabies a mile off with that thick black hair and those big blue eyes."

"Yes, other than Waycross, we've got a definite 'look' in this here family," she said. "Folks know it's us for sure when we're strollin' down Main Street, the whole kit and kaboodle of us."

"A sweet little baby is a welcome change in here, I can tell you," Herb said, straightening his tie. "We mostly get people here who've arrived at the end of their lives. It's nice to see a little one just starting out. It gives you hope, you know?"

"I do," Stella replied. "The sheriff here was just sayin' somethin' similar out there in his car."

Manny held out his arms to Stella and the baby. "Let me have him. The hard part's done, now that you've got him fed and changed."

"Are you sure?"

"Of course. You were in here, sticking mashed bananas in his mouth, while I was in the back with Herb and what's left of Dexter C." He nodded toward the pictures Herb was spreading across the top of his massive desk. "You may want to take a look at those."

At that moment, Herb laid down a particularly gruesome shot of the damage done to the back of the victim's head, and Manny added, "Or you might not want to look. It's up to you."

"You know me better than that, Manny Gilford," she said, handing Macon Jr. over with an eagerness that made her feel a bit ashamed. "I'm the kinda gal who looks at anything and everything she can and lives to regret it an instant later."

Manny took the child from her, turned him so that his back was to the desk, and, balancing him on his knees, began to give him a gentle, bouncy ride.

Out of habit, Stella gave them a quick once-over to make sure Manny was supporting him properly, and he was. One big hand was behind the baby's head, the other covering his back.

She didn't have to worry.

Her grandangels were, and always would be, in safe hands with Manny Gilford.

Feeling like a free adult and not a granny for the first time in what felt like ages, she turned her attention to Herb and his grisly autopsy pictures.

Even seeing the body at the crime scene the day before wasn't enough to prepare her for the visual spread out in front of her.

"This is tough stuff, Sister Stella," Herb told her as he finished slapping the last ones onto the desktop with the skill of a Las Vegas blackjack dealer. "You've got a stronger stomach than any woman I know. Any man, either, for that matter."

"Ever' single one of my grandkids had the flu last winter. Bad. All at the same time. So I assure you, I can handle it."

She tapped one of the photos, taken at the cemetery, and said, "Even that one there, with the back of his head busted open."

"There were five licks in all," Manny told her. "Three to his head—one front and two rear—and a couple to the body. Herb tells me that one to the back of the skull was the fatal blow."

Stella looked at the next photo and saw it was a facial shot and the forehead also bore a deep, long wound across it. "What about this business on his noggin'?"

Herb donned his official coroner face. "That wound you're looking at on the forehead is the only one on the front of him. And there was some dirt and grit in that gash. All the other wounds were clean, no dirt, no rust, no splinters. I didn't find a speck of anything in them. Nothing."

She looked closely at a photo of the body lying facedown on the steps. "That's because, when he got hit from behind, he fell forward and smacked his head on the sharp edge of one of them stairs."

"How would you know that?" Herb asked, impressed.

"I'm raising eight grandkids. Believe me, I know ever' way there is under the sun for a body to get hurt. Fallin' downstairs is bad, but you can get hurt fallin' up 'em, too. Cordele chipped a tooth that way a few months ago."

She picked up another picture and studied it. In that photo, the victim was lying prone on Herb's stainless-steel table in the mortuary preparation room.

In that close-up shot she could clearly see a lesser head wound beside the worst.

"Herb says the body blows wouldn't have been fatal," Manny told her. "The second head strike wouldn't have done it either. It's only a hairline fracture. Probably delivered after he was down."

"Just for good measure," she said dryly.

Herb nodded. "Considering the amount of damage I found under the scalp beneath that first blow, I'd say he was probably already unconscious and well on his way out the back door, so to speak, when he hit the deck. Er, the stairs."

"It would take a strong person to deliver a blow like that," Manny said. "One strike and hard enough to be lethal. Probably a male."

Stella shot him a stern, but playful, look. "In case you men haven't heard, us gals have been liberated now, and we can look at disgustin' pictures and not toss our cookies, just like you guys can. Some of you anyway. Not only that, but if we're stinkin' mad enough, we can hit somebody and send 'em into the Promised Land, if we've a mind to."

"I won't argue with you, Stella," Manny said. He grinned at

Herb and added, "I know better. Especially if I'm standing in her kitchen, and there's a fourteen-inch skillet on the stove."

She snorted. "Don't even start with the Stella Reid Skillet Massacree story. I don't wanna hear it. Bud had already busted Florence's lip and knocked one of her teeth loose. She came runnin' to me for help. He broke through my screen door so's he could grab her and do worse. He deserved what he got."

"He did, and it was one less thing I had to deal with," Manny said. "Some days I threaten to fire Merv and deputize you, Stella May."

For a few seconds, Stella thought of what it would feel like to carry a badge, wear a sheriff's uniform, help people who needed it, and lock up those who made life miserable for their fellow men, not to mention the women.

She could see why Savannah wanted to grow up and have a career in law enforcement.

Perhaps Savannah had "caught the bug" from her.

But it didn't matter. With eight children under her roof, women's liberation or not, she wasn't likely to ever be free of her familial responsibilities, free to do anything so exciting.

Which made her all the more grateful to Manny, that he included her in his adventures.

He has no idea how much this means to me, she thought. But when she looked across at him, holding her grandson and watching her as she searched the photos before her, looking for hidden truths, she saw something in his eyes. Admiration mixed with affection.

He knows, she told herself. *That man knows everything about everyone around him all the time. He knows what this means to you, and he trusts you. So git yerself busy and help him.*

"For now," she said, "let's just figure this one out. We got us a murderer runnin' around free as a naked jaybird. Dexter Corbin was a horse's hiney and a half, but he didn't deserve . . . that." She waved a hand toward the pictures.

"No, he didn't." Manny noticed that Macon Jr. was rubbing his eyes with his chubby baby hands, so he laid him down in his arms and gently rocked him as his eyes closed.

Stella turned to Herb and said in a soft voice. "What do you reckon the killer hit him with? A two-by-four?"

"Like I said, there were no splinters. You'd think that any kind of board would have left a few."

"A crowbar? A lead pipe?"

"Maybe," Herb said, "But there weren't any telltale signs of grease, motor oil, or rust to point definitively in that direction."

"Could have been a *clean* pipe," Manny said.

"Or a baseball bat, or a billy club, or a majorette's baton," Herb replied, sounding weary. "Who knows, Sheriff? You will, if you're ever fortunate enough to find the murder weapon, whatever it may be."

"Okay, let's move on," Manny said, suddenly looking as tired as Herb sounded. "What else do we know?"

Stella picked up a second picture where the victim was lying facedown on the steel examination table. "These two discolored areas," she said pointing to a couple of round marks, one on the right shoulder blade and the other on the small of the back. "What are they?"

"Those are the two body strikes," Manny said. "The ones to the head are long, like from a club or pipe. Those two on the back could have been done with the same instrument, only with the end of it."

"Like a really hard poke?" Stella suggested. "Maybe to check and make sure he was dead?"

"Good guess," Herb said.

"That's cold-blooded."

Manny nodded. "Everything about this is cold-blooded."

Stella recalled what Cindy had said about Dexter's late-night summons. "You gotta find out who called him that night, Manny," she said. "It's bound to have been the killer, luring him out there to the graveyard with skullduggery on his mind."

He snickered, and she knew instantly what he was thinking.

"Okay, okay," she said, "I know I sound like Savannah after she's read a Nancy Drew book, but still . . ."

"I'm going to make some calls and see if any other law enforcement agencies had any kind of tracer on his phone or, better yet, were surveilling it. But I doubt we'll be that lucky. Once we have a suspect, then maybe we can nail him with his phone records, depending on the company's sophistication wherever he is."

"If he's local, we're out of luck," Herb said.

"Okay," Manny said. "Let's concentrate on what we *do* have. Herb, your official ruling on this is going to be manner of death: homicide; cause of death: cranial blunt force injury."

Herb nodded solemnly. "Time of injury would have coincided with the time of death."

"Then he died instantly?" Stella said.

"Few of us are fortunate enough to literally die instantly," Herb said. "After a serious injury, it takes a while for the body's vital organs and systems to shut down, one by one. But with the damage done to his brain, Mr. Corbin would have almost immediately gone unconscious, and with that loss of blood, he would have died quickly thereafter."

"Reckon we can be grateful for that," she said, feeling compassion for the man she had scarcely known and, basing her opinion of him on all she had heard, hadn't wanted to know. "Do you have a time of death?"

"I did my best, but that's one of the hardest things you can ask a coroner," Herb told her, and she was struck with the depth of his humility.

Some years back, Herb had accepted the position simply because no one else had wanted it. Not a physician, the only knowledge of the human bodies he possessed consisted of preparing them for burial, but he was quite skilled at that.

Then, a young woman named Prissy Carr was murdered, and poor Herb was expected to earn his keep.

At the outset, Herb had been lost, terribly incompetent. But he had rallied, read every forensic science book he could find, took every course he could, and even traveled to Atlanta three days a week to learn his trade.

Now they were seeing the benefit of his dedicated learning.

Stella was as happy for her old friend as she was for her community.

"You did pretty well with the TOD," Manny assured him. "Nobody expects you to get it down to minutes and seconds."

"I'd be happy to hit the hour," Herb replied. "Maybe I should just get a board, toss a dart."

"Eh, you can do better than that," Manny said. "Tell Stella what you've got so far."

"Okay." Herb took a deep breath and plunged ahead. "There were no signs of animal scavenging yet, thank goodness. The body was cold to the touch and still."

"Which tells us what?" Manny asked, quizzing him.

"The body had cooled and was stiff. That means no less than eight hours, or it would have still felt warm. But no more than thirty-two hours, or the rigor would have faded."

"Good," Manny said. "What else?"

"I checked the livor mortis, the lividity, for blanching."

"Huh?" Stella searched her memory for any record of any such thing and found nothing.

Isn't "blanching" a fancy way to say, "Boil a vegetable for just a minute?" she thought.

"After death, without the heart pumping blood through the body, gravity takes over," Herb explained. "It causes the blood to settle in the lower areas of the body, whatever parts are closest to the ground or whatever they're lying on."

"That sounds like a handy thing to know," Stella observed.

"It is," Manny told her. "Sometimes the location of that discoloration can tell you that the body was moved some time after death."

"But that wasn't the case with Dexter," she said.

"No, it wasn't," Herb replied. "The lividity was in the face and the front part of the body, as it was supposed to be, considering how it was lying. The blood spatter also confirms that the injuries occurred there."

"What did you say about 'blanching'?"

Herb reached over to Stella, took hold of her forearm, and turned it over to show its underside. He pressed quite firmly on her skin with his thumb, then released it.

"See there?" he said. "See that white spot that my thumb made when I pressed down and pushed the blood out of that area?"

She nodded. "I did see it, for a second. Then it disappeared."

"That's because you're alive. Your heart is still pumping. Blanching happens even after you die, but not forever. Only for eight to twelve hours. Twelve hours after death, that doesn't happen. No blanching."

"All right," she said, "then he was dead at least eight hours, but no more than twelve."

"Exactly."

Herb looked so proud of himself that she hated to ask him to be more specific, but she couldn't help herself. "Can you get it any closer than that, Brother Herb? Four hours is an awfully long time. It could make a big difference in an investigation, like when you're trying to verify people's alibis and stuff like that."

He drew a deep breath and started to pick up the pictures, one by one, off the desktop. "I also measured the algor mortis, the body temperature, how much it's dropped."

"Now that I've heard of!" Stella said, excited to be on familiar ground. "It drops a certain amount each hour or somethin'.'"

"It does," Herb said. "We use something called the Glaister Equation."

"Sounds complicated."

"It isn't. When I took his temperature at four o'clock yesterday afternoon, there in the cemetery, it was 81.3. The normal human temperature is 98.6. That's a difference of 17.3 degrees."

"He had cooled off 17.3 degrees from the time he died until you took his temperature?"

"Right, and the body tends to lose about one and a half degrees per hour."

"Then you'd divide that 17.3 degrees by one and a half? That's it?"

"That's it. Eleven and a half hours."

Stella looked over at Manny, who looked a bit less convinced. "So," she said, "that would mean he was killed about four a.m.?"

"Theoretically," he replied, "I'm sure Herb got the temperature right and the math is correct, but they tell us to establish a window of three to four hours around that estimate."

"A four-hour window would mean between two a.m. and six a.m., right?" Stella asked him.

He gave her a big smile and, again, she knew they were thinking the same thing.

"That," he said, "would include the time that our lady with the cartoon cat voice said he received an important business call and took off without telling her where he was going."

She nodded thoughtfully. "We've just got to find out who called him. 'Cause it sounds to me like that was the murderer, settin' our man Dex up for a nasty execution."

153

Chapter 18

After their visit with Herb Jameson, Stella, Manny, and little Macon Jr. headed back to the sheriff's station house. As they walked through the door, Stella looked down at her watch and said, "I can't hang around long. School's gonna be out pretty soon. I have to pick up the kiddos and go back to being a granny."

"I understand," Manny told her. "Thank you for the time you've already given me. When I'm with you, the day seems to fly by."

"For me too." She smiled up at him, feeling a bit sad. "Even when I don't want it to."

They walked into the reception area to find Augustus sitting at the desk, cleaning his Colt Trooper.

He looked as out of sorts as when they had left him.

With little more than a glance in their direction, he shoved the weapon back into its holster and began to pick up the pieces of the cleaning kit.

"What's up?" Manny asked him as he walked toward the desk

with a purposeful stride, letting his deputy know it was time for him to vacate the chair. "Anything new since I left?"

"No," was the brusque reply as he grudgingly rose from the chair and waved a hand toward it, indicating surrender.

Manny waited as the deputy took his time removing the cleaning supplies and some paperwork he had apparently been working on from the desktop.

Finally, Manny leaned toward him and said, "Don't hurry on my account, Deputy. But once you're finished with your housekeeping, I'd like to fill you in on the particulars of the case we're now working on."

That got Augustus's attention, and he even seemed to cheer up a bit.

His hands full of the desk clutter, Augustus turned to Stella and said, "Before I forget, Miss Elsie Dingle called about half an hour ago. Said she couldn't get you on your phone at home, so she figured you were out in the field with the sheriff."

Stella's heart started to race. "Is everything okay?" she asked, fearing what the answer might be.

"From what I gathered," Augustus replied. "But she asked you to call her as soon as you can. Preferably before school's out."

"Oh, okay. Thank you," Stella said. "Manny, I'm going to run outside to the phone booth, quick-like, and see what she wants."

"You'll do no such thing." Manny motioned toward the phone on the desk.

Stella shot a quick glance at Augustus and saw the look of disapproval, which he wasn't trying to hide at all.

"Uh, sir," Augustus began. "That phone is for official business only. She's a civilian."

"How many calls have you received today, Deputy Faber?" Manny asked him, his face flushed with anger.

Augustus hesitated, thought it over quite a while, considering the simplicity of the question. "Just the one from Miss Dingle, sir."

"Did you make any calls yourself?"

Another, even longer hesitation. "I did, sir."

"To whom?"

"My wife."

"So, the only time this phone has been used since you came on duty was those two calls?"

Augustus gave one curt nod.

"Then I think we can allow a citizen of McGill to use it for a minute or two. A civilian who has spent her morning assisting me with a murder case on behalf of this department. I think we can grant her one lousy, rotten telephone call, if you don't mind, Deputy?"

Augustus shrugged. "Yeah. I guess it'd be all right. Hopefully, nobody'll call in with an emergency while she's on."

"You didn't seem too worried about that when you were whispering sweet nothings to your wife earlier," Manny told him.

"I'll make it short," Stella said, picking up the phone. "Just a second, I promise, to see what she wanted, to make sure the kids are all right."

"Make your call and take your time, Mrs. Reid," Manny told her. "This isn't the Dark Ages. Not even here in little McGill. We actually have *two* lines, for exactly that reason."

Stella wasted no time dialing Elsie's home number.

Elsie answered right away, but to Stella's relief, she sounded her usual, happy and peaceful self when she said, "Hello. Is this Stella?"

"It is. I'm here at the sheriff's station, and I heard you called me. Is ever'thing okay?"

"Better than okay!" was the jubilant reply. "I just found out I'm on vacation for the next week! The judge and the missus left this mornin' for a cruise that they forgot to even mention to me.

With them gone, there's nobody to cook for, and I won't have to lift a finger around here for ten days!"

"Wow! That's the best news I've heard in ages! Nobody deserves a break more'n you, darlin'."

Stella was overjoyed for her friend, but she did wonder why Elsie had taken such an extraordinary measure as calling the station house to deliver news that could just as easily be shared later in the day, after Stella had returned home.

As though sensing Stella's curiosity, Elsie proclaimed, "I got nothin' at all to do here, and I'm so bored I'm thinkin' of paintin' my toenails, just so's I can watch 'em dry."

Stella chuckled and looked over at Manny, who was jotting notes in his black book and pretending not to be listening.

Augustus had opened the gun cabinet in the corner of the room and replaced the cleaning kit. He was making a show of checking and rechecking the department's weapons stowed there.

Stella was pretty sure he, too, was eavesdropping. She hoped Elsie would deliver some more timely news pretty quick. Stella hated the thought she and her friend might be monopolizing the station's communications frivolously, as Augustus had not so subtly suggested.

"I'm sorry you're bored, darlin'," Stella said softly, "but there's not a lot I can do."

"There sure is! You can cure my problem in a jiffy, and I can help you out while we're at it."

"Okay. How's that?"

"When you pick up them kids from school, you bring the whole kit 'n' caboodle of 'em out here to the Pattersons' and dump 'em off, includin' the baby. Have Manny come, too. That way you can leave that panel truck here, so's I can haul 'em all around when I've a mind to. Then you can go hang around with the sheriff for as long as you need to and solve that murder."

"Elsie! You can't mean that!"

"Well, maybe not as long as you need, but up to ten days, when the Pattersons come back from their cruise. If you two ain't got it solved by then, heaven help you. In a town this little, it ain't like you got a bottomless pit of suspects."

"Elsie, you finally get a break, but you want to spend it watchin' eight rambunctious kids, including a little baby who's still not sleepin' through the night? What kind of vacation would that be for a hardworkin' woman like yourself?"

"A fun one! An interestin' one, for them and for me! They'd have a ball explorin' this old place. I'll show 'em around and tell 'em all the secret, historical stuff that most folks never heard of. All of it ain't nice, but the younger set needs to know the truth about what happened back then. This would be a perfect time for me to share it with 'em."

There was a momentary silence as Stella thought of her own mother, a Native American, who had labored alongside Elsie's mom, a black woman, in the cotton fields of the Patterson plantation all those years ago. She recalled the horrors they, and so many like them, had endured.

"Some of those stories, Elsie. I don't know if I want the younger ones to know what happened back then," Stella began.

"Don't worry, sugar. I'll take their tender ages into account. I'll watch how much I say, who I'm sayin' it to, and how I tell it."

"Of course you would," Stella replied. "They would love it. Truth be told, those kids have a better time when they're with you than anyplace on earth. Plus, the Patterson place. Like most people in town, they've only been there a couple of times, and they haven't seen what it's like behind the scenes."

"You know, of course, you can drop by as many times a day as you want to or have the time to. Day or night."

"Oh, I would! I can't stay completely away from my babies for days on end!"

"I know. You'll miss them even more than they'll miss you."

"I have no doubt of that."

"You could even spend the night here in the big house if you want. Lord knows, there's plenty of guest bedrooms."

A flood of emotions surged through Stella, conflicting, confusing, and wonderful.

A few days when she wouldn't need to make a zillion peanut butter and jelly sandwiches, bandage scraped knees, change diapers. A few nights, if she chose to fully accept Elsie's offer, to actually sleep the entire night and not wake to every movement, burble, and coo in the bassinet beside her.

She couldn't even imagine such a thing.

Glancing down at Manny, who had set his pen aside and was looking up at her with a questioning expression on his face, she thought of what it might be like to spend time with him and not be distracted, looking at her watch every minute to see when she would have to leave him and run back to the house.

It all seemed far too good to be true.

So good that she felt terribly guilty for being so happy.

"I don't deserve a friend like you, Elsie," she said, "but I'll take you anyway, and I'll accept your kind offer. Bless your heart."

"Oh, shush." Stella heard Elsie's laughter, loud, throaty, and filled with joy. "Go get them kids from school and bring them and that truck of yours over here. Don't even go back to the house for clothes. I'll run 'em over there after dinner to pack up some stuff."

Stella could hardly speak, but she managed a simple, "Thank you, darlin'," before she hung up the phone.

"Well?" Manny asked. "Everything okay back at the ranch?"

"As a matter of fact, everything is fantastic, amazing, and wonderful, back at the Patterson place. Elsie offered to let me drop the kids, all of them, over there right after school. She said she'll watch them a few days for me."

"*All* of them?" Manny asked, astonished.

Stella nodded.

"Does she know how many of them there are?" he added teasingly.

"She's got a rough idea, and apparently, that's enough."

"Wow!" he said.

"Yeah!" She allowed the smile that was building inside her to burst through and light her face. "She needs my truck, though, so's she can drive 'em around if she wants to. They won't begin to fit in that little Mustang of hers."

Manny anticipated her next request before she could even ask. He stood, tucked his notebook into a top drawer, and said, "Augustus, you're back on the desk. I have an errand to run. If you need me or you hear anything new about this case, you know how to get me."

Augustus answered with a barely discernible nod and went back to studying the weapons in the gun cabinet.

Manny walked over to Stella, nodded at the baby in her arms, and said, "I'm gonna miss that little guy there. I've gotten used to having him as a mascot."

"She says we can visit any time we've a mind to," Stella assured him, and herself, as she bent down to kiss the top of Macon Jr.'s sweet-smelling baby head. "I have a feelin', after that first night with precious little sleep or none at all, she'll be happy to hand him back."

Chapter 19

Stella pulled her panel truck over to the curb in a place where Manny could park his cruiser right behind her and, more importantly, in a place where her gang of grandangels would see her on their way to the school bus.

She had trained them to always look in that area for her, in case she had decided to pick them up rather than wait for them to get off the bus at home.

Once the bell rang, it didn't take long for them to come spilling out of the front of the building and racing toward her.

"Here they come, sugarplum," she said to the tiny one behind her in his baby seat. "This is the beginnin' of the closest thing to an adventure that you've had so far in your short life."

He answered with one of his baby giggles that went straight to her heart. Truly, it was the sweetest sound on earth. Turning in her seat, she looked at him over her shoulder. Now fully awake, he gave her a bright smile.

"You know," she said, "for a very short guy with not a lotta hair and nary a tooth in his mouth, you're pretty darned handsome."

Again, he laughed, as though he had understood every word she'd said and had found it hilarious, taking no offense at all.

For a moment, the excitement of having her granny-free days and spending unlimited time with the good-looking man sitting in the sheriff's cruiser behind her dimmed. "I'll miss you most of all," she told the baby, feeling like Dorothy bidding farewell to Scarecrow in her favorite movie.

Then she saw Savannah bounding across the lawn toward her. The girl who, any day now, would no longer be a child. She was blossoming into a beautiful young woman, whom Stella knew would continue to be a wonderful friend and confidante in the years ahead.

But Stella knew she would miss the little girl version of Savannah. Her innocence, her relentless optimism, her unwavering conviction that doing the right thing in this world would result in a carefree life.

Stella knew that all her grandangels would become adults, and from time to time, she would long to be able to see, hold, and comfort the former versions of them. These times were precious, when she still actually had the power to make the majority of their troubles go away, to ease most of their sufferings with a tight hug, a bandage strip, some disinfectant, and a comforting smile.

Adult problems were seldom so easily solved.

She watched Savannah's face and knew the instant she spotted the sheriff's vehicle.

Yes, there it was, the wide grin, the sparkling eyes, all present when the girl had a "Sheriff Manny sighting."

Stella saw her hesitating, obviously torn between joining her grandmother or going over to the cruiser and greeting Manny.

In the end, Savannah gave him a vigorous wave, then hurried toward the truck.

As she opened the front door and settled into the front seat, she said, "Sheriff Gilford's right behind you. Did he pull you over? Were you speeding? Got a taillight out?" Then the girl gave her a searching look and a bit of a smirk and added, "Or is he just saying, 'How do?' to you, like he does every chance he gets?"

"Since you ask," Stella said, choosing to ignore the insinuations, "he's followin' us over to the Patterson estate. The judge and his wife are away on a cruise, so Elsie offered to babysit you kids for me for several days. There at the Pattersons'."

Even as she spoke the words, Stella felt guilty. Terribly guilty. She felt like she was going to be dropping a litter of orphaned puppies off at the local animal shelter.

What a horrible, rotten granny you are! she thought as she waited for Savannah's reply. But she didn't have long to wait.

"Yippee! Yahoo! Wow! Oh, wow!"

Hmm. The kid ain't overly devastated, she silently observed. *Not so's you could tell anyway. If she's plumb heartbroken at the thought of my absence, she's hidin' it real good.*

"I can't wait! This is totally awesome, Gran!" Savannah was saying, bouncing on her seat and waving her hands. "How long do we get to stay with her?"

"I don't know yet. Reckon it depends on how it goes."

"It'll go just fine. The rug rats are always on their best behavior when they're with Elsie."

Stella was silent, trying not to take her granddaughter's statements personally. Savannah was an intelligent, well-mannered, loving child who would never utter a word that she thought might hurt her grandmother. Obviously, she had intended no offense.

Savannah was observant enough to notice the lack of response to her statement, and, as always, she was quick to make amends.

She reached over and put her hand on Stella's forearm. "That came out wrong, Gran. I just meant, you know how kids are. They always behave better for someone outside the family than they do for the person who's actually raising them."

"I completely agree with you, darlin'," Stella assured her. "Everyone behaves better when they're with our sweet Elsie. Even me. There's just somethin' about her that brings out the best in folks. We're all better people for havin' known her."

Savannah nodded thoughtfully and smiled. "I can't think of a nicer thing to say about a person than that. Somebody should write that on her tombstone someday."

"Good idea. If we outlast her, we'll see it gits done."

One by one, the rest of the kids piled into the rear of the truck. As was their ritual, they took turns leaning over the back of Stella's seat and giving her a peck on the cheek.

As they settled into their appointed seats and began to buckle themselves in, Stella shared her news with them and received the same joyful reaction as Savannah had shown.

"Eeeee!" screamed Jesup, a normally quiet, moderately morose seven-year-old.

"Coconut cake every day!" yelled Vidalia.

"For breakfast, dinner and supper!" Marietta added.

"Can we go swimmin' in the river?" Cordele asked.

"That'll be up to Elsie, Cordele. If she says so, it's fine by me. The currents aren't strong at all there by the weepin' willow tree."

"I'm not Cordele," was the quick reply. "Today I'm Cordelia."

"You're so silly with that business, Cordie," Waycross said. "Gran has enough trouble keepin' track of us all as it is. What if ever' one of us decided to change their name along with their underwear ever' mornin'."

Cordele flared, "Well, some of us just don't wake up every mornin' feelin' like they wanna be called after some Georgia town like the rest of her family. Some of us like bein' different once in a while."

"Settle down back there, Waycross . . . and Cordelia," Stella said as she did a quick head count, then pulled away from the curb and onto the road with Manny close behind. "I don't wanna go dumpin' grumpy kids off on Elsie."

"We won't be grumpy with her. We never are," replied the softest voice in the group, the one belonging to quiet, gentle Alma. The girl was nine and older than two of her sisters, but except for the baby, she was the smallest of the brood. A tiny, fey child, Stella often thought the fairies might have dropped her in a flower garden to be discovered by her less than gentle, quiet, or fey mother.

"I know, sweetie," Stella told the girl. "You'll all be good as gold and have a wonderful time."

"But what about Annabelle? Does she have to stay there at the house all by herself? She'll starve and die from loneliness."

Annabelle?

Stella had to search her tired and tattered mental files a while before she accessed the necessary information.

"Oh, Annabelle. Of course. Your little hurt kitty. The only one outta the batch that you couldn't find a home for."

"Nobody wanted her," Alma said, her voice tremulous. "They don't think she's pretty because her tail is crooked."

"She walks funny, too," Marietta added for good measure. "All crippled up and goofy looking. Nobody wants a ugly cat with a bent-up tail and a messed-up foot."

"I do! I want her!" Alma protested.

"You can't keep her!" Marietta persisted. "Granny said so. We've got too many mouths to feed already. If I can't have a dog, then you can't keep that stupid, ugly cat."

"Quiet down back there, before I just turn this truck back toward home and call this adventure of yours to a halt."

Stella softened her voice as she addressed Alma. "We've spoken about the kitten before. Alma, you get to keep nursin' her until her foot's all better, and then you'll need to find a home for her if you can. You did such a good job finding homes for all of those kitties after their missus passed on. You'll find one for this one, too."

"But she's Valentine's friend. They lived together, and now she's the only one he gets to see when he comes to our house."

"I'm sorry, honey, but we can't keep ever'thing you rescue. I'd have a house burstin' at the seams with dogs, cats, toad frogs, pigeons, and goldfish."

Stella looked in her rearview mirror at the downcast little face of her own miniature Florence Nightingale. "Don't worry, honeybunny," she told Alma. "Elsie loves kitties and might let you bring her over to the Pattersons, and if she doesn't, I'll be home every morning and night. I'll be sure to feed her and pet her and make sure she feels loved. Okay?"

She was rewarded with a smile and an eager nod.

As Stella drove on down the highway, Manny right behind her, she couldn't help getting excited about the prospect of trying to solve this new case with him. Considering how little he had to work with, he would need all the assistance he could get.

In the back of the truck, the baby slept and the other six chattered away, discussing their hopes for their impromptu adventure.

She glanced over at Savannah and saw an odd look on her eldest grandchild's face.

"You're thinking about the case, aren't you?" Savannah said.

"Yes, I was, as a matter of fact," Stella replied. "I wish you were along for this one. You were a lot of help before."

Savannah flushed under the praise, and the smile on the girl's face reminded Stella that she wasn't the only one in the family who loved mystery solving.

"Actually," Savannah said, "when we get to Miss Elsie's, I've got something to tell the sheriff."

"You do?"

Savannah nodded. "It's something that Waycross told me. I think he should say it to Sheriff Gilford, too. I'm pretty sure it's important."

Stella would have asked her what it was, but she was already pulling the truck off the highway and onto the narrow, hard-packed dirt road that led to the rear of the antebellum mansion.

More importantly, it led to the old carriage house.

It led to Elsie Dingle, the best friend Stella had ever had.

As far as Stella was concerned, the best friend to be found in the entire world.

Chapter 20

Long ago, the massive building, which was still known as "the Carriage House," had been home to the Patterson family's fine horses and elegant carriages. Later, after automobiles had replaced the horses, the upstairs had been converted from a hay loft into a large and elegant apartment for the plantation's overseer.

But for years, its occupant had been Elsie Dingle, the Pattersons' personal chef.

Judge Patterson was widely known for his love of fine food and his penchant for entertaining folks with equally discriminating palates.

When little more than a child, Elsie had distinguished herself, working in the kitchen as an exceptionally talented cook's assistant. Though she had begun at the bottom, scrubbing pots and pans and sweeping the floors, Elsie had become known as someone with both a gift and a talent for cooking, especially baking.

As a result, over the years she had been promoted, and eventually, she had become the head chef in a kitchen where her ancestors had once worked as slaves.

Even the persnickety judge knew her value and, upon her insistence that she couldn't sleep in the main house because of all the "haints," as she called them, he had remodeled the old overseer's apartment to her personal tastes and, after some considerable negotiating on her part, signed a contract with her that she could live there for the rest of her days, if she chose to.

Stella was proud of her friend. They had both endured difficult childhoods and had raised themselves above their raising. Elsie more than Stella.

But Stella didn't begrudge her friend one bit of her success. She knew all too well how hard Elsie had worked for the right to serve governors, judges, celebrities, and powerful heads of business at her table.

Then there were all the blue ribbons that decorated her kitchen walls. Prizes she had won in cooking contests all over the county.

As always when driving onto this elegant, if aged, estate, Stella felt more joy than sadness.

Yes, she and so many others had labored and suffered on this soil. But now it was so much more. It was her friend's home, and that made the old, historical estate a place of happiness, rather than sorrow.

Time had changed things here for the better, and since Stella knew that was a rare occurrence in the sad, old world, she was grateful.

She parked her panel truck, filled with her precious grand-angels, beside the carriage house and watched as Manny pulled up next to them in the cruiser.

She was excited to think they might actually have some new, unexpected information from her grandson.

"Waycross," Stella called back to the boy, "I hear you've got somethin' to tell the sheriff."

"It ain't a big deal. Just somethin' about some screens . . . there in the graveyard," he replied.

Instantly, she was all ears and excited. "Screams? You heard *screams* there in the cemetery?"

"No. *Screens*," Savannah explained, since her brother was already piling out of the truck, eager to get his Miss Elsie adventure under way. "He heard the man's voice in the graveyard say something about 'screens.'"

"Screens" weren't nearly as intriguing as "screams," but Stella grabbed Macon Jr. and the diaper bag and hurried around the side of the truck. She wanted to alert Manny to the possibility of some additional, hopefully valuable, information.

"Waycross, git yourself back here, sugar," she called out to the boy, who was already halfway up the long, outside stairway that led from the ground to the door of Elsie's apartment. "I'm sorry, but you gotta talk to the sheriff before you get busy playin' or eatin'."

He looked disappointed, but he begrudgingly fought his way back down the stairs, against the flow of his female siblings, who were heading upward.

She saw Elsie open the door at the top and begin to welcome each child inside with a kiss on the cheek and one of her famous soul-healing, if potentially rib-cracking, hugs.

The aroma of something divinely chocolate drifted downward from the open door at the top of the stairs.

"Here, let me take him," Savannah said, reaching for the baby. "I'll get everybody settled up there while you and Waycross and Sheriff Gilford talk."

Stella smiled at her, then held the infant close to her chest for a long moment, kissed his head, told him she loved him, and handed him over.

"Thank you, sweetheart," she told Savannah. "In case of an emergency, or if you guys need me for anything at all, you just call me at home. If I don't answer, then I'm probably hanging out with the sheriff, and you can get me through the station house. Okay?"

"I know the drill, Gran," Savannah said, standing on tiptoe to kiss her grandmother's cheek. "There won't be any emergencies. You just relax now and enjoy not having to worry about all of us for a little while. I'll help Miss Elsie, and everything's going to be just fine."

Manny had gotten out of the cruiser and was walking up to them.

His eyes twinkled as he watched the kids disappearing into the carriage house, one by one. "You'd think this was Christmas morning and Elsie was Mrs. Santa Claus," he said. "I've seen kids less excited to be arriving at Disney World."

"You'll be excited, too, Sheriff, once you hear what Waycross remembered," Savannah said as she walked away with her baby brother in her arms. "It's an honest-to-goodness clue. If you can't figure out what to do with it, call me and I'll tell you."

He laughed and turned to Stella. "Oh no! Now I'm under the gun. Can't let a kid outsmart me, even if it's your genius grand-daughter."

"Who has a talent for sleuthing."

"For nosiness, is more like it," he said. "But of your many qualities, I'd say pure, unadulterated curiosity is the greatest of you Reid gals' virtues."

"Why thank you. That's high praise . . . I reckon."

Waycross trudged over to them, as energetically as a fellow wearing lead underwear. His impatience was as obvious as the plentiful freckles on his flushed face.

"Can we get this over with in a jiffy?" he asked. "I gotta get up there before my sisters mow through all them chocolate cookies Miss Elsie baked, and I'm left with none at all."

"I'm quite sure Miss Elsie baked more than enough for all of you, and she'll make sure you get your share."

He smirked. "I know she will. That's what I'm afraid of. I was hopin' to get *way more* than just my share."

Stella tousled his curls and said, "What's this thing Savannah's talkin' about? Somethin' you overheard there in the graveyard? Somethin' you just remembered?"

"Yeah, I told her about it at recess, and she got all fired up about it. You know how twitterpated she gits over nothin'."

"Just tell me what you told her, son," Manny said. "Then I can decide if it's worth getting excited about or not."

Waycross shifted from one foot to the other, thinking hard. He grimaced as though concentrating was an exhausting effort. "Okay, Sheriff. Do you remember when you asked me what that guy and that lady were saying to each other?"

"I sure do," Manny replied. "You said you couldn't make out any of their words. Though I figure you must have heard and understood a word here and there, because you thought they were waiting for some guy, and he hadn't shown up yet."

"Yeah, that's it. Last night, when I was goin' to sleep, I remembered he said something about screens."

"Screens? Like, screen doors, or sunscreen, or a TV screen, or . . . ?"

"Yes, sir. I remembered that while he was complainin' about gettin' stood up by the fella, he said somethin' like, 'I can't wait around here all day. If I don't get that ol' geezer's window screens up, like I promised him I would, he'll be chewin' up nails and spittin' out barbed wire, and he'll be spittin' it in my direction.'"

Waycross laughed at the joke and added, "I thought that was funny, so I remembered it later on."

"It *is* funny, Waycross." Manny dropped down onto one knee to be face-to-face with him. "Better yet, it's not just humorous, it's potentially very valuable information. Thank you. I owe you one."

"One what?"

"I'll think of something."

"Cool." Suddenly, the smile on Waycross's face disappeared, and he looked a bit perturbed. "So, Savannah was right?"

Manny laid his hands on each of the boy's shoulders, looked him squarely in the eyes, and said, "Son, would you like me to tell you something? It's so important that if you remember it and apply it your life will be so much easier and happier in the years to come."

Waycross opened his big baby blues all the wider and said, "Sure. I like 'easy' and 'happy.' What is it, Sheriff?"

"You're going to be surrounded by women most of your days—if you're lucky. Once in a while, they're going to swear that something is true, and you're going to disagree. Just remember, they're almost *always* right."

"Really?"

"Yes. We guys don't like to admit it, but it's just the plain truth. Accept that fact right now, and you'll have a much happier life. I promise you."

Waycross glanced over at his grandmother then turned to Manny and sighed. "Okay," he mumbled, without enthusiasm. "If you say so. But do we have to let 'em know that we know that?"

"Absolutely not! Never let them know that we know that! It's a secret, just between us guys."

Waycross nodded Stella's way. He whispered, "But my granny. Now she knows that we know."

"I know." Manny nodded solemnly. "But that's okay, because she already knew it."

Waycross sighed. "Now I'm really confused, Sheriff."

Manny stood, gave him a companionable slap on the back, and said, "Aren't we all, Mister Reid? Aren't we all?"

Chapter 21

"I can't believe I actually asked myself, 'What would Savannah do next?'" Manny told Stella as he pulled the cruiser into the parking lot of McGill's one and only hardware store. "Maybe she's the one who should be running for sheriff, not me and that aggravating Augustus."

"She'd be better'n him any day," Stella agreed.

"No doubt about it. That cowboy's all hat and no cattle."

"I've come to realize that since I've known him. Here all this time I thought it was him who was the best of your deputies."

"I've only got two and one is Merv," he said, shaking his head. "It's not like Augustus had a lot of competition."

He took the keys from the ignition and nodded toward the store. "Let's go follow up on this hot lead, provided by those grandkids of yours, God bless them."

"They'd be thrilled if you got somethin' good from it."

"Savannah would. Waycross might, if today's interrogation didn't end up costing him the lion's share of Elsie's cookies."

"Well, yes. There is that matter of the cookies."

As they left the vehicle and walked up to the store's front door, Manny placed his hand on the small of Stella's back.

It was a simple and innocent gesture, but she felt it throughout her body. It felt like affection. It felt like protection.

It felt simply wonderful.

"I'm glad Elsie did this for you," he said. "For us, actually."

"I still can't get over it," Stella replied. "Like, who offers to care for eight children, just out of the goodness of their own heart?"

"You did, darlin'," he gently reminded her. "You not only offered, but you insisted! Quite loudly, as I recall."

"That's different. They're my flesh and blood."

"But Elsie considers all of you her family."

"I couldn't love her any more than if she was my true-born sister."

"I know that, and so does she. I'm happy for you both."

As they walked through the front door, the brass shopkeeper's bell sounded, filling the store with its cheerful chiming.

Stella breathed in the unique smell of a hardware store: freshly sawn wood, paints, stains, and various oils.

Even better than the aroma of the place was the broad, friendly smile given to her by the man who came out of a back room, wiping his hands on a dirty rag. He then removed a soiled work apron and tossed both onto a nearby counter.

His T-shirt had as many smudges and discolorations as the apron he'd been wearing, and so did his jeans and his hands.

Stella assumed from their red hue that he had been staining some wood.

"Nice shade there, Emmet," she said. "That'd look good on my kitchen cabinets."

"I'd sell you a quart of it, if you like, Miss Stella. I'd even show you how to use it."

There was a light in his dark eyes that suggested he might be conveying a little more than his usual interest in one of his customers.

Stella was surprised. She'd known Emmet Carothers her whole life, but never considered him anything but the fellow she'd gone to school with, a guy who now sold her bits and pieces of this and that whenever she had to perform some do-it-yourself home repair.

She glanced over at Manny and saw that he, too, had noticed the shopkeeper's feeble attempt to pique her interest.

Manny seemed less than thrilled. But he was all business when he told Emmet, "Sorry, Mr. Carothers. We don't have time for a class on the ins and outs of wood staining today. But I do have a couple of quick questions for you, if you don't mind."

Emmet shrugged and looked a bit put out, but he said, "Okay, Sheriff. What can I do for ya?"

"Anybody that you know of around here replacing screens on their house right now?"

"Um, well, I'm not sure, but—"

"Has anybody been in here to buy screen in, say, the last few weeks?"

Emmet nodded. "As a matter of fact, yes. Two guys."

"May I ask who they were?"

"Jesse Wainwright and Tyrell Grymes."

"They came in together?"

"No. Separately. Jesse was in a few weeks ago. He said he needed to replace the screen on his back door, because his cat did a number on it, trying to get outside to fight a stray tom that was on the back porch."

"And Tyrell?"

"He was in last week, bought a ton of my best stuff. Said he's changing all the screens on Old Man Jonsey's windows. Something about how they're full of holes, and the mosquitos are feasting on Mr. Jonsey at night when he's trying to sleep."

Manny gave him a brief smile and a curt nod. "Thank you, Emmet. That's all I needed to know. Good day to you."

In less than a minute later, Manny had ushered Stella out of the store, doorbell jingling, and back to the cruiser.

"That didn't take long," Stella commented, as he opened her door for her.

"Not nearly as long as Emmet there would've liked," Manny said. "He was obviously enjoying the view."

As he stepped aside so she could slide inside, she looked up at him and tried to read the expression on his face. Was he angry? Jealous, maybe?

She wasn't sure.

When he got in with her and started the car, she decided to find out.

"You do know, don't cha, that I got no interest at all in Emmet or his stain. I was just makin' polite conversation, warmin' him up for you, so to speak."

Manny looked surprised, then shook his head. "Of course I know that, Stella May. If he knew you half as well as I do, he wouldn't have bothered to ask you about staining lessons."

He backed the cruiser up, then pulled back onto the highway.

Once under way, he reached over, covered her hand with his, and gave it a little squeeze. "The only sort of stains that capture *my* girl's interest are bloodstains at a crime scene."

She laughed. "You know me too well, Manny Gilford."

"And before all's said and done, I'm looking forward to getting to know you much, much better."

She sighed, sank back in her seat, and tried not to think about how quickly her knees had gone weak.

Nope, she thought, *that Emmet Carothers can just be as interested as he wants to be. The boy don't stand a chance.*

* * *

Manny drove them straight to the old farmhouse, which sat on the edge of town, not far from Stella's own modest little place.

The home was one of the oldest in McGill, and it showed every year of its age.

Long ago, it had passed the "needs a new roof and paint job" phase and progressed to the state of "needs to be torn down before it falls on somebody and smashes 'em flat as a flitter."

"I'll be the first to admit that my porch is a bit off kilter," Stella said, as they reached the end of the dirt road and the house. "But this here place is leanin' so bad that it looks like it needs a walker just to stand up straight."

"I know." Manny shook his head, taking in the sagging frame that was pitched to the right at an alarming angle. "The town council had a meeting about it last year. They talked about condemning it, forcing Mr. Jonsey to move out and live in a safer place."

"I bet he threw a conniption fit about that!"

"You have no idea. Fortunately, Doc Hynson's on the council, and he could tell by his red face, purple ears, and bugged-out eyes that Jonsey was in danger of having a stroke, so they all backed down. Figured he'd live longer if they left him there and he took his chances with the roof caving in, rather than make him leave and risk him dying from the stress of the ordeal."

"Good choice, I'd say," Stella agreed. "It's usually best to just let folks be stupid, if they've a mind to."

"They're going to be anyway, and you save yourself the trouble."

He parked the vehicle next to Jonsey's past-its-prime pickup and looked around. Toward the back of the yard sat a black, barely maintained, older Pontiac Trans Am. The gold and orange firebird decal on its hood was missing a few feathers and didn't look like a phoenix who would ever rise again.

"That's Tyrell's Pontiac back there," Manny said. "I'd recognize it anywhere."

"You know him well?"

"Better than I'd choose to. I've arrested him several times, usually in the company of Dexter Corbin."

"Really? For what?"

"Mostly drugs. But they always showed up to court with expensive lawyers who got them off or pled the charges down to next to nothing."

"How did a couple of peckerwoods like those two afford expensive lawyers?"

"I always wondered that myself. Wait for me," Manny said as he opened the cruiser's door to get out.

"Really? I thought since I didn't have the little one with me, I could go with you on whatever you did."

"That's what you thought, huh?" he asked with a playful grin. "Tyrell Grymes is a felon, not to mention my number one suspect in a murder case."

"Oh, pooh. We both know Tyrell's only at the top of that list you're carryin' around in your head because you ain't got nobody else on there. It's easy to be number one when you're the only one."

"Be that as it may."

"Plus, those felonies he committed, was any of 'em acts of violence against grandmas?"

When Manny just quirked an eyebrow but didn't say anything, she knew that was as good as a no.

"To your knowledge, Sheriff Manny Gilford, has Tyrell Grymes ever raised a hand against anybody?"

"What is this? Am I on a witness stand here?"

"Okay, that's a no, too. So, I reckon it would be safe for me to go to the door with you."

"Oh, you *do*, do you?"

She nodded most emphatically.

He gave her a long, searching, doubtful look.

She decided to play her last card. "If I was a man, would you even give it a second thought?"

"Probably not."

"Well, there ya go. I rest my case."

"Because there's not a man on this planet that I care about one fraction as much as I do you, woman."

She gulped. "Oh. I . . ." She had no answer for that. None she could force herself to say at the moment.

But her argument had been more effective than she'd thought. She could see him wavering as he looked from her to the house and back again.

"Okay," he said. "You can come with me if you promise me faithfully that if anything, anything at all, starts to happen, you will instantly turn around and run, not walk, back to the vehicle and call the station house."

"You wouldn't want me to stay and help you out?"

"No!"

"Okay! I promise. I swear I'll desert you in your time of need, turn tail, and run like a chicken out here to the car and call them worthless deputies of yours to come help you out."

"That's exactly what I want you to do."

Stella muttered something under her breath.

"What did you say?" he asked.

"If you must know, I mighta said somethin' about lettin' people make their own stup . . . I mean, less than ideal decisions."

"Grrr."

As they left the car and walked up to the front door of the house, Stella looked at what was probably the living room and dining room windows. All freshly rescreened.

"Them mosquitoes must've been pretty fierce," she commented, "for Mr. Jonsey to spring for new screens on this old house."

"People do have different priorities," Manny said as he knocked hard and long on the door. "Some folks like roofs that don't leak."

"Or fall in on ya at an inopportune moment."

"And some people are rabid about mosquitoes. Apparently, Mr. Jonsey leans toward the latter."

"Ever'thing around here leans," she said, looking at the porch beneath her feet and the columns it supported. "This here house is like that Leanin' Tower o' Pizza."

"Pizza? I think you mean the Leaning Tower of Pisa."

"You lean your way, and I'll lean mine."

The door opened, and an elderly fellow stuck his head out. He had wiry white hair and an equally snowy beard, except for the two brown tobacco juice stains that led from the corners of his mouth downward.

From the way he was squinting, Stella decided he was having trouble seeing and recognizing them.

Of course, she had seen Old Man Jonsey, as folks called him, many times before. But she hadn't spotted him around town in a long, long time, and she was sad to see how much he had aged. He had been losing his hearing for years, and apparently, his eyesight was failing as well.

"Good afternoon, Mr. Jonsey," Manny said in a voice louder than his usual. "Sheriff Gilford here with Mrs. Stella Reid."

"Sheriff?"

"Yes, sir," Manny replied. "Don't worry. There's nothing wrong. I just need to talk to Tyrell for a minute. I understand he's doing some work for you here."

"Work? That guy? He's worthless and dumb to boot. I swear that boy could fall up a tree."

"Is he here?"

"Back there on the rear porch, makin' a nuisance of hisself. I swear I'm gonna go bankrupt, payin' for all the screen he's wasted."

Manny gave the older man a kind, compassionate look and

said, "Mr. Jonsey, I've got some good news and some bad news for you."

"What's that?"

"The good news is, you don't have to worry about Tyrell wasting your time and money for a while. Maybe even a *long* while. The bad news is, you're going to have to find some other knucklehead to finish putting up your new screens for you."

When Stella and Manny rounded the side of Mr. Jonsey's house, they found Tyrell Grymes, a spindly limbed guy, dressed in a faded blue T-shirt and torn jeans that seemed to hang off his gaunt frame. His haggard face looked far older than his twenty-something years. What one could see of it anyway. His features were mostly concealed by long, dirty auburn hair. His sallow and pock-marked complexion suggested a lack of health.

He was sitting on the steps that led from the lawn to the back porch, working hard at rolling a joint.

The instant he saw Manny, he fumbled what he was doing and the marijuana that he had so carefully spread on the flimsy rolling paper fluttered to the grass at his feet like so much green snow.

"Damn!" he said. "Damn it all!"

With a mournful expression on his face, Tyrell stared down at his intended herbal treat, now hopelessly lost among the long grass that was in desperate need of mowing. Then he looked up at the lawman, whose pale gray eyes seemed cold and stern at first glance, but they twinkled with a hint of perverse humor.

"Oh, Mr. Grymes. What am I going to do with you?" Manny said as he sauntered over to the overgrown delinquent and pulled him to his feet. "Since you were thirteen, I've been telling you that you're on the wrong road. But here you are, still plodding right along, headed for purgatory. Or worse."

"You gonna bust me for one spliff?"

"That depends," Manny said as he twisted Tyrell's arms behind him and handcuffed his wrists.

"On what?" Tyrell wanted to know.

"On how much you tell me about something a lot more important than a joint you didn't get to smoke."

Stella watched Tyrell's face closely.

He didn't look confused. Though she could tell he was pretending to be as he said, "What's that? Huh? What's up, bro?"

"I'm not your brother, Mr. Grymes."

"What should I call you then?"

"Sheriff Gilford will do just fine."

Manny gave him a nudge to start him on his way around the side of the house, heading toward the front.

Stella followed closely behind, watching, listening, learning.

"Whatever you think I did wrong, I didn't do it," Tyrell protested as Manny took him to the cruiser.

"What in particular do you think that I think you did, that you didn't do?" Manny asked.

"Huh?" This time, Tyrell was way out of his depth. He shook his head and said, "You cops. You're always out to confuse us guys."

Manny grinned back at Stella.

She stifled a giggle and said, "Doesn't seem like a job you'd have to work too hard at, Sheriff. Looks about as easy as gettin' a wet foot walkin' through a mud puddle."

Chapter 22

Inside Manny's private office, Stella found an extra one of the infamous, uncomfortable, rusty chairs and unfolded it a discreet distance away from his desk. She tucked herself into the corner of the room by the file cabinets and settled herself on the chair. From there she could observe what was going on, hear what was said, and yet not attract attention to herself.

Manny sat behind his desk. Directly across from him, Tyrell Grymes squirmed on his own flimsy folding chair.

To his right sat Deputy Augustus Faber, who looked perfectly at ease. Pleased, in fact.

To Tyrell's left was Deputy Mervin Jarvis. As Stella watched him, she wondered if she had ever seen Merv looking anything other than sleepy. From his droopy eyes to his perpetually mussed hair to his wrinkled uniform that had fit him much better thirty pounds ago, everything about "good ol' Merv," as townsfolk called him, suggested that when he wasn't on the job Deputy Jarvis was in his bed. Sound asleep. Probably still wearing the uniform.

When Manny, Stella, and Tyrell had arrived at the station

house, Faber had been getting ready to leave, having finished his tour, and Mervin was coming on duty.

Manny had invited them both to sit in on the interview.

Stella doubted that he wanted their input about what they heard. She suspected he had done so more out of courtesy.

They had both seemed eager and pleased to join in.

Much to the dismay of Tyrell, who was peeking suspiciously at them through the curtain of dirty, russet hair hanging down over his face.

"I feel kinda ganged up on here, Sheriff Gilford," their detainee said, nodding toward Augustus, then at Mervin. "Does it take three of you guys to squeeze me here?"

"Who's squeezing you, Mr. Grymes?" Manny asked, as he opened his black notebook and began to write in it. "We're just having a friendly chat. I took your handcuffs off. Merv gave you a soda there. We're just trying to make you feel at home."

"If I was home, I'd be smokin' my spliff and watching the Braves play the Cards," Tyrell grumbled.

"You might not want to mention that again," Augustus said, "the bit about the marijuana. Remember you're in a sheriff's station house being questioned."

"Ain't you on parole, good buddy?" Mervin asked him, sticking his thumbs inside his belt and leaning back in his chair, which creaked ominously, complaining about his more-than-ample girth.

"I'm done with that," Tyrell let him know most indignantly. "Been three weeks now."

"Three weeks?" Manny said. He shook his head. "Three whole weeks you kept your nose clean. That must be some sort of record for you, Mr. Grymes."

Tyrell gave a long, liquid sniff. "I don't reckon you brought me all the way in here to your station just to insult me, Sheriff. What is it you want with me?"

"I want to know where you were, let's see . . ." Manny glanced down at his notebook. ". . . around two forty-five yesterday afternoon."

"Home."

"Doing what?"

"Watchin' television."

"With anyone else?"

"No. I was by myself. My girlfriend and me split up a few weeks ago."

Manny closed the notebook and slowly, quite deliberately put his pen on top of it. "Mr. Grymes, I don't usually ask a question that I don't already know the answer to."

"If you know the answer already, why ask me?"

"To see if you'll tell me the truth or if you'll lie to me."

Tyrell looked down at his hands, which were tightly clenched together in his lap. "Do you think I just lied to you, Sheriff?"

"I'm sure you did. Because I know exactly where you were at that time, and so do you. Are you going to tell me the truth, or are you going to sit there and keep lying to me and dig the hole you're in even deeper?"

Stella could practically hear the gears spinning between Tyrell's ears, as he tried to determine the best way out of his predicament.

Manny appeared to sense his conflict, too, because he said in a softer, less confrontational voice, "Come on, Tyrell. You and I haven't always seen eye to eye over the years. But you know I've always treated you fairly, right?"

Tyrell hesitated, then gave Manny a slight nod.

"Okay, so spill it. Let's hear the truth, and then we'll sort it out and see what we've got."

"You won't believe me if I tell you. It's, well, weird."

"I've heard plenty of 'weird' in my day. Let 'er rip."

"I was in the cemetery."

"Why were you there?" Merv asked, suddenly awake and curious.

" 'Cause somebody asked me to meet him there."

Augustus leaned forward in his chair, staring at their interviewee with the same sort of intense, searching cop eyes that Stella frequently saw when Manny questioned someone. "Who?" he asked. "Who did you go there to meet?"

"I can't tell you, 'cause then you're gonna think I did somethin' wrong, and I didn't."

"If you refuse to tell us, we'll think that for sure," Manny told him. "Who asked you to meet him there? Who were you waiting for?"

Tyrell looked to his right, saw that Augustus was staring at him intently.

He glanced to his left at Mervin, who appeared to be nodding off again.

"Okay, I'm gonna tell you. The guy who asked me to meet him there was Dexter."

Manny studied his detainee for a long time before he said, "How did he ask you? Did he phone you or . . . ?"

"No. He texted me."

"What exactly did the text say?"

"It said, 'Meet me graveyard ASAP peach orchard gate.' "

"What time did you get the text?"

Tyrell thought for a moment. "I didn't look at my watch, but I reckon it was just a few minutes before I got there, 'cause I was at the fillin' station, gassin' up when I got it, and that's just down the road a piece from the cemetery."

Stella watched Manny lean forward, close enough that Tyrell looked uneasy.

"Was Mrs. Cindy Corbin with you at the filling station when you got that text, or did you meet her there at the graveyard?"

Tyrell seemed confused. "What? Why? No, she weren't with

187

me at the gas station. Ain't me that brung her to the cemetery. She got there on her own steam, she did."

"Why was she there?"

"I don't know. She said she got a text, too."

"From Dexter?"

"Yeah. Her and me 'bout ran into each other there at that gate by the peach orchard. I didn't know who she was, and she didn't know me. We was all suspicious-like when we first laid eyes on one another. Took some explainin' before we figured out that he'd sent for both of us."

"Dexter sent for you," Augustus said. "Are you sure it was him?"

"Course I am. Said so right there on my pager."

Augustus and Manny exchanged looks.

Mervin's eyes were closed, his breathing slow and deep.

"Okay, Tyrell," Manny said. "Did you walk around the cemetery, you and Mrs. Corbin?"

"A bit. There in the old part, since that's where I met up with him before."

"When you were doing drug deals," Augustus said. It was a statement, not a question.

"We had some business dealings once in a while. Car business. I was workin' on findin' him a Corvette that didn't have too much mileage on it. Dex could hardly sleep at night for wantin' himself a 'Vette. But before I could find one for him, he up and bought a brand new one when he went to Vegas."

"We both know you had more than 'car business' with Dexter Corbin over the years," Manny told him. "I busted you myself for cocaine possession right there in that graveyard. He let you take the rap for it, as I recall, fine fellow that he was."

"Yeah, well. Dex had a bad streak. Not to speak ill of the dead, but he did. I won't deny it. A mile-wide streak. But that day, all I had on my mind was selling him a 'Vette. I told that Vegas gal he married all about it, and she told me he'd already bought one, a new one, while he was back there in Nevada. After I heard that, I just left."

Augustus gave an unpleasant snort and said, "Yeah, right. You met Dexter Corbin in a deserted place to talk about a car deal. It wouldn't have had anything to do with the ton of cocaine that Dexter brought back with him from Las Vegas, right?"

Stella heard Tyrell gasp. The look on his face was like that of a boxer who had just received an unexpected uppercut to the solar plexus.

But what bothered her more was Manny's expression. He had obviously been taken aback and wasn't happy about it.

Glaring at Augustus, he said, "Deputy, please expound on the question you just asked."

The arrogant, self-satisfied sneer that Augustus gave Manny was enough to make Stella wish she had a frying pan and five minutes alone with Augustus Faber.

"I'd be glad to, Sheriff," Augustus replied. "Since you obviously weren't getting anywhere with this case, I've been conducting an investigation of my own. In my spare time."

Manny's eyes went positively glacial, but he only nodded and said, "Continue."

Stella silently gave him high marks for self-control in the face of extreme provocation.

Augustus lifted his chin a couple of notches and said, "Word on the street is that Dexter Corbin was connected to OC there in Vegas. They say he went there to score a ton of cocaine and bring it here for distribution in Atlanta and Chattanooga. I can't imagine he wouldn't have mentioned that fact to Tyrell here, his right-hand man."

Manny turned to Tyrell. "Is this true, Mr. Grymes? Did your friend, Dex, go to Las Vegas to do a drug deal with organized crime elements there?"

When Tyrell didn't reply, Manny slammed his open palm

down on the desk, causing everything on it to rattle and nearly upsetting Tyrell's half-consumed soda. "Well? Answer me!" he said, his voice booming in the small office.

Stella's eyes widened.

Even Merv woke up.

"Yeah!" Tyrell said. "He told me that he was doin' that, and I told him I didn't want any part of it. I'd just got off parole, and the last thing I'd wanna do is to go back inside. I can't stand bein' locked up!"

"But you hotfooted it out to the cemetery as soon as you got that text," Augustus said. "That doesn't sound like a guy who was running away from trouble. That's more like one who's eager to jump into the thick of it."

"I never seen him!" Tyrell exclaimed, his voice shrill, his face flushed. "I swear to you, he never showed up."

"There's a good reason why he didn't meet and greet you there at the graveyard," Manny told him. "He was already dead."

"What? I heard his body was found in the graveyard." Tyrell started to shake violently. "But are you tellin' me he was already dead when I was walkin' around in there? I might've passed right by his carcass and not even known it? Oh, lord."

"Yes, his body was there, sprawled out, plain as day, on the stairs of the Patterson crypt," Manny told him. "And you want us to believe that you didn't see it? Neither you nor his widow?"

"I don't know about her, 'cause she was still there when I took off. But I didn't see nothin' like that. For all I know, ever' dead body in that graveyard was underground, where they belonged!"

Tyrell covered his face with his hands, breathing so hard and fast that Stella thought he might pass out at any moment.

She looked at Manny and tried to read his eyes. She couldn't tell if he believed Tyrell or not. Manny had a reputation for having his poker face in place at all times.

Augustus was leaning back in his chair, his arms folded over his chest, wearing that irritating, exceedingly smug look that made Stella wish she could toss him off the nearest bridge and watch him splat in the muddy river waters below.

Merv was nodding off . . . again.

"Tyrell," Manny said, his voice soft again, "put down your hands and look at me, son."

Eventually, Tyrell did as he was told. Stella was surprised to see tears in his eyes.

In that moment, she remembered all she had ever heard and seen concerning his family. The severely alcoholic mother, the father who died in prison, the older brother who had been killed in a fight over a broken bottle of beer.

Other than a brief time in his first and only year of high school, when Tyrell had distinguished himself as a gifted hitter on the baseball team, his life had been unremarkable. Except for his rap sheet.

Now, as Stella watched him being interrogated, it occurred to her that Tyrell was just another one of those young men who hadn't been able to rise above their raising.

Her heart ached for him.

At that moment, she was glad she wasn't a law enforcement officer. If he was guilty, if he was bound for prison and another lengthy, soul-scarring incarceration, she wouldn't have wanted to be the one who sent him there. Even if he deserved it.

"Tyrell," Manny said. "I have one more thing to ask you, and whatever you do, tell me the truth. I promise things will be better for you if you do. Okay?"

He sniffed and nodded. "Yes, sir."

"Where were you the night before you got that text?"

Tyrell shrugged. "Home, I guess."

"You're going to have to do a lot better than guess," Manny told him. "Think it through and then answer my question again. The truth, the whole truth, and nothing but."

Literally squinting from the exertion of concentration, Tyrell reconsidered, searching his memory. Then a light came on in his eyes. "Oh, yeah! I remember! How could I ever forget! I was home all right, watchin' *Dallas*!"

The moment Stella saw the almost rabid gleam of fan mania in his eyes, she believed him.

The sun had hardly risen the morning after that particular episode of the beloved television show had aired when her neighbor, Florence, had hightailed it to Stella's back door, coffee mug in hand and the same look of mad delirium in her eyes.

The show season had ended on a cliffhanger, and for Florence Bagley, the world had stopped, and life as she had known it was hardly worth living.

"Did you see it, Sheriff? Did ya?" Tyrell was rattling on. "Oh my lord! I about jumped outta my skin there at the end!"

"No, Mr. Grymes," Manny said. "Tell me about it."

"Well, Pam Ewing was drivin' along the road in that cute little red Mercedes of hers, and she ran smack into the side of a big ol' truck, and there was a great big explosion, and that car burned up with *her in it*! Lord, I 'bout lost the six-pack of beer I drunk just lookin' at it there on the TV."

"Sounds pretty dramatic," Manny said in a flat tone that suggested far less enthusiasm than Tyrell's.

"It was! What a shame. That pretty little Mercedes all blown to smithereens. It was almost more'n I could take."

"I can only imagine. But putting the season cliffhanger of *Dallas* aside for the moment, can you tell me what you were doing later that night? After the show was over, late into the night and the early morning hours?"

"Not much. It liked to've wore me out watchin' that. I went to bed. Yep, I turned in early and went right to sleep."

Stella saw Manny's shoulders sag a bit. He sounded a little disheartened when he asked, "Tyrell, tell me the truth now. Did you sleep alone that night, or did you have company?"

"Naw. Since my girlfriend walked out on me, I've been all by my lonesome."

Augustus seemed to be the only one in the room who was in a good mood. Stella heard him chuckle before he said, "That's too bad, Tyrell, my man. You picked a bad time to suddenly become a single, sleep-alone sorta guy. You're a felon with no alibi when he needs one most. Your life's about to circle right down the toilet, dude, fast and furious."

Chapter 23

Later that evening, after another quick and casual meal at the Burger Igloo, Manny drove Stella home.

They sat on the porch swing, sipping a final cup of coffee, with Valentine sound asleep at Manny's feet and Alma's kitten, Annabelle, curled up and purring on Stella's lap.

She stroked the tiny feline's soft fur as she watched a host of fireflies perform their fairy-like courtship among the azalea bushes and boxwood hedges that bordered her small and modest lawn.

But Manny's mood was far from fanciful.

Stella could tell he was having a difficult time controlling his temper when it came to his deputy.

"I don't blame you," she said, reaching for his hand and giving it a friendly squeeze. "He should have come to you with that news he had about Dexter picking up a drug stash in Las Vegas and him bein' hooked up with organized crime."

"Yes, he should have," Manny agreed, clasping her fingers tightly. "He knows to come to me with anything he's got, as soon as he gets it. Holding back like that, it doesn't help the case, the people involved, or the town, for that matter."

"Are you going to discipline him for it?" she asked. "If you need any help, I have a tree full of switches in the backyard, and I'd be happy to make a contribution to the cause."

"Thank you, Stella May," he replied. "I'll keep that in mind. But to be honest, I have to admit that I didn't fill him in right away on what I know, either. Especially what Waycross heard. That was the only substantial break in the case. We knew about it, and I didn't bother to tell him. I kept it to myself. I can't really fault him for doing the same."

"Funny, I didn't think that was so bad at the time."

"Me neither. But with the shoe on the other foot . . ."

She turned and looked up at him. She was surprised and sad to see him so troubled. Usually, Manny was upbeat and positive. For all the years she had known him, she had only seen him looking like this—down and maybe even defeated—once before.

When his beautiful, young wife, Lucy, had died.

Like Stella, when she had lost her husband, it nearly destroyed Manny to lose his wife. Eventually, he had picked up the broken pieces of his soul and patched them together enough to continue a meaningful life. But it hadn't been easy.

The last thing Stella wanted was to see him go down such a dark road again. Or a path that even remotely resembled that road.

"Please don't take it so hard, Manny," she said. "I can't stand to see you sad."

"I don't think I'm sad as much as I'm tired, Stella. I've been doing this job for so long, and it seems to just be getting harder all the time. This was once a town where the worst thing I had to deal with was some kids overturning an outhouse or throwing eggs at a billboard. Now we've had murders and suicides and sexual assaults, beatings and robberies, and the drugs. Oh, these damned drugs, Stella! They just make everything so much worse."

"They do. It's true. But there's only so much you can do to prevent that. It's a sign of the times, Manny. They're just everywhere now. You can't push back a flood with your bare hands."

"That's exactly what it feels like. I keep pushing, and it all just slips through my fingers."

"I know. No wonder you're tired."

"I *am* tired, darlin'. Sometimes I think . . ."

When he didn't finish his sentence, she leaned into him and gave him a little nudge in the ribs with her elbow. "You think . . . ?"

"Maybe Augustus would do a better job. I don't care for him as a person, but he's no dummy. He's a good cop. He's younger, way more ambitious than I'd ever want to be."

"He's a jerk."

"He is. But he plays by the rules. Usually."

"The people of this town love *you*, Manny. They feel safe because you're in charge."

"Eh, public opinion is badly overrated. Being sheriff isn't a popularity contest, you know. Sometimes, being everybody's friend actually works against you. If they like you and believe that you love them, then they figure they can get away with more."

"You do have a soft spot for old ladies who jaywalk and disabled veterans whose parking meters have timed out."

"Not to mention girls named Savannah who have library books in their possession that are badly overdue."

She laughed. "You should be ashamed of yourself, lettin' desperados like that escape the clutches of the law."

"I lay awake at night struggling with the guilt."

"As you should."

"Don't tell anyone."

She rolled her eyes. "I won't. It'll just be our little secret."

He put his arm around her shoulders and pulled her closer to his side.

"I wonder sometimes how it might be to just have a normal life," he said, "like yours."

She choked, then laughed so hard that tears came to her eyes. "Normal? *My* life? Heaven help us, Manny! Do you really think raisin' eight young'uns at my age is normal?"

"Not compared to the average mom or grandma out there. But you don't have to drag at least one or two drunks up the stairs every night and toss them in a cell. When is the last time you threatened to take a guy to the vet and have a certain, um, appendage removed if he didn't stop peeing on the street in front of God and everybody?"

"Elmer Yonce?"

"Of course."

"I've threatened to rearrange Elmer's body parts a few times when he's decided to display his . . . shortcomings . . . in my immediate vicinity."

"Wow, he's a braver man than I am, doing a thing like that within striking distance of *you*! Braver or more stupid."

"Those two ain't mutually exclusive. I've seen folks who are brave as a bigamist, but they couldn't find water if they fell outta a boat."

They sat in companionable silence for a long time, soaking in the sultry night air, which was scented with roses, lilacs, and jasmine from Stella's flower garden, blooming right around the corner of the house, and the underlying fragrance of the ubiquitous Georgia pines in the forest nearby.

"This is nice," he said, as he reached over and tickled the kitten under her chin. In return, she rubbed her tiny face against the back of his hand. "Sitting on a porch swing with you, petting a cat, listening to my dog snore . . . I like this."

"I do too," she said, "and there ain't even any little faces peekin' through the curtains at us. I must say, I do miss 'em, though. The place is way too quiet without 'em."

"Yes, it doesn't seem right without them spying on us. Like you and Elsie and Savannah were doing when I was out here reading Augustus the riot act."

She rested her head on his shoulder. He leaned down and kissed her hair.

"As long as you weren't cuddlin' him and kissin' him it's okay. I'd get mighty jealous if I saw somethin' like that."

"No danger of that happening. Not ever. Kicking his backside, now that might be a possibility."

She pulled away a bit so that she could look up at him, into his eyes. "Are you gonna mention any of this mess tomorrow at the picnic when you give your speech?"

"Naw."

"Why not? They say ever'thing's fair in love and politics."

"I think that's love and war."

"Same difference."

"True, but I choose to take the high road in these election campaigns. I don't want to start slinging mud now. Playing it straight's always worked for me before."

"You never had anybody run against you before. Not in a million years anyway."

"Point taken."

"You might have to fight to keep your job."

He was quiet for a long time, and when she turned and looked up at him again, she thought she saw the glint of tears in his eyes.

She couldn't be quite sure. The porch light was dim, and the moon hadn't risen yet.

"That's just it, Stella," he said, his voice more tremulous than she had heard it in a long time. Since Lucy.

"I don't know if I want this job anymore," he said. "Sometimes, I think I'd rather just have some peace."

Chapter 24

As Stella stood in the middle of the town park and looked around at all the people who had gathered for the picnic, Manny's one and only campaign event, she wondered how he could ever doubt that he had made a great difference in little McGill.

Anybody who was anyone had gathered, carrying signs bearing his picture and the words *Gilford for Sheriff!* in bright yellow letters. They wore T-shirts that the local merchants' association had provided with the same picture and the pithy, if not particularly original, slogan.

Children played with balloons and Frisbees, all bearing his name.

The makeshift stage, erected beside the swing sets, the sandboxes, and the slide, was draped in red, white, and blue crepe paper streamers and a sign that read: MANNY GILFORD FOR SHERIFF, AGAIN!

Someone had set up a boombox and the Judds were belting out the cheerful tunes "Rockin' with the Rhythm of the Rain," followed by "I Will Stand by You."

Everyone seemed in a celebratory mood.

Even Manny, who was milling among the crowd with Valentine on a leash, seemed to be enjoying the interaction with the townsfolk, adults, and children alike.

Some of the grown-ups seemed afraid to pet Valentine or even get too close to the giant, fearsome-looking animal. The kids, however, petted him, told him how beautiful he was, and some even hugged him around the neck and kissed his dewlaps and forehead.

The big mutt took it all in good humor, seeming to revel in the attention and soak in the affection.

Stella watched for a while, then turned back to the picnic table and her chore of the moment, arranging the deviled eggs she had made that morning on her best cut-glass platter.

Ordinarily, that crystal dish was used only on holidays and the occasional Sunday when special company came, but since it was Manny's "do," she'd decided to use the best she had.

With her work done, she reached into the infant seat nearby and scooped up the sleeping Macon Jr. and hugged him close to her chest. It felt so good to hold him again. Her arms had ached for the warmth of his small body cuddled next to hers. For the sound of his breathing and the sweet, baby smell of him.

Whether Manny solved this case soon or not, even if the older children wanted to stay with Elsie for the rest of their "vacation," Stella decided she had to bring this little guy back home with her before long.

A bit farther down the long table, Savannah and Elsie were placing all sorts of cookies on plates: chocolate chip and peanut butter ones on Savannah's plates and pecan sandies and date pinwheels on Elsie's.

Stella was astonished to see half a dozen plates mounded high with the delectable sweets. She spotted more in the grocery bags still sitting on the bench seats.

"Lord've mercy!" she exclaimed. "Did y'all stay up all night long bakin' them goodies?"

"Not past midnight," Elsie replied.

"I think we were done about eleven fifty-nine," Savannah added, laughing. "But the time wasn't all spent baking. We had to do a lot of sampling, too."

"Of course you did." Stella shifted Macon to one arm and reached over to nab a pinwheel. "No good cook serves somethin' without testin' it first to see if it's fit to eat."

Elsie sidled over closer to Stella, lowered her voice, and whispered, "What did *you* stay up all night samplin'?"

Stella gasped. "Elsie Dingle, I'm plumb shocked at your insinuations. You should be ashamed of yourself, gal."

Elsie giggled. "Well, you cain't say I didn't give you the opportunity, if there was somethin' you've been hankerin' to do and hadn't had the privacy to git 'er done."

Glancing over at Savannah, who seemed oblivious to their conversation, Stella said, "For your information, Miss Nosy Pot, we sat swingin' on the porch with his dog and Alma's kitten till ten or so, then he went home. I headed off to bed, went to sleep two seconds later, and, thanks to you babysitting this little bopper here"—she nodded toward the baby in her arms—"I got the best night's sleep I've had in months."

"I'll have you know that he was good as gold, snoozed right through the night. Eight hours straight."

"He did not! You are lyin' like a one-legged dog!"

"He totally did," Savannah said from the other end of the table. "Didn't hear a peep out of him."

"Well, if that don't beat all. What did you do to him?"

"Nothin'. I just told him if he cried, he'd stir up the haints, and they'd start floatin' up and down the halls, makin' a nuisance of themselves."

Stella nodded thoughtfully. "I must admit, that wasn't somethin' I ever thought of tryin'. But I can understand why it worked."

Savannah finished her cookie arranging and folded the brown paper bags they had been brought in. As she put them into a box under the table with the other picnic paraphernalia, she said, "Thank you, Gran, for letting us stay at the mansion with Miss Elsie."

"Y'all seem to be havin' a good time."

Stella recalled how when she had first arrived at the park her grandangels had swarmed all over her, showering her with hugs and kisses, which she gratefully returned. But the moment she'd asked if they were ready to return home, they had protested loudly and run away to play on the swings and slide.

So much for missing your granny, she'd thought. But she was greatly relieved that no one was grieving her absence.

"Your brother and sisters didn't seem in any hurry to come home," she told Savannah.

"They're having a blast. Me too. She told us stories last night that I'll never forget."

Elsie looked at Savannah with true maternal love in her coffee-colored eyes. "That's why I told ya them stories, darlin'," she said. "So they won't be forgot. Them soldiers who died gettin' operated on, stretched out on that big ol' table there in the dining room, they suffered too bad for words to even describe. They lost their precious limbs, and many lost their lives in that terrible war. All that fightin', death, and destruction. That's what it took to end the awfulness that happened right on that there plantation before the long, bloody war put an end to it."

Savannah nodded solemnly, put her arms around the much shorter woman's shoulders, and gave her a sideways hug. "I'd read about the Civil War in school, of course. But seeing that table, touching it, looking at the walls around me and thinking what went on in that room . . . it made it real. Awfully real."

"I'm glad to hear that, darlin'," Elsie said. "It needs to stay real for each generation of you young'uns that comes along. Our country had to pay a terrible price to right its wrongs. We gotta keep fightin', too, cause the human heart don't change, and we're capable of makin' the same mistakes all over again if we ain't careful."

At that moment, Murphy Jackson, one of the city council members, walked by their table. When he glanced their way, he seemed to notice that Savannah had her arm around Elsie. For the briefest moment, he gave them a distinctly disapproving look and a slight head shake that clearly communicated his disgust to witness the small intimacy. Then he lifted his chin and walked away.

"Unfortunately, Elsie," Stella said, "you're quite right about that. We're always gonna have those among us who've decided to think a certain way and stick by it."

Savannah watched the councilman's retreat, his stiff gait, his upturned nose. "Better not rain this afternoon," she said. "Mr. Jackson there'll be in danger of drowning for sure."

As they shared a companionable laugh, Stella spotted a new face among the crowd. Not new to her, but to the town's festivities. It was Cindy Corbin who was walking toward her, dressed in a pretty, bright pink sundress, a lime green silk kerchief tied jauntily around her neck, and her thick blond hair twisted into an elegant updo.

But in spite of her colorful clothing, Cindy's walk lacked any youthful energy or joie de vivre. The old folks in the town might have described her as "draggin' her tracks out."

"Is that who I think it is?" Elsie whispered.

"If you think it's the new widow, then you're right," Stella replied.

"Wow, she looks really sad," Savannah observed. "But you can't blame her."

"Good afternoon, Mrs. Corbin," Stella greeted her as she drew closer. "It's nice to see you here today. So glad you could make it."

Stella carefully laid Macon in his stroller, then held out her hand to Cindy, and the young woman shook it.

Stella couldn't help noticing that even her handshake was that of an exhausted woman, limp and brief.

She didn't look nearly as perky as she had the day before, when Stella had watched Manny interview her.

Wonder what happened between now and then? Stella asked herself as she studied the woman's face.

The young widow had dark circles under her eyes, and in spite of the fancy updo, her blond hair appeared to need a shampoo.

Stella glanced around to see if she could spot Manny. When he had given Stella a ride to the park earlier, he had expressed a desire to speak to Cindy again, since he had heard she'd been in the park with Tyrell.

This would be the perfect time if he were nearby. But he didn't seem to be.

So, Stella thought she would take a stab at conducting a casual interview. At least, she hoped it would appear casual to her interviewee.

"I was thinkin' I might run into you today," Stella told her. "Though I didn't expect you'd be out and about, what with your loss being so recent and all."

Cindy shrugged her bare shoulders and said, "I couldn't just sit there in that awful old house all day. I'm gonna be leavin' town tomorrow. Right after Dex's funeral. So I thought I'd come and get a look at what I'll be missing."

"Leaving? Missing?" Stella's interest was instantly piqued.

"Yes. I can't stay here. I have to leave right away."

"You have to? Why?"

Cindy avoided her eyes for a moment, looking down, then

glancing around at the ever-growing crowd with something that looked a lot like fear.

"I mean," she said, as though searching for just the right words, "I want to leave. I was hoping I'd be making a new start here in a small, friendly town, but things don't always turn out the way you hope they will, do they?"

"No, they don't, hon," Stella told her. "I'm so sorry."

"Me too," Elsie piped up. "For your loss, that is. That's a mighty heavy blow you got dealt, you bein' so young and all."

Cindy's expression instantly became cold and hard. "Not as hard as the blows my husband received. At least I'll survive. His were fatal."

"Oh." Elsie cleared her throat. "I beg your pardon, Mrs. Corbin. That was a poor choice of words on my part."

"It's okay," Cindy replied, instantly warming to Elsie's sincerity. "You didn't mean anything by it."

"I'm sorry, too, about Mr. Corbin," Savannah offered, her voice soft and kind.

"Did you know him?" Cindy asked her.

"No. Not personally, ma'am," Savannah replied. "I mean, here in a town this small, everyone knows everyone's name, who their family is, where they live and work and all that. But I didn't really know him."

"I haven't heard a kind word about him since I arrived here in McGill." Cindy reached up and toyed with the knot on her scarf. "At first, I blamed it on the town. But then I had to admit that a whole town full of people wouldn't hate a man unless there was good reason. Plus, I got to know him better, so . . ."

"I wouldn't say we hated him, Cindy," Stella said, placing her hand on the young woman's forearm and patting it. "*Hate* is prob'ly too strong a word. Some of us just went outta our way to avoid him when we could."

"Was it his temper?" Cindy asked. "Was that why he had the reputation he did?"

Stella decided to answer her honestly. Grieving or not, the woman deserved to know the truth. "I doubt I need to tell you this, darlin', but Dexter drank too much, and when he did, the alcohol brought out the worst in him."

"Yes, I realized that. After we got married. That's the risk you take when you marry quick, like we did." Cindy paused, took a deep breath, then continued with her fact-finding. "Did he hurt people? Like beat them up and stuff like that?"

Stella searched her memory before answering. She wanted to give as truthful a reply as possible. "To my knowledge, he didn't actually do anybody any physical harm. But he seemed to enjoy calling them up in the wee hours of the mornin' and threatenin' to. That don't go over so good."

Elsie added, "Most folks don't cotton to a person who's threatenin' to come over that very minute and shoot 'em dead right in their own homes."

Cindy looked stricken. "Really? Dex did that?"

When neither Stella nor Elsie said anything, Cindy turned to Savannah. "Did my husband say things like that to people in this town?"

Savannah looked miserably uncomfortable, but she locked eyes with Cindy, nodded, and said, "Yes, ma'am. I do believe he did. I heard it from a lot of people, all saying the exact same thing, so I figure it was true."

Cindy shook her head. Tears flooded her eyes and spilled down her cheeks. "I really *was* a fool to marry that guy. But when he was talking about this little town where everybody helps everybody and there's only one streetlight, and you can walk down the sidewalk without anybody stealing your purse or assaulting you, I thought how wonderful that sounded, compared to Las Vegas."

"Yes, I reckon it would be a change of pace," Stella agreed. "Where are you fixin' to go, when you leave here?"

"I'm moving back to La Paz, a little town about the size of this one in northern California. *La Paz* means 'peace' in Spanish. I grew up there. My dad owns a feed store, and he'll give me a job. It sure isn't as exciting as Las Vegas, but it's peaceful, and I think I'm due for some of that."

"I think you are, too, sweetie," Stella said. "Peace is right up there with love and hope when it comes to the important things in life."

"I only went to Las Vegas because I wanted to be a dancer. I thought there'd be a lot of opportunities there and . . ." She struggled for the next words and looked sick at heart when she spoke them. "But I wanted to dance for the joy of it. I made money dancing in Vegas, but there was no joy in it. Quite the contrary, in fact, considering the kind of dancing I was doing."

"In your hometown you can work for your dad or at some other job," Stella told her, "and you can dance in your spare time just for the pure joy of it."

"That would be nice."

Stella thought of Manny and asked herself what he would want to know if he were talking to this woman, whose husband was lying in Herb Jameson's funeral home.

"I was just wonderin' 'bout somethin'," she said, trying to sound casual. "Somebody I know said they saw you the day before yesterday in the cemetery."

For a moment, Cindy looked frightened. Stella knew her statement had upset her, and she wondered why.

"Yes. I did go there. Just for a little while."

"Is somebody buried there who you wanted to honor?" Stella asked. She felt a bit insincere, asking a question when she was pretty sure of the answer. But according to Manny, that was standard procedure in law enforcement.

"No," Cindy replied. "Dex paged me and told me to meet him at the cemetery. Right away. So I took off over there, and I didn't see him, or anybody except this hayseed named Tyrell. He said Dex had paged him, too. It was weird."

"Yes, that's a stumper, all right."

"But now, according to what that coroner guy told me on the phone a while ago, I understand that Dex was already dead. His body was lying there in the graveyard, not all that far from where I was walking around. It makes me feel sick inside to even think about it."

"I'm sure it does," Stella said. "I'm so sorry."

"Why don't you have a cookie, Mrs. Corbin," Savannah said. "It'll do you good. Miss Elsie and I made them last night, and they're pretty tasty, if I do say so myself."

Savannah took Cindy's arm and gently coaxed her down to the other end of the table where the cookies were spread. Cindy leaned over the table to get a couple of the pecan sandies.

Stella heard her say, "I love these. They're just like the ones my mom makes."

"She'll probably make a huge batch of them when you get back home," Savannah told her as the two of them chatted on about cookies and their power to comfort someone feeling down.

"Oh, look," Elsie said, pointing to the main buffet table, which had been set up near the stage area. "They're startin' to put the food out. We oughta get your eggs and our cookies over there before the table fills up, and we ain't got a spot to put 'em."

But for once, Stella's mind wasn't on food.

She was thinking about a young widow who, if her words were to be believed, was wandering around a cemetery looking for her husband. Her husband who was lying dead only a few yards away.

It seemed improbable.

But then, so did cold-blooded murder in a quiet, sleepy little town like McGill, Georgia.

Chapter 25

"You gave a mighty good speech, Sheriff! Totally awesome!" Waycross called to Manny from the swing sets, where the boy was working hard at swinging as high as he possibly could.

"Thank you, Mr. Reid," Manny called back. He turned to Stella and Savannah, who were standing beside him, and asked, "Did he really listen to it, or is he buttering me up so I'll take him fishing, like I said I would?"

"No, he knows the trip down the river won't happen till after the election," Stella told him. "I reckon his praise is genuine."

"You did give a totally awesome speech, sir," Savannah told him, her eyes sparkling with girlish admiration and obvious affection.

Stella had to admit, Manny Gilford was a major hit with her grandangels. He never missed an opportunity to connect with them, collectively and individually. He showed concern about their problems and delighted in their joys. She knew they felt safer in a world where Sheriff Manny Gilford was in charge, and she was infinitely grateful to him for giving them that.

After having a mother like Shirley Reid and an absentee father like her own son, Macon Sr., they desperately needed all that Manny offered.

But for the moment, Stella and Savannah had a couple of things to offer Manny, other than the assortment of cookies Savannah had wrapped in a napkin, just in case he had been too busy or distracted to grab some off the tables when the mob had descended on them.

"Wow! These look awesome. Thank you," he said as he accepted the cookie-stuffed napkin and unwrapped it. "What was it you ladies needed from me?"

"For once," Stella said, "it's what you need from us."

He looked confused but said, "Okay, what do I need from you?"

"We had a long talk with that Mrs. Corbin lady," Savannah said. "Well, Gran did mostly. I just gave her cookies. Tell him, Gran."

Stella filled him in on everything she could recall that had been said during that conversation, including the fact that Cindy admitted to being in the graveyard with Tyrell, that she was later spooked to hear that she had been near her murdered husband's body, and that she was intending to leave town the next day.

"Do you believe all of that?" Manny asked her. "Did she seem sincere?"

Stella nodded. "She did, Manny. I believed every word of it. Well, except for when she told me that she had to leave town right away. When I asked her why she had to go, she got weird on me for a minute there, and she changed her story from 'I have to leave' to 'I want to.'"

"You think she's afraid to stay?"

"She looked afraid, glancing all around, like she was dreading running into somebody."

"Maybe somebody's leaning on her," he suggested.

"That's what I thought, and especially after I heard what Savannah had to say."

Manny turned to Savannah. "You got something for me, sweetie?"

Savannah nodded, looked around to make sure no one was close enough to hear, and said softly, "I saw something I don't think she wanted me to see. Wanted anybody to see."

"Okay. What was it?"

"She leaned over to stock up on those pecan sandies that she loves so much, and when she did, the neckerchief she was wearing slipped to the side a bit. That's when I saw the bruises."

"Bruises? You saw bruises on her neck?"

"Yes."

"Are you absolutely sure, Savannah? I believe you, but this is really important, honey."

"I know. And I'm very sure."

"What did they look like?"

"Fingertips."

"What do you mean?"

"You know, like when somebody grabs another person and digs their fingers into them." She turned to Stella. "Remember how Marietta got mad at Vidalia for borrowing her new barrette without permission, and when they fought over it, Marietta left those five round, black bruises on Vi's arm?"

"Yes, I do, child. Did these marks look like those?"

"Yes, but I only saw two of them, not five. And there were a couple of long bruises, too, leading up to those round ones. Like if somebody's fingers were around someone's neck, choking them, with their fingertips digging in really hard."

Stella watched as Manny's expression changed from relaxed and interested to angry.

"Okay," he said, his voice tight and clipped.

"I think that might be why she was wearing a scarf around her neck," Stella said. "Her outfit was pretty, her dress matchin' nice with her shoes and her purse, but the green scarf didn't go with the rest of what she had on at all."

"Might've been the only scarf she had, since she just moved here," Savannah suggested. "We figure she was wearing it to hide those bruises."

"Thank you. I'm glad you shared this with me, ladies," he said. "Very glad."

"I suppose it could've been Dexter that was responsible for them marks on her," Stella suggested. "Maybe the two of 'em had a big fight, and that's why he left the house, not because he got a business phone call, like she said. It'd make a lot more sense."

"But, Sheriff," Savannah said, "you didn't see the marks I saw when you questioned her there at the house?"

"No, I didn't. But her hair was covering her neck," he said. "I'm not sure I would have seen them even if they'd been there."

Stella nodded. "That's right. It was hanging down all around her shoulders. Today she had it in a cute updo."

"Then they might have been there," Savannah said thoughtfully, "and you didn't see them. Maybe they had a fight, like Gran said, and maybe she went after him to teach him a lesson or worse, to make sure it never happened again. She wouldn't be the first woman to get her canful of that sort of thing."

"No, she wouldn't," Manny agreed. "But she didn't seem that type to me. I can't see her beating him like that. Shooting, maybe. But a hands-on beating takes a lot of rage or meanness or both. I didn't pick up mean or rage off her. Just sadness."

"I agree," Stella said. "Maybe some desperation thrown in for good measure, but I can't see her doin' what I saw done to that man, even if he did lay hands on her before."

"Did you run a check on her, Sheriff?" Savannah asked, sounding like a seasoned detective.

Stella stifled a snicker, but when she glanced up at Manny to see if he found her granddaughter amusing, she saw he was considering the girl's words as seriously as he would anyone else's.

"Yes, we did," he replied. "As it turns out, she has no record at all. Not even a parking ticket."

"That's too bad," Savannah said, giving him a sympathetic look. "That narrows down your suspect list to . . . what? One?"

Manny nodded. "I'm afraid so. Unless we get something new and substantial soon, we're pretty much down to Tyrell Grymes."

He sighed, and Stella thought he looked very tired, not to mention downhearted.

He looked at her, shook his head, and ran his fingers through his wind-mussed hair. "The worst part about having Tyrell as our one and only suspect is, I don't think he did it, either."

Stella slipped her hand in his and said, "I know, Manny. No gettin' around it. 'Tis a sad situation. Plumb pitiful, in fact. No two ways about it."

At that moment, Stella glanced over toward the main food table, where most of the goodies had been cleared away. She saw two of her currently least favorite McGillians standing there, loading the few remaining desserts into a box that was, no doubt, headed back to their house. With or without the blessings of those who had brought the food to the event.

"Well, if it ain't Miss Jeanette Parker and her blessed momma," Stella muttered under her breath.

"What?" Savannah asked.

"Y'all are gonna have to excuse me for a minute. I need to go have a word with those two over there."

Manny looked at the table, saw the pair and what they were doing, and said, "I'll go arrest them, if you like."

"On what charge?" Savannah wanted to know, looking worried.

"Theft of potluck confections, maybe?" he replied. "If they're your grandmother's or Elsie's baking, it'd be considered grand theft and a major felony."

"No thank you, Sheriff. They're all mine today," Stella said as she walked away. "*All* mine."

When Jeanette and her mother spotted Stella walking toward them, they jumped and hurried to rearrange whatever was in the box, no doubt in a way that they hoped would conceal the stolen goods.

"Don't worry," Stella told them. "I won't mention you scarfin' up the leftovers to the sheriff. I'm sure, good Christian gals that you are, you'll be droppin' 'em off at the shelter over there in Holtville, so's the homeless folks can enjoy 'em."

"Um, we . . ." Jeanette began.

"I'm sure the next time I drive over there to donate stuff myself, they'll tell me how much they appreciated your generous gift today," Stella said, giving the woman a sly look. "I'll be sure to ask them how much those poor folks enjoyed Elsie's lemon pie in particular."

"Yeah, okay," was the lukewarm response.

Looking pointedly down inside their box, which was now loosely covered by Jeanette's sweater, Stella added, "They'll like all them pecan sandies that Elsie and Savannah stayed up half the night to bake, too. I'm just so glad to know they're goin' for a good cause. Otherwise, I'd have taken 'em home myself. Lord knows, I've got eight children to feed, compared to your one."

Jeanette's mom gave her a stony look and said, "You want your dang cookies back, Stella? Is that what you want, 'cause if you do, I'll give 'em to you, right here and now."

"No. That's okay. I'd rather you drive all the way over to Holtville and give 'em to the shelter. That'd give me a warm, fuzzy feelin', thinkin' of you doin' that and them poor, homeless people enjoyin' 'em. Charity is its own reward, they say."

The woman muttered something like an obscenity under her breath, and Stella laughed.

Then she turned to Jeanette, and in an instant, her demeanor changed from chatty to grandma stern. "I've been needin' to have a word with you, young *lady*," she said, placing a sarcastic emphasis on the last word. She looked the girl up and down, taking in the extremely short black latex skirt, the skintight, midriff-baring top that was cut low enough to expose the minute amount of cleavage her push-up bra had created.

Stella felt anger toward the girl for her unkindness to Waycross. But even more than that, she felt pity for her. The child couldn't be advertising her "wares" any more effectively if she had rented the oversized billboard on the highway at the edge of town.

Stella knew all too well where that sort of promotion would lead. Mostly, it would mean heartache for Jeanette herself.

Jeanette propped one hand on her hip and tossed her hair back over her shoulder. At least, she tried, but it didn't move much, due to the extreme amount of mousse holding it in place.

Stella figured an F4 tornado wouldn't dislodge it.

"I have nothing to say to you, Mrs. Reid," Jeanette said. "Especially if you're going to speak to me in a disrespectful tone like that." She turned to her mother. "I don't have to talk to her, huh, Mom."

It wasn't a question. By her tone and her cocky attitude, Jeanette was making it clear to her mother what she expected.

Mom wasn't so sure. "I, um. What is it that you want to discuss with her, Stella?"

"I'm sure she knows. Don't you, Jeanette?"

"I have no idea, and I'm busy right now."

"You have time for this. It won't take me long to say my piece."

Stella stepped very close to the girl and looked deeply into her eyes, trying to see the soul within. Was she truly as cruel as her actions suggested? Or was she simply unaware of the harm her words caused?

"You hurt my little grandson deeply the other day, Jeanette. By the time you got done saying all those ugly things to him, his little heart was just about broken."

She waited for her words to sink in and watched the girl closely for her reaction.

"I didn't say anything all that bad to him," she snapped back. "He sure didn't need to go tattletale to his granny about it, that's for sure."

Okay, Stella thought. *That's strike one.*

"He didn't tattle to me," Stella replied. "He didn't even come home to me, like he does every day. After you got done spewin' your ugliness all over him, he ran away from the school grounds, cryin' his eyes out."

Jeanette shrugged. "If he'd cry about a little thing like that, he's a sissy and needs to toughen up."

Strike two.

Stella fought to keep her voice calm when she said, "A *little* thing like that? A little thing like bein' called a *bastard*?"

Jeanette's mom gasped. "What? Jeannie, honey! You didn't!"

"She did," Stella told her, "and my grandson knows the true meaning of that word, too. He knows there's a lot more to it than just bein' called a jerk or a jackass."

"It's not my fault he gets called stuff like that," Jeanette protested. Then she smirked and lifted one eyebrow. "It's his momma's fault for being such a drunken slu—well, you know what she is. I'm not the only one in town who calls him that, behind his back anyway. The Ginger Bastard. That's what they call him. When they ain't calling him worse."

Stella felt a blinding rage sweep through her that felt like red fire. She lifted her hand, determined to slap that evil, simpering grin off Jeanette Outhouse-Seat-Bottom Parker's face.

But she couldn't.

Later, she would wish she could say it was her own self-control, her spiritual maturity that had kept her from striking a child across the face with all her might.

But she couldn't.

She would always remember that it wasn't any sort of discipline on her part. Because when she needed it most, her self-restraint had failed her. Completely.

It was Sheriff Manny Gilford's hand, closed tight around her wrist.

Chapter 26

"Thank you for not lettin' me make a fool of myself yesterday, Manny," Stella told him the next morning, as they drove away from her house in his cruiser, heading for the cemetery.

"You making a fool of yourself was the least of my concerns, gal," he told her. "I was more concerned about you, an adult, striking an underage minor."

"Yeah, well. There was that, too." They rode along in silence for a while, and then she said, "When you brought me home last night, I was tired and cranky, and I don't believe I said thank you."

"You're welcome. It was no trouble. I just intervened like that to save myself having to cuff you, arrest you, read you your rights, do all that paperwork. Worst of all, I would've had to search you for weapons, too, and neither one of us would have wanted to suffer through a horror like *that*."

"Heaven forbid." She giggled. "I had no idea how close I came to destruction there before you snatched me back."

"You were roller-skating along the edge of the precipice there. Next time you see that rotten girl Jeanette around and I'm nearby, do it again. It was the closest thing I've had to fun in a while now."

She grinned up at him and clucked her tongue. "That's so sad, darlin'. You're gonna make me cry, talkin' like that."

"Life's hard and then you die."

"The early bird catches the worm."

"Old habits die hard."

"A watched pot never boils."

She laced her arm through his and tugged. "Come along then. We got us a funeral to go to. It's bound to be crowded, considerin' how beloved a figure ol' Dexter Corbin was."

"There'll be a big turnout, you'll see. There's only one thing that brings more folks to a funeral than love does."

"Hate?"

"You got it. That and murder."

Stella knew Manny had been right about his attendance predictions when they left the highway and headed down the narrow road toward the cemetery. She had never seen so many cars parked along that small stretch that led to the gate. Not only were both sides of the road filled, but another row of vehicles were parked just off the pavement at the edge of the cotton field.

Dexter Corbin had caused quite a stir in little old McGill. His former enemies and neighbors had drawn together to wish his soul a quick journey to its final abode. Which most figured was the bowels of Hell.

"I think ever'body in town's here today," Stella commented as Manny drove farther and farther down the road, looking for a parking place.

"Everyone in the county, I'd say." He glanced at his watch. "They got here early, too. I thought we'd be among the first to arrive."

She pointed to a bright red Corvette, sitting in a prominent spot near the gate, beside Herb Jameson's hearse. "The widow's here. Looks like she drove herself, too."

"Did I tell you I went out to her place again last night before I turned in for the night?"

"No. Did you ask her about the bruises?"

"Sure. I even made her show them to me. They're pretty bad. Looks like she had a close call."

"Did she tell you who did it?"

"Not at first. But once I'd convinced her that I wasn't leaving until she told me, she said it was Dexter, like you thought."

"I knew it!"

"I told her I heard she was leaving town today, but I didn't want her to go until we got this wrapped up."

"Did she agree?"

"Kinda. Wasn't too convincing. I'll remind her again after the service here."

"What else did she say about that wife-beatin', mud-suckin' sorry excuse for a husband of hers?"

"Not a lot. She was pretty close lipped about him, and I'm not sure why. It's not like he's any sort of threat to her now. Maybe she's protecting his memory."

"I wouldn't. If a guy laid his hands on me, I'd tell ever'body what a low-down, rotten skunk he was."

He laughed. "I'm sure you would, Miss Stella, and that's reason enough for most guys to watch their behavior around you."

She gave him a searching, suspicious look. "Is that supposed to be a compliment?"

"Of the highest sort. Rest assured."

"Okay."

She pointed to an area just off the road. It was little more than a path but provided a snug parking spot. "There ya go. You can squeeze in there."

As he maneuvered the large vehicle into the small area, he

said, "That's the trail that leads to the peach orchard and the east gate. It'd probably be faster if we just cut through there."

"Good thinkin'," she said. "They're probably buryin' him in that new area in the back. I hope so anyway. Don't want him too close to anybody we know."

Manny laughed, looked her over, and shook his head. "You're some piece of work, darlin'."

"Well, I don't! The soil where my momma and Art are buried is holy ground. I don't want it tainted with the likes of that ornery Dexter Corbin."

As they got out of the car, Manny pointed to a spot nearby, a little alcove among the trees and bushes. "That's where Merv and I found Dexter's car," he said. "Had it towed to the garage."

"Nothin' in it?"

"Nothing to speak of."

"He must've come through this east gate, too. Funny how popular this entrance got all of a sudden, after ever'body in town forgot all about it."

"Yes. Funny," Manny replied thoughtfully.

As they left the road and walked into the orchard, Manny slipped his arm around her waist and gave her a squeeze. "Don't worry, honey. If you don't like where this skunk's being buried, you just say so. We'll come out here first full moon, dig him up, and relocate him wherever you want."

"Yeah, right. I'm pretty sure there was somethin' in your sheriff oath about you not robbin' graves."

"I didn't see anything like that on the contract."

"It was probably in the fine print on the back."

"Might've been. I didn't read all that. Didn't have my glasses."

As they continued to walk through the orchard, Stella thoroughly enjoyed the experience. The late morning sun had warmed the nearly ripe fruit and filled the air with its sweet fragrance. The color of the peaches themselves was Stella's favorite color, though it was difficult to describe other than "peachy." The long, curved leaves were graceful and made a slight swishing sound as the breeze swept through them.

"It's pretty in here," Manny said. "Makes me wish we didn't have a funeral to attend."

"I was just thinkin' the same thing," she replied.

"Funny how often that happens."

"Ain't it, though?"

His arm tightened around her. She responded by slipping her arm around his waist.

Sooner than she was ready, they had reached the end of the orchard rows and were approaching the cemetery's side entrance.

Many, many years ago, there had been a road leading to this gate and cotton fields stretching into the distance. But some time back, the land had been sold, divided, and planted with these peach trees and the pecan trees beyond.

Now the "east gate," as it was known, was hardly ever used. Most folks in town were unaware of its existence.

As they approached the gate, a simple, wrought-iron affair set between some stone pillars with short stone walls extending in each direction, Manny said, "Hey, what the heck?"

"Guess somebody left it open," she commented, thinking that was what had surprised him. "Maybe it was Tyrell or Cindy."

"Not that. I don't care if it's open or closed." He held out one arm, as though to stop her from going through, and said, "Wait. I have to see if this is what I think it is."

He bent down and stared at the top bar of the gate with its pointed finials. Then he studied the ornamental roses and leaves on graceful vines that curled from one straight, vertical picket to the next.

Finally, he touched one spot lightly with his pinky and stared at the dark residue he had collected.

"This has been dusted," he said.

"Dusted?"

As a housekeeper, the first thing Stella thought when she heard the word *dusted* was the can of furniture polish under her kitchen sink and her feather duster. "I doubt anybody's cleaned that for a hundred years," she said.

"Dusted for fingerprints, darlin'," he told her. "Look, see that powder. I'd recognize it anywhere. I tell you, somebody who knew what they were doing collected fingerprints off that gate."

"Wouldn't that have been your job?"

"I would have. Actually, I should have, or told Augustus or Merv to do it."

"Augustus, not Merv."

"True. Merv would have come back all proud after collecting a full set of his own prints." He shook his head and looked upset. "I should have dusted this myself, Stella. I swear, I haven't been thinking straight lately."

"Don't go beatin' yourself up about it, darlin'. You've had a lot on your mind lately." She glanced down at her watch. "You can figure it out later, Manny. We gotta get down there, or they'll start without us. Somethin' tells me the town ain't gonna beat around the bush when it comes to stickin' Dexter Corbin in the dirt."

Chapter 27

Stella was right. The town might have shown up en masse to see Dexter Corbin off, but they didn't linger over the task.

Pastor O'Reilly spoke the traditional words about the resurrection and the life, dust to dust and ashes to ashes. But those were the only pronouncements over the mortal remains of McGill, Georgia's, least liked son.

When the kindhearted minister was finished and asked if anyone had anything they wanted to say, no one did. Not even Corbin's young widow. The pastor stuttered and stammered and turned a bit red, obviously embarrassed that he had even asked.

After closing with a quick prayer, he folded his Bible, shook the widow's hand, and made as graceful an exit as he could manage.

"I guess he didn't know Dexter very well," Stella whispered to her neighbor Florence, who was standing beside her next to the grave, pretending to sniffle into her handkerchief.

Florence wasn't crying. She had no tears to shed over the likes of Dexter Corbin. But she never missed an opportunity to show off her fine, linen hanky with its Hardanger lace.

"Reckon not," Florence replied between sniffs. "I hope the

widow there paid Pastor O'Reilly well. The man done perjured his soul saying that Dexter was beloved and is up there in heaven right now, lookin' down on us. I reckon he's otherwise occupied, runnin' from pitchforks and wishin' he had a gas mask for all them sulfur fumes."

"I think Pastor O'Reilly will get a pass for his little white lies," Stella said. "He always tries to think of good things to say at somebody's grave. He said Lulamae Christie was generous, and we all know she was tighter than a bull's hiney at fly time. Plus, Pastor's sorta an innocent guy. He don't rub elbows with the likes of Dexter there, so he don't see the worst of 'im and his kind, if you know what I mean."

Florence nodded and dabbed daintily at the end of her nose with her kerchief. She turned and looked Stella up and down. "I see you're wearin' your funeral dress. The one I bought you for Art's funeral."

"Yes, Florence."

"The one I paid a bundle for."

"I know, Flo."

"It still looks good on ya, even after all these years."

"Thank you, darlin'."

"It's a little snugger across the butt than it used to be."

"Uh-huh."

"Funny how the material shrunk there but not up top around your boobs."

Stella looked around the gathering for Manny and saw him deep in a conversation with Herb Jameson on the other side of the crowd. She ached to hear what they were saying and longed to escape Florence.

She's sweet. One of the kindest, dearest friends I've ever had, Stella told herself, *but if I don't get away from her in the next thirty seconds, I'm gonna throw her down in that grave with Dexter. Then she'll be* his *problem. It'd serve him right for layin' hands on his wife in anger.*

225

Stella made a show of staring down at her watch and said, "Oh, would you just look at the time! I gotta go, Flo. But it was nice seein' you today. We gotta start gettin' together more!"

As she raced away from her beloved friend, she wondered if she, like Pastor O'Reilly, might have to answer for these untruths at some point in the future.

"I don't think so," she whispered as she fought her way through the crowd, working her way to Manny. "I can't imagine you'd hold it against me, Lord. You know her as well as I do, if not better. I'll betcha sometimes you're tempted to hurl at least one little lightnin' bolt in her direction."

She arrived at the spot where Manny and Herb were conversing just in time to hear Herb say something about the test results and "positive for alcohol and drugs."

She hadn't made her escape from Florence one minute too soon.

Both men nodded, acknowledging her arrival, then continued their chat. "How much alcohol?" Manny asked.

"His BAC was 0.10," Herb replied. "You would've nailed him for DUI if you'd caught him driving to the cemetery that night."

"What kind of drugs did he have on board?"

"The tests show some marijuana, but the big one was cocaine. I told you I thought I saw white powder in his nose and some on his gums. The tests show it was coke, for sure."

"That would explain him bein' off his rocker and hurtin' his wife," Stella said, "if he snorted that stuff before he choked her."

"He choked her?" Herb asked with a quick look in Cindy's direction. She was standing, sadly alone, by the grave as the citizens of McGill glided silently by, glancing down at the coffin at the bottom of the freshly dug grave, then moving on with little more than a nod in her direction.

Stella resolved that before she left the cemetery she would offer some genuine condolences to the poor woman. No, she hadn't been married long, and her husband had been a rotten one, but she was still a young widow, not even thirty years old.

"Yes, she says Dexter choked her the night he died," Manny answered Herb, "basically on his way out the door after they'd had a fight."

"Another reason not to mourn him too heavily."

Stella said, "Manny, after she admitted they fought before he left, did she take back that 'he got a business call' story?"

"Not at all. She was quite adamant about that. Claims he left to go meet someone about some business."

"Did you ask her about the drug angle?" Stella asked. "What Tyrell said about him and organized crime there in Las Vegas?"

"Yes, I did. At first, she held back. Then she claimed she hadn't actually seen any drugs or heard anything. Then she admitted that he had a large black suitcase with white trim around the edges that he kept a close eye on, but he never opened it. At least, not in front of her. When she asked him about it, they got into an argument. In fact, she said that was what the fight was about the night he died, when he choked her."

Stella couldn't help getting excited about the idea of a large black suitcase with distinctive white trim. "Did you ask her about the suitcase, where it is now?"

"Sure I did. In fact, she let me search the house. I couldn't find it. There's not a lot in the house, and the case she described was pretty big, so I don't think it's there."

"Shoot." Stella felt her mood plummet as quickly as it had soared.

"Yeah. That's what I said. Or something close," Manny replied.

"Hey, Sheriff, Herb, Mrs. Reid," said a friendly voice behind them.

They all turned to be greeted by a cheerful face and one of the more charming fellows in town.

He had to be charming. He sold used cars for a living, and Dick Ferdinand was good at what he did.

"Dexter got a good turnout, didn't he?" Dick said, surveying the now thinning crowd. "A lot of cheerful faces, for a funeral."

Stella looked around and realized he was right. Almost any burial had a few distraught loved ones. Tears flowing. Mourners who needed to be comforted and were.

But she had to agree with Dick that there wasn't one wet eye to be seen. No hugging or hand-holding going on.

Though Dick himself did look a bit downcast.

"Did you know Dexter very well?" Stella asked.

"Not at all. Just saw him around town, off and on. We'd never even spoken until about a month ago, when he came to my lot, looking for a late model Corvette."

"He did?" Stella was surprised. *How many Corvettes did one guy need?* she wondered.

"Yes. Got me all excited, too, because he seemed very serious. Said he didn't think he could spring for a brand-new one, so he came to my lot to see what I had or what I could find for him. I didn't have what he wanted, so I spent a long time looking, lined up a few for him to look at. Next thing I hear, he's gone to Vegas, and when he comes back, he's got a new bride, *and* they're driving a brand new 'Vette."

"Ouch," Herb said. "That must've hurt."

Dick shrugged. "Eh, that's the sales business for you. Until you've got the cold cash in your hot little hand, you don't have a deal."

"It's not that different from law enforcement," Manny said. "Your work isn't done until he's arrested, charged, convicted, and incarcerated. A lot can go wrong on that long road."

Dick nodded and pointed out a bald fellow in a black suit and a maroon bow tie standing near the grave, looking down into it at the lowered coffin.

"Take Vinnie there. Corbin came to him all excited about the prospect of buying the Weston house up there on the hill, over-looking the town. Vinnie says it's one of the nicest houses to come on the market hereabouts for ages."

"What would Dexter Corbin want with the Weston house?" Manny said. "That place is huge."

"Five bedrooms, three and a half baths," Dick said. "Seems Dexter was gung ho about getting a family going with this new gal of his. Was gonna surprise her with it. He told Vinnie his rich uncle back in Las Vegas died and left him a bundle, and he was anxious to spend it."

"Sounds like it," Manny said.

He gave Stella a loaded look, and she knew he was thinking the same thing she was. That black suitcase with the white trim must have held a king's ransom in cash or drugs.

More important, it was certainly enough to get you killed. Es-pecially if you lived in a tiny town where everybody knew your business even before you did.

Who had known Dexter Corbin's business?

He'd been running around buying, or at least suggesting he was ready to buy, big-ticket items with no concern for their cost.

He might as well have hung a big ol' sign on his back, Stella thought. *One that read: "I'm an idiot with more money than I know what to do with. Come and git it."*

Chapter 28

When Manny and Stella pulled up in front of the sheriff's station the next morning, Stella looked down the street at the crowd gathering around the town center's gazebo.

The old, quaint structure had seen better days, having been built over a century before, but it looked like an elderly lady decked out in her Fourth of July dress. The red, white, and blue bunting, draped gracefully around its lower half, had been used over and over for many years. The red had faded into pink and the once deep blue into a shade fit for a baby boy's nursery walls. The white was as dingy as a well-worn bath towel whose owner had never heard of bleach or bluing.

But the sight of the gazebo and its festive décor set Stella's heart to racing for what it represented.

"Election day," she said. "It's here, Manny."

"What's that, honey?" He turned off the engine and pocketed the keys.

"This is it," she said, nodding toward the gazebo and the crowd gathering there. "By the end of the day, you'll know."

To her surprise, his face reflected nothing but quiet indifference.

That wasn't normal for Manny. As a strong-minded, passionate man, he harbored deep feelings about most things in life.

"Ain't you excited?" she couldn't help asking. "Worried? Happy it'll be over, and you can celebrate your win? Something?"

He turned in his seat, gave her a long, affectionate smile, and said, "I'm feeling a lot of things right now. Either way this goes, I have a strong sense my life is going to be changing soon."

"For the better," she said, putting every ounce of faith and optimism she could into those three words.

He reached over, ran his fingertips across her forehead, then down her cheek, smoothing the always wayward black curls away from her face. "I hope so, Stella May. I sure do hope so."

"Ever'thing's gonna be just fine. You wait and see. We'll be celebratin' somethin' fierce come evenin'."

To her surprise, he bent over and placed a kiss on her forehead. Usually, he didn't do that sort of thing in public, but he was in a strange mood, and she didn't know what to expect.

A whimpering sound came from the backseat of the cruiser. When Stella turned around, she saw Valentine, standing on the seat, his enormous head brushing the headliner.

Manny glanced back at his pet and laughed. "Yeah, yeah, you want to skedaddle. No mushy stuff for you, huh?"

The dog barked and danced on the seat with impatience.

"Let's get going," Manny said, "before he starts eating my interior back there."

They got out of the cruiser. Manny clicked a leash onto Valentine's collar, and they walked to the station house.

Along the way they encountered numerous townspeople who wished Manny well.

"Me and mine, we're voting for you, Sheriff. We're hoping you win!"

"I talked three of the guys at work into voting for you, Manny! Sure hope you beat the socks off that stuck-up son of a sidewinder, Augustus."

"That deputy of yours can't hold a candle to you, Sheriff. Don't you worry. This town is behind you all the way!"

Stella could tell Manny was happy to escape inside the station house with her and his dog. He had never liked being the center of attention, and every election year, she had seen him quietly endure the heat of the spotlight.

This year's way worse, though, she thought as they entered the reception area and Manny released Valentine from his leash. *He didn't cotton to this election rigamarole before. This year, he puredee hates it.*

"How's it going, Deputy?" Manny asked Mervin, who was sitting behind the desk, looking more asleep than awake.

"Okay," Merv replied.

"Has Augustus reported in this morning?"

"No, sir. Not a word. Were you expectin' him to?"

"Yes. I phoned his home last night and left a message for him to return my call as soon as possible."

"Sorry, sir. Quiet as a mouse peein' on a cotton ball here."

"How about Tyrell and Cindy Corbin? I left messages for them, too."

"Nope. Not a word from anybody. But there is one thing. . . ."

"What's that, Deputy?"

"The light's burned out on the desk lamp here, so I wasn't able to get nothin' done." He pointed to the chair he was sitting on. "Chair's hinges are squeakin' again, too, but I couldn't find the oil. Tried to glue it, but that didn't work. Came loose the first time I sat down on it."

Manny gave him an "Are you serious?" look, then shook his

head and sighed. "Maybe you could hop over to the drugstore and get a new bulb for the lamp."

"What kinda bulb?"

"How about the kind that's in there now?"

Merv squirmed around, leaning sideways, trying not to fall off the chair in the process. Eventually, he accomplished his goal.

By laying his head on the desktop and peering upward he could see the bulb in the gooseneck lamp.

Stella tried not to giggle as Manny reached deftly across the desk, unscrewed the bulb, and laid it on the desk.

"Take that across the street, put it in Fred's hand, and tell him I said I need another one of these."

"Okay. Yes, sir. I got it. I'll get some oil, too, for the chair."

Manny drew a deep breath and said, "If you squirted glue in there, I think the oil ship might've already sailed."

Merv looked confused for a moment, then shrugged it off.

He stole one quick, sly glance at Manny, who had strolled over to the watercooler and was filling Valentine's bowl.

Seeing his boss was distracted, the deputy pulled out the bottom drawer of the desk and removed a small, metal cash box.

Stella saw him reach into the container and sort through the change until he had a handful of quarters.

Without even a glance in his direction, Manny said, "Get your hands off those quarters, Deputy Jarvis. Take a couple of dollar bills. No detours to the pizza joint. Play Pac-Man on your own time with your own quarters."

The coins jingled loudly as they went back into the box.

A pouting Merv shoved two dollars into his shirt pocket, grabbed the bulb from the desk, and headed out the door.

Stella couldn't stand it. Her curiosity simply got the best of her, and she had to ask the question that had been haunting her for years.

"Why in heaven's name, Manny Gilford, did you hire that

boy? I'm pretty sure there's a stump in a Louisiana swamp with a higher IQ than his."

"The stump didn't apply for the job."

"Seriously? He was the best you had to pick from?"

"He was my only choice. People talk a lot about how they'd like to be a cop, how they think they'd be great at it and all that. But you'd be surprised how few folks actually pursue it as an occupation. When push comes to shove, they'd rather sit in front of their televisions at home and let somebody else wrestle drunks out of bars, break up domestic squabbles, chase a fleeing felon down a busy street at ninety miles an hour, you name it."

"I see your point. It's romantic thinking about it, but actually doing it . . ."

"Exactly. Besides, Merv's not a bad guy. Just a bit dim-witted. He's dedicated and does what he's told."

"If you explain it very carefully."

"Several times, and draw him pictures with circles and arrows and write a paragraph on the back explaining . . ." He shook his head. "But he's basically kind, not to mention brave."

"I know he is. I recall hearin' that he faced down Momma Cora Belle's big gold rooster when it jumped on her and started scratchin' her somethin' fierce. That chicken from Hades tried to take her eyes out, poor lady."

"Well, I'm afraid that's not the best example. It wasn't Merv's shining hour. He took six shots at that rooster and missed it every time. He had to finish it off with his shoe. He did manage to kill her water pump and one of her pink plastic flamingos there in her yard. Shot its head clean off. Poor woman cried, I heard."

"She thought a lot of them three birds. Won 'em in some kinda gas station contest down in Orlando, when she went down to visit her daughter and go to Disney. She said it was the only time she'd ever gotten anything for free in her whole life."

"I know. We had to pay her for the one he broke. I still think twenty-five dollars was a bit steep. More than a lawn decoration's worth."

"Maybe it was five dollars for the bird, and twenty for punitive damages. The infliction of emotional cruelty or whatever. Them things were Momma Cora Belle's pride and joy; may she rest in peace."

They laughed, and for a moment, Stella thought how nice it was that his heavy, troubled mood seemed to have abated.

But they didn't have long to enjoy it, because within seconds the front door of the station house flew open, and Savannah raced inside. Her face was red, her breathing ragged as she said, "Gran! Sheriff! I'm so glad you're here! You gotta come quick! Augustus is about to make a speech there in the gazebo about the election and all. I heard him telling one of the reporters what it's going to be about."

Savannah turned to Manny, her eyes filled with concern and alarm. "Sheriff, you need to prepare yourself. You're not going to like the speech he's about to give. Not one little bit."

As Manny and Stella followed the girl out the front door of the station, Stella had a sick, sinking feeling in the pit of her stomach and deep in her soul.

She knew her eldest grandangel all too well, and Savannah wasn't the sort to overstate something. Not at all.

Whatever was about to happen in the gazebo, it was going to be bad.

Chapter 29

Even before Stella and Manny reached the gazebo and the crowd gathered around it, she noticed the news vans parked on the side of the street.

They seldom saw those vehicles in their little town. There was no local news station, only a small paper, and the publisher didn't own a van.

Any time reporters appeared on the streets of McGill, everyone knew they had come from Chattanooga or Atlanta, and they weren't there because something wonderful had happened.

But as she followed close behind Manny, who was working his way through the crowd to reach the gazebo, she studied their faces, and they didn't appear particularly alarmed. Only excited.

When they reached the front and were at the foot of the gazebo, she saw Deputy Augustus Faber standing in its center. He was beaming, telling the townspeople how he had invited the media there to hear him announce some exciting news that they would all be happy to hear.

Stella turned and looked behind her at Savannah, who had followed her and Manny into the crowd. A few feet away were the rest of Stella's grandchildren and Elsie, waiting to hear the announcement, like everyone else.

The children were looking her way, waving. Alma was blowing her kisses, which Stella returned, feeling the warmth and happiness they always brought her, in spite of the present circumstances.

Elsie, however, didn't look so happy. For once, her lovely smile was gone, and her eyes were troubled. She was staring up at Augustus, a look of strong disapproval on her face.

"I don't want to take you all away from your important jobs today," Augustus was saying, as he made sure he was speaking directly into the microphone and looking into the nearest cameras pointed at him, "and, of course, you know what that job is. Voting!"

He laughed hard at his own joke. There was a smattering of titters among his audience.

Stella saw his wife, Gloria, standing nearby with her sister. Neither of them appeared as happy as Augustus.

But then, neither did anyone else present. He was positively giddy.

That nincompoop's so full of hisself, Stella thought. *If he swells up any bigger, he'll pop the buttons right off that uniform jacket. He looks like the dadgum toad-frog who caught two flies with one lick.*

She glanced over at Manny, who had his calm and collected sheriff face in place.

"I have a very special announcement to make this morning," Augustus was saying, "regarding the murder of Dexter Corbin."

Stella heard some gasps among those nearby, and she felt Savannah move a bit closer to her and slip her hand into hers.

She looked up at Manny and saw that his neutral face had disappeared. His gray eyes narrowed, and his jaw tightened as he glared at his deputy.

Boy, if looks could kill, we'd need to be givin' ol' Gus some CPR right now, she thought.

"I know you'll all be relieved to know that I have solved this homicide and uncovered the killer."

"The hell you have," Stella heard Manny mutter through gritted teeth.

"Yes, that's right," Augustus continued once the crowd's exclamations of surprise and excitement had abated. "After an extensive investigation on my part, I am happy to tell you all that you can now sleep soundly in your beds, knowing that the killer has been unmasked."

Stella watched, feeling like she was watching a train wreck, happening in slow motion, right before her.

She saw Manny take a step closer to the gazebo and heard him say, "Deputy Faber, what are you . . . ? This isn't the time to . . ."

Augustus ignored him and continued his speech. "The murder was committed by a miscreant well known to us here in McGill. One Tyrell Grymes, a hardened criminal, a longtime threat to our community."

"No," Manny said, shaking his head. "Deputy, stop this. No charges have been brought against anyone."

"I have irrefutable evidence that Grymes slipped into our cemetery in the early morning hours and bludgeoned Dexter Corbin to death with the very same baseball bat that Grymes used when he played for the McGill school team back in high school."

"He found the murder weapon?" Stella asked Manny. "When?"

"I don't know," Manny answered, "but this is not how we do this."

Manny quickly mounted the gazebo steps, strode across it, and stood toe-to-toe with his deputy.

The two men had an old-fashioned stare-down that finally ended with Augustus glancing away, turning his attention back to the cameras. But he seemed no less arrogant when he said, "For those of you who may not know it, this is your present sheriff, Manny Gilford. But so you don't confuse us, I am the one you'll be voting for today, because you are sick and tired of hoodlums in our fair town, literally getting away with murder."

"Sheriff Gilford!" one of the reporters shouted. "Is it true that you've caught the killer? Have you arrested him?"

"No," Augustus interjected before Manny could answer. "Tyrell Grymes is not incarcerated. He's on the run because Sheriff Gilford here decided to set him free."

"Tyrell Grymes was released because there is no credible evidence against him," Manny told the reporter.

"Except his fingerprints on the cemetery gate, which I collected myself," Augustus proudly interjected, "and the murder weapon, bloody and with Grymes's fingerprints all over it, which *I* found in the peach orchard, after your present sheriff and his other deputy had supposedly searched it."

"We did search it. We searched it thoroughly," Manny protested. "Deputy Jarvis and I covered every inch of that ground and there was no—"

"It wasn't on the ground, Sheriff," Augustus said. "It was stuck up in a tree, in the fork between two large branches, four trees away from the gate on the right. If you or Deputy Jarvis had bothered to look up, you would have found it, as I did."

Stella felt her heart sink as a look of deep embarrassment and rage washed over Manny's face.

This looked bad for him. Whether members of the crowd believed and supported Augustus, or whether they considered him an arrogant jerk, Manny appeared to have no control over the situation at all.

He looked incompetent, and he looked weak.

Sheriffs can't afford to appear either, Stella thought with a sinking feeling that was a mixture of anger and despair.

Augustus had done his job well. But the deputy wasn't content to stop there. "So, I'm asking you, members of the public and the media, to be on the lookout for Mr. Tyrell Grymes. I have a picture of him that I will give to you news folks. Please distribute it as far and wide as you can. We must use any and all means at our disposal to capture this desperate, dangerous murderer before he kills some other innocent person."

"Enough!" Manny roared the word, and the sound of his deep voice filled the town square.

The crowd caught its collective breath and was utterly silent.

Even Augustus looked surprised. He whirled around and stared at Manny with something akin to fear in his eyes.

Manny stepped forward and put his hand on Augustus's shoulder. Stella could tell he was digging his fingers into the young man by the whiteness of his knuckles and the way Augustus flinched.

"Deputy Faber, you will end this news conference this moment, or I will place you under arrest. Here. Now."

"On what charges?" Augustus shot back, but his voice trembled when he spoke, and his face was turning paler by the moment.

"Inciting violence against a person who, at this moment, has not been charged with any crime, let alone murder."

Manny turned to the reporters and their cameras and said, "Mr. Grymes has been a person of interest in the case. He was questioned, as were several other persons in the course of this investigation. No warrant has been issued for his arrest or I would have been informed."

Manny released his grip on Augustus and said, "If Deputy Faber here has, indeed, uncovered new evidence, as he claims, he should have followed proper procedure and informed me of his findings before making an irresponsible, public announcement like this. I will question him, evaluate his claims, and if I find they have any merit, I will gladly inform you myself."

For once, Augustus seemed at a loss for words. He simply stood there, silent and angry.

"My deputy is right about one thing," Manny continued. "This *is* election day. I hope you will all perform your civic duty with pride. I know you to be a town filled with folks who possess more than their share of good common sense. For those of you who hadn't yet made up your minds about who you would support, I trust that all you've seen and heard here in your town square these last few minutes will aid you in making your decision. Have a good day. We'll see you later, after the counting's done."

Murmurings rippled through the crowd, followed by a long, loud round of enthusiastic applause.

Even the reporters seemed happy, satisfied with what they had achieved.

Maybe there hadn't been a proper briefing about the solving of a murder, but they had recorded some juicy conflict between a well-known sheriff and his deputy.

In the absence of true news, airing the sheriff department's dirty laundry would have to do.

Stella watched as Manny turned to Augustus and said, "You. Come with me."

As the two men descended the gazebo stairs, Augustus looked like he might be sick at any moment.

Stella turned to Savannah and said, "Thank you for comin' and gettin' us. Wouldn't have missed this for the world."

"Do you think Deputy Faber really found the murder weapon?" Savannah asked as the two men walked by them, heading toward the station house.

"I don't know. But I'm sure gonna find out," Stella told her as she quickly fell into step behind them.

"And let us know!" Savannah called after her.

Stella turned, gave Savannah a smile and a nod. Then she blew her grandbaby a kiss.

Yes siree, she thought as she followed Manny and Augustus to the station, then on inside. *This should be interestin'.*

Chapter 30

"I don't know what you're all steamed up about, Sheriff," Augustus began the moment they entered the station.

"Steamed up?!" Manny shouted. "Car windows get steamed up. You are in mortal danger, boy. I'm thinking of all the ways I can turn you into a suspicious smell in an attic or basement somewhere."

"Am I supposed to take that as a threat?"

"If you're smart you will!"

"I'd think you'd be pinning a medal on me or at least congratulating me for solving your case for you."

"Augustus Faber, you had best shut your mouth," Manny shouted back, "or as I live and breathe, I will slap you nekkid and hide your clothes!"

Stella watched the two men, standing inches apart, bristling like a couple of roosters getting ready to battle for a harem of hens.

She glanced over at the desk, where Merv sat. He had been practically standing on his head, trying to reach beneath the lamp and screw in the new bulb. He had stopped messing with the light and was frozen in his awkward position, the side of his face pressed against the desktop, his body contorted in a sideways pose.

As he listened to the heated exchange, his eyes grew larger by the moment.

Stella couldn't stand it anymore. She strode over to the desk, grabbed the lamp by its highly adjustable neck, and twisted it around until she could see the socket. That done, she snatched the bulb from Merv's hand, screwed it in, flipped on the light, and readjusted the lamp to its proper position.

"Good lord, Deputy Merv," she said, pulling him up to a full sitting position. "Didn't your momma ever teach you nothin'?"

Meanwhile, Manny and Augustus were still going at it, although Augustus had said a bit less since hearing the death threat.

"You had no call to do that, Augustus," Manny said, "other than some stupid, underhanded ploy to influence this election. Which I hope you noticed did you way more harm than good."

Augustus grumbled something under his breath, which Manny chose to ignore.

"Why didn't you bring me that evidence, assuming you weren't lying and actually found some."

"I found some. Right where I said I did. All I had to do was dust that gate and look up once in a while when I was searching the orchard."

"Are those gate prints really Tyrell's?"

"They are. I checked them good against his files. He's got a nasty scar on his right thumb. Makes it pretty easy."

"And the ball bat?"

"Got his prints all over it."

"That's not surprising if it's his bat, now is it?"

"It's his. I compared it to a picture in the high school yearbook. It's got some weird, colorful strips of tape he wound around the grip."

"Is there blood on the bat?"

"There is. Hair too. Herb Jameson says the blood is the same rare type as Dexter had. AB negative. Rarest there is."

"Is that weapon in Jameson's custody now?"

"It is."

"And the fingerprints you lifted?"

"Also with him."

"If Herb Jameson was examining fingerprints and a potential murder weapon, why didn't he say anything to me about them?"

"Have you seen him yet today?"

"No."

"I took them to him right before I came here. He'll probably call you soon. He'll verify everything I've told you."

"Did you attempt to contact Tyrell?"

"I did. I went out to his place, intending to take him into custody, but there was no sign of him. His next-door neighbor said he saw him pack some duffel bags into his car in the middle of the night and then take off. My suspicion is that he skipped town. We'll probably never see him again."

Manny walked over to his desk, tossed the old lightbulb into a nearby garbage can, then sat down in the chair recently vacated by a baffled and nervous Merv.

For a moment, Manny paused to close his eyes tightly and run his fingers through his hair.

Stella knew it was a gesture that he used when he was particularly tired or upset about something.

She knew he was both, and her heart ached for him. More than anything, she wished she knew what to say or do to comfort him.

Finally, he looked up at Augustus, who was standing nearby, not appearing half as cocky as he had before in the gazebo.

He looked like a man who had bit off more than he could chew and had choked on it.

Manny cleared his throat and said in an even, calm voice, "Deputy Augustus James Faber, as of this moment, I am relieving you of duty. Place your badge and your weapon here on the desk."

Stella watched as ever-changing emotions crossed Augustus's face: incredulity, confusion, anger, and sadness.

"Really?" he whispered.

Manny gave one small nod. "Really. You're fired."

As Augustus reluctantly unpinned his badge, Manny said, "This never had to happen, Deputy. I appreciate the fact that you found evidence I failed to uncover myself. I would have been happy to give you the credit and the praise you deserve there in that gazebo today. I would have gladly honored you in front of the whole town. Election be damned. But no, you had to do it your way. You put a person in danger who hasn't been charged yet, painting him as a dangerous murderer, which he may or may not be."

Augustus took his weapon from the holster on his belt, removed the bullets, and, having made it safe, laid it carefully, almost reverently, on the desk next to his badge.

"You embarrassed yourself, your family, and me," Manny continued, his voice still calm and even. "You shamed the entire sheriff's department, portraying us as fools, whose right hands don't know what our lefts are doing. We aren't like bankers and grocery clerks and used car salesmen. We face life and death situations on the job, and we can't afford to look foolish. Having our credibility in question can get us killed. And it endangers the members of the public we're sworn to protect and serve."

When Augustus didn't reply, Manny continued. "I'm deeply disappointed in you, Augustus. You were a good cop, but in the past twenty-four hours, you've made some very bad decisions."

Manny opened a drawer, swept the badge and gun into them, then closed and locked it. "I never thought I would say this to you, but I don't want to see your face for a very long time, Mr. Faber. Do you understand?"

Augustus nodded curtly, avoiding eye contact with Manny.

"Okay," Manny said, as though the simple word was a period to a long sentence. "Leave my station house."

Augustus turned sharply on his heel in a pseudomilitary manner and marched out of the building, slamming the door behind him.

Manny sat in silence, staring at the closed door.

Stella and Merv looked on, equally quiet, for what seemed like a very long time.

Finally, Merv gave a long, low whistle and said, "Wow!"

Manny looked up at Stella, his eyes full of pain, and said softly, "Yeah. Wow."

As the day wore on, Stella was aware that Manny was becoming more and more troubled. His usual effervescence was gone, he had little to say, and when he did, it seemed like a great effort on his part.

Late in the afternoon, after the two of them had stood in a long line to vote, they were walking out of city hall when he stopped in the middle of the sidewalk, turned to her, and said, "Merv's got the station. With everybody voting or at home watching the Braves, I don't think much is happening for the rest of the day."

"I was thinking the same myself. Why don't you go on home and get some sleep? Later, you can come over to my house, and I'll cook supper for you, then we'll come back to town for the election results."

"I have a better plan," he said.

"Let's hear it."

He had a strange look in his eyes, and she had a feeling something unexpected was coming.

"How about *you* go home with *me*, and we spend the rest of the afternoon and the evening together?"

Not sure exactly what he was suggesting, she felt her pulse rate quicken. "Don't you want to be here in town when the returns come in?"

"Not particularly. He'll win, or I'll win, and to be honest, darlin', I don't care which it is. I just want to go home, build a fire in the pit outside, and watch the sun go down on the river. It's been a long time since I've done that, and I want to do it with you. I really, really need to be home. With you."

He seemed so hurt. Not broken but deeply wounded. There was a distinct tone of desperation behind his voice that she hadn't heard since his Lucy had died.

How could she say no?

On the way to Manny's cabin by the river, Stella rolled down the cruiser's window and filled her lungs with the rich aroma of the magnificent pine trees that grew more and more dense as they neared the river.

In the backseat of the cruiser, Valentine was doing the same with his head stuck out the window and his dewlaps flapping in the breeze.

Soon, the moist, earthy smell of the water itself blended with that of the trees and made Stella feel wonderfully at home.

She couldn't help recalling when Manny and Lucy had frequently invited her and Art over to their cabin for a barbecue, a swim, and a game of Monopoly. Their place had felt like home to Stella.

The cozy cabin, the sound of the water running nearby, the rustle of the trees in the wind, the smell of the hickory sticks burning in the stone barbecue pit Manny had built from river rocks.

It feels like it was another lifetime, she thought as they drove. *So far removed from this one.*

The enormous pines and her abiding friendship with Manny seemed the only remnants of that time.

Oh, and the cabin, she added when they rounded a curve in the road and saw it, sitting at the river's edge. Its honey-gold logs glowing in the late afternoon sun. The stately fireplace chimney that Manny had also built by hand, laying rock upon rock.

"I just love comin' here," she said.

"You do?" He seemed surprised.

"Sure. Bein' here reminds me of the good ol' days, bein' young and lighthearted. Thinkin' only fun times were ahead."

She was silent a few moments and added, "Little did we know then, huh?"

"Yes. It's a good thing we didn't know. We wouldn't have enjoyed those times so much if we'd known how soon they would end. *How* they would end."

"Now that I'm older, I realize," she said, "we gotta keep that in mind ever' day. Hang on to the good stuff and get rid of the bad, just in case."

"That's why I asked you here tonight," he said, reaching for her hand. "I want to create and savor another good time. One we can both remember till our dying days."

"Which will, hopefully, be a long time off," she added quickly.

"Hear, hear." He laughed. "There are way too many good memories for us to make. It can't be over anytime soon. By the way, what would you like me to fix for dinner?"

"You still cook?"

"Of course. Shall I grill us some steaks?"

"Oh, would you? You used to grill 'em outside on that stone fireplace do-whacky you built, and they were the best I ever ate!"

"Steaks it is."

* * *

Once dinner had been cooked, served, and eaten with gusto, Stella and Manny went inside the cabin, as the sun had set, and it was turning cool outside.

Stella did the dishes while Manny built a roaring fire in the stone fireplace.

Having finished the tidbits of steak trimmings that had been thrown to him, Valentine retired to his bed, a round, overstuffed sheepskin affair situated next to the hearth.

Totally contented, the dog curled into a tight ball, draped his long, graceful tail over his nose, and went to sleep.

"That pooch of yours looks mighty content with his lot in life, now that you've got him."

"Yes. We get along well. He's no bother and good company."

She brought two mugs of the fresh coffee she had just brewed into the living room area and handed him one. "The night turned nippy awful quick."

"It sure did." He glanced over her lightweight dress, set his mug on a nearby end table, and said, "I'll be right back."

He disappeared for a moment into the bedroom on the other side of the cabin, then reappeared with a thick, pale blue Aran cardigan with traditional Irish patterns knitted down the front and back and the sleeves.

Wrapping it around her shoulders, he said, "There. That'll keep you warm."

"In an Arctic blizzard," she said, adjusting the enormous garment, feeling like she was lost inside it.

But it was a feeling she didn't mind because the wool smelled like Manny: an intoxicating mixture of his shaving lotion, coffee, fireplace smoke, and . . . him.

Wearing it was like receiving a long, affectionate, reassuring hug from him, and not having to pull away and end it.

"Have a seat here," he said, patting the cushion of the large leather sofa. "Get yourself comfortable."

She sat down and felt herself sinking deliciously into the soft, smooth leather.

The cabin wasn't as feminine as it had been all those years ago when Lucy had sewn frilly floral print curtains for the windows and sofa pillows galore to match.

This was a man's home. Simple but quality furniture, sophisticated black-and-white nature photos on the knotty pine walls.

Manny had made the cabin very much his own, and Stella felt, saw, and smelled him all about her.

She couldn't recall ever feeling so warm, safe, and protected.

He grabbed a couple of oversized throw cushions and tossed them onto the coffee table.

"There you go," he said, as he reached down, lifted her legs and feet, and placed them on one of the pillows. "A woman who does as much as you should put her feet up any chance she gets."

He grabbed a large Native American blanket woven with red, white, and black patterns and spread it over her lap, legs, and feet.

Then he stood up and looked down, surveying his handiwork. "How do you feel now?"

"Like a princess," she said. "A snug-as-a-bug-in-a-rug Cherokee princess."

"Good, since you are one. Well, half Cherokee, half Irish." He moved one end of the blanket aside, sat on the sofa next to her, and propped his own legs and feet on the other cushion. "And you're a princess in my house. Always will be if I have anything to do with it."

He pulled his half of the blanket over his legs and snuggled in close to her.

After taking a sip of the coffee he said, "Now isn't this a lot nicer than hanging around in town, waiting for election returns?"

"Yes, but how will we know once the votes are counted?"

"We'll turn on the radio later. I'm sure they'll announce it."

"You're very nonchalant about all this election mess, Sheriff Gilford."

"I reckon I am. As I get older, I'm starting to figure out what's important and what's not."

"Are you telling me that being sheriff isn't important?"

"Not as much as it once was."

"Then what *is* important to you?"

He thought a moment, then said, "My relationship with you."

She was taken aback. Of all the things he might have said, she hadn't been expecting that.

"Why, thank you, Manny," she stammered. "It is to me, too."

He turned to her, his heart in his eyes, and said, "You don't know what it means to me, Stella May, just spending time with you. I've felt alone all my life. I never understood why. Figured it was just part of my makeup. But when I'm with you, I don't feel alone."

"Really?"

"Really. I can be in a room with a hundred people, and I feel apart from all of them, so different. Alone. Then you walk in, I see your face, I hear your voice and I'm not alone anymore. It's the strangest thing. I can't explain it. But I treasure it."

"Oh, Manny. That's about the nicest thing anyone ever said to me."

He leaned over and kissed her forehead. It wasn't his usual quick peck. It was long, lingering. "I was feeling pretty rough today, after that disaster with Faber, that whole news briefing, having to fire him. I hated it."

"I know you did. I'm sorry you had to go through that."

"But once you said you'd come back here with me tonight, it was all right. You have a way of changing whatever's going wrong in my life and making it right."

"I'm mighty glad that's the case," she said, wishing she was half as eloquent as he was.

"Now, sitting here with you, so close to you, it's like the black fog that I felt closing in around me earlier today, it's lifting. Sometimes, it feels like that darkness is going to swallow me whole. Being in law enforcement, you see so much."

His voice caught in his throat, and he had to pause, regather himself. Tears shone in his eyes as he stared at the fire and said, "Stella, my world . . . sometimes it's dark, really dark. It's hard. Cold. Sharp. A blade that cuts so deep. Leaves . . . scars."

"I'm sure it does," she said, reaching up and stroking his cheek. "I'm so sorry, Manny."

"That's okay, sweetheart. You don't need to feel sorry for me. I just want you to understand that you . . . you're the opposite of all that. You are sunlight and softness and warmth and healing. When I'm with you, close to you like this, all that other . . . it lifts. It fades away."

Tears rolled down her cheeks as she looked up at him and saw more love in his eyes than she had ever received from anyone.

Including her dear Arthur.

She saw that he was looking down at her lips, and she knew what he was thinking.

Her heart began to pound, and her breath quickened.

For the first time all evening it occurred to her that she was alone with an extremely attractive man in a romantic cabin in the woods. There was no one to judge or even to form an opinion, because no one but the two of them even knew she was there.

"I'd love to kiss you right now," he said, his voice deep and husky. The sound of it went through her, warmer and stronger than the coffee in the mug she was clutching far too tightly.

She was about to say something like, "Please do. As quickly as possible."

But then he said, "I'm not going to, though."

"You aren't?" she asked, trying not to sound too disappointed.

"No. Because I don't want you to think that's why I invited you here. When it's not."

"It's not? I mean, um, I didn't think it was but . . ."

"I'd be happy to have it be more," he continued, "but I know you're a principled lady with strong convictions about certain things. The last thing I'd ever want to do is jeopardize our friendship."

"Oh, well, yes. I, uh . . ."

"So I just want you to know that I'm content to sit here with you like this. Close like this. With you."

"Okay," she said. "I understand. I appreciate that."

I reckon, she added silently, thinking how nice it might have been to receive another Manny kiss like the one he had given her in her kitchen on Christmas morning last year.

Boy, did that man ever know how to kiss! It was a Christmas gift she would never forget, to be sure.

How could she when she relived it a dozen times a day in her memory? At least.

But kiss or no, she decided she wanted a bit more than sitting side by side on the sofa.

Slowly, she turned to him and pressed her hand against his shoulder, gently pushing him sideways.

"Darlin'," he said, surprised. "What are you doing?"

She slid off the sofa and onto her knees, making room for him. "Lay down," she told him, coaxing him to raise his long legs, stretch out on the couch, and place his head on its cushioned armrest.

"Get comfortable. This is gonna be a long night," she added.

Once he was settled, she lay next to him and was happy to see that the cushions were deep enough to provide plenty of room for them both.

She snuggled against him, her feminine curves finding their complements against his male form. She could feel the heat of his body even through their thick clothing, and she was quite sure he could feel hers, too.

She reached down, took his hand in hers, and brought it up to her lips. She kissed it sweetly, then held his palm against her cheek.

"You've had a long day, sugar, and you need some rest," she told him. "Go to sleep now, hear?"

"No," he whispered. "I'm not going to sleep. I don't want to miss one moment of this."

She laughed softly then lay quietly for a while, delighting in the feel of his breathing and his heartbeat so close to her own.

"Thank you, Stella," he said. "Thank you for this gift."

"You don't need to thank me, Manny. I'm doing this as much for myself as for you."

"Really?" he asked.

"Yes. Believe me, you ain't the only one who feels all alone in this dark, cold, hard world. For me, there ain't nobody who makes that miserable ol' loneliness disappear quite like you do, Manny Gilford."

Chapter 31

Stella woke to the morning sun streaming through Manny's living room windows and the smell of fresh brewed coffee and frying bacon in the air.

She was pretty sure she had died during the night and gone to heaven.

But when she tried to sit up on the couch, her stiff muscles complained loudly, and her joints crackled like crispy rice cereal.

She glanced over at the dog bed next to the fireplace and saw that Valentine was in the same position as he had been the night before, curled into a tight, cozy ball, his tail draped over his muzzle.

At least she wasn't the only one who had slept in this morning.

"Well, look at you, sleepyhead," said a masculine voice from the kitchen area. "About time for you to rise and shine."

She groaned as she forced herself to stand and put her hand to her lower back. "I'm risin'," she said. "That shinin' business might have to wait till I've got a cup or two of that coffee in me."

Manny turned the heat down on the skillet and walked over to her. Wrapping his arms around her waist, he pulled her close and gave her a long, tight hug.

Then he pulled back and looked down at her, his eyes searching hers. "How are you this morning, Stella?" he asked. "Are you okay? You know, about . . . last night?"

"About the fact that I spent the night out here in the woods in the company of a man I ain't married to, and worse still, I slept with him?"

"Yes. That's what I'm asking."

She snuggled against him, gave him a winsome grin, and said, "I'm desperately embarrassed, scarred for life. I'll never get over the shame of it all."

He laughed. "Yeah, me neither. 'Tis an awful hardship, but I'll bear up."

She stood on tiptoe, kissed his cheek, then pulled away from him and headed for the coffeepot. "One thing you gotta know about me, Mr. Gilford, this 'gift of gab' my Irish daddy gave me, it don't kick in until the second cup of coffee."

She heard him clear his throat, then say, "That's *Sheriff* Gilford to you, missy."

Something in his emphasis got her attention. She whirled around and stared at him, wide eyed. "What?"

He gave her a grin and a nod.

Joy unspeakable bubbling up inside her, she started dancing a jig, and suddenly, her joints and muscles were sixteen years old again.

"You won!" she said. "You heard? How did you hear?"

"The mayor called to congratulate me. I had the phone turned down so it wouldn't wake you."

"I'm so, so happy. Congratulations!"

He gave her a quick bow. "Why thank you, Mrs. Reid."

"By what percentage?"

"I squeaked by with a mere 97 percent."

"Eh, that other three percent was probably the folks you gave tickets to or threw in the hoosegow."

"That's what the mayor said."

Stella thought of Augustus Faber and couldn't help laughing. "Poor ol' Gus. Bless his heart, losin' both his badge and the election all in one day. He must be feelin' lower than a snake's belly."

"In a wagon rut."

"I feel *real* bad for him," Stella said with a smirk.

"I know. Me too." He returned her grin. "But I'll get over it."

After breakfast had been eaten and Stella had tidied the kitchen, Manny asked her to go outside and sit with him.

"I have something I need to discuss with you, sugar," he said.

His tone didn't give her reason for optimism. His former levity had faded, and instinctively, she knew she wasn't going to like what she was about to hear.

They walked outside, and he led her to a pair of Adirondack chairs, near a stone fire pit.

The morning air was fresh and pine sweet, and Valentine raced by them into the woods, his nose low to the ground, working like a bloodhound's as he explored an intricate realm of the senses that humans could never imagine.

"You still workin' on turnin' that mutt into a drug-sniffin' K-9?" she asked.

"Absolutely. We missed our session last night because, well, we had a lady over for company, but I intend to keep it up until he's good at it. Should come in handy someday."

Once they were settled in their chairs with their refilled coffee mugs in hand, he said, "I'd like to talk to you about your grandchildren, Stella. Or your 'grandangels,' as you like to call them."

"Uh-oh. Did you have to arrest Marietta?" she said half-joking.

"No, but if she doesn't stop nabbing things there in Fred's drugstore, I'm going to have to one of these days. He can only afford to lose so many Snickers bars and hair barrettes."

"Oh no. Okay, I'll give 'er another talkin'-to."

"Actually, I'd like to ask you something about Waycross."

"All right. Spit it out."

"These trips he makes to the cemetery to talk to Art. What's that about, in your opinion?"

"Are you askin' me if he's actually talkin' to his grandpa or just pretendin' he does?"

Manny looked a bit taken aback by her bluntness, but he thought about it a moment, then said, "Yes, I guess I am. What do you think?"

"I don't know."

"Well, that's honest."

"I truly don't, Manny. When he first talked about it, I thought it was just one of his weird little Waycross things he does."

"Like painting mustaches on the figures in the town's nativity scene?"

She blushed. "That was the height of his criminal activity, but yes. He's not your average, run-of-the-mill kid."

"I've noticed."

"Honestly, I figured it was his way of copin' with not havin' a daddy around like he oughta have. It's a hole in his heart, the way that son of mine ignores him and the rest of the kids. I reckoned he was just fillin' that space any way he could."

"That's what I figured, too."

"But sometimes I wonder."

"Why?"

"He says things that I can't account for. One Memorial Day, when I took him to put flowers on Art's grave, he 'listened' to his grandpa and then told me that Art said he liked my hairdo, 'cause it was the way I used to wear it when we were courtin'."

"Did Waycross have any way to know that?"

"No way at all. I'd never had my picture taken with it like that for him to see. I hadn't worn it that way for ages, long before the boy was born."

"Hmm. I can see why you'd think there could be something there beyond the boy's imagination and his need for a male figure."

They were quiet for a few moments, then Manny said, "Anyway, it got me thinking, and with your permission, I'd like to follow through on that fishing business I talked to you about before. If I wouldn't be overstepping, I'd like to be more present in the boy's life, do some 'guy' stuff with him."

She was deeply touched and could hardly speak. When she finally could, she said, "Manny, that would be wonderful. I know he'd treasure any one-on-one time you could give him. That child thinks the sun rises just to hear you crow!"

"Great! I was hoping you'd say that." He seemed happy, but only for a moment. She understood why when he said, "I'm afraid I also need to talk to you about Savannah."

"Savannah?" Of all her grandchildren, Savannah would have been the last one she would have thought Manny was concerned about, let alone want to discuss with her. Especially with a troubled look in his eyes. "Why her?"

"I hate to be a tattletale. Normally, I just keep this sort of thing to myself and let families work out their own problems. But it's *your* family, and I'm afraid it's serious. Or could become so soon."

"You're scaring me, Manny. What's goin' on?"

"I'm just concerned for her well-being." He drew a deep breath and plunged in. "Okay. How much do you know about Tommy Stafford?"

Instantly, Stella knew. She understood why Manny was worried and what this conversation would be about.

The knowledge didn't make her feel any better.

"I know he's a tomcat on the prowl, and Savannah's got a great big crush on him."

"He *is* a tomcat. The worst in town, and that's saying something. I don't mean to scare you, Stella, but the truth is, I've peeled that boy off more than one girl in the backseat of a car, parked out in the tulies. He's not even seventeen years old yet, and if he keeps this up, he's going to be personally responsible for a population explosion here in our little town."

"I don't think he's gotten far with our Savannah," Stella said. But the moment the words left her mouth, she realized they were more of a wish than a statement of fact.

Manny's ensuing silence didn't set her mind at ease.

Stella didn't want to ask, but she had to. "Was . . . was she one of them girls you peeled him off of?"

"No," he replied, "but I did see them parked by the river a few weeks ago. He wasn't on top of her. They were in the front seat, vertical, and fully dressed when I knocked on his side window. But they were going at it, hot and heavy, and considering his track record, I don't know if that would have been the case five minutes later."

"Five minutes? Lordy, he works fast."

"The worst ones always do, and that boy's a damned jackrabbit."

"Oh, man. I was afraid this would happen. Her bein' an early bloomer and all."

He nodded. "She's that all right. She's lovely, Stella, and men of all ages notice a beautiful girl a mile off. She's also sweet and kind and trusting."

"Which makes her ripe, low-hangin' fruit for a Casanova like that."

"I'm sorry to say it does."

"I wish he wasn't so dadgum handsome," Stella complained. "I know grown women in their forties, even older, who watch him across a crowded room with goo-goo eyes. It's no wonder their daughters fall for his charms."

"He's far too good-looking for his own good," Manny agreed. "Plus, he's learned the power of throwing the word *love* around."

"Most boys figure that one out at that age."

"Unfortunately, yes. Anyway, I just wanted to tell you that if you haven't had the old 'birds and the bees' talk with her . . ."

"I gave her that talk a long time ago, and she knew all about ever'thing even then. Shirley liked men and didn't care who knew it, even the children livin' under her roof."

"That's too bad. I hate it when kids have to grow up too fast because of their elders' foolishness."

"But I'll talk to Savannah again, Manny. I will. It's one of them talks you have to keep givin', while prayin' it'll take."

"Unfortunately, at that age, biology speaks louder than grandmothers."

"Not this grandma. I can turn the volume up higher than you might think."

He laughed. "I can imagine. I want you to know that the speech I gave him after I found him with your Savannah was loud and clear, too. I told him all sorts of ways I would make him pay if I caught him with her like that again."

"You did?"

"Absolutely. With them both underage, there's not a lot I could really do, but I didn't feel the need to tell him that. Instead, I threw around some terms like 'statutory rape' and 'contributing to the delinquency of a minor.'"

"Did that shake him up?"

"Not enough to suit me. So I mentioned the fact that testicle mashing, and radical circumcision could be performed right in the backseat of my cruiser."

"Ouch. That must have got his attention."

"Not so's you'd notice. Smart-aleck kid told me he had been circumcised when he was born. So I assured him it could be done again, take off another couple of inches. With a rusty knife and a pair of pliers."

"Why, Manny Gilford, I'm shocked! To think you would terrorize a young boy in that manner, I'm surprised at you."

Manny shrugged. "I don't care. She's *your* Savannah and that makes her hands-off for the likes of him. It's not as if he doesn't have a long line of other silly girls waiting to do his bidding."

"Like Jeanette Outhouse-Seat-Bottom Parker?"

"Caught him with her last week."

Stella mulled that over. "Yes, I'm gonna have to talk to my girlie about this. Not that it'll do a lick o' good, but I have to try. Soon, too."

Manny thought for a moment, then said, "Why don't we go get her and bring her out here for the day? I have to go into the office this afternoon, but the two of you could stay here and have some quality one-on-one time with each other."

"Really? Sounds too good to be true. It's been such a long time since I had the luxury of a few hours with Savannah alone. I think it'd do us both a world of good."

"Then let's do it. We can go get her from Elsie right now."

"Let me phone Elsie first, make sure she can spare her. Savannah's most helpful with the little ones. Elsie might need her to keep them corralled."

"Then go give Elsie a call. I'll throw a stick for Valentine."

"Better yet, work on them drug-seekin' skills."

"Good idea. Hey, Valentine! Leave that squirrel be and come over here, boy!"

Chapter 32

Stella was happy to see how impressed Savannah was with Manny's cabin when they walked her inside.

"You live here, Sheriff?" she said, gazing at the furniture, the fireplace, the photos on the walls. "This is a beautiful place to live. Especially for a guy."

Manny laughed as he walked to the refrigerator to get iced tea for both ladies. "Us men aren't supposed to have any taste, huh?"

"I didn't mean it like that," she said, blushing.

"No offense taken." Manny handed them each their drinks, then, with a quick sideways glance at Stella, added, "I need to get to the station house. I put out that APB on Tyrell yesterday. Merv said we haven't had any responses yet, but, being it's Merv, I want to check for myself."

"No problem," Stella said. "Us girls will hang out here for the day. You can leave Valentine if you want."

At hearing his name, the big dog jumped up from his cushy bed by the fireplace and gamboled over to them, his tail wagging furiously.

"I'm sure he'd enjoy playing at the river with you ladies rather than hanging out with me at work."

Savannah knelt on the floor and pulled the dog to her. She laid her head on his and cooed sweet nothings to him as she scratched behind his ear.

She looked so sweet, innocent, and young. Stella felt a tightening in her throat and the sting of tears in her eyes.

Inviting the girl to the cabin should have been a wonderful treat for them both, but Stella felt dishonest somehow, since Savannah had no idea what was coming.

Or did she?

Several times, Savannah had shot her a look that suggested she might be suspicious. Though Stella decided to chalk the notion up to her own sense of guilt.

Stella didn't like being sneaky about anything. She considered it cowardly. If you didn't think you were doing anything wrong, why would you care who knew about it and what their opinion might be?

She wasn't good at "cunning" or "crafty" and didn't intend to get comfortable with either.

Wanting to just get it over, she said, "Let's get goin', darlin'. Grab your flop-eared buddy there, and let's make some tracks down to the river."

"I might be gone when you get back," Manny told them as they headed outside. "I'll leave the door unlocked."

Stella waved to him, he gave her a sympathetic "It'll be okay" look, and the females and Valentine left the cabin.

Once they reached the river's stony bank, they hadn't walked more than fifty feet when Savannah suddenly stopped. She gave her grandmother a sad look and said, "He told you, didn't he?"

Stella opened her mouth to make a denial, but she couldn't.

The last thing she wanted was to drive a wedge between her

grandchildren and this man who had become so important to her and to them. Especially, Savannah, who was obviously his favorite, and who loved and admired him so much.

But when Stella recalled all the speeches she had given her grandchildren about the virtues of telling the truth, she just couldn't make herself deny the obvious.

Savannah wasn't stupid. But she was still impressionable. Stella knew it was important to be a good example and practice what she preached.

"Yes. He did," she replied. "He told me this morning."

"I figured he would." Savannah looked down at her skater-style Vans, her pride and joy and a birthday gift from Manny. "I knew as soon as I heard we were going to stay at Elsie's, and you'd be having private time with him."

"He didn't enjoy telling me, honey. Not one bit. He tried to handle it on his own first, but—"

"Like to scare the bejabbers out of Tommy."

"Uh, yes. But Tommy didn't scare so easy, and since he saw you two together, Manny's seen him with other girls, doin' way worse with them than he did with you."

"Who!"

Stella was shocked to see how angry her calm, sweet, little Savannah was. She looked like she was ready to throw a hissy fit and snatch someone bald in the process.

"It doesn't matter who."

"It matters to me!"

Stella turned to face her and put her hands on the girl's shoulders. She was shaking badly and looked like she was about to cry.

"Darlin'," Stella said, trying to search for the right words. This was a rocky path that she hadn't walked before and wasn't sure how to proceed. "Tell me the truth. Did that boy say he was your one and only sweetheart?"

"Yes, he did! He most certainly did, or I never would've . . ."

Stella caught her breath. "Woulda what, honey?"

Savannah started to cry. Pulling her granddaughter to her, and hugging her tightly, Stella said, "You can tell me, sweetheart. You really can. I'm too old and seen way too much to be shocked. And I won't be cross with you. Sad, maybe, but not mad."

Savannah pulled back from her and said, "I wasn't stupid, Gran. I didn't let him do anything to me that would cause a baby. Okay?"

Stella felt a flood of relief that made her knees weak. "Okay. I'm glad of that, honey."

"But I did let him do a few, well, little things that I wouldn't have ever let him do if he wasn't my one and only boyfriend. He said he loved me."

"Some boys have a different definition of the word *love* than us girls do, darlin'."

"I know. To Tommy it probably means, 'I want to get nasty with you tonight and act like I don't know you exist tomorrow.'"

"Well, I don't think that's what most guys mean. I'd like to give 'em credit for bein' a little better than that. But from what I hear and have seen with your Tommy feller there, I'd say he's one of the worst ones you could keep company with. I know he's pretty to look at but—"

"Yes, he is. But that's not why I like him. He makes me laugh, and he's interested in detective and police stuff, like me. That's why I like being around him."

She paused, grinned a bit, and added, "It doesn't exactly stink that he's gorgeous, and he's a good kisser, too."

"I reckon he oughta be. From what I hear, he's had enough practice!"

They laughed together and Stella made a show of smoothing the girl's unruly black curls and straightening the collar on her sweater. Then she laid her hand on her granddaughter's cheek and said, "Savannah, you've always been truthful with me, so I believe all you've told me today."

"Thank you, Gran," she replied, sniffing.

"You're welcome. But I'm going to ask two things of you in return for my gift of trust."

Savannah gave her a wry smile and said, "Gee . . . could one of those things be not to hang out with Tommy Stafford anymore?"

"You're beautiful *and* brilliant. Go figure."

"Okay. I wasn't going to anyway after what you told me about the other girls. What's the second thing?"

"I'm gonna ask you not to hold it against Sheriff Gilford that he told me. He cares for you, very deeply. He'd walk on hot coals to keep you from harm."

"I know he would. I'm not mad at him. I'm surprised it took him this long to tell you."

Suddenly, they heard a disturbing noise. Valentine barking. The tone of it was frighteningly loud and had a definite sound of urgency about it.

"Oh no," Stella said as she looked down the beach, where the noise was coming from. "What in tarnation has he got hold of? A bear? A bobcat?"

Though she couldn't see anything, just the rocky riverbank and its surrounding shrubs and trees, she started to run in that direction.

When she realized Savannah was right behind her, she whirled around and said, "Go back to the cabin! See if Manny's still there!"

"But you might need help!"

"Go, Savannah! Run! Tell him to bring his gun! If he ain't there, bring me the skillet on the stove."

Savannah hesitated another second or two, then took off, racing back to the house. Stella continued on toward the barking that was getting louder by the moment, a mixture of plaintive distress and fear.

For a moment, Stella paused, reached down, and picked up the largest rock she could see. Then she continued to run.

"I'm coming, Valentine!" she called out to the animal, realizing how silly she looked, and hoping to high heaven it was something smaller than a bear.

Preferably *much, much* smaller.

Less than two minutes later, Manny and Savannah found Stella, kneeling on the river's rocky bank. Her arms were tight around Valentine, who was still barking, but he seemed less frightened and upset than before.

"There, there, boy," she was saying. "It's all right. You're okay. What a brave boy you are."

"Stella!" Manny shouted as they approached. "What's going on? Are you all right?"

"What is it, Gran? What's the matter?" Savannah asked, running up to her and grabbing her by the shoulders.

That was when both Savannah and Manny saw it.

The cause for Valentine's alarm and Stella's sadness.

Nearby, half in the water and half on the bank was a sodden mass that wasn't instantly recognizable.

"It's a dead body," Stella told them. "Another one."

"Drowned?" Manny whispered.

Stella knew he was reliving the horror of Lucy's passing and her heart broke for him.

"No, Manny," she said. "I don't think so. There's a head wound."

Manny knelt beside the body, studied it for a moment, then said, "Yes, an ugly head wound. Just like Corbin's."

"Who is it?" Savannah asked her grandmother. "Can you tell?"

"From that long, stringy, reddish brown hair hanging down over his face, I'd have to say, I'm pretty sure it's Tyrell Grymes."

Manny got up from his knees, looked at Stella, and nodded. "It's him all right." He sighed and stuck his weapon back in his holster. "I guess I can cancel that APB."

Chapter 33

At two o'clock that afternoon, Stella and Savannah sat on the edges of their metal folding chairs and listened intently to Manny's end of the phone conversation he was having with Herb Jameson.

Stella was fiercely interested in every word he was saying, but she couldn't help thinking how different the cozy warmth of the night before had been compared to her present circumstances.

The horror of what they had seen earlier, not to mention the removal of the body from the riverbank to be transported back to Herb's lately very busy mortuary, was a sharp contrast to lying peacefully in Manny's arms throughout the deliciously long night hours.

For just a moment, Stella looked over at her sweet granddaughter, so new to the wicked wiles of the world, and she felt a bit guilty. Was she a hypocrite, warning Savannah about the evils to be found in the arms of a man, when she had just spent the night with Manny?

Oh, shut up, you old harpy, she silently told the critical voice in her head. *Some tender cuddling with a fine man like Manny, who had no intention whatsoever of taking advantage of me, is a world away from what that pile of wet goose poop had in mind for our poor little Savannah.*

With an effort, she pulled herself back to the present and what Manny was saying to Herb. "Okay. Even without opening him up yet, you're sure that blow on the head would have been fatal?"

He listened to the response and nodded an emphatic yes to Stella and Savannah. "Do you have any idea what it was done with? What sort of weapon?"

Again, he listened to Herb and then repeated. "Blunt force to the cranium, but . . . harder? Something harder than a bat. And smaller in width. Gotcha."

A few more seconds passed as Herb continued to talk. Stella could hear his voice through the phone, but could only discern his tone and mood, not actual words.

"Are you sure?" Manny asked. "Did you test it or . . . ? Okay. You did. You're sure it's grease. Dirty grease. Not clean motor oil. All right. Thank you, my friend. I sure appreciate you calling me with that. Yes, I did want to know it as soon as possible, and anything else you come up with."

The telephone rang on the desk, but Manny was saying, "Of course. As soon as you can predict the time of death, that's one of the most important things."

The phone continued to chime, and Stella pantomimed to Manny if she should answer it in his office. He nodded vigorously as he said, "I know, Herb. Submerged in water like that, it makes it hard."

Stella raced to Manny's private office and grabbed the phone, cursing Merv the whole time for overextending his lunch break. His "Pac-Man" break was more like it.

"Sheriff's station," she said breathlessly into the phone.

"Who are you?" asked a hoarse, raspy voice that she didn't recognize.

"I'm Stella Reid. Who are *you*?"

"It doesn't matter who I am. I need to speak to Sheriff Gilford right now. It's important."

Something in the tone of the voice, its scratchy, gruff quality, caught Stella's attention, but she couldn't think why. "I'm really sorry," she said. "The sheriff's on another important call, but I promise you I'll give him your message just as soon as he gets finished with it."

There was a hesitation on the other end, as though the caller was considering their limited options.

"Okay," they finally said. "Here's what you need to tell him. I was near the front gates of the cemetery the night Dexter Corbin was murdered."

Stella's hands began to shake with excitement. "I understand," she said. "Please go on."

"At exactly four ten a.m. I saw a cruiser from the sheriff's department pull up to the gates. It stopped right there in front and a guy wearing an official uniform got out of that car and walked into the cemetery. He was there for fourteen minutes, and then he came back, got in his car, and drove away."

Stella's pulse was pounding so loudly in her ears, she could hardly hear what the caller was saying. "Okay," she said breathlessly. "Do you know who it was? Can you give me his description?"

But they had hung up, and all she heard was a dial tone.

Stella flew out of the office and back into the waiting room, her heart racing.

She was just in time to see Manny hang up the phone. When he and Savannah saw the look on her face, they both jumped to their feet.

"What is it, Gran?" Savannah asked.

"Is something wrong?" Manny wanted to know.

"Lord help us," she said. "I sure hope not."

As soon as Stella told Manny the details of the call, his demeanor changed drastically. Gone was the easygoing, kind, and gentle companion of the last evening.

The man at the desk was a law officer. Nothing more or less.

He pulled open one of the desk drawers, reached to the back of it, and took out a set of car keys.

Rattling them in his hand, he said, "Merv's cruiser is parked out back. That one first."

Stella had to stop herself from laughing. "Merv?" she said. "Oh, Manny. You can't think for a moment that was him."

"No. I don't. But I have to rule him out before I can . . ."

He didn't finish the statement because he was pulling a pair of gloves from another desk drawer. Then he was on his feet and headed for the rear door of the station house.

Stella and Savannah followed right behind him, and a moment later, they were all three gathered around Mervin Jarvis's official vehicle, the one he drove constantly, even on his days off.

The job had few perks, but a full-time cruiser was one of them. This car had been Merv's from the day he had joined the department.

Manny used the keys to open the doors, and he quickly searched the interior. Stella watched him, amazed at the speed and thoroughness with which he accomplished the task, until she remembered that he must have performed this procedure literally thousands of times during his lengthy career.

When he was finished, he opened the trunk.

That area took a bit longer, because it was all too obvious that Merv had been using it as a mini–storage locker for his personal items.

A few bags of empty beer bottles, some dirty laundry, a box full of soft-core porn magazines made it difficult for Manny to conduct a thorough search. Finally, he gave up and began to dump the stuff on the ground behind the car.

Stella noticed that he tossed a dirty sweatshirt over the box of magazines before removing it. No doubt for Savannah's sake.

She blessed him for it and thought, *Thank goodness for Southern gentlemen*.

"I didn't think you'd find anything," Savannah told him, as she leaned into the trunk to watch. "It's *Merv*. His elevator doesn't go more than one or two floors."

"I know, sweetheart, but, like I said, I have to eliminate him. There are only three cruisers on the roads hereabouts. I know I wasn't at the cemetery that night. So, that leaves Merv or . . ."

He grunted as he leaned down and moved some heavy barbells aside to get to the area where the spare tire was stored.

Peeling back the cover and exposing the spare, he gasped and whispered, "Holy shit."

Stella wedged herself between him and Savannah so she could see what had evoked such a response from her genteel Southern gentleman.

"I sure wasn't expecting this," he said, staring down at what they could now all see quite clearly.

"Are those bags of white powder cocaine?" Savannah asked, pointing to the items in question that were poked haphazardly between the wheel spokes.

"I'll have to test it to be sure," Manny told her, "but I'd bet dollars to donuts it is."

"Look at all that money!" Stella said, pointing to the rubber-banded stacks of cash that circled the outside of the tire.

"It's not unusual to find a ton of cash with a ton of drugs," Manny said dryly.

With his gloved hands, he picked up a nearby tire iron and held it up in the light to study it more carefully.

That was when they all caught their collective breath.

The ugly metal rod was covered with black grease. Except for its end.

"Blood," Manny whispered. "All over the first six inches of it. Lots of it."

Savannah looked closer and said, "Hair. There are long auburn hairs mixed in there with the blood."

Stella saw exactly what she was talking about. Several strands of lengthy copper-colored hair glistened in the sunlight.

"You've got your murder weapon, Manny," she said.

"Yes." He nodded. "But do I have my murderer?"

"It's Merv?" Savannah asked incredulously. "He plays Pac-Man and sits at your desk all day and answers the phone. And he drives around at night looking to see if anybody's stranded on the road. That's *all he does!*"

Manny studied her for a long time, the desperate expression on her usually sweet face.

Finally, he said, "I hope so. I would dearly love for you to be right, Savannah. You have no idea how much."

"What are you gonna do now?" Stella asked him. "What's next?"

"What's next is, I'm going to go arrest my one remaining deputy." He shook his head, closed the trunk, and locked it. "Damn. Now there's a sentence I never thought I'd hear myself say."

Chapter 34

Stella and Savannah waited in tense silence as Manny left to go to the pizza restaurant and collect Mervin.

After a few minutes, Stella said, "Is somethin' wrong, honey? I mean, other than the obvious, us stumblin' upon another dead body. We gotta put a halt to that nonsense."

She had hoped her morbid little joke would bring a much-needed bit of levity to the situation, but it didn't.

Savannah sat stone-faced and silent. Only her open eyes and the jiggling of her right foot suggested she was conscious.

"I know it was scary, what happened today. Plus us havin' our little talk."

"It's not that," Savannah said. "I did think when I got there it was going to be a nice day, you and me spending time together, and it did all go south pretty quick-like, once we started our walk, but that's not why."

The front door of the station house opened, and Manny strode in, closely followed by Mervin. Manny looked serious and upset. Merv just seemed confused and maybe a bit nervous.

"He hasn't told him yet," Stella whispered to Savannah as

both of them quickly vacated the chairs by the desk and stood next to the soda machine.

As Manny sat behind the desk and motioned for Merv to park himself on one of the chairs, Stella caught his eye.

She gave him a questioning look and motioned toward herself and Savannah, then toward the front door.

Manny shook his head and said, "That's okay, Stella. You and Savannah can stay. This isn't going to take long."

Stella whispered to Savannah, "We'll stay here. Don't say anything. Okay?"

Savannah nodded, looking positively miserable.

Manny turned to Merv and said, "This isn't easy, Deputy Jarvis. I don't know any way to sugarcoat it, or even if I should try. But I've searched your vehicle."

Merv looked shocked, then horrified. "You did? My . . . my cruiser?"

"Yes. I found some alarming articles in your trunk."

"Oh, oh, I . . ." He gulped, turned an alarming shade of purple, and suddenly developed a coughing fit that went on for so long that Stella was considering calling an ambulance.

"Do you want to tell me about those items?" Manny said.

Finally, Merv recovered himself. "Um, not really, sir. I mean, if I'd known you were going to open my trunk, I would have gotten rid of them. Or never put them there to begin with."

"I'm sure you wouldn't have, Deputy. They're quite incriminating, don't you think?"

Merv hesitated, then said, "I guess. Yeah. They aren't something you'd want your boss to see."

Manny stared at him for a long time, then shook his head and said, "Deputy Jarvis, do you think I'm talking about your girlie magazines?"

"Yes, sir. Isn't that what we're discussing here?"

"No, Merv. It isn't." Manny rubbed his hands over his eyes,

then breathed deeply and said, "Deputy, inside the spare tire well of your trunk, I just found bags of cocaine, stacks of money, and a bloody tire iron with hair on it that most likely belonged to Tyrell Grymes."

"What!" Mervin jumped up from his chair, his eyes wide, the veins on his forehead throbbing. "You found what? In my car?"

"That's right. Please sit back down in your chair and tell me how they got there."

"How they got . . . how am I supposed to know?"

"Did you put them there, Merv? Did you hide that stuff in your trunk?"

"Of course not! Why would I do a thing like that?"

"Did you kill Tyrell Grymes?"

"No! Manny! Of course not! Why would I kill Tyrell? Why would I kill anybody?"

Stella watched breathlessly as Manny studied his deputy. The silence in the room was unbearable as they waited for one man or the other to speak.

She glanced over at Savannah and saw tears in her eyes.

She caught the girl's attention and mouthed the words to her, "Do you want to leave?"

Savannah shook her head and whispered, "No."

Finally, Manny broke the long silence and said, "I'm going to ask you a very important question, Merv. Think hard and long before you answer me, okay?"

"Yeah. Okay. I'm thinkin'."

"Where were you at four last Sunday morning?"

Merv's eyes glazed over as he thought and thought. Then he snapped to attention. "Wait a minute. Ain't that around the time when Corbin got killed there in the cemetery?"

"Please just answer the question, Deputy."

Merv mulled it over for what seemed like forever, then said, "I don't know. I think I was on duty that night. Wasn't I?"

"Yes, you were. What were you doing at four ten that morning?"

Again, Merv squinted his eyes, furrowing his forehead with the effort. "I don't know, sir. I was drivin' around town, the way I'm supposed to, I reckon. I don't remember it 'cause it probably wasn't all that excitin'. But if I'd been doin' somethin' different from my usual, I probably *would* remember it. Don't cha think?"

Manny looked at him with a mixture of frustration and compassion. "I don't know, Merv. I don't know what to think."

Manny stood, walked around the desk, and stood beside Merv. "I hate this, Merv," he said. "I can't tell you how much I hate this. But I'm going to have to read you your rights, and honestly, I'm telling you as a friend, you really do need to call a lawyer, buddy, 'cause you're gonna need one."

"You're arrestin' me, Sheriff? Really? But . . . but I didn't do anything!"

Mervin started to cry as Manny pulled him to his feet and took a pair of handcuffs from the back of his belt.

"No! Stop!"

Everyone jumped and turned to Savannah, who had shouted the words. She was sobbing as she ran over to Manny and tried to take the handcuffs away from him. "You can't arrest him, Sheriff. You can't. He didn't do anything. He's innocent."

Stella hurried to her granddaughter and put her arms around her. "Savannah, sweetie. What are you doin'? You can't interfere in somethin' like this. Sheriff Gilford is doing his duty, and you can't get in the middle of that no matter how you feel about it."

"Deputy Jarvis didn't kill Dexter Corbin at four ten a.m. in that cemetery."

"How do you know that, Savannah?" Manny asked her, his eyes searching her face intently. "Tell me, now."

"Because he wasn't anywhere near there at four ten. He was way out of town, down by the old, deserted lumber mill on Hollow Road."

Manny gave her a small, knowing nod. "How do you know that, darlin'?"

"Because that was where I was. With Tommy Stafford. We were parked there, talking and . . . stuff . . . and Deputy Jarvis came up and shined his light on us and told us to leave. So we did, and he followed us all the way back to town, I guess to make sure we got home all right."

"That was you in that car, Miss Savannah?" Merv asked, his facial expression turning from terrified to hopeful.

"It was," she admitted.

"I thought you were that Jeanette Parker gal. She's the one that Stafford boy is usually, er, talkin' to in his car."

"It was me that night," Savannah said. "I admit it."

She turned to Stella. "I'm sorry, Gran. I sneaked out the bedroom window and met him on the highway. I also kinda lied to you when you asked me about me parking with him. What I told you was the truth, but it wasn't the whole truth. I let you believe it was just one time. It's been more than that."

Manny took a step closer to Savannah and said, "How can you be so sure it was that night, darlin'? It's critically important that you're right about this."

"I know for sure. The next day Tommy must have told somebody at school what happened, 'cause Jeanette Parker found out about it. She threatened to clean my clock there in the lunchroom. I told her to go ahead and try, and she backed off. But that afternoon, right after school, she went after Waycross. She knew she could hurt me by hurting him. She's like that."

"Okay. So it *was* the night of the murder that you saw Deputy Jarvis," Manny said. "But how about the time? That's equally crucial. We can't have any mistakes about that."

"There's no mistake. I'm sure it was four ten a.m." She ducked her head, blushed deeply, and said, "I know because I was keeping a really close eye on the clock on Tommy's dash. I told him that I absolutely, positively had to be back home and in bed before five, because that's when my baby brother usually wakes up and wants his bottle."

"You wanted to make sure you were in bed in case I went into your room to look in on you," Stella said.

Savannah nodded. "I'm so sorry, Gran."

Stella felt the sting of betrayal, but it was mixed with pride that her granddaughter would confess something so personal and embarrassing rather than stand by and see someone falsely accused.

When it was truly important, Savannah had come through.

As she watched Manny put his cuffs away and offer Savannah a tissue for her weeping eyes and drippy nose, Stella told herself, *She put herself in the hot seat to save an innocent guy. You can't really ask much more of a thirteen-year-old.*

Once Manny got Merv settled down and convinced him that he was officially "unarrested," even reinstated as the on-duty deputy, he turned to Stella and said, "I'm going out to Tyrell's house to look around. Want to come with me?"

Stella looked over at Savannah, who, like Merv, was less forlorn now that the storm had passed.

"Go ahead," Savannah said. "I'll find my own way back to the Patterson place."

"How?" Stella asked.

"I'll go to the library and shelve books until Miss Rose closes up. She'll drive me there. She passes right by it going home."

"Are you sure you want to do that, after all you've been through today, sweetcheeks?"

"Yes. I feel good now. Like what I did before that wasn't good worked out for good in the end."

"A healthy outlook," said Manny. He turned to Stella. "Before I go anywhere, I have to bag up that evidence we found, label it, and put it in the safe."

"Fine," Stella told him. "I'll walk Savannah over to the library while you do."

"Gran, you don't need to take me over there. I could find my way to the library with my eyes closed and my feet tied together."

"Then let me get a blindfold and borrow some of Manny's leg-irons and we'll see how long it takes you to get there." Stella walked over, took her granddaughter's face in her hands, and said, "Our walk along the river wasn't nice at all," she said, "and I feel bad about that. You and me, we need to do stuff like that more often, and we will. Startin' right now. We'll even duck inside the Igloo and grab a couple of cones for us and a shake for Miss Rose. Okay?"

"Okay!"

Savannah's eyes sparkled, and her smile was so wide that Stella felt a bit guilty. It was so easy in life's hustle-bustle to forget how precious the little things, like attention and an ice cream cone, meant to someone you loved more than life itself.

"Then let's get goin'."

As they headed out the door, Stella heard Manny ask Merv if he thought he could handle some honest-to-goodness detective work.

"Sure!" was the response.

"Then get on the phone while I'm gone and try to find a phone number for Cindy Corbin. I believe she told Stella she was headed back to her hometown, La Paz, California."

"Yes, sir! I'm on it, sir!"

Merv was a man snatched from the cruel jaws of death. Or at least, an undeserved murder sentence. He was joy and relief personified.

"Hey, Merv," Stella called out before she headed out the door with Savannah, "try the local feed store. It's a little town, so there's probably only one. She said her dad owns it."

"Thank you!" was his jubilant reply. "Thank you, Stella! I owe you one! You too, Savannah!"

"Boy, he's a happy camper," Savannah said as they closed the door behind them and headed down the sidewalk toward a cold confection and the library. Two of her favorite things in life.

"He sure is, darlin'," Stella told her. "You can take a lot of satisfaction in that, 'cause you're the reason why. If you hadn't come forward and told your truth like you did, he'd be sittin' in a jail cell right this minute, and Sheriff Manny would've been heartbroken to put him there."

"Worse than that," Savannah said, looking terribly serious for her young years, "a cold-blooded murderer would have gotten away with killing Tyrell. Maybe Mr. Corbin, too."

Stella was surprised at her words. For the first time since she had received that mysterious, anonymous call, she realized . . . Savannah was absolutely right.

The killer was still out there.

Chapter 35

When Stella and Manny arrived at the shabby, tiny shack on the edge of town that had been Tyrell's home since his mother had kicked him out of hers, on his eighteenth birthday, they were full of hope that a search of the place would reveal something about how he had died.

But an hour later, they emerged from the dump of a house tired, dusty, and without one bit of evidence or a new clue.

All they had to show for their troubles was the lingering stench of stale cigarette smoke and Tyrell's body odor in their sinuses.

"Glad you came with me?" Manny said as they walked back toward the cruiser, parked on the sidewalk.

"I reckon," she replied halfheartedly. "Ain't my idea of a good time, goin' through somebody else's grubby clothes and dirty dishes. I got plenty of that at home. But it's always nice spendin' time with you."

"Same here. Thank you for your help and for making a nasty, frustrating task a lot nicer."

They were about to get into the cruiser when a lady Stella recognized came running out of the house next door to Tyrell's. She was waving at them, an intent look on her face. Her pink night-gown and chenille robe fluttered around her as she ran, making her look like an enormous, distressed pink bird.

"We got company," Stella told him. "She's the new clerk there at the grocery store. Moved to town a few months ago."

"Yes. I know her. I think she wants to talk to us."

"Sheriff!" the woman shouted. "Mrs. Reid! Hold on!"

When she reached them, she was out of breath, huffing and puffing from the exertion. Stella thought she seemed pretty upset about something.

She didn't have to wonder what it might be. Murder was a big deal in any town, and in a tiny town, news traveled fast.

"Is it true? Is Tyrell really dead?" she asked. "I heard that he's dead. I can't believe it!"

"Yes, ma'am," Manny told her. "I'm afraid it's true. His body was found this morning, down by the river."

"Oh, I hate hearing that." The lady started to cry, and Stella could tell she was truly heartbroken by the news.

"Were you close to him?" Stella asked her.

"I was, yes. My kids grew up and moved away a while back, so I kinda adopted Ty. I brought him supper every night. He was so skinny. I was worried about him starving to death. But I never thought something like this would happen!"

"That was most generous of you to take care of him like that," Manny told her. "I don't think a lot of people felt that kindly toward him. It's good to know someone cared."

"Underneath those drugs and all the problems they caused him, Tyrell was a good boy. The only person he ever really hurt was himself. You can't say that about everybody these days."

No, you sure can't, Stella thought, recalling the terrible wounds on both Dexter and Tyrell. The blood and hair on the tire iron.

"I was afraid something bad had happened to him after I saw him light outta here three nights ago. He usually stops and waves to me when he comes and goes, but he was in such a hurry. Just ran out and got in his car and peeled outta here. I never got the chance to tell him good-bye."

Stella noticed that Manny was listening to her very carefully and had a certain "alert" look on his face. She wondered what he'd heard that had piqued his interest.

"Ma'am," he said, "Deputy Faber told me that he spoke to Tyrell's next-door neighbor about seeing him leave that night. Was that you?"

"He did talk to me. Knocked on my door and asked me if I'd seen Tyrell lately. Nobody lives in that house on the other side of Tyrell's, so I must be the neighbor he told you about."

"Can you tell me what you told him? Exactly what you said, if you remember."

"Sure. I just told him what I told you. That I saw Tyrell run out of his house, get in his car, and take off, quick-like. I was surprised when he didn't wave to me like he usually did. That streetlight there is bright, and I know he must've seen me standing there on the curb, taking my garbage out."

Manny glanced up at the light she was pointing to, then said, "How about the duffel bags?"

"What duffel bags?"

"The ones you said he threw into the car before he left."

"He didn't have no bags. Didn't have anything at all in his hands that I could see."

Manny glanced at Stella, and she could feel her own pulse quicken.

Then he turned back to the woman and said, "Ma'am, this is very important. Are you telling me that you didn't say anything at all about Tyrell loading up his car before he left?"

"I never said anything like that to anybody. Why would I? That's not what happened. He just ran out, got in, and drove away. Simple as that. You must have misunderstood what that good-lookin' young deputy said."

"Yes," Manny agreed with her. "I think I've 'misunderstood' my deputy all along."

"That dirty, rotten son of a gun lied to me," Manny said the moment he and Stella got back into the cruiser. "He told me that bit about the duffel bags to give me the impression that Tyrell was fleeing the area."

"I wondered about that when I saw the half-eaten plate of tuna casserole there in the kitchen," Stella said. "If that sweet lady took Tyrell supper ever' night so's he wouldn't starve, he would've devoured the whole plateful before he went anywhere. Young men like that who don't get enough good cookin', they'll eat anything that ain't tied down. And all of it. He must've had a good reason to leave in a hurry like that."

"I have a feeling he got a call. Or maybe a page. Something sent him hightailing it out of here. Someone."

"Someone, like the only person other than you and Merv who drives a cruiser?"

"The person who was seen in the cemetery that night? The only person other than Merv and me who know where the extra keys to our cruisers are kept?"

Manny reached for his radio and called the station house. "Merv, did you get that phone number for Cindy Corbin yet?" he asked.

"I sure did, sir," was the crisp, happy reply. "I tracked her down. I even spoke to her. She's workin' today at her daddy's feed store, but she said you could call her anytime. She'd be happy to hear from you."

"Good work, Deputy. Ring her up and patch her through for me."

"Will do, sir."

A few moments later, Manny was speaking with Cindy.

"Good afternoon, Mrs. Corbin," he said. "I'm glad to hear you made it back to your family safe and sound. Are you doing all right back there in California?"

"I am, Sheriff. Thanks for asking. It's good to be back home again."

Manny glanced over at Stella and said, "Mrs. Reid sends her regards, too."

"Tell her thank you. She's a nice lady."

"She is that, indeed." Manny's friendly tone became more serious when he said, "We've had some new developments back here on your husband's case, and, Cindy, I need to ask you some very important questions."

There was a short pause, and then she gave a tentative, "Okay."

"But first I want to assure you that you have nothing to worry about from anyone here. Nothing at all. Anyone you might be concerned about, anyone who may have threatened or coerced you in the past, they're no danger to you now. Do you understand what I'm saying to you?"

Another long silence and then, "Yes, Sheriff. I believe I do."

"Okay. First, I want to ask you who left those marks on your neck. Who choked you, Cindy? Was it really Dexter?"

Stella heard Cindy give a little gasp, and then it sounded like she might be softly crying. "No," was the barely audible reply.

"Was it Tyrell?"

"No."

"Who choked you, Cindy?"

"You won't believe me if I tell you."

"You'd be surprised what I'll believe at this point. Tell me."

"That deputy of yours. I think his name is Farber."

"Faber?"

"Yeah. Him. Young, kinda short. He's got a blond mullet."

"Why did he choke you?"

"He'd told me to leave town and never come back or else he'd kill me. I told him I wasn't going anywhere until I saw my husband buried proper. He lost his temper. That's when."

Stella saw Manny take a deep breath and close his eyes for a moment, as though trying to process this difficult information.

Finally, he said, "Do you have any idea why he was insisting that you leave town?"

"I think he was afraid I'd tell you what I know. Well, at least what I *think* happened to Dexter."

"He's not going to hurt you again, Mrs. Corbin. I promise you that. So tell me what you think."

"I figure that somehow that deputy got wind of the fact that Dex had scored a bunch of coke and was selling it to the bigger dealers in the area. I think it was your deputy who paged Dex at four that morning, probably pretended to be somebody else, and got him to go to the cemetery."

"Do you think it was Faber who killed your husband, Cindy?"

"I do. And I think it was him who got in touch with me and that Tyrell guy the next day, using Dex's pager, telling us to meet him at the cemetery."

"Why would he do that?" Manny asked.

"So I'd be out of the house long enough for him to search it. When I got home from the cemetery, our place was ransacked and that suitcase, the one Dex kept locked all the time, it was gone. I never saw it again."

Manny nodded thoughtfully. "That makes sense, Mrs. Corbin. All of it. You have no idea how helpful you've been. Thank you."

"I'm glad, Sheriff. It feels good to help you and not be so scared." They could hear her sniffling and blowing her nose, but she sounded genuinely happy. "If he's the one who killed my husband, I want you to make him pay for it."

"Oh, I'm going to, ma'am, and he'll pay a price for hurting you, too."

He wished her well, signed off, and turned to Stella, a stricken expression on his face. "He did it, Stella. Augustus murdered Dexter, then stole the drugs and cash from his house. He lured Tyrell and Cindy to the cemetery. He did it to get Cindy away from her house so he could steal the suitcase."

"The same with Tyrell," Stella added, "so's he could steal his baseball bat."

"That's right. He told Tyrell to use the orchard gate so he could lift his prints off it later. Then he killed Tyrell and tried to make it look like he'd fled the area."

"That way he could not only blame the murder on Tyrell, but on election day, he could wow the voters by claimin' he'd solved the case."

"Right. But he must've not counted on Tyrell's body washing ashore or anybody finding it. When you did, he had to frame somebody for that, too. Poor Merv was an easy target."

"Not a very good one," Stella said, shaking her head, "since the boy ain't got a bit of guile in him or the sense God gave a cabbage. He couldn't plot the makin' of a peanut butter and jelly sandwich, let alone a murder."

The radio crackled and Merv's voice came through, excited and incredulous. "Sheriff? Come in! Pick up!"

"I'm here, Deputy. What's up?"

"I just got a call from Augustus's sister-in-law, Norma. She said to come over to her house right away. Said it's mighty important. Do you know where she lives?"

"Uh, no."

"I do!" Stella said. "She's on Madison Street, over by the old elementary school."

As Manny pulled the cruiser away from the curb, Stella thought back on the anonymous phone call she had answered at the station house earlier. That deep, raspy voice. The fact that she couldn't tell if it was male or female, but somehow, it had sounded familiar.

A light switched on in her head. "It was her, Manny!"

"Who was what?"

"That anonymous call we got about seeing the cruiser pull up in front of the cemetery at four ten that morning. The voice was too high for a guy, but too deep for a woman. I thought it sounded kinda familiar, but I couldn't place it."

"Norma?" he asked. "Her voice is deeper than most women's."

"Now that I think about it, I'm pretty sure it was her."

"She never did like Augustus and didn't mind who knew it."

"Most folks in town would probably say the same. Let's go!"

Manny flipped on his red and blue flashing lights and stepped on the gas.

Chapter 36

Stella and Manny arrived at the attractive, newly built contemporary home on Madison Street, and when Manny knocked on the frosted-glass door, it opened almost immediately.

Although Norma was dressed and groomed as usual in her trademark bold colors and garish makeup, she looked as though she hadn't slept in days.

Through her life, Stella had seen plenty of people who were in crisis, and at a glance, she knew this woman was in the midst of one.

"Sheriff, Stella, come in," she said, grabbing Manny by the wrist and literally pulling him over the threshold. "Thank you for getting here so quickly."

"Glad to be of service, Norma," he said. "We got the idea that maybe you have a problem."

"*Have* a problem?" she said with a derisive sniff. "We've *had* a huge problem for a long time, but we're finally, *finally*, going to do something about it."

"We . . . ?" Stella asked.

Norma pointed toward the living room and a large sectional sofa. In the middle of it sat Gloria Faber, looking small, fragile, and pitifully vulnerable.

Even from the entryway, twenty feet away, Stella could see the woman trembling. She could tell by her red, badly swollen eyes that she had been crying for a long time.

Probably a lot longer than anybody knows, Stella thought as she walked into the room and sat down next to her.

"Sister Gloria," she said, laying her hand on hers and gently patting it. "We're here now. Ever'thing's gonna be better from here on out. Whatever's wrong, the sheriff's gonna help make it right for you. Okay?"

Gloria nodded ever so slightly.

Well, that's a start, I reckon, Stella told herself.

Manny hurried over to her and started to sit down on the other side of her, but when he saw the woman jump and cringe at his sudden movements, he backed off and sat farther away on a different section of the sofa, well out of reach.

"Mrs. Faber," he said, "we just want to help however we can."

"Please don't call me that!" she said in a voice that trembled but was loud, firm, and insistent. "From now on, nobody's going to call me that name again."

Stella felt a thrill that she was careful to hide. There was nothing quite as soul satisfying as hearing a person who had been living in chains for far too long rip away their hated restraints and toss them to the floor.

"Good for you, sugar!" she said. "I'm proud of you."

"God knows, it took her long enough," Norma said, standing in front of Gloria, her arms crossed over her chest, a disdainful look in her eyes as she stared down at her sister. "She could've done this a long time ago and saved us all a lot of misery."

Manny raised one hand, cop style, and told Norma, "These are matters of the heart, ma'am. No one can set the timetable for another person's heart. Only they know when it's time."

"No," Gloria said. "My sister's right. If I'd come forward before, Dexter and Tyrell would still be alive." She drew a deep breath and shuddered. "Who knows what else he's done?"

"Can you tell us what you believe he's done?" Manny asked.

His voice was gentle, but it was deeper and louder than most, and Stella could feel Gloria's hand tighten around hers when he spoke.

Stella had a feeling it would take a very long time for Gloria to feel safe with men again, and that made her sad.

What a shame, she thought, *with so many truly good, loving men in the world, that victims like her go around scared to death of half the people they meet.*

"We already know some of the bad stuff he's done," Stella told her. "I think you wanna tell us what you know, too. Is that right?"

Gloria nodded. "He hurts people," she began tentatively. "He threatens them to get . . . stuff."

"What kind of stuff?" Stella asked.

"Anything he wants that they've got or can give him. He comes home from work with all sorts of things: drugs, money, expensive cameras, jewelry, VCRs, things like that."

"What does he do with it all?" Manny asked.

"I guess he sells it to somebody. I see it come in, and then, the next day it's gone, and he's got all this extra cash in his wallet."

"That's not all," Norma said. "Tell him about the hookers, Glor."

Gloria blushed bright red. "He . . . he comes home and brags about how he caught some girl somewhere turning a trick, and how he gave her a stern 'talkin'-to' instead of arresting her. But I know he, well, makes bargains with them."

"How do you know that?" Manny asked, his face dark with anger.

294

"I just do."

Norma spoke up. "She's a wife. She does his laundry. Women know these things."

"Okay," he said. "Gotcha. The old 'lipstick on his collar' business."

Norma snorted. "More like on his shorts."

"Oh, sorry."

Stella saw a flush creep up Manny's face and would have found it funny under less serious circumstances.

She leaned closer to Gloria and said, "What does he do to you, sugar?"

"He hits her!" Norma interjected. "He's been hitting her since their honeymoon, and for no good reason!"

"There's never a *reason* for a man to strike a woman," Manny said. "Just lousy *excuses*. What sort of excuses does he give you for what he does?"

"The latest one was the worst." Gloria pulled her hand away from Stella's and placed it over her throat. "He claimed I caused him to lose the election. He said, there by the gazebo, when he had that news conference, I was looking all sad and mad and disapproving, and people saw that and didn't like me, so they wouldn't vote for him."

"You do know that's a pile of steamin' horse manure, don't cha?" Stella said. "That sorry excuse for a husband of yours made a jackass of hisself that day, and that's why he lost. Besides, all those people he's mistreated behind closed doors, they probably couldn't wait to get to the votin' booths to cast their votes for the sheriff here. Your husband's got nobody to blame but hisself."

"Thank you, Sister Stella," Gloria said softly. "That means a lot."

Stella noticed that she still had her hand to her throat, which was covered by a turtleneck.

It occurred to Stella that the day was rather warm to be wearing a turtleneck.

Slowly, carefully, she reached over and slipped her fingertip inside the top of the neckline. "May I?" she asked softly.

Gloria hesitated, then started to cry again. But she nodded.

Stella braced herself for what she might find as she slid her finger farther into the neck of the garment, then pulled it down.

Dark purple lines. Round spots, the size of a fingertip. Bruises like the ones Savannah had spotted on Cindy Corbin.

Stella replaced the cloth, once again concealing the injuries. Then she turned to Manny, who had been watching her intently, and said simply, "The same."

He turned to Norma and asked, "Was it you who made that anonymous call to the station house earlier?"

She nodded.

"You saw someone driving a cruiser and wearing a uniform go into that cemetery at four ten in the morning?"

"It was me," Gloria said. "My sister called for me, because I was afraid to. But I was the one who witnessed it."

"Tell me about it, ma'am. How you happened to be there, exactly what you saw. The whole thing."

Gloria drew a deep breath and settled back into the sofa, obviously steeling herself for what was coming.

In a gesture that Stella thought was, perhaps, out of character for Norma but touching, she hurried to her younger sister and sat down close beside her.

Norma put her arm around Gloria's shoulder and hugged her. "I gotcha, kid," she said. "Just tell them the truth, and then you won't have to carry it around inside you like you've been doing. Let it out."

"Okay." Gloria turned to Manny. "Here's what happened. We had a big argument that night over the fact that he was, well, doing things with those prostitutes. I told him I wouldn't go to bed with him anymore because I'm afraid of catching that awful

AIDS thing that the president told us about. I heard it's here now, too, or it's going to be soon."

Manny nodded. "Yes, it is. Please go on."

"He was so mad. Madder than I'd ever seen him before. He said he'd, you know, have relations with me any time he wanted to, because he was my husband, and it was his right." She started to cry. "Then he . . . proved it."

Manny bit his lower lip, looked down at the floor, and said, "Did he force you, Gloria?"

She nodded. "Yes. He choked me, too. I even passed out. He told me later that he liked that and to expect more of the same in the future."

Stella glanced over and saw that Norma had tears rolling down her face.

Stella had never felt a kinship toward this brash and bombastic woman the way she did at that moment.

"I'm so sorry, ma'am," Manny told her. "He'll pay for that, along with all the other things he's done."

Gloria gave him a quick, grateful nod and continued. "Anyway, we had that fight, and he did what he did. Then he went out to the garage and was doing something out there for a while."

"Do you know what?" Manny asked.

"Yes. I snuck out to the kitchen and caught a peep at him through the door crack. I had a feeling he was fixin' to do something bad to me, so I thought I needed to keep an eye on him."

"What was he doing?"

"The first thing he did was send a page to somebody."

"Do you know who?"

"No. I couldn't see up close. He was on the other side of the garage. I thought it might be one of his 'professional' girlfriends, setting up a so-called date or something. But then he started to rummage around in the front of his cruiser."

"And?"

"He got a buzz on his pager. He looked at it and gave a little laugh. Then he took a pair of his old gardening gloves off a nail on the wall and put them on. Next, he opened the trunk and took out a baseball bat, one I'd never seen before."

"Can you describe it?"

"Just a regular bat, but it had all different colors of tape wrapped around the handle. Anyway, he opened the car door and tossed the bat inside."

"Where inside the car?"

"The front floorboard. Passenger side. He did something else weird. He took off his gloves and threw them inside the car, too. On the passenger seat. Then he got into the car and left."

"What did you do?"

"I followed him in my car."

"You did?" Stella asked. "How'd you get goin' that fast? Fast enough to catch up with him?"

"It was pretty easy. After he pulled out of our driveway, he turned left. That meant he was heading for the highway. So, I jumped in my car. I was just wearing a long T-shirt and my underwear, but, well, I didn't care. I took off in that direction."

She glanced over at Manny and added a bit sheepishly, "I broke a few traffic rules and went over the speed limit, I'm afraid."

"We'll give you a pass, considering," he said. "Please, go on."

"I spotted him up ahead. We were the only two cars on the road at that hour, so it wasn't hard to see his lights up ahead of me. I hung back, so he wouldn't think he was being tailed. Then I saw him turn off the highway and go up the hill toward the cemetery. I was sure he was going there because there's nothing else up that way but peach trees."

"Did you follow him all the way to the cemetery?" Stella asked, surprised that this timid, humble woman would do something so dangerous. Especially after she had just been viciously attacked.

"I did," she said. "I was careful. I went really slow and turned off my lights. The moon was nearly full, so I could see okay without them. I didn't go all the way up. Just far enough to see the entrance and his car. I parked over on the side of the road behind some trees and shrubs."

"That must have been really scary."

"It was, Stella, but so was living my life. I was afraid every day, and what he did to me that night proved I had every reason to be scared. But I sensed he was going to do something bad. Really bad. I thought if I knew what it was, I'd have a good excuse to leave him."

Stella was amazed as she heard the woman describe her thought processes. *I would've figured I had a good excuse to leave the first time he hit me,* she thought. *But like Manny said, hearts follow their own timetables.*

"On the phone, your sister said something about seeing him go into the graveyard." Manny pulled his notepad and pen from his pocket. "Did you actually see that yourself?"

"I did. He got out of his car, put on those garden gloves, got the bat, and went inside. He was in there fifteen minutes."

"Is that the exact time or an estimate?" Manny wanted to know, scribbling in his notebook.

"Exact. I remember looking at the clock on my dash when he went in. It was four ten. Then again when he came back out at four twenty-five. It seemed important. Maybe I've been a cop's wife too long."

Manny scribbled in his notebook and muttered, "You've certainly been *that* cop's wife too long." Looking up from his writing, he said, "So, he came out of the cemetery and then what?"

"He unlocked the trunk and put the bat and gloves in there. Then he got back in his cruiser and drove away. When he passed me there on the road, I prayed he wouldn't notice me parked over there in the bushes. He didn't, and thank goodness he didn't. If he had, he probably would've killed me, too."

"You had a close call, Gloria," Manny said. "No doubt about it."

Norma hugged her sister a bit tighter as they all contemplated how differently Gloria's story might have ended.

Finally, Stella said, "Did you have any idea what he'd done in that graveyard?"

"No. I followed him because I thought he was meeting some woman. But the baseball bat and the gloves? Who takes those on a so-called date with a hooker?"

"You must have been surprised," Manny said, "when you heard Dexter Corbin had been killed there in the cemetery that night."

"Oh, I was horrified," she said. "Augustus told me himself. He said, all cocky-like, 'They found that Corbin guy in the graveyard with his brains beat out. Serves him right. He never was worth a plug nickel.' I figured it out right away, and I've been scared to death ever since."

"After Augustus left the cemetery, what happened then?" Manny asked. "Did you follow him?"

"No. I was behind him, far behind, until he turned toward town. I went the opposite way and headed back to our house. I didn't want him to get home before I did. Then he might realize I'd followed him and kill me for sure."

"Good thinking." Manny folded his notebook closed and stuck his pen back in his pocket. "Gloria, we believe there was a large black suitcase filled with cocaine and cash floating around at one time. Dexter Corbin had it, then it disappeared. I believe Augustus may have it now. If he does, can you think where he might be hiding it?"

"Does that black suitcase have white trim on it?" Gloria asked.

Stella's heart skipped a beat. "It sure does," she said. "You've seen it?"

"I did. I don't remember what day, but Augustus brought one home with him. Said he'd seen it on the side of the street. Someone had put it out for the garbage fellows to pick up. He thought he'd use it for something or other downstairs in our basement. He's got a lot of hobbies and spends most of his spare time down there."

Manny locked eyes with Stella, then said what she was thinking: "I need to spend some time there myself. Gloria, to the best of your knowledge, where is Augustus right now?"

"He left a little while ago, said he was going fishing."

"How long is he usually gone when he's fishing?"

"Hours."

"Good. While he's away, would you grant me permission to search your basement?"

"Sure," she said. "I'm going to help you put an end to all of this. He can't keep hurting people. And worse. He has to be stopped."

Manny jumped to his feet. He said to Norma, "Is there someplace out of town that you can take your sister? Somewhere that Augustus would never think to look?"

"Sure. I have an old boyfriend who's got a vacation cabin in Cedar Hollow. I'm sure he'd let us stay there as long as we want, and Augustus has never heard of him."

"But I need to go home," Gloria said, "to get my toothbrush and some clothes."

"I've got a new toothbrush in the medicine cabinet, and you can borrow some of my clothes."

Stella snickered when she saw the horrified look that Gloria gave her sister.

She felt a bit more optimistic about the battered woman's future. Yes, her past few years had been dark and painful, her body injured, her self-esteem trampled. But if she still cared that much about her personal appearance, Stella believed she would eventually find all the lost pieces of herself, put them back together again, and be all the stronger for it.

Chapter 37

When Manny and Stella got back into the cruiser, Stella was shaking with excitement and Manny had the look of a hungry eagle about to snatch a big, juicy salmon from midstream.

"We have to find that suitcase," Manny said as he stuck the house keys Gloria had given him into his shirt pocket and started the engine. That's the piece of evidence we need to nail him. I just hope he didn't get smart and pitch it into the river along with Tyrell."

He grabbed the radio and called the station. Merv answered right away. "Okay, Deputy, listen to me carefully and do exactly as I say."

"Ten-four, Sheriff."

"Close up shop there, nice and tight, then meet me at Augustus's house. Bring Valentine, too."

"Augustus's place? I don't wanna see that guy! He tried to frame me for murder."

"Do as I say, Merv, and do it right now! He won't be there. We're going to search his residence. Now, repeat back to me what I just said to you."

"Close shop, Valentine, Gus's."

"Yes, and do *not* tell *anybody* where you're going. Got that?"

"Close shop, Valentine's, Gus's, don't tell!"

"That's it. Make tracks."

Manny replaced the microphone and pulled out of the driveway. Once they were on their way, Stella said, "Do you really think he's gonna remember all that?"

"Probably not. Merv does well to remember three things at a time. That was four. He's definitely out of his depth."

"Which one do you figure he'll forget?"

"I don't know. But if he shows up without Valentine, I'm gonna make him get down on his hands and knees and sniff all over the basement until he finds that suitcase."

Stella and Manny had already been at the Faber residence for nearly twenty minutes before Merv made his appearance with a happy, bouncy Valentine on the end of a leash.

"Sorry," he said when he found them in the basement, searching through the many cupboards, boxes, and cabinets that nearly filled the area that was as large as the entire house above. "I was almost here, and then I remembered that I forgot Valentine and had to go back for him."

Manny was kneeling beside a stack of boxes that were shoved against the wall, but he rose, gave Stella an "I told you so" look, then held out his hands to Valentine.

"Come here, boy," he said, and the dog instantly bounded toward him, tongue lolling, practically dancing for joy as he ran. He acted like he hadn't seen his master in years.

Manny took the leash from Merv and said, "Deputy, I'd like you to go to the bathroom upstairs and get me a small, clean towel from the linen closet."

Merv looked terribly confused. "But, sir, where's the linen closet?"

"Never mind. I'll fetch it," Stella said, as she ran up the steep wooden staircase.

As she neared the top, she heard Merv say, "How come she knows where Augustus's linen closet is? What's a linen closet?"

Predictably, Stella found the closet in question in the hallway, next to the bathroom. She quickly grabbed the smallest towel she could find and raced back downstairs with it.

She found Manny kneeling next to Valentine, stroking the dog's ears, and telling him what a good boy he was. When he saw her, he said, "Discreetly hand it to me. Don't let him see it."

He stood, put one hand behind him, and she made a quick transfer without the "K-9 for a day" being any the wiser.

Manny leaned over, put his head close to the dog's, and said in a highly animated voice, "Valentine! Seek!"

Instantly, the animal's demeanor changed. Instead of a goofy pup, he was a professional on a mission. He began to run around the room, sniffing everything he passed, stopping, smelling certain areas again and again, then moving on.

They watched breathlessly as he explored.

Let him find it, Stella prayed silently. *Please, please help him.*

The dog barked, so loudly that the sound filled the large room and bounced off the cement walls. Then he began to paw at the bottom edge of a filing cabinet.

"You got it, boy?" Manny asked, hurrying over to him. "Is it under there?"

Manny attempted to shift the cabinet by himself and managed to move it a couple of inches.

"Here, let me help you there," Stella said.

"It's very heavy, darlin'," he replied. Then to Merv he said, "If you can lift those barbells that were in your trunk, maybe you could lend me a hand over here."

Merv seemed to snap out of his trance. He scurried over to

Manny and huffed and puffed as the two of them scooted the metal cabinet aside a few inches.

That was when Stella saw it. Manny too.

"It's the suitcase," they exclaimed in unison.

"Really? Wow!" Merv said, staring down into a hole in the floor and seeing the black case and its white trim crammed inside.

The dog howled and pawed at the case, tail wagging furiously.

"I know, boy," Manny told him. "You'll get your treat in a second. I promise. Hang on."

Once the cabinet had been moved far enough, the men were able to tug the suitcase free.

Manny had it open in a heartbeat.

Inside were five large bags of a white powdery substance and more cash than Stella had seen in her life.

"Look at this, Stella," Manny said, pointing at something else inside. "Two pagers. How much do you wanna bet one of them was Dexter's and the other Tyrell's?"

"That's good, isn't it?" she said. "That's enough to nail him, huh?"

"It sure is."

Closing the suitcase lid, Manny held the towel out to Valentine, who instantly sank his long fangs into it and began to shake his head vigorously, initiating a spirited game of tug-of-war with his master/trainer.

"That's his reward?" Stella asked, laughing.

"The only one he ever wants. Other than a bit of bacon for breakfast and some steak trimmings for dinner," Manny replied.

Watching the dog's antics and seeing the suitcase with its incriminating evidence inside, Stella could feel a swell of relief and joy rising inside her. They had him! The nightmare was finally over.

Then she felt something else. Something that felt like a boa constrictor suddenly wrapping itself around her throat. She tried to scream, but she could barely even breathe, as yet another twisted around her waist and pulled her backward against something . . . someone!

She realized they were lifting her off her feet, dragging her backward.

She smelled something terrible, a combination of familiar but foul scents. Fish. Sweat. Fear.

A few seconds later, a more sane, less terrified part of her brain realized she was being held by two arms. One around her neck. The other around her waist.

She also realized if she didn't do something fast she was going to slip into unconsciousness. Or worse.

She turned her head and shoved her chin into the crook of the elbow, finding a space to breathe.

Her head cleared a bit, and she could see Manny staring at her, rage and horror on his face.

She heard Merv swear. Valentine growled.

She heard the man behind her, the one who was holding her so tightly against him that she believed her ribs were breaking.

"I'll kill her!" he shouted, his voice exploding in her left ear. She recognized it instantly.

Augustus.

"I'll kill her!" he yelled again. "I'll do it right here in front of you if you don't give me that suitcase right now!"

Kill her? she thought. *Kill me? He's threatening to kill me? Now?*

None of it made any sense to her until she saw the glint of the knife blade he was holding in his right hand, only inches from her jugular. A terribly sharp knife. A fish-fileting knife.

Then she fully realized her situation and her knees buckled beneath her.

For half a second, she thought she might fall out of his arms, but he was stronger than she had imagined and grabbed her all the tighter.

"No!" he shouted in her ear, spraying his spittle on the side of her face. "You stand! Damn you! Stand!"

"Stop!" Manny took a quick step toward them, reaching for his gun.

"No!" Augustus put the blade against her skin beneath her left ear. "You draw your weapon, I'll slit her throat. I will."

Stella knew he meant it. She could hear it in his voice.

Manny must have known it, too, because he held up both hands, palms out.

"No," he said, his voice suddenly calm. "No, Augustus, that's not going to happen. I'm not going to pull my weapon, and you aren't going to cut her."

"I will if you don't—"

"No. You won't." Manny pointed at Stella, and his face took on a scary look. Rage. Contained. But barely.

"That woman," Manny said, "she's *my* woman, Augustus. *Mine.* If you hurt my woman, I will draw my weapon, and I will put a bullet through your head, here and now. I will. You will die *today*! I swear it!"

Manny waited a moment for that to sink in. Stella felt Augustus behind her, his breath ragged, his muscles tightening, his arms squeezing harder and harder.

Once again, she could feel herself sliding toward unconsciousness.

"Drop the knife," she heard Manny saying, as though from far away, as a blackness, thick and suffocating, began to close in on her.

"She has eight grandchildren to raise. Come on, you're not a heartless bastard. Drop the knife now, Augustus. Drop the knife. Live another day."

Miraculously, she felt the arm around her waist loosen a bit.

Then the one around her neck.

It was only a slight difference, but she could breathe again. The darkness began to slide away from the edges of her vision.

She saw Manny. Much closer than he had been.

He was looking past her, at the man behind her. Staring. His pupils were huge, black.

"You have nothing to gain by hurting her," he was saying, his voice tight but still calm. "Let her go. Augustus, just let . . . her . . . go."

He did.

Suddenly, Stella felt herself released. Shoved hard. Weightless. Flying. Crashing into boxes, cabinets, the floor.

She looked up and saw images flashing. One after the other, so quickly she couldn't process them.

Merv, his mouth open, frozen.

Augustus. His hand. The knife.

Manny moving toward him.

"No!" she screamed. "No, no, no!"

Merv whimpered.

Something roared. She saw an enormous, dark shape burst through the narrow space between the two men, separating them. A growling mass of black and brown fur. Snarling. Glistening fangs.

An instant later, she saw Manny's fist crash into Augustus's left jaw, and she heard a distinct cracking sound, as well as a loud moan from Augustus.

The next moment, Stella realized Augustus was lying on the floor near her. She tried to roll away from him, then realized he wasn't holding the knife anymore.

His right wrist was in Valentine's mouth, and the dog was biting, growling, shaking Augustus with a fury that was frightening to watch.

Manny kicked the knife across the floor to Merv, who gathered his wits enough to stoop down and retrieve it.

Then Manny reached down and grabbed the dog's collar. "Leave it!" he told him. But either Valentine didn't hear him above his own growling, or he wasn't ready to release his captive just yet.

Manny pulled harder and shouted, "Val! Leave it! Leave it, boy! That's enough!"

The dog seemed to come to his senses, suddenly aware of the large man tugging on him. He released Augustus but sat back on his haunches and continued to glare down at him, as though daring him to move.

Manny bent down, and with one smooth, not-so-gentle move, he flipped Augustus onto his belly, then yanked his arms behind his back and cuffed him.

Then he hurried over to Stella. He grabbed her and pulled her closer to a table light where he could examine her.

His eyes were frantic, his hands trembling when he ran them over her throat, checking for wounds.

"I'm okay, Manny," she told him, wanting that terrible, frightened, heartbroken look to leave his face. "Really, darlin'. Don't fret. I'm okay."

He turned to Merv and said, "Get upstairs and call an ambulance."

She noticed he was rubbing his right hand with his left, and she remembered that cracking sound when he had slugged Augustus.

"You didn't break your hand, didja, darlin'?" she asked.

"I'm not sure. I heard and felt something break, but I think it was his jaw."

He pointed to the quivering, bleeding mess that was Augustus Faber on the cement floor.

They both watched him for a few moments. Then Stella said, "You should've let Valentine chew on 'im a little longer before you pulled 'im off. Just think, a few more bites, and you wouldn't've had to feed that pooch supper tonight."

Manny looked down at his dog, who had walked over to sit at his feet, staring up at him with adoration in his big brown eyes. "Oh, this boy gets a steak of his own tonight. A big, juicy one."

He looked down at his woebegone prisoner. "I wish I could've waited a while longer before calling a halt to it. But how would that look? A guy who's been in my custody walking into court with a broken jaw, missing an arm?"

She shrugged. "Once the judge and jury heard what that mangy polecat's been up to, I doubt they'd hold it against ya."

Chapter 38

Stella sat at her kitchen table and looked around at the precious faces she had missed so badly. She had been away from them for only seventy-two hours, but it had felt like months since she'd seen them, heard their sweet voices, held them close.

She looked down at tiny Macon Jr. in her arms and touched his soft infant skin. He was gazing up at her with what, she was sure, had to be pure baby love.

The kids had been beautifully cared for by Elsie, who was back at her own home, taking it easy, recuperating, after being thanked copiously over and over again by the Reid clan. But Stella could tell that even with all of Elsie's loving care, her great cooking, and all their adventures on the Patterson estate, they were happy to be back in their humble house. Happy to be back with her.

It was a thought that gave her more joy than anything on earth. Even the satisfaction of helping Manny capture a killer.

"I've been thinkin'," she said, having decided to share her new resolution with them.

"Oh yeah? With what?" Marietta asked, batting her eyelashes.

"Ha ha. Ain't you the smarty-pants," Stella responded with more good-natured tolerance than she would have demonstrated before her break from them. "I've been thinkin' that I'm fixin' to start somethin' new around here. I intend to plan special little outings with each one of you. We're gonna talk about it ahead of time, and we'll choose someplace special we'd like to go together. Or maybe there's somethin' nice we'd both like to do here at home. Just you and me."

"Can we play with my kitten?" Alma said. "Make a little yarn ball for her and show her how to have fun with it?"

"Absolutely, Miss Alma. I'd love to do that, and that ain't all. I was thinkin' these past few days, and I decided you can keep her. One little kitty ain't gonna make all that bigga difference in my grocery bill."

"Oh, thank you, Granny! Thank you!"

"You're welcome, puddin'. Now what would the rest of you like to do on your special day?"

"Could we go pick some blackberries together?" Cordele asked.

"I wanna play with paper dolls with you."

"Can we dress up like we're princesses and drink tea and talk all proper?"

The requests continued to pour in until Marietta said, "I want you to take me to Atlanta and buy me a whole bunch of fancy new clothes like Cyndi Lauper's."

Stella gave her a look and said, "How about we sit on the front porch swing and look through some JCPenney catalogues and talk about what we'd buy if we had a million zillion dollars to spend?"

Marietta considered the compromise carefully, then nodded. "Okay. That ain't near as good, but it'd be all right, too. I guess."

Stella saw Savannah sitting quietly at the other end of the table, a gentle smile on her face. But her eyes suggested a trace of lingering sadness. Assuming it was because of their previous, ruined time together, Stella said softly, "You and me, Savannah girl, we could take another trip out to Sheriff Manny's cabin and go for a walk along the river. A quiet walk. No big talks. Just for the fun of bein' together."

The sadness disappeared in an instant, and the girl's eyes twinkled with anticipation. "I'd *love* that, Gran. But let's take a path in the opposite direction. If we find another body, we'll just keep walking and pretend it isn't even there."

"You got it, darlin'. I'll be lookin' forward to that myself."

Waycross held up his hand. When Stella nodded and told him to speak his piece, he said, "I'd like for me and you to go back to the cemetery again. I need a fun time there to get that last time and Mr. Horton's hollerin' outta my head."

"Me too, grandson. Me too. We'll go first thing tomorrow morning."

As Stella and Waycross entered the cemetery, she looked down at the happy, peaceful look on his face and was glad she had adopted this new one-on-one policy for each child. What she hadn't realized was that it would provide a much-needed break for her, too.

Savannah was sitting in the truck with baby Macon, having offered to do so. It was a cool, pleasant day, with a taste of the autumn to come in the air. They would be fine for a while.

The other children had been dropped at the library for Miss Rose's reading hour. Stella had called Rose ahead of time to make sure that a gang of five wasn't too much for the small library or the elderly librarian. Stella had been assured that it was a "more the merrier" situation, and Rose was positively tickled that she would be guaranteed an audience that large, even if no one else showed up.

Stella's "special Granny time" with Waycross might be short, but it would be meaningful for both of them.

The simple, well-trodden path through the cemetery entrance was a journey in healing for both of them.

As they passed Michael the Archangel, they took turns placing a kiss on his big toe.

"Does that really work, Granny?" he asked. "Does it give you good luck, messin' with his toe like that and him just bein' a statue?"

"I think it works if you believe it does."

"Then it's the believin' that works, not the toe-kissin' business?"

"I think if you believed it would bring you luck to kiss your own big toe, that would work, too."

"But what if—"

"Waycross Reid, maybe we could listen to the birds and enjoy the sunshine on our faces and stop wonderin' about ever'thing just for a little while."

"Yeah. We could do that."

He slipped his warm, little-boy hand into hers as they walked quietly toward Arthur Reid's grave. When they arrived, she handed him one of the two bouquets they had picked from her flower garden before they had left the house.

He had chosen the ones for his grandfather's grave. Blue bachelor buttons and snapdragons, because he had proclaimed them the least "sissy-fied" of the other flowers there.

She had chosen roses and carnations for her mother.

"You wanna talk to him by yourself for a little while," she asked him, "in case there's some manly-man stuff you wanna discuss?"

"Yeah. I do. I definitely do."

"Okay. Sounds important. I'll be back in a bit."

She walked away and took the longer path to her mother's resting place, a walkway that wouldn't lead her near the Pattersons' crypt. She had already decided it would be a long time before she would venture that way again.

She walked up to the simple stone, engraved only with her mother's name, birthday, and death date. Her years had been too few and too hard.

She had deserved better.

"I hope that where you are now, you're gettin' the better things you deserved, Momma," she said. "I'm sure you are."

She sat down on the grave and laid her palm on the soft grass. "I'm doin' fine, by the way. I've been keepin' company with Sheriff Manny Gilford. He's the man I told you about, the one who caught your killer. Well, I helped him catch another one yesterday. It felt good. Justice feels good. Ask anybody who's had somethin' awful happen to 'em and didn't get any. But you got a bit, and now some other people got a little, so I'm glad about that."

She sat quietly wishing that she, like her grandson, could feel a closer connection to those lying beneath the grass. What would her mother say to her, she wondered, if only she had the childlike faith to believe, like Waycross?

"I guess I'll never know for sure," she said, as she got up from the grass and brushed off her skirt. "But if you can hear me, I love you, Momma, and I miss you. I'll see you again someday."

She left, and since she could tell that Waycross was still chatting away to his grandfather, she wandered among the gravestones, reading the inscriptions, seeing how many had passed at early ages.

Life is short, Stella May, she told herself. *Short and unpredictable. Don't waste a minute of such a precious gift.*

Finally, she saw Waycross rise and motion for her. She walked back to him and saw that he had a large, sly grin on his face. She wondered what mischief the kid could have gotten into just sitting on the grass talking to a gravestone.

"What's goin' on, kiddo?" she asked.

"We had a good talk, me and Grandpa Art."

"Oh you did, huh? Can you tell me what it was about, or is that some kinda guy secret?"

"No. It's no secret. In fact, he told me to tell you."

"Okey dokey. Lay it on me. What did he want you to tell me?"

"He said to tell you that Manny Gilford's gonna ask you to marry him."

"What?" Stella choked on her own spit. After her coughing fit, she said, "Are you being a Mr. Goofball?"

"No! Not a bit. He told me to tell you that the sheriff's gonna propose to you, and that you have his blessing. He said Sheriff Manny's a good man, and he'll take good care of you and us kids. He says you've been alone too long already."

Stella's knees went weak, and she sat down abruptly on the grass. On her dead husband's grave. She was shaking when she said, "Waycross, please. I know you love Sheriff Manny, and you'd like to see us together, but you wouldn't make up a thing like this, would you?"

To her surprise, he laughed. "Grandpa told me you'd say that, too. He said, just believe a bit more. Rub your big toe or somethin'. Whatever you gotta do but go for it. He said, 'Be happy, Stella, my sparkle star.'"

She couldn't hold the tears back any longer. The sweet pet name her husband, and *only* her husband, had called her during their most private moments . . . to hear it once again and under these circumstances, it was too much to be borne dry-eyed.

"Are you okay, Granny?" Waycross asked, crawling into her lap and throwing his arms around her neck. "I didn't mean to make you cry!"

"Don't worry, darlin'," she managed to say as she held him close. "It's happy cryin'. It's good for ya. Cleans out the soul."

After a few minutes, she was able to get control of herself. She took tissues from her pocket, wiped her eyes, and blew her nose.

As they stood to leave, he looked up at her, blue eyes shining, freckles glowing. He smiled his sweet, snaggle-toothed grin. "Then I reckon, right now, you must be sportin' the cleanest soul in town."

Chapter 39

"I hear this spending some special time with each kid business is working out nicely for you and the children," Manny said as he drove Stella through town, heading for the highway.

"Where did you hear that?" she asked. "Somebody's been spreadin' rumors behind my back."

He laughed, reached over, and took her hand. "Savannah dropped by the station house yesterday when you sent her to the drugstore. She wanted to know what was going on with Augustus."

"What *is* goin' on with that boy?"

"He's hating life at the moment. The DA is charging him with everything from drug dealing to trying to frame Tyrell and Merv, the two murders, assaulting Cindy Corbin, and, of course, choking and sexually assaulting his wife, not to mention his attack on you."

"Did he come clean and confess?"

"He's confessed everything, hoping his lawyer can cut some kind of deal, and he'll eventually get out of prison."

"I hope he don't."

"He won't. Don't worry. Cops don't go on trial that often, but when they do and they're found guilty, they pay for disgracing the badge, the way he did. He'll serve some rough time, too, right alongside some mean fellas he put behind bars. I wouldn't want to be him, I assure you."

"I cain't wait to testify at his trial."

"Me too. You wear an evening gown, and I'll rent a tuxedo for the occasion."

She burst into giggles. "Won't that courtroom be impressed with us! I want one of them strapless dresses with the big fishtail skirt, all bushy around the bottom."

"I'd love to see you in that."

"I wouldn't mind seein' you in a tux. You'd look like Mr. Tom Selleck in one of them James Bond movies."

He looked confused. "Selleck never played Bond."

"Well, he should've."

They traveled on in silence for a little while, and she began to reflect back on the events in the Fabers' basement. Some aspects of what happened would haunt her for the rest of her life. But other memories remained and warmed her heart when she played them over again in her mind.

"I don't think I told you yet how grateful I am to you for savin' my life," she said, squeezing his fingers.

"Oh, Stella, you don't have to thank me. Besides, Valentine was the hero of that little escapade. Without him, I'm afraid we might both be dead."

"Maybe. He is a hero and a half. But he ain't the one who kept his cool and talked that miserable Augustus into lettin' me go. You walked right up to that man, with him holdin' that sharp knife, knowin' he could stab you way faster than you'd be able to get to your gun. You put your own life in danger to save mine."

"I'm just so grateful it worked out okay. I couldn't stand to lose you. Certainly not like that."

They exchanged a look that said a lot about how traumatic the event had been for both of them. But in spite of that, the experience had been positive in a few aspects.

"So, I'm *your* woman?" she said. "As in, 'If you hurt *my* woman . . .'"

He winced, then grinned. "Sorry. That was a bit presumptuous, I'll admit. Heat of the moment and all that."

"No apology necessary. I liked it."

She heard him catch his breath, and then he said tentatively, "You did?"

"Yeah. I did. A lot."

He chuckled. "Good. I'm very glad to hear that."

She noticed that he had gone past the turnoff that would have taken them to the river and his cabin. He hadn't said where they were going, only that he had something to show her. Whatever it was, she was looking forward to seeing it. Mostly because the thought of sharing it with her seemed to make him very happy.

"I was surprised when Elsie called this morning and insisted on watchin' all them kids again," she said. "I'd have thought she'd got her canful of them from last time."

He just grinned and nodded.

"Then you called," she continued, "askin' if you could have a 'special time' with Granny yourself. Today ain't gone the way I figured it would when I went to bed last night. Not at all."

He lifted her hand to his lips, gave it a quick kiss, and said, "Sometimes a day brings troubles, sometimes blessings. We have to enjoy the good times while we can, Stella May."

"We do. We do at that."

Looking out her window, she saw the gates of the Patterson estate ahead. "Are we going to Elsie's?" she asked. "Are you and her in cahoots about this day we're havin' together?"

"We aren't going to the Pattersons' place," he said. "But we're not far away from our destination now. ETA, one minute."

"Okay, now I'm gettin' mighty curious, 'cause I noticed you

said we aren't goin' to Elsie's house, but you didn't answer the 'in cahoots' part of my question."

"Oh, look. Here we are," he said, as he slowed the cruiser and pulled off the highway onto a driveway lined with maple trees on each side. Beyond the trees, lush grassland extended for acres, all the way to the dark pine woods in the distance.

As they traveled farther onto the property, the road began to rise.

"What is this place?" Stella asked. "I don't believe I've been here before."

"I hadn't either until just the other day. I like it. I think you will, too."

The road curved sharply to the left, and once they had made the turn, Stella saw, perched on the top of the hill, a beautiful brick home with white shutters, a steeply pitched roof with dormers, and a massive, herringbone brick chimney with a gleaming copper cap.

A magnificent magnolia tree dominated the front yard, and brick-edged flower beds overflowed with blooms that even the green-thumbed Stella didn't recognize.

"This is gorgeous!" she said, gaping at the house, which seemed to stretch on and on and on.

"I'm glad you like it," he said as he parked the cruiser. "Let's get out and look around."

As he opened her door and gave her a hand stepping out, it occurred to her where she was. "I know! This is the Weston place! I've heard it was big and beautiful, but I never had a chance to come up here and see for myself."

Walking toward the house, she turned for a moment and saw the sweeping view below. From where she stood, she could see little McGill, all of it, from the tiny downtown area to the children's school, the residential areas, the cemetery, and the next property over, which was the Patterson estate.

"Wow," she said. "Can you imagine havin' a cup of coffee out here in the mornin' and lookin' at this view? These folks must feel like they're on top of the world."

She looked up at the many windows, all no doubt with their own wonderful vistas. "Are we gonna get in trouble comin' here, Manny? They probably don't like trespassers and gawkers."

"I got permission," he said, slipping his hand into his pocket, then pulling out some keys and jingling them in front of her.

"What? We're going inside?"

"We sure are. If you think the outside's nice, wait till you see the interior."

They passed through the broad entryway, with its sunlit atrium filled with tropical plants, Stella marveling at the idea of having a garden right inside one's home.

The living room astonished her. "This is bigger than the Pattersons' parlor!" she said. "You could turn a semitruck around in here! Just look at that fireplace goin' all the way up to the ceiling, and them big windows and the view, and all this fine leather furniture, and these wood floors. Boy, do they ever sparkle."

He draped his arm over her shoulders and said, "I want to show you something else I think you'll like even more."

He led her to the massive kitchen, with its granite countertops and black and white checkered floor tiles. The walls were a cheerful red, and through the large window over the sink, Stella could see the backyard and a lovely natural pond with cattails and water lilies.

"Oh my goodness," she said. "This kitchen is bigger than my whole house. And that back there looks more like a park than somebody's yard!"

"They tell me it has fish in it," he said, "and there's a barn out there big enough for a pony. Several, in fact."

"Can you believe that some people actually live this way, Manny?"

"No one's living here right now, darlin'," he said softly. "This house and the property are for sale."

"Well, a body'd have to be a Rockefeller or Mr. J. P. Morgan to afford it, and we ain't got a lot of them guys runnin' around McGill."

"Actually, it's not as expensive as you might think. It's not close enough to a city for business folks to commute. McGill's a fine little town, but it's not one people are flocking to right now. Plus, it's been on the market a long time. The bank that owns it really wants to sell it."

He pointed to an empty place on the wall between the kitchen and the breakfast nook. "I think that blank spot over there is calling for something, but I'm not sure what."

She studied him carefully. "Well, *I'm* not sure what you're talkin' about, boy."

"I think," he said, "the one thing this kitchen really needs is a cat clock. Right there in that bare spot."

She looked at him, trying to grasp the point he was making.

"I don't understand, Manny," she finally said, afraid to think anything at all.

"I love this place, Stella," he said. "I know it's grand and so much more than what either of us live in right now, but there's something about it that feels like *home* to me. I want to buy it."

"Buy it?" She looked around at the grandeur, the likes of which she had never seen before. "But how? You'd have to be a millionaire to afford this."

"I'm not a millionaire. But I've worked hard for a long time, and I've lived very simply. I've squirreled away money and made some good investments, and I don't mean to brag, but I'm sitting pretty, financially speaking. Since they've dropped the price considerably and are eager to sell, I can definitely afford it."

She tried to get her mind around the idea of this man, her Manny, living like a king up here on this hill.

Heaven knows, he deserves it, she told herself, *but—*

"But you'll be lost, rattlin' around up here all by yourself in this big ol' house, Manny Gilford."

He nodded and said, "That's why I say the place needs a cat clock in the kitchen. There are five bedrooms and two and a half baths. There's an office that could be converted into another bedroom, and an area downstairs that's just a big playroom now. It could be broken up into three more."

Stella's stunned mind couldn't take it in. Even if she could, she didn't dare. He couldn't possibly mean . . .

"All I need," he was saying, his heart in his eyes as he searched her face, "is a wife and about eight kids to fill it up. And the clock. I've gotta have a cat clock!"

"Manny, you don't know what you're sayin'. Me and them young'uns, we're a handful."

"I've got big hands."

"Those kids would eat you out of house and home."

"Stella May, for years I've wanted to help you, give you money to feed and clothe them. I've hated watching you struggle when it would have been so easy for me to lend a hand. But I know you'd never take money from a man who isn't your husband."

She stared at him, not allowing herself to believe what was happening. This house? A proposal? It was all too much. She felt like something deep inside her was about to burst into song.

But she didn't dare think it.

"Manny," she said, "I know you're too good a man to tease me, so I know you aren't. But I don't know for sure what's going on here."

"Shoot," he muttered. "I know I should've gone ahead and got the ring, but I thought you'd like to pick it out yourself."

He grabbed her hand. "Come with me."

He pulled her out the back door, across the patio, and toward the pond.

When they got to the edge of what looked like an illustration from the old fairy tale book that Stella read to the children at night, Manny turned her to face him and took both of her hands in his.

"Stella, honey," he said, "I know you're afraid. So am I. We've both loved and lost before under terrible circumstances. Hearts never completely heal from something like that."

He reached up and laid his palm against her cheek.

"We've been saying for years that we can't get together because you and Lucy were close, and Art and I were best friends. We've said you're too busy being a grandma and me a cop. But those were lies. Who are we kidding? You're fine with me being a sheriff. You love what I do. You even help me with it."

She thought back over the recent events. She wouldn't have missed a minute of it for anything. Not even what happened in the Faber basement.

"That's true," she said. "If I didn't have them kids to raise, I'd be after you to make me your deputy."

"I'd hire you in a heartbeat."

"But the children . . ." she began.

"Think about it, Stella," he said. "Do you really think those kids wouldn't be happier living up here, with their own bedrooms, room to romp around and play, swim in the pond, ride a pony, have a bit of privacy when they want it?"

She looked around her and imagined her grandangels running through the grass, Waycross throwing a fishing line into the water, Alma playing with her kitten on the lawn, and Valentine galloping across the grass. She saw Savannah reading a book in the shade of one of the maple trees.

It was too beautiful to imagine, but she *was* imagining it, and it seemed like heaven. It seemed right.

"They love me, those kids," he was saying. "I love them. I can help Waycross, fill in the blanks for him, give him some male company among all you gals, poor kid. I can keep guys like Tommy Stafford away from Savannah. Or at least give it my best shot. I can buy Marietta a new dress once in a while and pay for the vet bills when Alma brings home something that's been through the mill and needs doctoring."

Stella couldn't recall a time in her life when she was speechless. But now, when she needed to find the right words in the worst way, her mind was a complete blank.

"I know I'm messing this up," he said. "It looks like I'm bribing you with a big house and offers to help out with the kids, but that's just the practical end of it."

He cleared his throat, then said, "Okay, here's the romantic stuff. Stella, I love you with all my heart. I've loved you since third grade, when you helped me get an A on that test."

"I did?"

"Yeah, I copied your paper. Never mind. Moving on . . . I intended to ask you to marry me the day after I got back from college, but Art had just asked you, so, well, you know the rest. Anyway, I went by the cemetery the other day and told him I was going to ask you. I promised him that if you said yes, I'd take good care of you and his grandkids for the rest of my life."

"Oh my," she said, thinking of what Waycross had told her. "Did he say anything to you?"

"Not like he talks to Waycross. But I left the place with a strong sense of peace, like I had his blessing."

She smiled. "You did. Ask Waycross next time you see 'im."

"Huh?"

"I'll tell ya later. Go on."

He dropped to one knee in front of her, took her hand, and said, "Stella May Reid, I would be most honored if you would become my wife."

She fell to her knees and threw her arms around his neck. "Do you promise that you won't die before me, 'cause you're right, it's not about the grandkids or your long hours. I've been afraid, Manny. I've had a lot of losses, and I couldn't bear to lose two husbands in one lifetime. Especially if one of 'em was *you*. Promise me you won't die before me."

"I can't, darlin'. You know that." He kissed her cheek, slowly, tenderly. Then the other. "How about if I promise you that I'll try really hard not to, and we'll make the most out of every day we *do* have together for the rest of our lives, however long they might be?"

She thought about it a moment, then nodded. "Okay. Close enough."

"Yes?"

"Yes." She looked into his eyes, then at his mouth, so close to hers. She thought of how blissful it had been to lie in his arms in the cabin, and what it would be like to lie with him as his wife.

"We'll make the most of every day," she said, then added with a twinkle in her eye, "and every night."

He laughed, loud and long, then growled and, in one quick move, had her on her back, pinned to the soft grass.

"Okay, okay! I surrender, Sheriff," she said between kisses, sweet and tender at first, but then so fierce and passionate that she could hardly catch her breath. "I give up," she gasped. "You got me."

"This is a life sentence, you know," he told her, pulling her even closer.

She snuggled against him, loving him and the feel, the sound, the taste, and scent of him.

Reveling in the joy of the moment that had been so long coming, she whispered, "I wouldn't have it any other way."